The Unknown Masterpiece

The Unknown Masterpiece

AN ALIETTE NOUVELLE MYSTERY

JOHN BROOKE

Signature
EDITIONS

Cover design by Terry Gallagher/Doowah Design.
Photograph of John Brooke by Anne Laudouar.
Shoemaker painting on front cover by Willem van Nieuwenhoven (1879-1973). The author has unsuccessfully sought the family/estate of W. van Nieuwenhoven. In good faith, jb

Printed and bound in Canada by Hignell Printing.

We acknowledge the support of The Canada Council for the Arts and the Manitoba Arts Council for our publishing program.

Library and Archives Canada Cataloguing in Publication

Brooke, John, 1951 Aug. 27-
      The unknown masterpiece / John Brooke.

(An Aliette Nouvelle mystery)
Issued also in electronic format.
ISBN 978-1-897109-98-4

      I. Title. II. Series: Brooke, John, 1951 Aug. 27- .
Aliette Nouvelle mystery.

PS8553.R6542U65 2012   C813'.54   C2012-906322-3

Signature Editions, P.O. Box 206, RPO Corydon
Winnipeg, Manitoba, R3M 3S7
www.signature-editions.com

"We're both of us beneath our love, we're both of us above."
— Leonard Cohen
"Dance Me to the End of Love"

PROLOGUE

Top Basel Art Restorer Slain in Garden... Inspector Aliette Nouvelle may have noticed the item in yesterday's paper as she spread it open on the lawn. But lurid headlines screaming bloody murder had ceased to engage her. She wasn't jaded — she was a cop. A French cop. A murder in Basel, the Swiss city an hour down the road, was not her business. And she had other things on her mind that morning. Piaf was dead. Her closest friend, her staunchest ally. Almost nineteen years of partnership were over. Of course she had known it was coming. For the past three years the kindly vet had been suggesting that a quick and painless needle would put a dignified end to the limpy, hearing-impaired, perpetually shitty-bummed ignominy of Piaf's golden age. Aliette had always agreed wholeheartedly. Then resisted.

Claude Néon had had no choice in consenting to Piaf's presence when Aliette consented to move into the large house in the north end. Love me, love my cat. The old white warrior had explored every shadow in the garden. In the end, it seemed Piaf had dozed off in the dying autumn flowers and hadn't woken up. Aliette had arrived home the previous evening to find him lying there, dead stiff, spirit gone — no more Piaf to be seen in that grizzled old face. Sad proof that the body's just an envelope for the soul.

She called the vet. He gently advised her to put Piaf in a garbage bag and out with the trash. The inspector gathered that a garbage bag was the dreary fate of those cats left to die at the clinic where she had spent a small fortune on her friend. Or, said the vet, she could bury him where he lay. He added that pet cemeteries were available in the area but they were expensive and, in his opinion, slightly ridiculous. When, unasked, the vet pressed on, eager to assure her that a garden interment was not against the law, it suddenly occurred to Aliette that after all these years this good man had no idea she was a senior inspector with the local bureau of the Police Judiciaire and would probably already know the ins and outs of such regulations. Aliette did not resent this. *Au contraire*, she was touched. Piaf was the vet's focus, not her. She was merely Madame Nouvelle and her payments were always prompt. She thanked him for his advice. In leaving her to grieve, the vet told her pet psychology was central to his role and the death of a pet was always a family milestone. She did not tell him that now it was just herself and Claude.

The bereaved inspector had thought about her options for Piaf's final resting place overnight. The tragedy was compounded by the fact that Claude had no idea how to comfort her. This lack of empathy was at the heart of the larger thing weighing on the inspector's mind. Somehow the mournful night had produced an erotic dream about the kindly vet. The vet and Aliette. And a lot of animals who were sort of human, each of them damaged to the quick and needing to be cared for by someone who knew how, i.e., not Claude Néon.

She had awoken to the realization that their relationship was over.

Now she stood in the morning sun, weeping in her discreet way. Piaf would be buried in the garden, exactly where she'd found him.

After shrugging his permission, because it *was* his house and property, Claude had turned his attention back to his tennis club newsletter and finished his breakfast before going out to dig a cat-sized hole with his spade. Then he left for work, leaving her alone to say her final farewell.

Kneeling, she wrapped Piaf in newspaper and tied the bundle with a green velvet ribbon, an old one she'd had for years, that he'd always loved to kick at, and put the bundle in the bag. Yes, a garbage bag. '*Adieu*,' Aliette whispered.

Then she slowly lifted gentle shovelfuls of garden earth and covered her old friend.

Part 1

This side, that side

PIAF AS MARKER

For a while Aliette and Claude had walked to work together. Why bother trying to conceal what was never officially mentioned but universally known? A pleasant twenty-five-minute march along affluent streets with school children and professionals, then down through the park and past her old apartment, and on through the labyrinthine old quarter to the musty police building in rue des Bon Enfants. Different schedules had eroded this comfy ritual. The morning of Piaf's burial, Aliette headed out alone and was glad not to have Claude beside her. She paused in the park to gaze at the third-floor balcony where she and Piaf had shared beer and dreams... Arriving at the Commissariat, the inspector felt the weight of too much time as she climbed three flights of stairs. In no mood for morning chitchat, she went straight to her office, where she sat at her desk, morose, staring through her north-facing window. The sky was pale blue amid vague grey swathes of cloud where it met the rising Vosges. Summer was still making desultory gasps, but it was dying, mirroring back this futile sense of another year, not enough to show. She felt as if her life were collapsing behind her. It was not Piaf the cat. It was Piaf the marker, the mute evidence of an entire part of her life. Her best years? The notion was devastating. She stood, took her coat from the hook on the door and pulled it back on.

It was testimony to the ever-tenuous core of her heart that the inspector still paid rent to Madame Camus for the third-floor apartment beside the park. 'My pied-à-terre,' she joked whenever the subject of this 'needless expense' came up — because Claude was wanting her to contribute to the payments on the house. Needless? She had tried to see the future but it would not come clear, and so she always put another envelope in Madame Camus' mailbox at the start of each new month. Indeed, she often climbed the stairs to sit there for a spell. Because love matters and you had to care about it. You had to work at it. Wasn't work the crux? Claude Néon was proud of his tulips, but guess who'd soon taken over responsibility for the garden in the north end? Aliette watered and dug, planted, pruned and picked. And she tried to help him learn to tend it, but Claude had been happy to watch her do it. He said it stirred something deep and central to see her kneeling with her clippers and her trowel. That was nice to hear but did nothing to ease the encroaching ache in her lower back (like her mother was prone to), nor this evolving worry in her heart. Central, Claude? You can learn a lot about a man from observing him in his garden. Or with your cat. Perhaps she should dig Piaf up and put him in Madame Camus' tulip bed instead. Madame Camus had never expressed much love for Piaf, but she was at least a studious gardener. She'd won a prize for her nasturtium patch...

Monique, secretary-to-everyone-but-mainly-Claude, buzzed. 'You joining us for coffee?'

'Yes. No... I don't know.' The inspector sat back down. In her coat. In a muddle. It doesn't really matter where you put a body. A garden in the north end was just as good as a garden by the park. And the flat on the third floor was a stop-gap, not a final destination. In her heart Aliette knew she could not go back there in any permanent way.

Toward mid-morning, Monique buzzed again. Claude had something. Please come.

She headed down the hall. Monique asked, 'Are you OK?'

'Piaf died.'

Monique raced around her desk and hugged the inspector before the tears could start again.

Just in time. 'Merci, Monique... I'm fine. I'm good...' She breathed. She smiled.

Collecting herself, stepping into Claude's domain, she mused that if Piaf were to be cremated his ashes would fit into a cigar box, maybe a hand-thrown clay jar. 'I could keep him on my desk.'

Claude nodded but refrained from comment. Piaf was a private matter. They had to stick to the rule about leaving private stuff at home. And he knew that whatever he might say, it would surely be wrong and only add to the larger problem. Not easy trying to manage two separate relationships with the same person. Instead, he passed her the information just sent up from the municipal police detachment at Village-Neuf, a bedroom community thirty minutes away on the banks of the Rhine. 'You should check the situation. It's up your alley, or appears so.' A body discovered on the shore. Found by two kids that morning. 'If you don't want it, give it to Patrice or Bernadette, depending.' Inspector Patrice Lebeau was their Anti-gangs specialist. Inspector Bernadette Milhau, still a rookie, was focusing on Vice. A senior inspector knew whose skills fit with what crime. She also had tacit rights of first refusal on whatever case struck her fancy. 'But if he floated across from one of our neighbours, it'll be for you. Mm?' Her own unlabelled specialty being the borderland defining the murky legal edge of France. 'IJ's already gone down,' he added. IJ was Identité Judiciaire, their two-man forensics team. And now Claude smiled, trying to be encouraging — at least in his role as boss. At home, all he could do was dig in and hold his ground. 'Go. It'll help you get this off your mind.' Whether he meant Piaf or them was left professionally unclear, hanging in the space between.

She rose, robotic, file in hand.

He smiled again. 'I'm sure the right solution will come.'

Inspector Nouvelle descended to the garage and requisitioned a car from mechanics Joël and Paul. Sorry, the barf-green Opal with the fritzy clutch was the only vehicle not out or up on a hoist. Shedding her coat because it was a now sunny and rather humid early autumn day in Alsace, and in no big hurry — she was in mourning and mourners don't rush — she headed out of town, took the slower D201 down to D105, then went east. The sickly coloured Opal brought her thinking back to Piaf, his poor tummy, always full of fur balls and bugs and only God knew what…

CRIME SCENE

FRENCH SIDE

The longest river in Europe has its source in the Swiss Alps. Flowing west, the Rhine forms the Swiss-German boundary until making an abrupt jag north at Basel, where the Swiss briefly share the river with both Germany and France. The Rhine then forms the French-German line before entering Germany, where it flows on to the Netherlands and into the North Sea. The thirty-kilometre man-made canal separating the Rhine from ports serving the French shoreline dates from 1925; for most of those thirty kilometres the view of Germany is blocked by a finger-like *faux-isle* which is home to park and beach areas, government-owned farming sites, several hydro stations. The inspector's destination was a park-like stretch of shoreline at the mouth of the canal where it joins the actual river. A uniformed cop on the side of the road across from an industrial pump parts factory directed her down a well-worn track through the trees. Emerging from the forested area separating road from water, she could see beyond the tip of the finger-island to Germany on the far side. Aliette left the car and headed across fifty metres of scrubby grass and shrub-strewn terrain to the boulder-lined shore.

After almost ten years with the PJ force in this corner of the Republic, Inspector Nouvelle had dealt with lots of cases arising from the Rhine. Illegal immigrants. Illegal traffic. Drugs. And bodies. Floating, snagged in the rocks, dredged up from the mucky bottom, a body in the river usually meant a murder without a home as jurisdictions bickered to lay claim or, more usually, took steps to deny any. While the victim languished in a legal nowhere-land, the perpetrator gained the benefit of wasted time.

There were pockets of sand along the bank, large enough for a beach towel, maybe two. The place was probably fine for swimming, partying, lovemaking, quiet thinking—but you could never call it a bona fide beach. Jean-Marc Pouliot and Charles Léger of Identité Judiciaire were hard at it. Jean-Marc was marshalling the movements of half a dozen gendarmes trained to assist. The group, always strangely absurd in their snowy 'bee keeper' suits and bag-like boots to match, trooped softly, methodically picking through the rocky edges and shrubby growth. Charles waded in the shallows, looking like a bizarre long-billed rubbery-skinned amphibian thanks to the diving mask with the extended beak which plowed a course below the surface (his own rather clever invention, affording him a clear view while saving his back a good amount of agony). The inspector noted a snorkel moving parallel to Charles Léger slightly further out. Yet another diver surfaced near mid-stream. Then sank.

The usual yellow and blue tapes had been spooled out and widely stretched because of course the public had found its way past the road-side barriers. Indeed, there was a good crowd, mothers mostly, with dogs and prams, some senior citizens. Plus media. Husbands were at work. Kids were at school. Or most. The gendarmes had detained two adolescent boys.

It was hard for a cop fending off depression to be thrilled by these examples of emerging masculinity. Around fourteen or fifteen, both conformed to the large, hulking mode that mothers were producing these days: boys with bad skin and dirty hair, slouched, hands stuffed in low-slung baggy pockets while languidly shuffling to a self-conscious kind of choreography as they waited by a patrol car. Aliette's eyes registered wires extending from ears hidden under the unkempt hair to palm-sized devices clipped in belt loops. Drawing near, she could hear it, the way you hear it in the train—an undertone, a discordant din, the boring thump of bass.

Before she could present herself to the cop minding the two boys, Serge Phaneuf of the *Cri du Matin* rudely left an earnest local mother in mid-description of how it felt to have a murder in her neighbourhood and, notebook in hand, touched her arm. 'Got a name for me, Inspector?'

She waved him off, peevish. I just got here! And ducked under the barrier tape.

The gendarme got out of his car. 'Inspector…'

He handed her his notes and a plastic bag containing two expertly rolled joints.

'*Alors?*' Drugs and a body. She hoped these two boys hadn't swallowed something powerful enough to inspire them to go after a stranger on the shore and leave him dead. It was happening everywhere. She was in no frame of mind for the likes of *that*. The smaller of the two large teens was nervous enough to turn his music off and nod hello. His gigantic friend smirked in her direction through glittery eyes and continued to move to the beat. Aliette had nothing against children, but neither was she one who automatically loves them just because they are. This child entered into his relationship with the Police Judiciaire on a seriously bad foot. Stupid boy.

Aliette started in on the notes.

The boys admitted to skipping school. They had gone to get high by the river straight from breakfast, intending on passing the day. They had come upon the body — it was not clear at what time. Village-Neuf police had received a call at ten-twenty, a clumsy anonymous tip. From René, the nervous one. In less than the time it takes to drink a coffee and eat a brioche, a beat cop alerted to the source of the call found the two giggling boys making a mess at a table in the plaza McDo's. The beat cop detained them and confiscated their remaining pot. René admitted making the anonymous call. Threatened with severe punishment for playing dangerous games and carrying an illicit substance, they had insisted the information passed along in their call was the truth. They had taken the officer to their gruesome find by the river. Their parents had been informed. The local police might be prepared to leave it at that. The focus had naturally shifted from the boys' small crimes to this much larger one.

'Your call, of course,' added the gendarme as Aliette returned his papers.

The boys were called Hubert Hunspach and René Laprade. Hubert grooved. René was wary.

Inspector Nouvelle put a guiding hand on René's shoulder and walked him in a slow circle around the music-shielded Hubert. 'So, is this a good spot to come, René?'

René shrugged.

'Hubert's choice then?'

A nod, a quick sidelong glance at his friend. Yes, Hubert's pot. Hubert's spot.

The glittery eyes of the boy in question narrowed. A thumb casually moved to his belt and adjusted his sound level. He began turning slowly with a sullen sway, one ear tuned to his friend.

The inspector encouraged René. 'And you just walked down and found the man?'

'Pretty much, yeah…I mean, first we sat on a rock and, you know…'

'Lit up. OK. And then you found the body.'

'Just floating there.'

'Were you afraid?'

A shrug.

'Did you run when you saw it? The body?'

'Yes.'

'I have information saying your shoes and socks were still soaking wet when they found you at McDo. Why would that be, René?'

A shrug. 'Maybe we went into the water to make sure. You know?'

'Well, that makes sense. But why did you wait so long before calling the police?'

'It's like, um…we lost track of time.'

Nice to lose track of time, she thought. Even with a dead body on your hands. Maybe she could learn something from these boys. She asked, 'Who's the boss here, René?'

René did not understand the question. Or maybe he did. In any case, Aliette knew the answer. She told him, 'René, you're a good boy for calling the police, even if Hubert said you shouldn't. But you must also tell the truth despite what Hubert told you to say. Do you understand?'

'Yes.'

'And so?'

René considered. Hubert removed his earphones and faced her with his outsized adolescent arms folded across his chest, as if challenging her to a fight. 'He was dead!'

The inspector smiled, inviting him to tell her more.

'You could see it. Dead. Why would we be afraid?'

Good question. 'How close did you get to him?'

'Close enough to know for sure.'

'You see lots of dead bodies?'

A shrug. All teens have this basic move. Translates as: stupid question. 'Tons of 'em on TV.'

'I mean real ones, Hubert.'

'But it was just like on a show. The guy was floating there, just like on a show.'

'It's why we didn't run away,' René said.

'Did you touch him, René?'

A shake of the head, eyes diverted. 'No.' Horrible liar.

Hubert, very much the brains and the boss behind this operation, said, 'Just a sort of a poke. To make sure, you know? I mean, like, we didn't want him to be floating there and still be alive or anything. If he was alive, we would have helped him.'

'But he was dead and you were high and so you stood there and looked at him.'

That smirk. That shrug. 'There was nothing we could do.'

'So?...how long?'

'I don't know. It was very freaky. We just looked at him and wondered what happened.'

'And what we should do,' René added. 'Like, uh, we were in a bit of a bind, you know?'

'And he really was dead,' Hubert repeated.

'And you had a long day ahead of you,' noted the inspector.

Hubert did not like her tone. He put his music back on and turned to watch the ongoing IJ operation. His day was still in progress.

But René was properly contrite. 'Sorry.'

Aliette said, 'Well, someone was bound to find him.'

René asked, 'Can we go?'

Aliette asked, 'Do you care that the man was killed?'

René stared out at the river. That was a tricky question. 'I guess so.'

Aliette told him, 'We may have to talk to you again. Promise me you won't leave town.'

'Where would I go?'

She smiled and returned to the gendarme. 'What are we going to do with all these hard-hearted children who are so happy to look and touch but never feel?'

'I could think of a few things.'

'We don't need them for the time being. You can give them back to their mamas.'

'Fine.' He made a note.

'Is this a place you come to often?'

'Occasionally,' the officer replied. 'If the partying gets out of hand. Never for anything like this. Pretty quiet around here for the most part. At least during the day. Any trouble, it's those kind with their pot and beer, and it's usually after dark…Or the *pédés*.' Homosexuals.

'This is a gathering spot?'

'Sometimes. When the bars close over in Saint-Louis, they'll move the party over here. At least in summer.' This was punctuated with a cop shrug (which is a world apart from a stoned adolescent shrug). Translates as: What are you gonna do?

'Was there a party this past weekend?'

'It rained this weekend.'

'Friday?' Friday had been lovely.

'Not the kind where they needed us.'

'Merci.' She left the gendarme to release René and Hubert.

— ⁓ —

Jean-Marc Pouliot ushered her into the tent-like blind they had thrown up.

In fact there were two men found in the Rhine that day. The first, the man René and Hubert had poked and studied, was fortyish, tall and lean, fine features, good looking—absent the death-dulled stare, the matted, ratty hair. There was also the fact of a clean bullet hole in the centre of his forehead. And the side of his head had been severely broken open, battered with a sharpish object during the course of a struggle. Or perhaps falling on a rock.

A spiffy dresser—at least on top: stylish cream-toned lightweight suit coat, a navy tie with tiny ruby hearts in a running pattern, a two-toned shirt (with two more bullet holes). South of his trim waistline, one elegant but blood-stained grey silk knee-length sock remained on his right foot. A string-like brief (*le slip*) more or less preserved his modesty. Shoes, other sock, and trousers were not part of his ensemble. It certainly fit with the notion of a trysting spot.

Jean-Marc Pouliot let the plastic sheet fall back. 'We have his pants and one shoe.'

'Who is he?'

'Don't know. Wallet's gone.'

'Get a time?'

'Not really...' handing over the initial paperwork. The local medical examiner had done his job and left. 'At least forty-eight hours. Have to wait for a more exact time-frame.' Until *Médecin légiste* Rafaele Petrucci took over and performed a more extensive pathology investigation.

Their victim had spent a rainy weekend in the river. 'But he didn't float in.'

'No,' Pouliot agreed. 'I'd say the first two shots knocked him into the water. He may have floated from one shallows to the next, to where they found him, he was definitely in the river and it rolled him around some. But it happened here, that's sure.' The pants and shoe would add strong circumstantial confirmation. 'And we're gathering up some other things.'

The inspector was pleased to see they had recovered a pistol. It was laid out on plastic, on display in the sun. 'SIG 220,' Pouliot said. 'Standard police and army issue. Up to the task.'

'In the water or the bushes?'

'Water, but a pretty weak throw.' Adding, 'Five shots gone from an eight-round mag.'

Interesting. Three in the victim. 'Find the other two?'

'Casings, yes. Slugs from the misses, not yet. All these rocks, the river...' They would do their best. In Jean-Marc's opinion, the non-pattern of the casings suggested a rundown. 'Two shots to the stomach area—two casings over by the willow there…' Directing her view; 'where we found his pants and shoe. We found two more casings along a more or less straight path from there to those rocks. I'd say he tripped and fell there. Last casing from a *coup de grâce* to the head was in the sand directly below. Not where we found him, no. Like I say, he probably rolled with the currents a bit over the weekend.'

She could see it—a chase along these jagged rocks and bushy fringes. Then an execution. Both the victim's shins were a mess of cuts and scratches, some deep… his fingers and palms had also taken a beating. 'Hard to run along those rocks,' she observed.

Jean-Marc confirmed. 'Examiner says he fell more than once.'

She suggested, 'Maybe the chaser had some of the same difficulties, left something for us.'

'We're looking.' Then, in his usual low-key manner, Jean-Marc hit right on it. 'I'd say the gun's your best indicator. Such a weak throw. Too easy to find. I'd say someone panicked. Which probably means: not a pro.'

Merci, Jean-Marc. 'Think there was more than one?' Chasing the victim.

'Not clear…' Jean-Marc Pouliot scratched at an ugly red spot on his inner arm. The breeze was minimal, the horseflies owned the shoreline. 'Those kids didn't help us any. Made a mess.'

'No ID beyond a missing wallet?'

'No. His things might help locate him. His suit especially. We'll find his tailor.'

'Or we may get lucky with the gun.' She noted the serial number in her book. Snazzy clothes like that—maybe with a gang. Payback. Punishment. But her colleague was right: no pro would leave the weapon so easily found. Maybe some desperate soul fighting back against the gangs?

'And we have this guy,' Pouliot said, now kneeling to unfold a rectangular package carefully wrapped in plastic. It was a painting of an old man.

He's taking a break for tea, pouring the brew carefully into a cup, a cup without a handle held lovingly in the palm of his hand. Not a tea cup. More like a cereal bowl. *Un bol.* His tools, pliers and a punch are most evident, and several pots make a workaday shambles of his table. A dim light hangs above him. His rimless glasses are low on his nose, accentuating taciturn eyes as he concentrates on pouring his refreshment. A shoemaker's eyes. A boot rests in the middle of his table, a battered old thing, central to the table but almost lost in shadow, you'd have to think willfully forgotten for the moment by a man whose fate it was to fix too many. The pot of tea gets all the light. Refreshment. Diversion. A break in the day's quiet routine. It was a golden-seeming teapot, in a long-ago moment a painter had felt compelled to study...

It had been found soiled and ripped in the rocks along the shallows: a shoemaker at his work table with a pot of tea. Oil. In a dark and ponderous naturalistic style. Not at all modern. 'Late Romantic,' Jean-Marc surmised. 'Flemish or Dutch. Not French.' It was strictly a guess.

'Famous?' Meaning valuable.

'Haven't a clue.'

The gilt frame had been shattered, the shadowy plane in the top right corner ripped. The shoemaker, teapot and the resting boot were severely stained with mud and water. Maybe irreparably. She hoped not. 'Can they clean that?' Aliette Nouvelle wondered.

Jean-Marc Pouliot didn't know.

Thus two crimes committed at the unofficial park at Village-Neuf. Most would deem murder more serious than the destruction of a painting. But not all. It depends on your sense of inherent worth. A certain calibre of thief would not think twice about a murder in pursuit of what he wanted. A certain cop might find a ruined painting more interesting than a ruined man.

Climbing back up the bank, Aliette was thinking she would take the lead on this case.

The crowd had grown, the gendarmes were moving them back, more media had arrived, some were perched on the tops of trucks and cars, cameras aimed at the operation. Most of the attention was on the regional television news team. The reporter known as Cakeface (at least to the police) was conducting an interview with Hubert and René. Hubert's mother monitored the exercise with a grim wariness. You can always tell a mother: Easy. Hubert had her sallow face. Can a mother always tell what her child has been up to? Harder to know. Both boys giggled sporadically as Cake posed her questions and they gave their version of events.

Maybe they were just excited to be on TV.

Crime reporter Serge Phaneuf appeared in front of her again.

'Got a name for me yet?'

'Not yet, monsieur.' She headed back to her barf-green requisitioned car.

CRIME OF PASSION?

Returning to rue des Bons Enfants, Inspector Nouvelle gave Commissaire Néon the rudimentary details of the situation by the river and said she would take the lead. She hoped there were no links across the border, but she sensed there likely would be — Basel was a busy art centre. And hadn't she just read something about an art-related killing there? Where? She could not put her finger on it…

The body and the crime-scene findings were just now being delivered to the basement. She would have to oversee a quick exam and push for ID on the victim, then get the usual report and forms written up for the Prosecutor's office so she could move ahead, mandate in hand, without undue delay. It was shaping up to be a long day.

She told Claude not to expect her for supper. Claude was irked at the prospect of a Tuesday evening alone and made noises to this effect. Aliette was irked by that.

Apart from the fact it meant he'd have to cook for himself, Claude was…What?

Claude Néon was proving to be far more domestic than she ever would have guessed.

Odd word to hang it on, a tricky problem to confront. At first she'd put it down to peer pressure. The better the neighbourhood, the more evident the syndrome? The garden. His club. At first this aspect of the man she'd thought (felt sure!) was her true life's partner was a niggling mystery, a slight imbalance she believed would be righted with time. But it hadn't been. Now he was always far too disappointed when she couldn't make it home. Though they were two cops sharing a home, it was two different worlds and the gap was getting wider.

It was *supposed* to be a love built on a shared direction, a passion for the job. This domestic thing was an interloper, an unwanted guest installed in a room never properly prepared.

Claude knew the lot of the inspector. He'd been one too, before his sudden jump to police management. *Remember, Claude? Can you so easily forget the place you come from?*

It grated. Maddening when the heart says you just don't want the things you thought you did. It's not fear—you got past that. It's knowing you were wrong. And so disheartening, how the bitterness of self-deception is slowly, implacably revealed.

Today, facing Claude, everything grated a little sharper. Because her cat had died?

Oh, Piaf… A conflicted Aliette returned to her desk and began an initial report.

She did a search on the gun. It was not in the system. She made a call to Basel, seeking the same information and wasted the better part of an hour being politely shunted here, then there, then waiting yet again before being told they couldn't help her. She knew it was by design, ridiculous politics spearheaded by strange little xenophobic minds at all levels of the system, but mainly at the highest. It was past six, too late to contact a Swiss ally—she would sort out the gun tomorrow. There were colleagues downstairs also wanting to get home.

Despite all their work at the site, Identité Judiciaire had nothing much.

'All the skin and blood belongs to him…' Jean-Marc Pouliot reported, with a look through the door toward the morgue across the hall. 'And the gun. His hands are all over it. Plus some DNA from his skin where he kept it in the back of his waistband. Maybe traces of other hands on the gun. Maybe. Not enough DNA to read after a weekend in the river.'

'One person, both hands?'

'Working on it, Inspector… With my luck lately, it'll break down to three.'

'And perhaps a bit of fabric,' Charles Léger muttered. 'Synthetic. Like training shorts.'

She moved to his bench, looked through the scope at the tiniest morsel. Lighter than darker. Bluish, not white. 'Or a bathing suit?'

'Sure.'

'Or underwear,' Jean-Marc suggested. 'Again, very indistinct. An outer layer. Minimal contact with skin… Thing is, a lot of different people rolling around on the ground out there, or so I gather.'

Indeed. 'Thanks, messieurs. Please don't stay late on my account.' Though she knew they would. Adding, 'Tomorrow I'll have the gun.' Then she went across to the morgue.

Pathologist Raphaele Petrucci uncovered the cleaned-up corpse. 'The bullet killed him, no doubt there. I mean the one in his head. But the two in his gut could have done, if required. But dead before his little swim, that's sure. And smacked about the face and head with something hard.'

'Not the rocks while he drifted?'

'No…well, a bit. But the worst part of it is pre-swim.'

'Med Examiner says two days, maybe three.'

'I'll narrow it to Friday night. Saturday, early.'

Aliette's eyes drifted over the surface of lifeless flesh of what used to be a handsome man. A severe mish-mash of cuts and scratches on the legs and back and shoulders. 'Most of that's your rocks and thorns and the like,' Raphaele said. Sustained in being run down, tripping, falling in the rocks? 'Yes,' gesturing across the hall. 'IJ's got corroborating blood and bits of skin. But this mess around his head…' now demarcating the tighter, deeper cluster of wounds which had ruined the classic face, 'this is something else. A chair? Or a board?… Wood, not metal.'

'A picture frame?'

Raphaele Petrucci considered the gashes. 'Yes…Well, a hefty one. Could be. Why not?'

'Ask Jean-Marc to check the frame of that painting they brought back for blood.'

'I will.' Making a note.

After being whacked on the head he'd been shot by someone who'd missed twice. 'Easy to miss if you're running,' Petrucci suggested. 'Jean-Marc says the terrain going down from park level to shore is pretty rough. The cuts and scratches bear that out.'

'Yes…' Mulling it, the thought occurred: Or if you're scared, running for your life, looking over your shoulder, panicked, shooting, missing, running further, turning and firing again. Missing…easy to miss. Running! Finally getting lucky as the pursuer drew near. Was their victim the pursuer? Chasing someone with a painting, and a gun, wanting the one, discounting the other. Someone who shot him and *then* beat him around the head with the painting? And then, by virtue of a half-assed throw into the shallows, makes them a virtual gift of the guilty gun. But it was the victim's gun… She could not make sense of that scenario.

But he kept his gun in his waistband and his pants were off. The gun would have been lying there beside them. Someone could have taken him unawares—especially if he was having sex—and grabbed the gun. The object of his affections? Or a third person? … Turn it around. Their *victim* was running with the painting. The killer was wanting it. That was the more logical scenario. When the killer finally runs the victim down and finishes him off, he also—before? after?—administers a beating around the head with an ornate hardwood frame, then throws the painting away like so much garbage after a picnic by the river. And the gun. The victim's gun.

'The cuts around his head—from the frame—'

'If they are,' Petrucci cautioned. First let's link painting to murder in no uncertain terms.

'Yes, yes… But the cuts: are they before or after death?'

Raphaele Petrucci took a moment. 'I'll say just after death. He bled, but the river cleaned him up. Then again, these here…' indicating slightly ridged contused areas along the forehead, 'these are from being hit with the same thing, I'm positive, but the skin is unbroken. You'd expect bruising, but the blood didn't have time.' A non-committal smile betrayed his pronouncement. 'Yes: After. Kind of a fitful and completely unnecessary smack across the cranium after the *coup de grâce*, which was the bullet through his brain. Not that it matters.'

'No.' But with the *painting*? That mattered. Who would do that? Why?

She couldn't fathom it. The found gun and the execution style of the killing would not fit together in her mind. Nor the ruined painting. And the wallet? They keep the wallet. They wreck and toss the painting. They give *us* the gun. Or may as well have. At first glance, the thing was totally erratic. Garbage? The painting's a fake! Why else destroy such a thing so brutally? she wondered, staring at the body the way one tends to, willing it to tell her more.

Beside her, the pathologist kept rubbing his stomach as he perused his notes, a steady, circular massaging motion, as if he were pregnant. It disturbed her focus. 'Do you have to do that?'

'Oops!' He stopped. Then started chewing on his thumb, rueful. 'She's turning me into a fat person. Eats like a bloody horse. I'm helpless.' *She* was Nanette, a local woman given to cowboy boots and eating. They'd met at a crime scene. Raphaele boasted as to how he'd subsequently charmed Nanette with the culinary skills he claimed were 'instinctual to my kind.' Perhaps he had, but there was blowback: Dr. Petrucci's formerly trim line had been expanding. His comely Italian movie-star face was getting heavier too. There was a time when Aliette Nouvelle had not been able to resist it. A few others too amongst the ranks at rue des Bon Enfants, if Monique had her information right. It appeared Raphaele had met his match in Nanette.

The inspector focused. 'What about sex?'

'You know how it is — after a while, a good meal is just as enjoyable, often more so.'

'Our victim, Raphaele. Please.'

He sensed her pain. 'Sorry...and sorry about your cat.'

Merci, Monique. She accepted his condolences with an empty stare.

He went back to his notes. 'The time in the water cleaned off any outward signs. Peeing when he died would've washed out the urethra...' Rolling the body slightly. 'More scratching and abrasion on his buttocks. That may or may not be signs of some fun on the beach.'

'It's not a beach in any way, shape or form.'

'Nevertheless, they found him without his pants on. But, no — I see no signs of sex.'

'*Bon*...' Once again, the river was a murderer's best accomplice. 'Drugs or alcohol?'

'Nothing in his stomach. Have to wait for the blood work to come back.'

'Fingers? Dental?'

'All in the pipeline. Hopefully tomorrow.' Raphaele was unconsciously rubbing his tummy again as he pulled the sheet back over the victim, a contented victim of love.

She couldn't hold it against him. 'What's for supper tonight?'

'Tuesday? Pizza.'

'Enjoy it. Thanks. Bonsoir.'

She returned to her desk. On a humid evening at the far end of summer the skyline presented a washed-out skim-milk-bluish haze with traces of anaemic cloud, the weak pink sun floating low. She laid out all the paperwork from the day's interviews and processes. Each item was entered with due consideration. Because each item mattered. Because she would rather spend time becoming absorbed in this than at home fighting her anger at choosing the wrong man.

Shhh...Focus! Be a shoemaker. Fix a shoe.

Parameters: No drifting. It seemed certain the man was killed close to where he was found along that stretch of shore. Fine. Another key would be the dynamics. The possibility that the victim was in pursuit of the perpetrator, and somehow the tables had been turned. The shooter had gained control of the victim's gun. A shooter with an unsteady hand, an unsure shot, and a less-than-powerful throwing arm. And quite unaware of or blasé about forensic recovery techniques. An unsteady-handed shooter who panicked and threw the gun into the river. A pathetically short way. It pointed to a crime of passion of some kind.

Gratuitously breaking a picture frame over the skull of a man already dead supported that. In the context of murder, passion was anger. Anger out of control.

There were probably lots of delicate boys, objects of beauty who could not throw far. Or there were wives. Suspicious wives, and angry, tracking a philandering husband to a big surprise. Somehow the possibility of a woman as a central player in this dynamic made the notion of an unsteady-handed shooter more concrete. Inspector

Nouvelle was always loath to stereotype, but it was an image she could see. A wife. A gay husband exposed. And killed. Heat of the moment, loss of reason, a furious heart. Or a terrified heart? Back to the beautiful boy: Wanted, not wanting, breaking away… and with a cherished object, desperately chased, all ending in a tragic struggle. Either way, a crime of passion.

But…

But who?

No ID. The inspector's eyes rested on the empty space on the required form, a space waiting for the victim's name. The logic of the imagined dynamics of a crime of passion did not square with a wallet gone missing. Erratic. But a man could do that to you. A man could get your blood boiling so you couldn't think straight. Too angry to make a clear assessment of the results of your actions. Aliette knew the feeling. Who didn't? And no one angry enough to wreck that lovely old shoemaker would have the presence of mind to step into the water and find a wallet on the person of someone they had just killed. The painting was definitely before the wallet.

Unless there was no passion. Just a business thing. Art theft? Art fraud?

But why leave the shattered remnants of this obvious investigative direction?

She sat and puzzled, finally had to decide that a crime for commercial gain was not feasible. A crime of passion was winning the battle for primacy waged by opposing sides of her deductive instincts. The wallet was coming to the fore. Set against the other chaotic elements—throwing the gun, smashing the painting—removing the wallet could only happen within the context of a careful moment. Afterward. Quite a while after. She was thinking, No, the wallet's not part of the murder. She was asking herself, Was it two things then? A chaotic crime of passion and someone else's really dumb mistake? Sitting back and muttering, 'You deceitful little bastard.'

Requisitioning the same drab Opal from Georges the night mechanic, Inspector Nouvelle headed south again—to 34 circle Georges-Simenon in Village-Neuf, the recorded address of Hubert Hunspach, leader of an illicit expedition down to the river to get high.

HEADING FOR THE BORDER

FRENCH SIDE

Village-Neuf was a typical mix of charming old core streets surrounded by developments displaying varying success at fitting with the original idea. She found her way to one such development in a cul-de-sac on a rise off the River Road. The unofficial park area along the channel where she had spent the afternoon was five minutes away by car—the hulking pump parts factory, thrumming through its evening shift, marked the place in no uncertain terms. And likely kept house prices within a certain range. The Hunspach residence was designed in the traditional chalet style, exposed upper beams, base covered by light grey stucco, a balcony on the master bedroom above the front door, a terra cotta tiled roof. And clean: lawn in perfect trim, not a dead petal in the earth beneath the clumps of dying primary-coloured annuals. How would you ever guess an ugly boy like Hubert lived here? It was Papa who answered her touch on the ding-dong bell. A trim man with an austere regard. She'd bet a mid-level bean counter, at the pump manufacturer here in town, or over at the vast Peugeot factory, or possibly at one of the big pharmo plants that employed thousands in the area. She flashed her warrant card. 'I don't mean to disturb your supper, monsieur. I just need a quick word with young Hubert.'

'We eat early,' he said, his tone as unassuming as his front yard.

She supposed he'd heard several versions of his son's arrest.

Inside was equally neutral: pristine nordic wood, perfectly white materials covering *divan* and matching *fauteuil*, no carpet on the white tile floor, no photos or knick-knacks, nothing to read, just the requisite television and stereo system. Like an IKEA model, everything lighter than air. The inspector nodded *bonsoir* to Maman, Hubert and Sister, gathered in front of the regional news, about to enjoy their moment of fame.

It was just past seven-thirty. The regional report was already on. The job-killing realignment taking place at Peugeot was bigger news than a body in the river. But the body would certainly come next. Maman was pained when the cop demanded to speak to her son. 'Now?' she whined, displaying the same automatic wariness Aliette had observed during the interview in the park.

'*Désolé, madame...*' Sorry. Suggesting, 'Surely you were on the local edition.'

'But we eat during the local edition.'

'I want to see how I did,' Hubert complained. To Papa, not the cop.

But Papa pointed to the kitchen, and held the door for the inspector.

Sister, young but clever, quipped, 'Have to catch it rerun.'

'Fuck off,' Hubert said, heading for the kitchen.

'*Ça suffit,*' Papa warned as he pulled the door shut.

Alone with Hubert Hunspach in the spotless *eau-de-javel*-scented kitchen, the inspector did not mince words. 'Where's the wallet?'

Pissed at having to miss himself on the news, he avoided her eyes, sullen. 'What wallet?'

She flashed her warrant card again, to remind Hubert that this was no longer about being on TV. The gesture shook something loose. The boy grinned a dreamy grin, a quintessential adolescent move, the child taking over from the hulking almost-man, presuming the benefit of the doubt as to an innocence left over from childhood and the forgiveness that *always* came with that. Unspoken message: All kind of a joke — reporters, cops, dead people...

'Don't be *too* much of a twerpy brat, Hubert. It's really not becoming on a big boy like you.'

Which merely replaced the grin with a shrug: I have no idea what you're talking about.

Ordering him to sit, she laid out it. 'A man was murdered in cold blood. From the way it looks he'd have been in considerable pain, and a lot of fear. Then dead. Can you wrap your mind around that, Hubert? Dead. A fellow human being. It's the worst crime, murder—not fun at all, I don't care how much pot you smoked or how many shows you've seen, this is not a laughing matter. And more to the point, monsieur—'

'I'm still a juvenile.'

'Juvenile? Really? So far, all you are is a very dumb child. But if you have any knowledge of the circumstances connected to this crime, then you are a witness and you will be dealt with accordingly. And a wallet containing a murdered person's papers and other personal information is knowledge of the utmost essential kind, and if you are found to be withholding that knowledge you'll be charged and your life will change forever. Are you getting the picture here, Hubert?'

'He's *dead.*' This was so boring. 'He doesn't need his wallet. He doesn't need—'

'*I* need his wallet!' Standing, directing him to do likewise. 'Get your toothbrush, Hubert, we're going downtown where we can do this in a more businesslike manner.'

'Oh, for God's sake!'

Papa looked in. 'Do I need to call a lawyer?'

'You need to tell your son to grow up.'

Hubert Hunspach stomped out of the kitchen. His large feet in his thick boots made a lot of noise. Aliette followed. The father trailed the two of them up the stairs and into a poster-plastered bedroom in desperate need of fresh air. The boy yanked open a drawer and pulled out a wallet and threw it on the floor. '*Putain de flic...*' Whore cop.

Before an inspector could stoop to retrieve it, an embarrassed father had stepped past her and smacked the boy—a good hard one he might actually remember for a day or so. Then Papa gestured at the wallet. Pick it up or you'll get another. Resentful, so typically an oversized child in his outraged sense of having been wronged, Hubert picked it up and placed it in her hand.

'Merci.' A quick look inside. Then a flat smile for Hubert. 'The money too.'

The boy looked about to do a reprise of his kitchen act, but his father did a reprise of his look. Message received; staring straight ahead at nothing, sighing deeply—some days life is just so wrong—Hubert Hunspach pulled his own wallet from his droopy pants and handed over 300 euros and 75 Swiss francs.

'*Bon.*' The inspector bowed in receipt of it. 'Consider the fine paid and the matter closed. You're an extremely lucky boy.'

Hubert shrugged. Papa followed her down the stairs and showed her out.

She offered her hand, 'Sorry if that was a little rough.'

'I could file a complaint. You've no mandate. This is a private dwelling.' And, his eyes added, not everyone around here's a fucking *plouc*. Which translates to *rube*.

She nodded, all true. Countered, 'The quicker we can amass the proper information attached to these things, the better chance we have to solve it—I'm sure you've heard them say that?' Cooperative citizens were society's only hope. Aliette's hand remained extended. Reluctantly he shook it. She reckoned he knew his son deserved it. 'Bonsoir.' She returned to the car.

The recovered wallet gave her Martin Bettelman, French citizen, address just across the way in Saint-Louis, employed in Basel—the 'quick-through' pass card for the Swiss border people indicated a security firm called VigiTec. So, not a gangster. But suspiciously nice clothes for a security guard. In management? In any event, she could now assume a very probable relation between Monsieur Bettelman's employment in the Basel security industry and the painted shoemaker's uncalled-for wounds. This case would certainly have to go to Switzerland.

Inspector Aliette Nouvelle rolled her neck, rotated her shoulders, visualized a glass of beer. It had been a long and vexing day, a day now reduced to a humid blue line wavering between indigo and black, but she had no wish to go home. Not yet. She called the night desk from the car and requested a double-check on the identity card. It was confirmed. She headed for the border.

━ ━

Saint-Louis, last stop this side, is the site of the shared international airport. Thanks to the airport, thanks to industry, it's one big city from Saint-Louis on in to the middle of Basel. But the five-kilometre 'closed' road from the Swiss side into the Basel-designated side of the terminal is Swiss territory. You have to pass through a customs checkpoint in the middle of the terminal hall if you wish to cross to the French-side terminal. It's an efficient business arrangement, but the effects of this unnatural marriage spill over: The run-down street Martin Bettelman had called home seemed locked in permanent twilight thanks to the 24/7 glow of buildings and runways two kilometres away. It was past nine, too late for unwelcome police to come knocking when Aliette stopped in front of the dreary place on the wrong side of the ugly town.

Bettelman. Ground floor. Far end. Over-wrought odours and television sounds all along the hall. She knocked. 'What!' The door was yanked open to reveal a haggard face that fit perfectly with the frustrated voice, unwashed hair, noisy television, kid-evident mess, unattractive air.

'Good evening, Madame Bettelman?' Yes, yes, what the hell could you possibly want? 'My name is Inspector Nouvelle,' flashing her card and a sad smile. 'I regret to inform you...'

In response, Madame Bettleman kicked the door, more angry than distraught. 'Stupid ass!'

There was a sleepy '...Maman?' from somewhere behind her.

'Madame?' The inspector reached to place a restraining hand against the door.

Because Madame Bettelman was already in the process of shutting it. 'What?'

'Can you help me here?'

'Why?' Peevish, sighing, no hint of bereavement. Death made some people strange.

But the police were allowed in, the *télé* muted, basic information supplied. Her name was Lise. Yes, Martin worked as a security guard in Basel. Not sure where at the moment. Mostly galleries and museums, both private and public, they rotated them around — they being the agency, VigiTec. He'd been with them going on ten years. Since the kids... 'at least the bastard cared about them,' Lise muttered. 'Even if he didn't come home, he'd always show up for work.' Small consolation. 'It's a pittance, but it's regular...or was... Fuck!'

'...Maman?'

'*Dors, chérie…c'est rien. Dors!*' It's nothing. Just your stupid father. Go back to sleep.

'Do you know where he went when he didn't come home?'

'Off with his cunts… The clubs? Partying? I don't know.'

Aliette waited.

'So stupid. They think you can't smell the way a stranger smells. Always said he had a night shift, a favour, someone sick, a special exhibition, it always fit but none of it was true. I know the security guard business too—it's how we met. For my sins,' she added in a bitter aside to herself. 'And he knew that!… Really very stupid, my Martin. I could smell it all over him all the way round to the next night. *Putes.* Cheap as hell. Cheaper than all this…' Her home, her street. Lise Bettelman massaged her eyes, deflating. 'I didn't get it.'

Didn't get how he could be so stupid? Big mystery. Bigger disappointment. Not to rub salt, just to learn more, Aliette told Lise, 'He was wearing pretty nice stuff when we found him.'

'What kind of nice stuff?'

'Designer suit, high-end loafers, the whole kit. Straight out of the boutiques.'

'Shows you where his priorities lay. What a prick.'

'Did you confront him?'

'Sure, at the start.' Lise Bettelman paused to reflect, her tired face now beginning to collapse. But she hadn't booted him out, her beau Martin. She needed that cheque and he always managed it. But, 'what a useless waste of time!' Her anger surged back in. She pounded the door.

There was another fearful noise from a half-asleep child down the hall.

Aliette pushed gently. 'Beyond his…his cunts, did you get any sense of anything not right, I mean with his nights away from home?'

'Not right? What the hell else do you want?'

'I mean like against the law.'

'Ah. No…no drugs. He always went to work. They would've seen it, even if I didn't. They won't have druggies. Clients won't have it. Very Swiss. Everything neat and tidy.'

'I mean related to the clients. His work. Art. The things he was hired to watch over?'

Lise Bettelman snorted, bitter, 'If he was, none of it made it here,' gesturing at the cheap humidity-stained walls adorned with unframed, fraying posters.

'You say you worked down there?'

'Yeah. I should've stayed in school.'

'Does it happen? Stealing?'

'No one told *me* about it. But they wouldn't have. I was just a stupid girl. Still am. Fuck!'

'Did he ever mention anyone in Village-Neuf?'

'No. Maybe it's where one of his cunts lives…' But no, Lise Bettelman did not know who Martin's friends were. Didn't want to know. She knew the name of some club downtown. 'I mean in Basel — he lived there more than here. I found a card in his uniform.' She fetched it.

Zup. *Tanzen!* (dancing, in German). An address. The inspector puzzled over the pen-and-ink image of a pair of lederhosen, the traditional suspender-held, elaborately finished alpine leather shorts.

There were now two small voices complaining down the hall. Lise closed her weary eyes and zapped the muted *télé* into oblivion. She bit down on her lower lip, trying like a million other mamas to keep it together. *'J'arrive, mes petites.'* I'll be right there. Exhausted, miserable, she scratched at the scab on her knee, bare and white below the frayed cuff on a pair of cheap pale blue Decathlon all-purpose training shorts.

A not-unsympathetic cop was obliged to enquire, 'What happened to your knee?'

'How the hell should I know?'

'Please.'

'Oh, Jesus… Smashed it in the park.'

'Doing what?'

'Being a goddamn mother!' Adding, 'On the bloody steps to the slide?'

Aliette stood to go. She promised a social worker would be there first thing in the morning, sooner if Lise needed. That was shrugged off. 'My condolences, madame. We'll work on this, so at least you'll know.' Aliette did not mention there would have to be a gendarme sent along with the social worker, to take a swab from her mouth and a cutting from her shorts. It would be a formality. For Lise Bettelman, being a mother was a full-time job. Not a heck of a lot of time unaccounted for in the course of a day — no time to trail a shitty husband from the clubs in Basel to a riverside park and kill him for his selfish ways. But there was a gash on her knee and that fit. Poor Lise would have to suffer the additional indignity of a test. To be sure.

– 5 –
ZUP

Aliette headed for the checkpoint. It was closer than the house where Claude Néon would be staring at the television, waiting. And maybe someone at this club would be able to provide a bit of direction, a name she could add to her report. Fifteen minutes later, the Swiss officer was puzzled when she showed him the card for Zup. Perhaps he even grinned. He knew the location, more or less. 'Klein Basel. Straight ahead, over the bridge, right on Klybeck to Zahringer, right again… in there somewhere, near Alban market?'

Merci… I mean, *Danke*. Geneva spoke French. Here it was mainly German.

Basel occupies both sides of the Rhine. On the left bank, Greater Basel abuts on French territory. Klein Basel, on the right bank, touches Germany. Basel and Klein Basel are linked by six bridges. Crossing St. Johann Bridge, the inspector's eye settled for a wistful moment on the apartment blocks overlooking the Rhine and the promenade. Must be beautiful to have a place up there. One happy Saturday that now seemed unreal, she and Claude had enjoyed riding the cute green trams, marvelling at the fountains, so many of them, at corners, intersections, in squares and parks, from the ancient to the highly modern. They'd sat on a bench and gazed at magical Tinguely fountain, a large pool filled with fantastical mechanized metal creatures. Charming.

And there *is* that Swiss thing: they work at keeping Basel clean.

Klein Basel had been working class and drab. Its edges were still lined with factories and mills within easy reach of the docks. Lots of enclaves were still home to basic apartments filled with working people, Swiss and foreign. But the rebuilt centre had gained a reputation as the fun part of the city. The ultra modern Basel Trade Fair Tower rose thirty-nine stories from the heart of Klein Basel, in daylight shining richly under its sexy blue-tint glass façade. Shopping at the Claraplatz, directly off the Middle Bridge, was as chic as you could want — bistros, cafés, clubs, boutiques, galleries. Gentrification was proceeding apace along many residential streets. There was a pretty university campus at the southern end of Klein Basel. But, after exiting the bridge, Aliette was quickly getting confused in the still-gritty enclaves of the northern end. Her destination was in one of the plain old streets almost in the factory area. Finally daring to try her German, she asked directions. She found her way to the tiny close off Klybeck. Zup? There was no sign, but the music from inside and the dragon in drag by the doorway said she was there.

Well, not quite. It was a basilisk, more complex than simple dragon. The mythical lizard-like creature is Basel's heraldic beast, visible everywhere in the city's windows and doors. Stylized: Head like a cock, tail like a snake, wings like a bat. Said to live in springs and fountains. They also say that looking directly at a basilisk can kill you. Like the Gorgon.

Here at Zup an expertly carved and painted basilisk was fitted out in pinkish lederhosen, the rear end of his hosen not painted in to allow full room for its bum and creepy tail. The door opened immediately to the inspector's knock. A large caricature of a woman was packed into a Heidi-inspired alpine dirndl without a millimetre to spare. Aliette enquired, 'Zup?' In response, she — no, *he*; this was now past doubting — rolled out a long tongue. It wagged and darted, dragon-like and a bit obscene. The sides of his lewdly painted mouth pulled up in a grotesque grin, he uttered 'Zup!' So some Swiss are more polite than others.

Aliette could only smile and step inside. There was a cover charge — this communicated in the Alemannic Swiss German dialect so difficult for her pure French ears. Euros? Offering a ten. She had no Swiss francs. Lifting it from the inspector's fingers, the strange greeter turned dour.

'Ten more.' In English now.

Twenty euros to walk through the door. 'A joke, right?'

Another salacious, in-your-face display of tongue. 'Very special here!' And, 'We gonna give you a beer into the bargain.' Great. Merci. They were playing Frank Sinatra, if she wasn't mistaken, a fairly upbeat thing about that's why the lady is a tramp. Three couples danced. One couple had done it up for a Tuesday evening out at Zup, he in a tux, 'she' in a satin gown, pencilled brows, fake lashes and an incongruous 1940s kepi pinned at a jaunty angle anchoring a wavy wig. But a regular, at ease with her partner; no one paid the least attention. It was the new presence. A well-tuned French inspector felt all the eyes were on her as she made her way through a maze of tables to the bar, where, presenting her ticket, she was given a bottle of Boxer beer by a lovely blond man dressed in leather lederhosen shorts and nothing else. His hairless, well-pumped pecs were shiny against the dusty leder suspenders as he poured out half, then placed glass and bottle in front of her.

Sipping… Not bad. Nice to sample something new. Boxer. She smiled at the barman.

He cocked his head. 'What are you doing here?'

'Meeting someone.'

She understood why one might ask that question. She was the only actual girl.

She drank and perused the scene. Johnny Halliday was a jolt after Frank Sinatra. When Johnny finished growling, she turned to the barman. 'No Martin tonight? Martin Bettelman?'

His reply was a pained look. An abrupt shake of his head. *Bon.* Lise Bettelman had steered her straight. The barman knew Martin and was obviously chagrined at the sound of his name.

Sensing something, the canny cop mirrored the pained look with one of her own.

Empathy's an easy ploy. It moved the barman to exclaim, 'Such a waste!'

'Yes, a shame.' Voila: she saw anger flash across his boyish features as he uncorked a bottle, poured Scotch over ice in a glass waiting on a tray. Aliette encouraged his reaction to the missing Martin by looking hopeful. 'Don't worry. He'll be here. He's a regular.'

'Not with me. Never again.'

'No?' It was starting to come clear.

'Fucking con artist.' The barman lifted his tray and headed out to a table.

Like the basilisk guarding the door to Zup, the barman's leather shorts were minus a bum—his behind was there in all its tight and hairless glory as he passed among the patrons and bent to serve the ordered drink. The tuxedo-clad dancer was now seated at the next table. He gave the barman's behind an admiring pat and got a coquettish wiggle for his trouble. But it prompted the Heidi doorman with the horrid tongue to stride directly over to slap the admiring gentleman in the face and give him a piece of his mind. The elegant man was contrite and cowed, no match for Heidi. And his extravagant date did not look pleased with his less than elegant behaviour as she examined the red spot on his cheek. Heidi dragged her lovely barman back to the bar, where they argued in harsh German, an arm's length from where the inspector stood. They were Adelhard and Maximilian. They were oblivious to her presence. It didn't matter, she could hardly catch a word of it, though it was clearly a lover's quarrel. The glaring truth of Zup had left her feeling slightly stupid. She sipped her 'complimentary' beer and rolled with it, humming along with an unknown but not unpleasant version of "La Vie en Rose."

One often stumbled onto revelations, stupidly or otherwise. It was part of the job.

When she finished her beer, Max the barman was sulking. Adelhard, weird keeper of the door, was looking too mean for a foreign cop on an unofficial fishing trip to push any further. As for the rest of them, the inspector was arriving at the realization that her presence here did not mean much to anyone. She was heading for the door when a voice behind her asked in English, 'Are you lost?' It was the gentleman in the tux with the sneaky hand.

'I think I'm starting to get my bearings, thank you.'

'Ah, you're French.'

She smiled. In English, she asked, 'Are you a friend of Martin?'

The man returned the smile. 'I was...for one beautiful night.' The extravagantly gowned transvestite beside him stiffened, controlling automatic jealousy, assessing an out-of-place visitor. Her debonair chum patted her hand, assuring, 'But that's all in the past.'

'And Max?' Gesturing toward the bar.

'Same. Well, longer than a night, poor boy…Eh, Greta?' Greta nodded darkly to confirm. The bow-tied man told Aliette, 'Martin was our beau Français but now we seem to have lost him. Haven't seen him for weeks. But we all feel a little safer, if you know what I mean.'

'Maybe I do. Where would he get to?'

'Greener pastures, I'd imagine.'

'Another club around here?'

'Not like this.'

'No… Merci, messieurs…madame.' To the one pretending to be Greta Garbo. May as well play the game. She sensed she'd be returning. As the music flared and dancers rose, Aliette left Zup feeling poor Lise Bettelman didn't know the half of it where it came to Martin's cunts.

– 6 –

ANGEL ON A ROCK

Aliette was tired, but she was resisting going home. Claude would be in their bed by now and she did not want to be. Once back on French territory she stopped at a riverside lay-by and sat for a spell, going over the details of the case in her mind: a chaotic crime-of-passion scenario made the most sense. A visit to a gay nightclub added a new range of possibility. Yes, an outraged wife taking revenge fit. Poor Lise. Though a fine painting smashed and ruined on the head of the victim who was likely already dead still did not make sense, at least it was clearly related. Or could be. Martin Bettelman. Security guard. A gay security guard who minded some of the finest art around. Who had, it seemed, screwed his way through the regular crowd at Zup. What had he said, that elegant dancer?…they were safer without Martin. Why? Was it strictly sexual innuendo? Or had Martin brought something criminal into their madcap midst?

It was a warm night in the final days of Alsace summer, surely one of the last they'd have. The inspector started the car and continued on, in no great hurry, mulling, heading back to the scene of the crime. If the 'beach' was what they said it was — a dark meeting place for anonymous sex, a nexus of forbidden need — could violent death be a tempting extra? The Day-Glo-treated yellow-blue remains of a police barrier ribbon were clear and bright in the glow of the pump parts factory. The inspector turned off the road and bumped along the track through the trees, pulled up at the edge of the unkempt field, cut motor and lights and waited, peering into the haze of moist air rising off the canal.

Her eyes adjusted. She saw no cars parked surreptitiously among the trees. A tiny sliver of new moon made it impossible to see the shore from this distance. She sat with the window down a crack, listening, waiting for a car to come rolling into the woods and stop beside her. Or for someone to come walking out of the misty dark.

She smiled at the thought. She was comfortable. This was her job.

What I'm supposed to be doing, Claude.

Aliette Nouvelle had spent a strange six weeks sitting in a car with Claude Néon, driving the streets, searching for a man who was supposed to no longer exist. You could say it was how they'd met. She had been *his* boss, then. Claude had been her pain-in-the-ass assistant. She had found the missing man, but her methods were questioned. Claude Néon had won the promotion.

It was difficult to divine how those six weeks had led to passion, but they had. Eventually. Something to do with a sharing of experience too inchoate to define. Which is why it was a miracle. Eh, Claude? A miracle within a mystery. Now Claude preferred that she cook supper.

Brooding on what might have been and should have been was not constructive. It probably put her briefly to sleep. But something broke the spell. She jolted awake, then froze, alert.

What? Slowly rolling the window fully open. Eyes straining.

There was a faint cracking sound, stones or branches…Where?

The inspector exited carefully, stepped onto damp grass, walked cautiously toward the water, listening, watching. She had no gun. She never did. She had a can of pepper spray and a Swiss army knife Claude had given her after they'd argued to a stand-off as to her need for a gun. She could smell the water, then hear it. Water barely moving. She froze mid-step and listened. Sounds in the bushes to her left. She moved in that direction, eventually came to the edge of the bank and moved down the rock-strewn slope. Heard a splash downstream and froze again.

She crept closer. There: a figure on the shore.

Aliette took another step, careful, aware of her feet on doubtful purchase.

He was naked, standing on a large rock, perched there, white back, falling hair, lean buttocks, taut legs, an arm outstretched like a sentinel signalling. And so deathly white set against shapeless darkness. Like marble. A perfect, statuesque pose, strange and oddly beautiful.

Aliette Nouvelle did know how to process what she saw, except to feel that it was somehow remarkable, almost unworldly. Of course he did not have wings—but the image of an angel came to mind. Her impulse was to get closer, to see his face full on.

And so another breathless step, inching down and closer…

She slipped on a loose rock, cursing, '*Bordel!*'

She was on her feet in a second, calling, 'Police! Halt!'

But the figure on the shore dove into the dark canal and disappeared.

Not a trace, not a ripple, as she reached the place and stood there on the shore.

7

NOT JUST ANOTHER MORNING AT FEDPOL

SWISS SIDE

Agent Franck Woerli was pleased to do a favour for the French cop. As a member of FedPol, the Swiss Federal Criminal Police, Woerli's purview was both extra- and international. And his inclination was to do what he could to counter the small-minded actions of too many local counterparts. He knew all about the sort of petty-minded crap Basel City Police Commander Heinrich Boehler threw in the way of what should have been straightforward, coordinated information sharing amongst police. Boehler was devoutly pro-gun, very active in ProTell, the Swiss version of the NRA. He routinely blocked the sharing of gun registry information out of an inflated and retrogressive sense of patriotism attached to the national reputation for guarding privacy at whatever cost, and especially from foreigners. Franck Woerli was quietly ashamed to be even remotely associated with the likes of Heinrich Boehler. He was glad to make the call for Inspector Nouvelle. They had accomplished good things together, the latest being their central role in bringing down a trans-Euro hashish importation ring. About four years ago? Time flew. Woerli had been deskbound lately, investigating payroll fraud. But his desk had a phone and he had rank. He used it and extracted the required information.

He got back to her within the hour. The gun was registered to VigiTec, the security firm where her victim was employed.

'Merci, Franki. It's what I feared…' A pause. A pause he could feel. In that French voice he did enjoy, she put it to him. 'In the mood for some work, Agent Woerli?'

'I would love it, Inspector. Unfortunately I'm up to my ears in payroll tax fiddles. Not too exciting, to say the least, but with all the migrant workers flowing in, it's big a problem. And you know, a simple murder, I think you may have to work this one with the Commander.'

'But it's *not* so simple...' Aliette Nouvelle hesitated again at the other end of the line. Then, with a what-the-hell kind of sigh, she said, 'We also have a painting. Probably Swiss-owned.' She described the ruined piece found near the victim. 'Art means you people, not Boehler, yes?'

'Normally, but not absolutely.' Woerli paused to open the newspaper on the desk in front of him—they'd moved Monday's headline story to page three. 'You say Friday night?'

'Our best guess.'

'That makes two in...looks like the same day. Art-related murders, I mean.' He filled her in. Justin Aebischer, a well-regarded Basel art restorer, had been murdered on or about Friday afternoon or evening. Found Sunday on his back patio, sodden with the past weekend's rain, a bullet through his head. 'Not here. Biel. A village an hour out of town. Perp came up from the forest, through his garden and shot him. He worked there, studio's in his basement. So—'

'So that is interesting, Franki. Justin Aebischer. Did a painting go missing?'

'They are not saying much about that. As usual, it's someone else's business.'

In the same way Swiss democracy affords cantonal politics maximum leeway for laws and structures, the Swiss policing system confers maximum control on canton forces. Thus Heinrich Boehler could rule Basel City canton like the Sheriff of Nottingham. And whoever ran the Basel Lands force would have complete jurisdiction over the past weekend's murder in Biel.

'But, Franki, if a Swiss painting ends up in France?'

'But,' he said, quiet and patient, 'we won't know that until they decide to tell us.'

'No.' A pause. Franck Woerli wondered if the French cop could hear his weary resignation.

In that French pause, FedPol Agent Woerli reflected bitterly as to how he hated payroll fraud. Strictly numbers, dry as a bone. Only saving grace: it was an extra-territorial issue, no question, and he could actually close a case. Trying to work in a coordinated manner with the cantons was worse than frustrating. It was soul-killing. 'Excuse me? Sorry…'

She repeated, 'Do you know a place called Zup?'

'A place called Zup?'

'A club. A gay nightclub in the old city.'

'Can't say I do, Inspector.'

'No…' Another noticeable pause. 'Can you find out more about this Justin Aebischer?'

'I probably could.'

'Bring it to me. I'll buy you lunch. At the Rembrandt.'

She could not see it from France, but the offer brought a spontaneous smile. 'I would enjoy that. Give me a day?'

'Of course. Merci, Franki.'

'You are most welcome. I look forward to seeing you again.'

And to lunch. That Dutchman who ran the place where they met whenever he made the trip to the otherwise dull city up the road—van Hoogsomething?—was a genius with carp taken from the streams in the forestlands along the border. The pleasing thought of a special meal and a few hours in the company of Inspector Nouvelle left Franck Woerli staring out at the Rhine. A tiny section was always there, visible from his office in a sixth-floor suite on Freiestrasse, just where it met Eisenstrasse. The humidity had blown away with a pre-dawn shower. Today the river ran silvery and energetic on a blustery overcast morning.

A body. Art-related? He wondered what it held in store.

Amazing how a phone call will poke a hole in the greyness that settles on the soul.

He got up from his desk and went down the hall. To Cultural Crimes. 'Morning…'

Agent Josephina Perella was another mid-level senior rank veteran, fiftyish, Franck Woerli's contemporary, a career cop who'd studied in Florence, Paris and in Basel, of course. For the last dozen years she had headed a small but busy brigade dedicated to the investigation of crimes related to cultural artifacts, institutions and transactions. The art squad. Though her team's solve record could hold up against most any of their counterparts' across Europe, Josephina rarely smiled. A dour, largish woman, she did not smile when Franck Woerli appeared at her office door — just turned in her chair and fixed him with a questioning look.

'What can you tell me about Justin Aebischer?'

'Nothing more than I've read in the paper.' Her lack of emotion was a professional thing. Franck Woerli recognized it because he felt it himself. A weariness borne of too many years of systemic futility? He could not really call her a friend but he could always see it in her almond-shaped Longobard eyes. Franck and Josephina communicated in their silent way.

'I mean about him. Just got an interesting call from a French friend... You know him?'

She shrugged. 'In passing. Affiliated with the Kunstmuseum but hardly ever there lately — too much private work. Specialized in the Baroque. Very talented and highly regarded.'

'Is he gay?'

'I wouldn't know, Franck.' A certain frown added to the flat tone said Josephina did not want to get into sexual gossip. Franck doubted sex played much of a part in her life. Inspector Perella swung her chair back round to face her desk, as if to say that's all I know, goodbye.

Franck Woerli was wanting to impress Inspector Nouvelle with some useful information, and it was not just to justify the lunch she'd promised. He needed to. He badly needed to feel the spark that came from being actively involved in a real case — on the ground, as it were. He knew that Basel held the largest repository of art in Switzerland. The city's museums and private galleries were a source of civic pride and steady tourist trade. It also meant a lot of art went missing. Most files came to FedPol because most stolen art passed out of the country. When Franck Woerli asked Josephina Perella if a murdered VigiTec security guard found in the river on the French side with a painting on the rocks nearby might have a connection with any of her files, she was jolted out of her moody cloud. Perella spun back round, immediately intrigued.

'Name of Martin Bettelman.'

'Doesn't ring a bell,' was her immediate response. But Woerli sensed she was as excited as he by the possibility of taking part in something with warm guts. 'What painting?'

'They don't know...pretty bashed up. ID-ing it could obviously help.'

Josephina Perella's eyes darkened spontaneously. She went directly to her computer.

'No...' Martin Bettelman was nowhere in her directory. 'Worked for VigiTec?'

'Yes. For ten years or so.'

'A bashed-up painting on the French side?'...musing on it, running her cursor down her docket. She had directives and leads on missing pieces pointing to Germany, Scotland, Japan, Saudi Arabia, Los Angeles, Florida...But, 'I see nothing moving through France at the moment. Your friend's Fine Art group in Quai d'Orfevres are good at sharing. I suggest she call them.'

'But it could've come across from here—same day as this Aebischer, Josephina. Worth a look? A call?' He meant to the investigators at Biel. Did she hear the urgent thing he was suddenly feeling? 'I mean if art goes missing, you are the best source in the region and they—'

'The problem is, Franck, they wouldn't necessarily know. They don't know art from artichokes, most of them. More to the point, the business is so secretive. If someone brings a million-franc painting to Justin Aebischer for cleaning, they are going to be very, very discreet.'

He nodded, took two deep breaths. 'Mm, makes it hard.'

'Very. Does it matter if Aebischer was gay?'

'This Martin Bettelman was. Frequented some club in the old city.'

'Right.' Perella saw the obvious possibilities.

'They'd have to let you in, Josephina.' Let her in to the Aebischer investigation. 'And you might enjoy my friend on the French police. I've worked with her. She's good.'

'Maybe.'

Franck Woerli watched her weighing his proposition. He asked, 'You like fried carp?'

'If it's done right,' Josephina said. Again her eyes betrayed her.

'What if it's done perfectly?'

Woerli caught the traces of a smile. It was couched in consternation, but it was there.

Perella nodded in her dour way. 'I'll call my friend Dieter.' Dieter Taub was Head of Resource Allocation at VigiTec. 'When paintings go missing in Basel it's a good bet VigiTec has or has had contracts with the owner, be it gallery or home. Not certain, mind you—it's a competitive market.'

'OK, Josephina. You lead...' Franck Woerli realized he was smiling. The ball was rolling. Josephina Perella was acting like a cop taking control of an investigation. It did his heart good to see a sense of purpose there. It had been a while. He felt it reflecting back inside himself.

He was another cop who did not know art from artichokes. But he knew murder, and after too much time in the muffled world of tax fraud numbers he longed to be involved.

8

Our Murder, Their Painting

'So: Our murder. Their painting.'
  'Seems so.'

Claude hadn't woken when she'd crawled in beside him the previous night. She'd hurried out before he'd got down to the kitchen that morning. But once at the office, it was her duty to inform him of her movements on the new case. *Alors*: victim a French citizen employed in Basel as a security guard; gay or bisexual. She had feelers out concerning the club he frequented and possible links to a similar 'art-related' murder on the Swiss side, possibly the same day.

Commissaire Néon said, 'I really wish you wouldn't do that.' He meant going to Basel unannounced and uninvited. He did not dare mention the late hour of her return—two? closer to three. He'd been fast asleep. Claude knew their relationship was hanging by a thread.

Inspector Nouvelle did not respond to wishes. 'I have to. Sometimes. You know that. I had a beer at the bar, very low key. To them I'm some friend from across the border who was going to meet him. They had no idea. Probably still don't.' While the probable gay factor in Martin Bettelman's violent death was noted in her report to the Procureur, her visit to Zup was not. So Claude's ass was covered. And the victim's name had yet to be released. Claude's order. He was figuring they could keep it to themselves for another day, with some luck, maybe two.

Unless it was to their advantage to name Martin Bettelman.

'Depends if it's a love thing. Or a business thing,' suggested the inspector.

'Which is it?'

'I'll bet love. But paintings are worth money and there are too many possibilities to say for sure just yet.' She had told Claude about the bar, but not about the beautiful unwordly figure briefly encountered at the crime site in the dead of night. Everyone has their own sense of when information should and should not be released. It's called ownership.

'*Merde.*' Claude slumped in his chair. 'I hate these things.' He was speaking in his role as principal commissaire of the last PJ unit before the border. He could not care less about her sneaky moves in Swiss bars. He knew you did what you had to do. It was his fear of an international shit storm. 'Can't you call someone over there? Get them to pick up that end?'

'Already have. My friend Franck Woerli at FedPol's helping with the painting.'

'He'll stay clear of Boehler?' A mean-minded ownership freak if ever there was.

She assured him, 'As clear as humanly possible.' She knew Franki's views on Boehler.

Claude scratched at the spot in the centre of his thinning scalp. '*Pédés* in love, then?'

'Probably. Though there is the possibility of a lady. Lover? Business?'

'Mm.' To be determined.

'You have to practise saying homosexual. Or gay. No more *pédé.* OK?'

'Right, right, right.' The political part of being in charge could be a strain.

— —

An hour later, none of the media types camped in rue des Bons Enfants batted an eye when a police car turned into the courtyard. Aliette went down to receive the victim's widow.

Lise Bettelman was accompanied by Ginette Gromm, a social worker from the Saint-Louis detachment. Lise was on edge, scowling. As Raphaele Petrucci welcomed them and went about sorting papers, easing Lise toward the moment when the drawer was opened and the sheet pulled back, Madame Gromm quietly explained to Aliette that they had taken a swab and cut a sampling from her shorts. Lise had resisted loudly, insulted by the notion that she might be a suspect. Aliette advised Madame Gromm to assure Lise that it was strictly routine. Gromm advised that her client remained deeply resentful. Lise had insisted she was ready to ID her husband. But she would need a lot of counselling to deal with her resentment, not to say the shock. 'She wants to get it over with. For the children's sake,' Gromm confided. 'Which is good. I think we can begin to work toward some closure here.'

Closure? Aliette had begun to hear this word. It sounded manufactured. She doubted it had validity, given the context, usually violence, often death, against which it was being applied. But social work was not her métier, God knew.

Was closure synonymous with acceptance? Madame Bettelman's feelings for the father of her children had hardened. Upon viewing the corpse and signing the papers, she told Raphaele Petrucci, 'I don't care. Put him in the garbage. Burn him. Drop him back in the river.'

The pathologist was smiling gently, purring low, being his professionally sympathetic best. 'I'm sorry, madame. I meant, where should we *send* him? Once you've signed the release form, the deceased is no longer under our purview.'

The social worker was less solicitous. 'You have to take him home, Lise, see it through to the bitter end.'

'No.' Adamant, steely, she turned to leave.

Ginette Gromm admonished, 'But your children — they need to know the end point. You can tell them whatever you want. They'll certainly form their own sense of it as they grow up. But they need a name somewhere. A couple of dates. He's their father. It's only fair to them.'

'What about to me?'

'We've been through this.'

'I don't *want* him!'

Raphaele Petrucci began to rub his tummy as the women bickered. Aliette made a face. He caught her signal, clasped his hands like an attentive undertaker. When Ginette and Lise reached an impasse, Raphaele proffered the package waiting on his desk. 'And his effects.'

'His effects…' Lise Bettelman was stupefied, as if in a heavy narcotic trance, as she beheld the eight-hundred-euro suit which had been dried and folded, if not exactly cleaned and pressed. The silk tie. 'Silk socks? *Mon Dieu!*' And the single shoe. You didn't need the pair to guess the value. 'That fucking, sneaking, selfish…' Spinning away from the table.

'Lise…please.' Madame Gromm moved close and put a hand on the woman's arm.

'But it is absurd!'

'A lot of men who discover their sexuality later in life lead secret lives.'

'The money this suit cost would feed us for three months!' Fingering the soiled but still fine summer weight linen. 'Four! …the way I've had to stretch his shitty cheques.'

'He may have been in a lot of turmoil. This suit may have been the only thing to calm it.'

'Oh shut up! *I* know what calmed it…Bastard!' To Raphaele. 'I really don't want him.'

'And I really can't help you,' he replied. A sad smile, a slow shake of his handsome head. Most people whose fate brought them to this chilly place were lulled into providing the requisite information—which included the name of an undertaker to be contacted.

Lise Bettelman began going through the pockets of the high-priced suit, automatic and perfunctory, the way a woman does before she dumps a load of washing into the machine on Saturday morning. Of course IJ had been there first and they were empty. There was a large envelope on the table. She turned it over—sunglasses, reading glasses, a silver comb and a key chain spilled onto the table. Lise began examining each item with the same stark glance, like some scientist assessing—before dropping each item in the basket by Raphaele's desk. Aliette stepped forward with the recovered wallet. Lise grimly removed the bills, pocketing them. She began pulling credit cards. A cursory glance, then she let each one fall from her fingers. Opening her man's identity card, she tore it in eight pieces and tossed them over her shoulder like so many grains of salt.

The social worker tried a scornful, mothering tone. 'Stop it, Lise. You're only making more trouble for yourself. And your children!'

She was ignored. Gazing at the straight-on photo affixed to Martin's driver permit, Lise Bettelman pronounced, 'Martin Jean-Marie Adolphus Bettelman cheated his wife and children.' She dropped the licence into the waste basket. 'For sex. Can you believe it? Sex with men.'

The social worker was getting worried. 'You mustn't do that. You'll need those things!'

Lise sulked. 'I signed for it. All of it,' dropping the wallet, still thick with credit cards, into the basket, '*and I don't want it!* You understand? For my children...For my children's sake, I do not want this man in their lives. No stone, no dates. No part of him! Martin Bettelman's effects are garbage. His fucking credit cards too!' Now moving on to Martin's key chain.

Ginette Gromm tried again. 'You're his wife. You were married by a priest, we talked about this. You have to take him home. Take responsibility. It's your duty.'

'Not any more...not any more...' Lise muttered, flipping each key on the chain, studying it, ripping it from the ring, letting it fall with a clink on the floor. '*Plus jamais, plus jamais...*'

'Home, Lise. It's the only proper way to end this. You'll never feel right.'

Lise Bettelman's eyes grew wide, slightly crazy, as she stopped at a key. Staring at it. Then at the social worker. She took this one key from the ring. She let the rest of the keys drop in a clatter on the floor. The flustered social worker stooped to retrieve them...and the stuff in the waste basket. Madame Bettelman held this one key out to Raphaele Petrucci.

He shrugged — made no move accept it. No longer his problem. Sorry.

It was not a plea, it was a gesture: a tiny key was a wife's rhetorical prop as she told her audience of three, 'The home is where the heart is. Yes? His heart was not with us. No way! The one he gave his love to can take him home. Scum!' With a sob, she slammed the key down on the table, swept the pile of lovely clothes off of it, then kicked them where they lay on the floor — several violent kicks, as if somehow her Martin was still somewhere inside them.

Then Lise Bettelman ran weeping from the morgue.

Cursing, social worker Ginette Gromm left the mess on the floor and hustled after her.

The inspector briefly considered giving chase. If he was still out there, crime reporter Serge Phaneuf was sure to waylay the poor woman, offer her a ride, get everything he needed to start an international war between the French and the Swiss. But Aliette lingered in the morgue, very interested in this last key. The rejected credit cards might come in handy too.

She gathered them back into the envelope and took it back upstairs.

The courthouse, around the corner from the Hôtel de Ville, is called the Palais de Justice. Many around the Republic are brand new these days, as if designed for space age justice. Ours — much of it painstakingly reconstructed after a messy war — retains the vaulted Second Empire look and conservative feel to match the pervading local mindset. Aren't we all conservative at heart forever? The suite of offices housing public prosecutors and staff at the sunny end of the third floor is known as *le Parquet*. Claude had arrived by himself. Aliette knew he was avoiding her in daylight, the way she was needing to create some essential space at night.The commissaire and his inspector sat drinking coffee with Procureur Michel Souviron, quietly ignoring each other till Chief Magistrate Gérard Richand finally bustled in from his own suite at the far end of the hall.

'So,' Michel said by way of getting down to business, 'homosexuals killing each other in a park over art that probably belongs to the Swiss. Obviously we need a solid footing in Basel and this could be a problem.' The Swiss did not need the nuisance of a murder in France. They would, in their polite way, slam the door. All present knew he meant Commander Boehler.

'Almost impossible,' Claude confirmed.

Gérard refuted that. 'Not at all. We go in the back way.'

Resisting the obvious crass rejoinder, the urbane and always politically astute Proc smiled evenly at the ever-earnest magistrate. 'Meaning?'

'Stolen cultural goods,' Gérard replied. Though they might have to prove that before proving the murder of Bettelman. 'Painting first, murder second. I'll set up a temporary unit.'

Claude scratched his chin, eternally skeptical where it came to Gérard Richand's bright ideas. 'Even if we do, there's still no link between the murder and that painting.'

Aliette responded smartly to the commissaire's doubt. 'Sure there is.'

He was forced to face her and ask, 'Yes?'

'His head. And the picture frame.' Forensics and their pathologist had both confirmed this.

Claude pursed his lips. Sucking a lemon. He could not argue.

Pedantic Gérard began to quote the rules. With respect to customs offences involving narcotic drugs, arms and stolen cultural goods, customs officers carry out judicial investigations within special ad hoc units where they work jointly with judicial police officers. Such temporary investigative units are set up, at their discretion, by the public prosecutor or by the examining magistrate, who have also authority to appoint the special agent in charge of the unit, who may be either a judicial police officer or a judicial customs officer. '...that would be you, Inspector.'

'Could work,' Michel agreed. 'A bit messy, but yes.' He suggested Gérard prepare an Instruction for a two-pronged Rogatory enquiry balancing the murder of Martin Bettelman with the theft of an as-yet-to-be-identified painting. He would call Strasbourg to confer with the regional head of Customs. Then a caveat: 'I'll do my best with Grimm.' Prosecutor Artur Grimm was Michel Souviron's counterpart in Basel City Canton. Never as blustering as Commander Boehler, but just as difficult where it came to the politics of justice.

Gérard rather cavalierly waved this worry away. Given the usual attitude, he was sure Prosecutor Grimm would assign the case to the most junior magistrate in Basel City. Gérard was confident he could instruct legal rings around a callow Swiss.

'You've certainly thought about it,' Michel murmured, jotting notes.

'I respect fine art,' Gérard declared. He neglected to mention murdered security guards.

Was she only one who noticed that? Yes, well, maybe Martin Bettelman did not merit much respect... In any event, Aliette liked the notion of being a special agent. Gérard Richand had not showed such imagination since, well, she could barely remember. She'd long ago slotted those nights into a dormant category called Another Life.

'As for the painting,' Gérard went on, 'I've had it sent to a local restoration expert I happen to know. Very talented. In Kembs. Just up the road from our crime scene, as a matter of fact.'

Aliette, who knew her judge, instantly heard subtext. Not clear exactly what, but she felt vague alarm. 'I'm sure we'll be done well before that, Gérard. Doesn't it take months?'

'Even so. It would be a nice gesture to return it in the condition that it left, no?' He passed the forensics photo of the shoemaker to Michel Souviron — effectively his boss. The Proc studied the image. 'We really ought to have him cleaned and mended.'

Aliette said, 'But it does belong to someone. Do we have the right?'

'More than a right. An obligation.' Gérard had indeed thought about it. 'Given the context, I won't be surprised if no one claims it.' Voice dropping a tone, the judge opined, 'Those Swiss care more about their business reputations than a wretched security guard. We have to make our shoemaker as attractive as possible. Make someone want him back. We'll clean him up and put him on display. Someone will recognize it, at the very least. That will help us.'

'It could.' Procureur Souviron was impressed. Magistrate Richand had a leg up on this file.

'Do we have a budget?' Aliette definitely sensed an ulterior motive in Gérard's tactic.

Michel had no idea what said budget ought to be.

'We'll bill it back to whoever claims him,' Gérard said, overriding the point. 'If they want their shoemaker back, they pay. Or we sell him to the highest bidder.'

There! Aliette suppressed a grin but had to roll her eyes at Gérard's little machination. After a reasonable amount of time *Gérard* would buy the shoemaker for a nominal fee from the legal equivalent of the Public Lost and Found. He was investing the Republic's money as a hedge against a future acquisition. Sneaky Gérard. But if Michel went for it, fine.

Aliette was also feeling an extra-legal obligation to mend the battered shoemaker.

If Claude saw through Gerard's self interest, he let it go by. Not much of an art lover.

But the commissaire left the meeting with the consoling thought that Customs would officially lead the charge across the border. Claude knew that the ones who led the charge were the ones who were killed. He emphasized that he did not mean her. He meant the Office.

Aliette accepted this with a shrug.

She stared out the cab window for the balance of the ride back uptown.

- 9 -
JOSEPHINA'S ROLE

FedPol Agent Franck Woerli had gone for lunch. So Agent Josephina Perella left a note with a list of gallery addresses on his desk with basic instructions on how to proceed, and went down to the garage for a car. Once out of the city, she took a longer but more picturesque route, destination Oberwil. She glided past harvest-rich fields, grazing livestock, the odd farmer on a harvesting machine. Not that she enjoyed the scenery. She brooded. Any links in this thing would surely lead through Basel and that had to be controlled. On hearing her reasons, a visit to the Aebischer murder site had been graciously arranged by Basel Lands Commander Berger. He was a soft touch, the diametric opposite of his bloody-minded Basel City counterpart. After gleaning what she could, Josephina would confront Marcus Streit — the letter he'd sent had to be dealt with, there was no avoiding it now. The thought of a Reubens torn and sodden from a weekend in the Rhine left her feeling ill. She could not even begin to contemplate dealing with the French. Just over an hour later, upon entering the Basel Lands police detachment at Oberwil, Josephina Perella realized she had never felt so alone.

The receptionist's buzz produced Inspector Hans Grinnell, the officer in charge of the Aebischer investigation. He was younger than herself by half a generation, and as fit and clean-cut as the junior football coach the photos on his desk showed him to be. His sand-coloured corduroy suit was stylish, but his farmer brush cut ruined the effect. Agent Perella was glad when, after providing tea and a biscuit, he informed her straight off that he had no particular interest in art.

She told him not to worry, few cops did, she hoped her expertise might be of help.

Grinnell said there was not much more to be told than had been reported. He called up a file and turned the screen. Josephina Perella dutifully perused the Basel Lands forensics team's scant collection of indicators: the bullet from the victim's brain, but no casing found; a photograph of a casting of a shoe sole taken from the lawn — 'a hiking boot, killer came up from the forest'; photos of some markings along the killer's likely trail; one unfinished glass of beer, pieces of another unused glass smashed on the patio flagstone, one empty bottle, one full — opened, Boxer, indicating a social occasion barely begun, violently occluded. 'Pretty clear he knew his visitor, which gives one to wonder why he arrived from that direction,' Grinnell mused. 'Apart from wanting to conceal a murder, of course. There are always lots of hikers on a nice day. We could put out a call for possible sightings...we'll see. There are some other things that might happen first.' A shrug. 'That's about it just now,' Grinnell concluded. 'Plus he was gay.'

'And so was the man the French found. Martin Bettelman.'

Grinnell nodded. 'Which is why you are here.'

'That and the fact both Bettelman and Aebischer worked within the art community,' noted Perella. 'And the time frame. Seems too tight to be coincidence.'

Hans Grinnell did not react. He was waiting to hear more.

First she confessed, 'Not many of my cases involve murder.' And she sipped her tea. 'But the art community is small. The gay element reduces it further. When we received that call this morning the links were there, and it occurred to me that if I can find something in his desk as to clients, contacts, etcetera, well, we might make some progress.' She bit into her cookie.

Grinnell leaned forward. 'Still, I'm intrigued as to why you would receive such a call.'

Josephina blanched. Her nerves were fogging her antennae. She wondered, What else did they know about Justin Aebischer? 'I don't understand, Inspector.'

'Why call a Federal art cop about a security guard killed in France?'

'Oh. Well… But they didn't call me. It was my colleague. He has worked with the French investigator. She needed help identifying the gun — to get around Boehler?' Grinnell nodded. He knew Boehler too. Josephina was glad for that. 'They saw the links, he brought it to me, I talked to Bettelman's employer, got a little more — here I am.' She smiled and hurried past the moment, gently asking if he could maybe show her any pertinent business materials found at the scene — contracts, client lists, an agenda book, that kind of thing? Grinnell said no, the victim's desk and papers were an unfathomable mess. She said much of the art business was not exactly regular and suggested that, given an hour at Aebischer's studio, she might notice something useful in that vein. She expressly made no mention of a painting found with Martin Bettelman.

And neither did Hans Grinnell. 'So you're thinking crime of passion?'

'Yes. Or something like it. The thing is, no one has mentioned if anything was stolen.'

'No. We're in a bit of a holding pattern there.' Grinnell folded his arms and waited.

Josephina swallowed. She was not doing this right. '*Was* anything stolen?'

The Basel Lands cop's grin broke wide and bright, just this side of laughter. 'Agent Perella, I thought you'd never ask.' She gaped. He shrugged. 'We don't really know.' He turned to the forensics report on his screen. 'I'll just send this along to your shop, then let's you and I go see.'

Grinnell's smile had a unreadable edge. He made her nervous. He seemed to want to.

— —

Josephina Perella followed Hans Grinnell out to an isolated cul-de-sac on the farthest edge of the village of Biel. The twenty-minute drive gave her time to calm down, get her priorities in order. The crime scene was the last property up a winding hill lined with chalet-styled homes. On the outside it was a mundane example of Swiss alpine design. Two uniformed officers were keeping the site secure. Grinnell exchanged greetings and introduced Josephina, and they went in.

Inside, Justin Aebischer had effected simple but tasteful changes to enlarge and brighten the place, for himself and no one else, this was quickly apparent. Grinnell led her down to the basement, to a beautifully opened room. They walked directly out onto a patio with a view looking over the forest and all the way to France. Josephina followed him to the edge of a cared-for garden, already showing signs of missing Justin. 'Here,' he gestured. 'Whoever did it came out of the woods. Went back the same way.' She dutifully studied the garden, the path down to the woods. It meant nothing. When Grinnell finally ushered her back inside, through the stylish recreation area and into the victim's workroom, Josephina's heart was banging in her chest.

Justin Aebischer's studio was nothing special. He did not need the very latest technology—that was available in the lab in the basement at the Kunstmuseum if a job required it. But he had the tools he needed and, more important, the reputation he'd built as one of the very best. Opening cupboards, the fridge, Josephina Perella perused the place where Justin Aebischer had performed his magic. She was in her element now—a slow tour through his tools and materials helped calm her rattled nerves, giving her eyes a chance to see correctly.

Knowing Hans Grinnell would not know what she was seeing helped.

But she could not poke around forever. Lifting back the thick plastic drape, Josephina Perella saw what she had come to see. Hans Grinnell joined her. 'A Reubens, apparently.'

She heard his insinuation loud and clear. 'Apparently?'

The canton cop was pensive, gazing at the work. 'Still waiting on a definitive answer, Agent Perella. I'd be very interested in your opinion. I gather your expertise includes forgery?'

'I have dealt with dozens of instances, Inspector.'

'And would you authenticate this painting?' So saying, he retreated, leaving her to study it.

Impishly titled *Post Chase Pleasures*, surely a product of the famous Antwerp studio, her best guess circa 1620: a hunting scene, now considered the Flemish master's obscure specialty. Actually, a *post*-hunting scene. No sign of the hunting party. A smallish study of a beagle, away from the pack, contentedly licking its anus. An afterthought, almost certainly. Probably an old master's joke, maybe in reply to friend and sometimes partner Frans Snyders' own variation on the theme, it would have been something kept in the studio for the private entertainment of the artist and his cronies. But these artistic jokes had since found their way into collections and were now highly prized, precisely for their quirky lewdness. Baroque animal porn, Flemish style.

Josephina knew it was easily worth a million US dollars.

Or one just like it. Somewhere.

Re-emerging from the protected area, resolved, professionally grave, she told him, 'In my opinion this is the original. It's not quite finished. Looks like light damage. The red was in the process of being re-deepened, if one can put it that way. I would say he hadn't yet got to the blues.' Grinnell shrugged. She explained, 'Justin Aebischer was known for his skill at bringing back original colours with original materials—almost an alchemist the way he could zero in on the right pigments and medium. Many were proprietary secrets, highly sought. And that's four hundred years ago. Justin could see them. It's very impressive. It's a shame he didn't get to finish. His poor client. With Justin gone, they may have to live with colour discrepancies forever. Or cheat it with new technology, of course. Have they been around?'

'Not yet.' Grinnell smiled oddly. 'I'm expecting them to come knocking any day now.'

Although murder was outside her ken, Josephina Perella knew a strategic cop smile when she saw one. She didn't like it. Needing space, she turned away from Hans Grinnell and began to go through Aebischer's desk, busying herself with documents until, bored, Grinnell drifted back out to the garden. She heard him chatting with the uniforms and felt herself relax.

She found Aebischer's business cards in a small box at the back of a middle drawer. *Reubens & Associates*. Justin Aebischer could work flawlessly in a range of styles but it was common knowledge within the trade that the majority of Aebischer's commissions fell within the Baroque period, as advertised on his ludicrous card. *Reubens & Associates*. Cheeky, if not stupidly careless, even in a very specialized market. But it didn't matter now. Did it?

Josephina Perella cast a glance toward the garden.

When every inch of the desk had been thoroughly inspected, she sat back, turning to the patient Grinnell, exasperated. 'I cannot believe no one has called looking for their painting.'

The Basel Lands cop indicated negative.

Which confirmed what she already knew.

What she did not know: Was Grinnell playing straight with her? All she could do was push him. Staying in role, Josephina Perella folded her arms under her expansive breast in the manner of the older, senior cop. She added incredulity to exasperation. 'And you've contacted *no one*?'

'We're in contact with the Kunstmuseum. They came and had a look. They'll send some appraisers. They will help find the client.' He shrugged, sensing her skepticism. 'There are no documents. We looked, believe me. They're gone. *If* they existed.'

'But if that's the case, why didn't they take the painting back to their vault?'

'They offered. I asked them to leave it. Just to see.' That shrewd smile: His case. His way.

Without losing her temper but making sure Grinnell knew she found his methods wanting, FedPol Agent Perella wondered how the Basel Lands police could leave a 'very valuable!' work of art virtually unguarded for…'What? Almost a week now?' The place was isolated, easily accessible to anyone who knew the victim and what he had been doing! Two uniforms were easily eliminated! 'I mean, Inspector Grinnell, this is a genuine artistic treasure!'

Grinnell smiled. 'We're comfortable with it. The place is sealed. And—'

'That's all well and good, but I'm still not certain as to your cavalier—'

'And you're on tape, Agent Perella. Every move. Please…' Another sort of smile said, I'm not an idiot, Frau. 'We know what were dealing with here.'

Josephina stopped dead, peering around the room.

Grinnell said, 'The Museum people agreed it might help to leave the work here for a while, for the very reasons you're so worried about. A temptation too great to resist?' He sniffed. 'It's just a strategy where no other has occurred. Or the beginnings of one.'

Josephina was mulling. 'And Aebischer's bank?'

'We tried. Didn't get too far. His client ordered them not to reveal any information.' Grinnell's dry expression was universal: This is Switzerland, don't forget. The ones who could own a Reubens were also the banks' most valued customers. A closed loop and then some.

Josephina Perella felt that her best move now would be to shut up and go back to the city. She had found out what she been needing to know. The more she talked, the more harm she did.

Opening the plastic drape, gazing at it one last time. 'It seems authentic to me.'

Grinnell stepped close. 'I used to have a beagle. They do that. Disgusting. Worse than cats.'

— —

After leaving Hans Grinnell, Josephina Perella stopped at a quiet spot beside the Birsig River to gather her scattered wits. An unmitigated disaster. She'd got what she'd come for. But she had no idea what she'd given away. The Basel Lands inspector had been laughing at her.

She breathed for a good quarter-hour before opening her phone. Franck Woerli answered. 'Franck? Josephina. Just leaving Biel. Since I'm in the neighbourhood I thought I'd drive over to see one of Aebischer's fellow restorers. Marcus Streit. Consults for us regularly. He might have a sense of who Aebsicher was working for. There's nothing useful at the scene.'

'That's not good... Nothing here, either.' A weary-sounding Woerli recounted a frustrating afternoon visiting the galleries on her list. He had got no cooperation at all. 'Worse than bankers.'

Josephina commiserated. 'Welcome to my world, Franck,' adding, 'Sorry for disappearing. After talking to VigiTec, I sensed a certain urgency with this. Had to have a look for myself. But, dead end, I'm afraid—I mean from my perspective. We'll try again at the galleries. We really do need to get some kind of lead as to who Aebischer was working for and they would have it. I know how to get them talking... You received the Basel Lands forensics file?'

'Yes. Gone to the registry and over to France. Some results tomorrow, I hope.'

'Should help… Best call it a day, Franck. I might be late. We'll talk tomorrow.'

Woerli reminded her of their luncheon date in France.

'Looking forward to it.'

Signing off, her will evaporated. She sat there fighting tears. From that spot by the river Josephina Perella could see a hillside that she knew. There was a green patch at its peak, isolated in a swath of forest, enticingly sunny in late afternoon. Two kilometres north and you were over the line in France. She had passed days of freedom hiking and picnicking in those forests with the man she loved. And making love. On a hill overlooking France. In a glade beside a stream. He knew some lovely places. She'd never done such a thing before. Not many men fancied a largish woman. Fate sent the odd one to share her bed from time to time — just enough of them, always transient, to ensure an abiding sense of lonely entrapment, in her skin, in her job. Fate had never said it was the least bit sorry. When the man she loved proposed a scheme, Josephina Perella had said yes, with no remorse or shame.

She had so badly wanted it to work. And it had! Perfectly… How had this happened? If the copy was here, then the Reubens was in France. Ruined? The thought made her mind stop. Josephina took her gaze away from the hills and sat staring at the river, moment by moment exquisitely dappled in the lowering evening sun. Come on, Josephina, think! Martin Bettelman somehow gets wind of Justin's contract — probably in a bed somewhere. Bettelman kills Justin and takes the painting, leaving Justin's copy there for the world to find. He takes the painting to the French side? To whom? She had no problem seeing Bettelman being gunned down after the delivery — it happened all the time to naïve and greedy thieves. But then they destroy the thing?

Not priceless, but up there, top tier. It just did not make sense.

No rhyme or reason for this aberration came through the gentle motion of the river.

But it calmed her. And after more empty minutes, her willpower and focus regathered, more or less, she started up the car and headed for a hamlet on the border, heart tightening, struggling to cope. She would not give in to panic. She would work with Franck Woerli, the

French police as well. Stay right in middle, that was her role, and prove she could handle a crisis.

Josephina Perella wasn't very brave. But she was trying to be. For *him*.

Twenty minutes later she turned up a sylvan drive. Marcus Streit was another solitary artisan. Same trade as Justin Aebischer but a different kind of man. Older. Less talented. Less daring. His lawn was scruffy, his chalet in need of paint and newer, larger windows, a thorough cleaning of the mossy shingles. But his advice was always good. Josephina knocked.

Silence. Forest silence. She went in. He was sitting on the divan, sad looking, always that lovely slightly sad thing that pulled her to him, as if toward something in herself. 'It's gone,' she reported. 'The copy's there. I blew some smoke, but it can't last.' The tears were pushing. She fought them, fought panic. 'I cannot understand how a Reubens got torn apart and left in the river with that horrid little thief. Can you help me with that? Please!'

'Calm down, Josephina. Calm...' She tried. She watched him breathing, looking into her. 'Josephina, the Reubens is not in the river. It's somewhere safe with the Basel Lands police.'

'What are you talking about? How?...If the copy's on the table...' She stopped. It dawned even before he spoke the words, quietly damning.

'Did you even ask your colleague what painting they found?'

'Well, no, I...I saw the link to Justin and I...you said I had to go see which one was there. I just assumed...I—' She rubbed her pounding temples. Her mind would not pass that point.

'And you did, Josephina. Now we know. They've laid a trap.'

'Yes.' Slipping into a vague place, instincts backfiring. '...And you sent me.'

'That's your role. I certainly can never tell one from the other.'

'Yes. My role.' Then it occurred to wonder, 'But where is Marcus?'

'In the kitchen.'

She found Marcus Streit dead on his kitchen floor. One bullet through his head. She knew she should not have come here. Josephina was shaking as she stood over the body. She had to keep control of her fear. Police are *meant* to be brave. He stepped into the kitchen.

She asked, as stern and businesslike as she could manage, 'Did you need to do that?'

'Yes. Very necessary. We're closing it down, Josephina. Completely.'

'But why? Marcus couldn't hurt anyone. Could he?'

'I know for a fact he could.'

The fear tightened to where it hurt. Her breathing stopped.

He said, 'Who else could have alerted Justin's client to Justin's work?'

'Who is Justin's client?'

'Someone who'd have never known the difference but for Marcus Streit.'

'Then how did that horrible country cop ever—?'

'Because Justin's client went to him. Obviously.'

'Which means Bettelman killed Justin for—' For love? She was baffled.

He was shaking his head, rueful, arms out. 'Josephina, you're still not seeing it right. We're shutting it down. The threat from this inspector and Justin's client is too great. Not to the Reubens. To the entire enterprise. Our clients have standards, Josephina. This falls far short. They cannot be compromised... Justin had to be shut down too. Obviously,' he murmured, taking her in his arms.

Obviously? 'What are you telling me?'

He smiled into her eyes. His sad smile.

'You killed Justin.'

'Had to. Josephina...had to. The risk is just too great. We disappear for a time. It's all or nothing, this service we offer. For people like ours, it has to be... You see?'

She was enfolded in his arms, shaking, sobbing now, desperately needful, her body heaving until both these actions seized up with a sudden intake of breath—the reaction to the blade entering through her cushiony side. It did not hurt much. The betrayal hurt far more.

There was an absolute loss of any notion of what to say as he watched her. So she only watched him. Josephina Perella watched his face turn vague. Grey. Then gone.

'My poor Josephina.'

Laying her out on the floor beside Marcus Streit, he began going methodically through her pockets, her valise, her purse, thinking how Josephina had been useful, but clearly, in a crisis, she was not that good. Which meant a liability. Confidence and confidentiality, these hold an intricately sourced transactional system in ever delicate balance. Reputation is everything.

Yes, so tragic how Josephina had become a liability during this difficult time.

MORE ROLE-PLAYING AT ZUP

SWISS SIDE

Inspector Nouvelle left the office early, went home and changed her clothes, added makeup. It was not her usual look: a short (and now too snug!) black leather skirt over red autumn-weight tights, the collarless, cream-coloured wool top with the sequined outline of a cat she'd purchased on impulse and never worn. And a pair of blue sling-backs, sexy but a pain to walk in. Slightly down-market? Aliette hoped she looked like a distraught wife out looking for her slimy husband. She threw her trusty blue mac on over her tawdry disguise and left a note on the kitchen table. Claude would have to fend for himself again tonight. The shoes were a bother, she stumbled more than once on her way back to rue des Bons Enfants, where, without stopping at the third floor, she requisitioned her favourite car and headed back to Basel.

She was early. She found herself some fast food, a French newspaper. A careful look at every page told her Martin Bettelman was still nowhere in the mind of Basel; his status as a body found in the shallows on the French side of the Rhine remained safely undisclosed.

Later, flashing the discarded credit card as she stepped into Zup, Adelhard the doorman was apprehensive. Adelhard was just as strange in his Heidi dirndl this fine evening, but not so outrageous in his greeting. Perhaps it was not the first time a wife had come looking for an errant man. Avoiding her eyes, he indicated that the cover charge would be tallied at the bar.

It was much the same scene as the night before — couples at tables, some more into their roles than others. Macho roles framed in gay irony. Sleeveless T-shirts, leather jackets. Johnny? Alain? More likely American. Kitschy sentimental music added another layer of cinematic irony to the scene. There was no one in drag tonight but Adelhard. No black ties.

Max the barman shrugged, shook his head, No, Martin had not been in. Aliette slid Martin's card across the bar to Maximilian. 'Two Boxers, please. Put one on for yourself.'

Like Adelhard, he turned wary when he noticed the name on the card. 'That's you?'

'The least he can do if he won't show his face is buy me a fucking beer.' A bitter wife made no bones about the fact. 'I earned it. And you too, Max. I guess he owes you something too, no? This is about dishonest bastards playing with hearts. Mm?'

He returned the credit card without processing it. 'It's on me. I mean us. I mean...' He stared past her. Poor Max. Martin Bettelman left him emotionally conflicted.

She leapt. '*What* do you mean, Max?' Angry, refusing to be mollified by free drinks.

Frazzled, Max put a Boxer beer in front of her. 'Why are you here?'

'To confront the prick.'

'Forget it.' His forlorn eyes said it was a useless thing to attempt to do.

'And I want my things back...from our place. I bought half the stuff in that place and I want it back. When he comes in here, I'll drag him there by the ear!'

'Really?' Max smiled grimly. He seemed amused by the thought.

But the woman who was Lise deflated, sighing, 'No, I don't know what I'll do.' She sipped her beer and let her sense of hurt resurface. 'But I will do something. I will...'

Max opened a beer for himself. 'Doubt it'll do much good. It didn't do much good for me. Martin just laughed. Soon the whole place was. I could've died...' surveying his happy clientele, rueful with the memory. 'He didn't give a damn. Confronting Martin, that was one of the worst nights of my life. Why don't you just go and get your stuff and to hell with him?'

Lise stared down at the bar. 'I'm afraid to.' To give substance to her claim, she slowly rolled her sleeve back till the bruise on her bicep was blatant. That it had come from a hard bump against the shed door the morning she buried Piaf in a daze of sad confusion didn't matter; tonight it served as a wronged wife's defining mark. Max gazed knowingly. She would not open her shirt to show further proof, but she gently rubbed the area below her breast and gazed back.

'I know what you mean,' said Max. 'The dumb part was I liked it.'

'At first, sure. Marty's an expert. I'd melt. Melt and moan.'

Max blushed. 'Until he turned mean. Wouldn't listen. Wouldn't discuss. All he could say was, That's it, get out, and add a few good kicks to get me out the door.'

'You didn't kick back?' He was no pipsqueak, this Max. '*I* sure as hell did. Bastard.'

Max shook his head. 'Don't know how. Not when it's like that.'

She sipped her beer. Turned and watched the dancers. Frank Sinatra...*do bee do bee do.*

Leaning close to her ear, Max said, 'He's got my albums. Bowie, Bette, Sinatra, Nomi. Everything! We've had the same reel going for a month. Addie's getting crazy.'

Lise nodded. 'Your regulars too, I'd imagine.'

Max nodded, dewy, remembering nights with Marty. 'We danced.'

Lise frowned into her bottle. Turned back to the crowd. She had till closing time.

Ordering her next beer, she openly contemplated Max, assessing, like a team commander might, sizing him up for a mission. Finally decided, 'We could go together.'

'And do what?'

'Knock on the door. Demand what's ours.'

'What if he's not there? He hasn't been much, lately.' His voice dropped to a whisper, and he glanced at the door, as if Adelhard might hear across the busy room. '...I've passed by.'

'I have this.' She held the key from Martin's keychain between her finger and her thumb.

'Well...' Max was tempted. But no... 'Addie would freak.'

Adelhard: tending the door, slotting in the music, and watching them carefully.

Someone called for drinks. Max attended to it. She was again jolted by the sight of his trim, bare bottom as he took his tray out to the table. And another jolt at the sight of Addie's hand just there as Max paused to share a word, likely about herself. Martin's wife. Yes, Addie's brightly painted Heidi eyes were clearly weighing her in a different light.

Lise stared back, coldly daring Adelhard to challenge her presence, her right.

She drank. Max worked. The soft jazz tones of some American were replaced by David Bowie's regal baritone. *Oh, Oh, Oh…oh! My little China Girl.* The drinkers liked it. They were getting up to dance. While Max glared at his lover, smirking on the far side of the room.

Jealousy is mostly useless. But a cop saw leverage there. And three beers had an effect.

Lise, qualmless, beamed a fuck-you kind of smile at Heidi. Heidi tweaked the music up.

Draining her glass, Lise slid from the bar stool. 'I think Addie misses Major Tom. Thanks for the beers. I guess I have to do this myself.' She gave Max a pat on his perfect bicep, grabbed her purse and coat. Ignoring Adelhard, she stepped into the street. Where she waited, cooling off, tamping perspiration from her face. The night was cool, she did not want to catch a chill…

It did not take too long till Max stepped out of Zup. She heard an exchange of cursing in German. Adelhard had pushed the issue. Max had responded. Good. With no idea of their destination, she began moving up the street. This would be tricky. All bluff.

'Where are you going?'

'*B'en*…my car?'

He snorted, still in high dudgeon from his standoff with jealous Adelhard, and headed the other way. Her cheap heels clacked as she hustled after, solicitous. 'Are you all right?'

'We can walk it… I need some air.'

She fell into step beside him and slowed the pace, letting the despondency of love abused fill the space between them. She was careful to let Max lead. 'We spent some lovely nights in these streets,' Lise mused, desolate eyes on the cobblestones, playing it shamelessly.

Ten minutes later he had picked up the pace—indeed, Max was hurrying as they turned in to Mulheimerstrasse. She sensed Max was desperately hoping 'Marty' would be there. Poor guy. A mixed sense of guilt and pity helped her keep the face she needed to be Lise. They passed a few more cross streets along Mulheimer. There was nothing of the sexed-up renovated Klein Basel along this stretch, no overpriced boutiques. These shops and cafés were for the people who actually lived in the quarter. Finally, Max stopped in front of a block. Five floors built above street level, entrance between a fabric shop and a butcher. She noted a dozen buzzers.

Max waited for her to open the door and lead the way. But which door?

With one last push of brash pretending, Lise commanded, 'Buzz him!'

Max stepped back and looked up. At the top floor? The dormer? 'Not home.'

'He could be in bed.' With someone else was clearly implied. 'You ready for that, Max?'

Max's eyes tightened. 'Are you?'

'I want what's mine. If we disturb his shitty little fun, that's just too bad.'

Max seemed to agree. 'So, you've got your key...' He gestured, Let's go.

'But just walking in on him...well,' Gently massaging her bruised arm, letting some wifely fear play up. 'I mean, you never know. Right, Max?' Nodding at the bank of buzzers, willing Max to do this one last thing. 'We'll give him time to get his pants on.'

Max took a deep breath and put his finger on the top buzzer, left side.

No response. She indicated, try again. He did. No response. No light came on. Nothing.

'OK,' sighed Lise. 'Ready or not, my darling bastard...' She took the key from her purse.

It worked and they climbed the dark stairs to a door at the stop, where it worked again. They entered a small dormer apartment. Three small rooms: salon/kitchen, bed and bath. Cold, silent. No Martin, obviously. No one to pay the heating bill. What stopped the role-playing inspector dead in her tracks were the paintings. Not on the wall. The only painting on the wall was a small, cheaply framed reproduction of a kitschy alpine scene. Aliette Nouvelle was staring at the paintings on the floor, standing in five neat rows, extending from the base of the wall to the middle of the main room. They were protected underneath by a padded mover's mat.

Max paid short shrift to this discovery. He went straight to the bookcase and began sorting though the music discs, urgently separating out several in a pile, as if afraid Martin might suddenly appear.

Aliette tried not to be too fascinated as she likewise took stock. The paintings were coupled back-to-back, then frame-to-frame, ensuring each canvas was shielded from hooks and framing tacks, or pointy gilt edging. Flipping through, there was no one piece that immediately jumped out at a cop whose eye had never been particularly trained — no Picasso, no van Gogh — but she recognized modern, old and very old. There were at least fifty.

When a flabbergasted Lise wondered where all these paintings could have come from, Max glanced over and shrugged. 'Mm, yeah, looks like a few more than the last time I was here.'

'When was that?' she asked, momentarily letting the cop slip through the guise of Lise.

'Spring,' Max mumbled, methodically removing albums to a growing pile. 'He always had some lying around. Not much for art, myself... Said they were for his work.'

Max was far more interested in making sure his own collection was still all there.

GAME CHANGER

The ballistics report from Basel Lands forensics forwarded by FedPol Agent Franck Woerli meant PJ Inspector Nouvelle would not have to become a special customs agent after all. Like the ones taken from Martin Bettelman, the bullet removed from the head of Justin Aebischer was unmarked. A comparison done against the French ballistics by the Swiss Registry included the retrieved gun and filing marks on scratched-out numbers and barrel profiles. It was not one hundred percent sure, but almost: the bullet pulled from Justin Aebischer was part of the same batch and had been fired by the gun registered to Bettelman. It meant Martin Bettelman could have murdered the Swiss earlier on Friday, prior to his own slaying. Aliette was mulling it, seeing a larger pattern beginning to form, when Monique buzzed. A call from Basel.

'Good morning, Franki, I got the file. Someone's definitely —'

Franck Woerli interjected, stating dully that he'd have to cancel lunch.

There was a moment of dark silence. Very dark, she could feel it. She asked, 'What's happened?' He played the stoically reticent cop for maybe fifteen seconds, then told her. She could hear his heart collapsing. 'But how? I mean, I'm sorry, Franki. Where?'

'The roadside, outside the city. A farmer found her.'

'Do they have someone in mind?'

'This restorer she'd gone to interview. Streit...Marcus Streit. Colleague of Aebischer, apparently.' Franck Woerli struggled through an explanation. 'At first she said the Aebischer killing was none of her business. But your news, Bettelman, the painting—like you and I,

Josephina saw the possible link. She found out where Bettelman had been working lately and sent me off to talk to the gallery people while she drove down to talk to the Basel Lands cop in charge. She thought if she could have a look at the scene, she might...' Woerli stopped to regroup. 'I sensed she was really excited. We were going to meet last evening but she called to say she wanted to see this other contact, Streit, in the same business as Aebischer, and not far from the scene. Said maybe he'd have some insight into Aebischer's life, work, his clientele. That's all. This morning I get a call from Oberwil. Came in about a minute after I sent the specs on the Basel Lands ballistics to you. So sudden...' Aliette heard Woerli breathing through an extended pause. Heavy. Burdened. She would not push him. She had lost colleagues in the line of duty. 'Stabbed,' he finally uttered. 'Lying by the side of a road. He stabbed her and threw out of the car. Poor Josephina.'

'Marcus Streit?'

'It looks that way.' When he spoke again, Woerli's voice had dropped almost to a whisper. 'Josephina learned something, Inspector. And got caught in the middle of it. That has to be it.'

'The middle of what? ...Franki?'

'Probably some kind of art scam. What else could it be?'

Based on her previous night's discovery, Aliette was tending to agree.

Though she elected to keep the secret apartment and what it contained to herself. It was not the time to load up her grieving friend with revelations and ideas. And, international agreements notwithstanding, Commander Heinrich Boehler could and would still try to block her. She only asked, 'And the people looking into this other thing—the Aebischer case?'

'Inspector's name is Grinnell.'

'Who is not Basel City, but Basel Lands?'

'Totally different kind of people down there.'

'Which means?'

'He'll be here tomorrow to tell us what he knows and what he thinks.'

'So will I, Franki...so will I.'

'It's appreciated, Inspector. But I don't want you to... I mean, you know how it is.'

He meant Boehler.

Inspector Nouvelle thought Franck Woerli understood when he'd sent the ballistics. The game had changed: Two murders. Two countries. One gun. A French police officer now had a viable reason to go into Switzerland openly and actively seeking assistance. But at that sad moment her friend was in a fog. She tried to sound encouraging. 'We'll work around Boehler. You and I… We'll find this person. We'll solve it…' Trying to encourage him, but feeling she was speaking into a dark, desolate hole.

Better to simply wish him, 'Condolences, Franki. Try to rest. *À demain.*'

Then Aliette went down the hall—from one despairing man to the next.

Last night Claude had turned toward her, smelt the beer on her breath, then rolled away, back to discontented sleep. A part of her resented his disdain, another part was grateful. Who wants a screaming match in the middle of the night? At breakfast there was sullen silence, the right moment already past. Poor Claude.

But that morning she was obliged to report: fifty or so paintings stashed in a secret love nest in Basel. Apparently intact. One painting found ruined in France beside the murdered owner of the love nest. Gun and bullets indicating a chain of murder linked to art theft. No more need for Gérard Richand's cross-border legal manoeuvre. She assumed the Basel Lands investigators would be open to collaboration. 'Tomorrow, at FedPol. We'll see where that goes.' Given her path to Bettelman's pied-à-terre, gay romance was an obvious way in. Given the location, Boehler remained problematic. But from Basel to the murder at Village-Neuf, a bigger context now seemed clear. 'Voila.'

'Good job.' Claude stared at his day's agenda, unable to meet her eye. He was perplexed. Sad. 'You're going to ruin it,' he muttered. 'You're trying to ruin it. Why?'

She responded, 'I'm working, Claude. *Working.*' Not an answer, but all she could say.

He shook his head, flipped a page. To tomorrow? Today had barely started. With a shrug, Commissaire Néon let his agenda page fall back to the present and indicated the end of the briefing. She challenged him. 'But *why* would I try to ruin it? Why? Please find the answer.'

'I believe it's for you to give me that answer. It's you who can't seem to budge. Mm?' He waited. No, she couldn't find the proper words. Or was it that she just refused to?

They were both guilty. It was becoming intolerable. And such a waste of time!

He finally dismissed her. 'Carry on, Inspector.'

Because Claude felt it just as strongly, the intolerable weight of their shared mistake. Of course he did. And he knew there was nothing he could do to stop her from dealing with it in her own way. Ruin it? Blast it to pieces so time could move forward?

In her own way. Which she still could not grasp clearly. But what can you do but keep moving toward the wretched inevitable? She collected her things and left him. Your job, my job, two different worlds. She was torn between sympathy and guilt, essentially sick at heart.

— —

She drafted a memo to Instructing Judge Gérard Richand regarding Agent Woerli's new information on the gun, the coincident murders—but she didn't send it. Zup, Max, et al. and a pied-à-terre in Klein Basel were still too grey to disclose. She would wait till she'd met with this Inspector Grinnell. She informed Identité Judiciaire there would be no visit from two Swiss cops to view the painting found with Martin Bettelman. She called the Rembrandt, made her apologies to Willem van Hoogstraten…What next? What next?

Lunchtime found Aliette Nouvelle staring at the mountains, etched crystal clear that day.

She needed to see a different kind of man. She thought of the old shoemaker pouring tea.

She went down to the garage and rerequisitioned the car.

12

A DIFFERENT KIND OF MAN

FRENCH SIDE

The battered painting recovered with Martin Bettelman's remains had been sent to an address in Kembs, another small community on the Rhine canal twenty minutes north of the crime scene. The inspector knocked at a door on a pretty street running down to the water. A large man with flowing curly reddish hair answered her knock. She flashed her warrant card and apologized for arriving unannounced. 'Not a problem, Inspector.' Gregory Huet led her to his studio area in the back. A partial view of the river. A nice place to work. He offered green tea and kugelhopf. 'Just putting together my plan of attack here,' Huet said, pulling back the plastic draping. The shoemaker, stripped of the ruined frame, was on an easel surrounded by a battery of lights plugged to a panel. There was a camera on the work table. A bigger camera on a tripod. Various lenses. A notebook. 'First we have to look at it—as deeply as possible. And at all the different elements. Paint layers, paint composition, varnish, support, a new frame, obviously. But genuine. That is, if we want to put it back together the way the artist made it.'

'Can you do that?'

'*B'en*, if you let me.' This with a curt sniff. Gregory Huet had worked for the police before.

'Out of my hands, monsieur.' She had no idea how much time and expense would be required. The police do not ask for miracles, they only require certain information and they operate on budgets anathema to perfectionists. She changed the subject. 'Do you think he could be Turkish? I saw this teapot in a window the other day and—'

'I think he's Dutch. The boot. Turks don't wear boots like that. Or they didn't then. And the nose. That smock. European. The light, mostly. Everyone has their own tradition of light.'

'Ah.' Tradition of light? It didn't really matter where the shoemaker was from. The kugelhopf was excellent and Gregory Huet enjoyed musing aloud. Aliette listened, watching his large hand move through the shoemaker's dim yet richly golden space, pausing at certain points as he explained his thinking. She experienced an odd thrill when he parted another plastic curtain and allowed her a glimpse of the Watteau he had almost finished cleaning. '*Mon dieu!*' Not that she'd ever want a late eighteenth-century picnic in her home. 'For whom?'

'I won't tell you that, Inspector. Not unless you're investigating me. And even then.'

'I'm not investigating you. I'm investigating him.'

The shoemaker. Waiting. Next in line after Watteau.

Gregory Huet was a rangy man. Like Claude—though with more substance through his shoulders, chest and gut. And, like Claude, he stooped. She observed Huet hunched over the table, deeply alone within himself and his work, fingertips carefully feeling a web of cracked and chipped, badly yellowed varnished paint in the area of the shoemaker's lamp. Like a blind man reading Braille. One of his lights was parallel to the painting. 'What's that one for?' He flipped a switch on a panel, the room went dark, the light splayed a powerful beam across the surface of the image, revealing the extent and depth of the web of cracks, a mottling of chipped spots showing varied colouring. Then Gregory Huet restored the light in the room and turned his attention back to his guest. 'You seem interested. You a collector like my friend Monsieur le Juge Richand?'

'No, not at all. But yes, I am attracted to this man.'

'Good. Why?'

She challenged him. 'You tell me.'

He accepted with professional equanimity. 'You see something of yourself.'

'Which something would that be?'

'The something that becomes engrossed in a problem. This shoemaker is a serious man. His work is the main thing. He's taking a break. But the teapot, and the light, and the way he cups the bowl so fully in his palm, and his concentration as he pours, this is what makes you know you respect him. I'd guess the thing you respect is something you feel inside yourself.'

That sounded right. She had to add, 'And his solitude.'

Huet looked at the battered shoemaker. Sniffed, 'Well, yes,' as if it went without saying: Work. Solitude. Dignity as a self-contained elemental energy flowing out of the craftsman and into the craft. A job to do, a job well done. Simple.

Aliette asked, 'Dutch? …Not as old as Watteau.'

'Probably a hundred years younger.'

'But not immediately recognizable.'

'One of hundreds…thousands.'

'Not worth much then?'

Gregory Huet had received the basics of the situation from Gérard Richand. 'In the grand scheme of things, no.' A smile, bemused. 'In and of itself, it could be priceless — in the sense of irreplaceable. But there are thousands of so-called priceless pieces in those gallery storage vaults. Steal one from a wall, they replace it in two minutes. No one will actually miss this shoemaker.'

'You do a lot of business in Basel?'

'Most of it. Occasionally a contract will come down from Strasbourg. Or a museum or an institution in the area. A school. A firm. A family.' She sensed he was referring to the Watteau. 'But if I need work, I drive down to Basel. They know me there.'

'And did you know this Justin Aebischer?'

'Not really. Not really my kind of person. I know he did good work. Much in demand.'

'So you don't know who he would have been working for lately.'

'Inspector, almost every contract I've ever had stipulates silence on this issue. I assume his would too. Those insurance types are sneaky bastards. They'll find out if you've been blabbing. And if you have…Well, reputation is everything. You know?'

She nodded. OK, OK.

'Justin had a different specialty. Baroque. Runs the gamut from Rembrandt to Velazquez, lots of Italians, very realistic, often highly dramatic, a lot of detail, and they gave us some incredible colours.

You've done a good deed if you can restore a sky to Reubens' original blue. Me, I'm a bit more modern. Rococo and onward.'

'And Marcus Streit?'

'Heard of him. Never met him…not sure what his line is.'

Aliette bit into her cake, sipped tea, gazed at the shoemaker. 'Could this one be a fake?'

'This?' Huet looked askance, not sure where she was coming from. 'No. Couldn't be. People don't kill each other for fakes. Not that I've ever heard of.'

'Unless the fake happened to be a party to a business deal gone bad?'

A shrug. 'I suppose. But I really doubt this shoemaker is faked. No, I'm sure of it.'

Inspector Nouvelle decided to share a little with a man she instinctively liked. 'My start point on this case is difficult. I can't understand why someone would do this to a painting. The man, yes, but a lovely thing like this?' She turned from the shoemaker, looking for ideas.

Gregory Huet thought about it. Asked, 'Was the man in the river the thief?'

'Don't know that either, I'm afraid. Not yet. One solid piece of evidence could bring it all together.'

Acknowledging this with a pensive grunt, Huet ventured, 'Price of art's all about potential value, Inspector. Even historic value is only potential value. This painting was on a wall in a gallery. Whoever took it assumed it was worth something. They saw a chance and grabbed it. Happens all the time. In fact it's become a bit of an epidemic. The galleries, they'll spend fortunes on high-end security systems but they can't seem to solve the problem of people lifting paintings off the wall, tucking them inside their coats and walking out the door. The thing is —'

'Value is only value if someone wants it.'

'Exactly. No buyer, no value.'

'So you might assume an amateur thief.'

'You might,' her host allowed. 'A professional will usually have a buyer lined up beforehand. A service, then payment. But as you say, deals can go bad. Your man in the river? Maybe there was a buyer but he had wrong instructions and took the wrong piece and Mr. Buyer said forget it. *Alors*, back to square one as far as making some money for his risk and effort. That could cause a fight. Poor old shoemaker gets caught in the middle.'

'Makes sense.' Another bite of kugelhopf, a sip of tea, enjoying herself. 'Or the buyer punishes his careless thief, is left with a stolen painting he doesn't want and can't price it without a whole lot of trouble. It's just a liability. He breaks it and leaves it.'

'Possible. Or it might not be about the money. Art's as idiosyncratic as the one who makes it. A question of passion,' gesturing toward the shoemaker. 'Same applies to the one who loves it? Sure. Love of art, I mean true love, is a two-way proposition, just as unfathomable as love between two people. Some thieves work strictly for themselves. This one, maybe because he wanted it. And then someone else decided they wanted it too. A battle. A victim.'

'*Un crime passionnel*,' she offered. To keep him talking a little more.

Gregory Huet chuckled. 'A lover's triangle, so to speak. And the shoemaker slipped away from both of them while they fought.' He looked out at the canal, beyond his garden and the River Road. 'Perhaps a barge plowed over him while he floated, thinking he was free.'

Free to get back to work on his boot? It was charming how Gregory Huet brought the shoemaker's stake in the matter to life. She knew there was no barge. The painting had been used as a cudgel on Martin Bettelman, a gay bar crawler who worked around art and (probably) stole it. But her host did not need to know that. Finishing her tea, dabbing crumbs from her lips, she smiled. 'Your work brings out the romance in you.'

He shrugged away the compliment. His notion of a free-floating shoemaker was whimsy, pure and simple. A lightening effect?

And Gregory Huet had more hair than Claude Néon. Soft red, almost chestnut coloured, that gentle curling at its edges… Oh, stop! What was the point in comparing men?

Because he was a man intensely interested in his work. She wished she sensed this at home.

In parting, she admonished, 'Fix him up, monsieur. Make him irresistible. We'll put him on the TV news. Someone will claim him. That will help us.'

Huet bowed. He would try. Aliette happily accepted another piece of kugelhopf.

'For the road,' said Greg. She was supposed to call him Greg.

'Merci. Where did you find this?'

'Find it? I bake it.' Obviously.

Claude Néon would never bake a kugelhopf. Never in a million years.

No. And neither would she.

13

INFO ON AN ANGEL

The Rhine canal was glinting silver sparks in the late afternoon and Inspector Nouvelle was gliding south, heading for the crime scene at the 'beach' at Village-Neuf, no particular strategic goal in mind, only because it was close, munching kugelhopf, getting sugary crust all over her skirt, thinking Gregory Huet should get a medal for his wonderful bundt cake.

One Christmas, in what seemed another lifetime, she had brought her mother an authentic kugelhopf form, sometimes called a 'turban' because of its resemblance to the wrap of the traditional headpiece. It was made of heavy pottery, with painted flowers, a gift from her new life on the far side of France. It had been received with much gratitude, enthusiasm, a big kiss. And then forgotten. Each time Aliette saw it hanging on the kitchen wall when she returned for a visit in Nantes, she felt a twinge of regret. You can't expect your ageing mother to love what you love. You can't expect her to change. No. And what about a man? A man like Claude.

Claude Néon loved the hope of a wife and family. This was the life deep inside his heart and there would be no changing it. Aliette had failed to see it until too long after allowing *her* life to be fused with his. Her hopes. Her body… Great body, that Claude. Energy to burn.

Perhaps one strategic reason for visiting her crime scene was to avoid going home to Claude.

Again.

As she passed the signs indicating the environs of Village-Neuf, she could see the waterway widening out ahead where the canal merged with the river. At the sign announcing the pump factory, she turned off the road and bumped slowly along the dirt track. There were a few cars in the wooded area today, a few men pretending to read newspapers, casually noting the new arrival. Leaving the car, popping the last bite of buttery cake into her mouth, wiping crumbs from her lips on her sleeve, she took her bottle of water and headed to the shore. The sun was still warm. She could sit and think about murder, shoemakers, love. She wished she'd brought a beer…

Thus it was that a momentarily emotionally suspended Aliette Nouvelle found Hubert Hunspach standing on a boulder, lanky arms outspread in silent praise, thick shoulders moving to the rhythm in his headphones. The same boulder: take away Hubert's clothes, replace day with night, it was a replay of the strangely ecstatic tableau she'd happened on two nights before. And the sincerest form of praise is mimicry—but you have to know who you are mimicking.

She approached. Hubert was likewise emotionally suspended, too preoccupied with his music lifting him to some other level to sense the intrusion of the police. When he finally turned, she knew he'd been smoking his pot again. As if to confirm it, Hubert registered her presence with a laugh, rather loud, like a deaf person's. It was not belligerent or mocking; more a laugh of stoned-out wonder. And he offered a broad smile.

What to do with this delinquent boy? Hubert stood, smiling blandly, bobbing to his music, not in the least concerned with a cop deciding his immediate fate. She decided there was no point scolding him again, or taking legal action. This blasé adolescent would learn, or not. Whichever, his value to her had nothing to do with the presence of an illegal substance. The inspector spent a good portion of her time talking to people who were quite removed from the daily grind thanks to one substance or another. The fact that they had a drug temporarily added to their perspective did not automatically delete what they knew. The information was usually still there to be gleaned. It was just a question of listening differently. *Asking* differently—going direct to the object of his dreaming. 'Is he really so beautiful, Hubert?'

'Totally. *Impeccable.*'

'Have you talked to him?'

'No way. I've barely seen him.'

'Has he seen you?'

'Even if he did, he wouldn't. He's up there. Like a god. I'm nowhere.'

'What's his name?'

A shrug. No idea. He turned back to the place of the beautiful vision and with a touch of his thumb he boosted the music high.

She had to yell. 'I saw him!'

He heard. '*Voyons!* Don't bullshit me. Removing his phones, facing her, Hubert Hunspach could not believe it. 'Where?'

'Here. Right where you're standing, as naked as that stone.'

This was a revelation. 'He's like completely white? Like a vision?'

Aliette nodded. Something like that. 'He dove into the river and disappeared.'

'You have to be able to do stuff like that. I mean, if you want to matter.'

'Yes, I think I understand that. Who knows him?'

'No one I know.'

'I think the man you found did.'

Rather than challenge this barely circumstantial assertion, from deep inside his adolescent soul Hubert Hunspach intoned, 'Death is part of love.'

An ancient sentiment and not untrue, God knows. The inspector wondered which heavy metal band he'd got it from. 'He may be at risk, Hubert.'

'No… No way. He's above it. He's safe.' Hubert gazed across the water.

'Does he live on the other side?'

'For sure.'

'I mean in Germany.' Not the land of the gods.

The boy hadn't the slightest clue. 'Doesn't really matter where he *lives*. It's like, his soul, you know? Out there. Far away. Safe on the other side.' This, Hubert knew for sure.

The inspector considered Hubert Hunspach dreaming of the benign far away, out there, a life safe on the other side. Today, without a murder, threatening police, noisy media circus, his resolutely normal family ready to pounce if he acted out, she perceived something needful.

And afraid? 'Do your parents know, Hubert?'

Stoned and otherwise preoccupied, it didn't matter, he knew exactly what she meant. Eyes glued on the distance, he admitted, 'Just my mum.' Giving his music another boost, moving with it into another wistful thought, he fairly yelled, 'If my mother could see him...' moving like he was dancing with a ghost.

Aliette called, 'Yes? ...What would happen if your mother could see him?'

'What?' Reluctantly lowering the volume a fraction.

'Why should your mother see him?'

'Because he's beautiful. Not *bad*...' then, 'Yeah!' This in response to something in the music only he could hear. 'If Maman saw him she would stop being so fucked up and understand.'

'What about your father?' He didn't hear that. Or else ignored it. She called, 'You should tell him, Hubert!' He shook his head with adamant force. No! She called, 'If I need you to come and look at pictures, we'll have to tell them.' But he would not respond to this advice.

And she couldn't force him.

The song ended. He removed his music and faced her. She tried again. 'You were here that night. I know you were.' A resigned nod, yes. 'So tell me, Hubert. A man was killed. Another one may be. This beautiful man—he's real and he may be in very real danger.'

'I didn't see anything. I was back there.' Gesturing at the woods.

In the woods. That was sad, but not her problem. 'Come down often?' A nod. 'Out your bedroom window?' Another nod. 'With your friend, René?' No. 'Does René know?' No. And some tears were starting now—yes, just a frightened kid. 'What did you see, Hubert?'

He blinked, looked past her. 'Just the usual. Cars. Fogged up windows. Then there was noise over by the river. Like here. Like yelling. And some pops. Sounds like pops... I went to see but everyone was running the other way, just wanting to get away. So I ran too.' Voila.

She tested this. 'This was the night before you and René found him?'

'No. Friday.'

Bon. Truth. 'You didn't come on the weekend?'

Hubert wiped his tears. 'I never come on the weekend. Too much happening. Friends, all that, I can't just... Weekends are when I pretend.' And it had rained.

'Can you give me any names?'

'No one has a name here.'

'Faces?'

He shrugged. Put his phones back on. She mulled and paced, looked across at Germany.

But then the song was over and they talked some more. About many things. He was not the worst kid in the world. He understood her feelings. She did not want to go home? Neither did he.

He seemed to be trusting her. At a certain point, she asked, Was he interested in helping her?

His eyes brightened. 'Like an informant?' *Un indic.* 'Like on the shows?'

'More or less, yes... Be my cousin, Hubert. Could you handle that?'

'Maybe...' What was he supposed to do?

'Keep an eye out. And talk to me.'

He considered it. He considered the shows. 'Cousins. Cool.'

'Good.' Maybe the beautiful man on the rock lived in the area.

Hubert doubted anyone as special as that could live anywhere as boring as Village-Neuf but promised he would keep his eyes peeled. And that he would be careful when he snuck out to come looking for sex in the park. She did not push him on that one; being careful was as much as she had a right to expect. Then he talked about his friends and who he thought might be 'like me' till inevitably it was time to go. Supper. Hubert's mama would be wondering. So would Claude.

Aliette promised she would be in touch. Hubert Hunspach walked away.

She lingered.

She was not an adolescent. She could go back home. Or she could go back to Basel.

She chose Basel. It was closer now — and closer in her mind. Martin Bettelman had brought a stolen treasure from his love nest to a public trysting place by the river. As a gift? A gesture of his passion for a beautiful man? Or was it nothing of the sort? The opposite. Strictly business. A deal? As she passed slowly through the rush hour at Saint-Louis, heading for the checkpoint, she realized something Gregory Huet had said was drawing her back to the tiny flat. She needed to have a closer look at the collected art in Martin Bettelman's fuck pad.

Baroque. Rococo? Maybe those pictures could help her understand a murder.

I'm working, Claude, working. Then I'll come home...

Thirty minutes later she found a spot along Mulheimerstrasse and parked. Working, working, working, working... It was like a stubborn mantra as she climbed the long, steep stairs to the fifth floor and again, thanks to Lise Bettelman's fit of disgust, let herself in.

Empty. Martin Bettelman's art collection was gone. The only thing left was the department-store reproduction of the mountain village scene hanging by the bedroom door.

➤ ➤

As night fell on Basel, Aliette Nouvelle was sitting in a corner café nibbling at a fast-food version of raclette, sipping from a glass of uninspired Swiss wine. She had been up and down the long stairs to Bettelman's hideaway, knocking on doors, interviewing — though hiding herself behind poor Lise Bettelman.

'Have you seen my husband? He came to move some things and didn't come home.'

She learned at least one useful thing. It was likely there had been two visits to the apartment that day. That morning residents had heard a lot of up-and-down. None had bothered to look. They assumed a tenant was moving in or out. As for vans being loaded down in the street, well, there were many vans in the street during the course of a day. And someone had gone up later on. She got varying estimations as to when they'd left. She gathered she had probably missed the second visitor by an hour, not much more.

A single visitor, or two different parties, not one piece remained. It was galling and chilling to equal degree. She had to assume someone was aware of her every move and had responded to her discovery by eliminating it. Her first impulse was to run to Zup. Obviously.

But no. She would not go back to Zup till she went in as a cop with a warrant, knowing exactly what and who she wanted. She knew in her gut it was not Max the bare-bummed barman. Unless he was a total fool... But again, no. Max had not been the least bit interested in those paintings, much less Martin Bettelman's 'work.' Had he the slightest idea? A security guard wasn't going to wear his uniform when he went out dancing. A man like Martin Bettelman was not going to let the dull truth get in the way of making himself as attractive as he felt he needed to be. And Max was guileless... No, he had only wanted his music back. He wanted his Addie not to be angry. He wanted to leave *le beau* Martin behind in the forgotten past.

But Max may well have gabbed. So, who amongst that happy crowd?

Aliette hoped her charade as Lise had not put the hapless Max at risk.

After her meal, in a phone booth on a corner, she said, 'Claude, I won't be home tonight.'

'Where are you?'

'Working.'

He hung up. He did not slam it. He just hung up. It was left for her to read it: Patience. Or a man losing hope? She purchased beer from a grocer and headed back up the long stairway. She had no children to put to bed. She had no husband. She had Claude, fading. And she kept having the nagging sense that Gregory Huet had told her something she already knew. But what? She drank beer and moved inside the cold apartment, looking at everything, looking out the window at the night. It was dark up here above the street lights. It was far from anything except her job.

Eventually, there it was, in front of her nose, stuck on the refrigerator door.

Good. Merci. One solid thing.

The inspector slept in Martin Bettelman's bed that night, in her underwear and coat.

She might be losing her mind — she probably was — but it would be on her own terms.

And, strangely, she slept deeply and well.

14

FRIDAY AT FEDPOL

SWISS SIDE

'Can we back up for a moment here?' FedPol Agent Franck Woerli was persisting in a futile battle. Turning to Agent Rudi Bucholtz, now nominal head of the Cultural Crimes unit. 'Let's get this straight. Was Josephina working on anything related to Justin Asebischer?'

'If she was, I was not informed of it.'

Woerli turned back to Basel Lands Inspector Hans Grinnell: 'To be clear: These boot prints in Aebischer's garden. How many sets?'

'One,' repeated Grinnell, his tone aiming for somewhere between patience and compassion.

Because Woerli's persistence was fluctuating between embarrassing and just plain sad.

They were in the board room at the Freiestrasse office. It was a bright morning. The swill-coloured Rhine actually shone on its way through Basel. A woman had brought coffee and a basket of pastries—sweet kuchen, creamy brioche. Inspector Nouvelle sat with three Swiss police officers: Franck Woerli, looking old and entirely defeated. Hans Grinnell, methodically destroying the credibility of the slain Agent Perella. Rudi Bucholtz, dutifully present but much more interested in the French cop across the table, his soft Saint Bernard eyes brazenly feasting. She ignored him, but she adjusted her hair.

In deference to their guest, they conversed in French, which, as public officials, they were all able to do. Grinnell was doing most of the talking. He was polite but relentless. He was also lying, or omitting something key—which amounts to the same sin. The

French inspector saw it clearly, but had no idea what he was hiding. So she listened.

Agent Perella had arrived at Oberwil in mid-afternoon. She was not interested in the murder of Justin Aebischer, not per se. 'She admitted it was not her area of expertise,' Grinnell noted. He characterized the visit as more of a consultation, 'to see if she could see something that might help with our investigation. Fair enough. I took her to Biel. She spent a long time going through his desk. And the painting, this Reubens the victim had been restoring, she studied it and declared it authentic. She couldn't understand why no one had come to claim it—was quite baffled there'd been no contact with the client at all. I told her no one had come forward. I said we'd been trying from many possible angles but had no luck.' Grinnell laughed softly. 'Then she gave me righteous hell for leaving such a valuable piece of art in such a vulnerable place.'

Franck Woerli was irritated. 'Why is that funny, Inspector?'

Grinnell stopped smiling. He hesitated. Yes, keeping something back. 'Your colleague was a bit, well, out of her depth. I mean in regard to the game she was trying to play. I'm sorry she's dead. I do mean to find the one who killed her. But she was involved in this.'

Mustering some anger from inside his gloomy torpor, Woerli smacked the table. 'No!'

'Yes,' Grinnell replied, calm, totally sure. Josephina Perella had been found on the edge of a farmer's field on a back road about ten kilometres from Marcus Streit's chalet. It appeared Streit killed her and left her for the crows. *Or* Streit and someone else—a third pair of tire tracks at his house. Streit's house was clean, but Perella had been there. A fine trail of hair from salon to the kitchen. And the footprints. 'She'd changed to the same hiking boots she wore Friday at Aebischer's. She was wearing them when they found her.' Perella's requisitioned FedPol car had disappeared, along with Streit. And maybe someone else.

Franck Woerli could not accept it. 'This is just wrong! Obviously she was onto something. She confronted them. And they killed her. She would never…' He closed his eyes and breathed. The notion that Josephina Perella had murdered Justin Aebischer was devastating.

Grinnell shrugged. 'The pattern on the sole matches the prints on the lawn at Aebischer's.'

Woerli flared. 'Everyone in Switzerland has a pair of those boots and you know it!'

'Matched perfectly,' Grinnell murmured. 'We've even matched traces of grass from Aebischer's lawn.' For Hans Grinnell, the boots sealed it.

Woerli pleaded, 'My colleague Josephina Perella was as dedicated and honest as—' He stopped. Stopped dead. Stuck for a metaphor to fit on Josephina.

'Agent Woerli, please…' Grinnell was perplexed by his reaction. He was not trying to be mean. 'I'm sorry, but sometimes we just don't know our colleagues.'

Rudi Bucholtz blinked and seemed to emerge from his erotic trance. 'She's a big walker. Sometimes Josephina left early if it was slow. To go walking? Last Friday was nice, as I recall.'

Hans Grinnell made a note. The look in his eye said, Thanks.

Bucholtz looked across the table, not sure if he'd said something right or wrong.

Aliette doubted he was thirty. She liked his long, thick, jet-black hair, lightly gelled to keep it back. His face was deeply serious. Black eyebrows over wide dark eyes created this effect. His lips looked like he'd been lapping up a bowl of soup. Slightly moist. She liked that. But the French cop was dismayed that this adorable Rudi would be so unsavvy where it came to choosing sides. She felt a loyalty to her friend Franki. She countered Rudi's observation. 'But Justin Aebsicher was killed with Martin Bettelman's gun, yes?'

Grinnell turned, as if just now aware of her presence. 'And so was Bettelman.' He had a flat smile, clear blue eyes. In good shape, recent haircut, wholesome. She guessed slightly younger than herself. She could see a wife and kids trailing behind as he led a Sunday hike. 'But that doesn't mean Bettelman fired the shot that killed my victim.'

'Well, no,' she conceded. 'Of course it didn't.'

'And that was Agent Perella's pretext for coming to see me,' Grinnell noted, adding, 'Yes, our enquiries have confirmed that Aebischer was homosexual and active in the Basel gay community.'

Woerli blurted, 'But you have to consider—!'

'That she could have killed this Bettelman too? Sure.' Grinnell reached for another sweet bun. 'But Bettelman is not my problem.' Sitting back in his chair, he nibbled. Sipped coffee.

The riposte left Franck Woerli limp, as if punched.

Aliette protested, 'But surely he is.' Someone Grinnell should be concerned with. '…With what I found at this club and at Bettelman's apartment, this has to be considered.'

Maybe encouraged, Woerli asked, 'And how could Josephina have had Bettelman's gun?'

To which she added, 'Or, *par contre*, where did Bettelman get Josephina's boots?'

Grinnell only shook his clean-cut head, moving on to the next bit of damning circumstantial. 'And the business cards in her purse confirm beyond any doubt that—'

Woerli cut him off. 'Was Martin Bettelman working Friday afternoon?'

'No,' Bucholtz reported instantly—before checking one of many sheets laid out in front of him. 'Scheduled for Saturday and Sunday. At the Kunst. He was posted at the Kunst.'

Woeful but still fighting, Woerli challenged Grinnell. 'How can you ignore this?'

Hans Grinnell rolled his eyes, vexed, beginning to lose patience with this Federal policeman.

But Aliette had to ask, 'What business cards?'

Grinnell pulled an envelope from his case, withdrew a business card and put it on the table. 'We found a box of these in Perella's purse.' It read *Reubens & Associates*. And gave a phone number. Nothing more. The two FedPols hovered over it, Bucholtz bemused, Woerli mystified. 'More to the point, I have Josephina Perella on surveillance video in the act of removing that box from the desk of my victim.'

'Oh, Lord!' Again Franck Woerli seemed personally insulted by this fact. 'When?'

The Basel Lands inspector offered a snide laugh. 'When she thought I wasn't looking.'

A listless Woerli picked up the card. 'What is this?'

'Exactly what it appears to be.'

'But there's no name…no…'

'Justin Aebischer served a special clientele. He didn't need his name.'

'But the number.'

'An answering service in Geneva. They have no idea who he is. They take messages.'

Aliette was finally seeing some method behind Grinnell's apparent disinterest. She asked, 'If Inspector Perella hadn't called with the Bettelman link, would you have called her?'

He smiled. 'I think we would have seen her at some point. We have the painting, after all.' Another sniffy laugh. 'Though I confess I don't know Reubens from ribbons.'

Franck Woerli was spiteful, ' You were lucky to have her best advice.'

Grinnell agreed. 'Before that, all I saw was a picture of a beagle licking its ass.'

Too mean. More silence. Even Agent Rudi Bucholtz was now looking at his senior colleague as if the man was the greenest junior in the place. Franck Woerli wasn't getting it.

'She's guilty,' Grinnell declared. 'It's just a question of how deeply, and why.'

Frank Woerli was bewildered. 'Guilty of what?'

'Murder. One or two, we'll see…We'll appreciate anything you can help us find.'

'And what else?' Aliette demanded, feeling her own frustration level rising.

A polite but completely cryptic smile. 'Surely murder's enough at this point, Inspector.'

It brought another impasse, all energy devolving to the man who'd called the meeting. A tear traced Franck Woerli's sagging middle-aged cheek. Swaying as if he might be sick, he got up and left the room. Poor Franki. But it was as good a moment as any—Aliette hated to add to his pain. She removed a business card from her own valise and added it to the one on the table. They were the same. 'It was stuck to the door of the refrigerator at Bettelman's secret love nest.'

Finally Hans Grinnell was interested. He jotted another note.

With Franck Woerli absent, Rudi Bucholtz was their official host. The French cop wondered, 'Would Agent Perella have legitimate reason to visit Marcus Streit?'

Rudi seemed pleased with the new responsibility. 'He consults here often.'

'What was she working on?'

'Usual sort of stuff. An Ernst that surfaced in a gallery in Edinburgh, a family here insists it's theirs. Paperwork having to do with Nazis hiding art in bank vaults—we normally don't get any of that, but she'd been getting a bit lately. A phony signature mark, maybe, on a supposedly just-discovered-in-an-attic Millet... I know Marcus was helping her find expert opinions on the Millet last spring.'

'And would Streit know Aebischer?'

'Surely. Old enough to be his father, but it is a small community.'

Echoing Gregory Huet, almost to the word.

She asked Grinnell, 'Any idea where they were headed?'

'The road they found her on is a straight line back to Aebischer's. An easy half-hour.'

'Perhaps she was thinking of showing him the painting at Aebischer's.'

'Perhaps. But she would not have got past my security.'

'But if they could, why would they be? Going to see it, I mean.'

Grinnell sat forward in his chair. He seemed to welcome an intervention by an actual investigator. 'Why indeed?'

'And why,' she had to wonder, 'if this is something bigger than a gay community murder, would Marcus Streit and maybe someone else leave those cards on her person?'

'Two possibilities come to mind, Inspector. Either Streit was unaware she had them and neglected to look before tossing her in the ditch. Or, more likely, this someone else knew we'd find what we found and has probably already killed Herr Streit as well.'

'And there are no traces of this someone else?'

'Not as yet.'

And it obviously wasn't Martin Bettelman. But someone had removed all the works from the dormer on Mulheimerstrasse. 'It means there may be more for us at this club,' she ventured.

Inspector Hans Grinnell nodded, maybe even smiled encouragement, but offered nothing by way of strategy. 'Us country boys know nothing of these things, madame.' It was his friendly way of saying he did not care about fifty or so paintings that had suddenly gone missing from a secret love nest in Klein Basel, nor the murder on French soil of its proprietor. He apparently felt he didn't need to care.

...Then a belated attempt at police diplomacy: 'Whatever you can dig up at this, Zup? — where on earth would they get a name like that? In any event, send it along, we'll have a look.'

Aliette bit her tongue, nodded her agreement. This Hans Grinnell was no ally.

Twenty awkward minutes later Franck Woerli had not returned to the table.

Agent Rudi Bucholtz finally suggested, 'Perhaps we'd better look at Josephina's files.'

— —

The same woman brought a lunch of sandwiches and advised that Agent Woerli had left for the day. Not feeling well. They ate in the airless office, poring through a murdered art cop's files. Whatever else, Josephina Perella had been carefully professional in keeping records of her moves and contacts. There were over a hundred documents — memos, correspondence, professional opinions — in both electronic and paper form bearing the name Marcus Streit, several as recent as that spring. About the Millet. There was no trace of the name Justin Aebischer in any of their dealings.

It was barely mid-afternoon when Hans Grinnell snapped his briefcase closed and offered his hand. 'Inspector, it was a pleasure.'

Aliette was taken by surprise. 'Where are you going?'

'Home. Got two matches after school.' As he moved to the door, Grinnell proudly explained his two sons' busy involvement in the junior soccer program at Oberwil. '...Apart from the fact I'm helping out with Willy's group, if I don't show up it will mean my wife will have to drive in two different directions at the same time. She will not be happy and I will suffer.'

The French cop blurted, 'Wait!'

'Yes?' Was that an order?

She blushed. 'Will I see you tomorrow?'

'I hope not.' Trying for a joke, missing completely. Realizing as much, Grinnell shrugged and stated that because the forensics search at Josephina Perella's flat had yielded nothing useful, there was nothing more for him here in Basel.

'But the galleries...I need...I mean, surely two of us...'

Hans Grinnell gestured toward Rudi Bucholtz: there's your man for the galleries, noting, 'I've done the galleries, Inspector.' And got nothing.

'But I should have a look around her apartment. You could—'

'No, that will not be necessary.' Grinnell was kindly as he moved through the door. 'Thank you for your help...' adding, 'Please. It's not personal. I'm sure you understand.'

She followed. 'Why won't you tell me what you have?'

'Because you do not need to know.' He stopped in the foyer. Sighed once. 'What I mean, with respect, Inspector, I don't see how you could help.'

'Would you please stop insulting me. Respect?...It does not play well, Herr Inspector.'

'As you wish.' Another phlegmatic sigh. 'Here's the story. Please listen. There is nothing in the Bettelman killing that comes anywhere near Josephina Perella and the role she had to be playing. Beyond her,' a shrug, 'it's all quite Swiss. Has nothing to do with you. It really doesn't.' He smiled: not trying to be a nasty bugger here, just averse to wasting precious time. 'Perhaps my investigation will open a door for yours. But first things first, yes? We'll be in touch.'

Then the lift arrived and he was gone.

Aliette Nouvelle found herself alone with Rudi Bucholtz—watching her, eyes wet and dark, gently quizzical. Waiting. Waiting to be led. '*Alors, monsieur?* No Franki. No Hans...'

'No Josephina. You could call Basel City. Ask them to escort you through her place.'

'Right.' At least Rudi had been following the flow and (maybe) had a sense of humour. 'Is there anyone special in her life I should talk to?'

'Only her mother.'

'Was Josephina gay?'

This brought the young Swiss up short. 'No idea. Never heard much at all about her private life except her old mother over near Lugano. We just thought of her as...as single.'

'Did your boss love art?'

Not an especially useful question, but Rudi took it at face value. 'Some.'

'Do you love art, Agent Bucholtz?'

'Some.'

'What about Reubens?'

'I appreciate it. But love...?' Agent Rudi Bucholtz took the opportunity afforded by a moment alone with a French cop to pronounce, 'It has to be a fake.'

She enjoyed the fact that he would dare to do this. She wanted to know more. '*Has* to be?'

'Why would someone kill Justin Aebischer and not take it?'

Which prompted her to recall Gregory Huet's considered opinion that the shoemaker found near Martin Bettelman had to be the genuine article. People did not kill for fakes. She said, 'You'd better come and see our shoemaker. We're having trouble identifying him.'

'Sure.' He met her eyes. 'Have you ever killed a man?'

'No. But some men have died on account of me.' She proceeded to explain that guns were a distraction in her work, not to say messy in her bag and about her person. She was trained to shoot, of course. To kill, if necessary. She hinted (falsely) that she could kill a man with her bare hands, if required. But she preferred to meet her adversaries on a higher level.

'We rarely do,' Agent Bucholtz responded. 'Kill. I mean the art squad.'

'I'm glad to hear it, Rudi...may I call you that?'

'Of course.'

The way he said it, the way his eyes stayed fixed on hers, Aliette Nouvelle heard herself suggest, 'And perhaps you should come and see Bettelman's apartment.'

'Why?' His soft gaze held steady.

But hers was softer. 'It's part of the investigation, Agent.'

'When?'

'Soon. Tonight?'

'Should I bring wine?'

'Beer…Boxer beer.'

Rudi Bucholtz nodded and made a note. Then he went to call Herr Dieter Taub at VigiTec, to ask if a French investigator might have a half-hour of his time on a Friday afternoon.

15

VIEW FROM VIGITEC

It took twenty minutes to walk it, across the Middle Bridge and straight up Clarastrasse. The Basel Trade Fair Tower was the city's tallest and highest-priced corporate redoubt. VigiTec headquarters were in a suite on the 27th floor. The blue-tinted glass filtered the light, creating an ambience of silent, shining purpose. VigiTec VP Resource Allocations Dieter Taub was a doleful Buddha, motionless in his sumptuous chair, shiny head and hairless face offset by heavily lidded cornflower-coloured eyes. The inspector wanted to ask if they'd met before, but the Buddha look is nothing if not monolithic and she dreaded the wrong words. Instead she thanked him. Herr Taub was kind to receive her at such short notice at this late hour.

His English was impeccable. So was his French.

Yes, Josephina Perella had informed him of Martin Bettelman's cause of death—he had heard but assumed suicide—and about Bettelman's gun when she'd called before heading off to her own 'very tragic' end. 'We worked with Josephina often.' When the inspector added the fact of the role of Bettelman's gun in the killing of Justin Aebischer, Taub said, 'It is quite against the rules for our staff to carry their sidearms when off-duty, and especially so for our French staff to take them across the frontier.' Yes, he'd met Justin Aebischer a few times—'he was affiliated with the Kunst Technical Department,' but their paths had not crossed for 'at least a year.' No, he hadn't been to the murder scene—not his business, but he was aware of the museum's efforts to help locate the client. 'As our list is fairly widespread, they thought I might be able to suggest a name or two. Problem is, they won't divulge the artist he was working on.'

And, he added, dry and laconic, giving out client names willy-nilly was never a good business move.

The inspector was not going to divulge Hans Grinnell's facts and suppositions regarding Perella's role in Wednesday's events in and around Biel. Nor about a secret apartment where upwards of fifty pieces of very likely stolen art had been stored, then disappeared with the murder of Martin Bettelman. What she wanted was information situating the slain art cop close to events in Basel. Close to Bettelman. Something to take back to France. Aliette placed the list of gallery owners Josephina Perella had given Franck Woerli in front of Dieter Taub. 'She thought one of them might provide information as to Justin Aebischer's latest contracts.'

Taub bowed, a quick dip of his bullet-like head. 'Yes. All my clients. I called them to smooth the way for Josephina's colleague. In theory, a logical place to start. Very logical. But—'

'But he gets nothing, she's murdered. Any sense of what's going on here, Herr?'

Taub morosely signalled negative. 'I don't know the first thing about Josephina's purposes and I would never ask. It's a tragedy. I can only assume she tumbled onto some kind of conspiracy and made a very wrong turn, but...' leaning forward a fraction of a millimetre, 'I can tell you that she had to know her colleague would get exactly nowhere trying to pry business information out of the likes of Rutger Mettler. Josephina knew these people. It's business, Inspector.' Big business. The private galleries open to the public were the tip of the art business iceberg. Vaults in basements were overflowing with art for sale. Files were bursting with notes regarding paintings on offer, paintings sought. Money was made by being in the middle and inventory information was proprietary. It was a fantasy to expect cooperation without the heaviest judicial pressure, which, on the spur of the moment, a FedPol agent did not have. May as well casually ask a banker for details of his currency transfers. The laws were made for the benefit of private business, not the Federal Police. That was the bottom-line reality in Switzerland.

'Meaning it's a one-way street.'

Dieter Taub caught her drift. 'Meaning it's difficult. Privacy and discretion? Oftentimes, when a problem arises there's only so much my client will permit me to share. Other times they'll ask us to sort it out without the police, regardless of FedPol's needs or networks. Or they write it off.' A shrug. 'I work for my client, Inspector. Josephina knew that.'

'But she would know markets? I mean black markets.'

'It was her job to know things like that.'

A pause. And very difficult to get the measure of Dieter Taub. She asked, 'How well did you know her?'

He looked into her eyes for an instant, slightly askance. But he understood. 'I knew her professionally. Same with poor Martin, as far as that goes. I have been in the same room with both of them on occasion, always for professional reasons.'

'Meaning the theft of a piece of art.'

'That's all that would ever bring us together, Inspector. I mean all three of us. Martin would describe what he saw or, more usually, didn't see. Josephina would bring gathered intelligence as to whom or where said piece might be headed. I suppose I should add that I consulted with Josephina countless times on issues related to my clients.'

'Such as?'

'Such as stolen art or forged art or missing art that has surfaced on foreign territory.'

'And she helped you?'

'If she could. As far as it went.'

'At these places?' Referring to the list.

'Sometimes. Usually at the Kunst. I'm in and out of there all the time. Biggest client. Always some issue or other to be settled. Josephina spent a good deal of her time there as well.'

'And Martin Bettelman was assigned there lately.' A nod. 'How difficult would it be for Martin Bettelman to remove paintings in the course of his duties as a security guard?'

Another nod. 'Yes, Josephina mentioned that you'd also recovered a painting.'

When she did not respond to that, he bowed again in the slightest way — an odd tick, it was like a headwaiter, or a circumspect psychiatrist — and opened the file that lay waiting at his right hand. Martin Bettelman had an unblemished history as a VigiTec employee going back almost fifteen years. He'd started off working the range of VigiTec clients, from banks to football stadiums to private homes, gradually settling into a rotation through the firm's cultural contracts. He had worked in every gallery and museum around Basel but was eventually more or less permanently posted at the Kunst, the venerable Basel Museum of Fine Art. 'They like it there,' Taub noted.' Lots of people, lots of variety... Involves more than just standing around, mind you. Our staff are trained in how to hang art securely, pack and transport, store at proper climate. It's a value-added service we provide.' Not cheap was clearly intimated. And, closing the file with a corporate sigh, 'no complaints about Martin... None.'

'But that's not what I asked, Herr.'

'Just so.' Dieter Taub bowed. 'We do try for perfection, Inspector,' now taking a ring-binder from a stack by his left hand and handing it across the table. 'We have to. Ours is a very competitive industry.' Aliette began flipping through laminated pages featuring photos and schematics of the latest security technology while her host explained. 'We're constantly upgrading our methods, and of course, that involves constant retraining of our personnel. But we are constrained by our clients' budgetary constraints. And, to be frank, by their sense of urgency in these matters. The mindset of the culture industry is not that of the security industry. What I mean is, it attracts a different kind of person. We do our best to push them forward. Case studies. General awareness. Each time a major art crime is reported anywhere in the world, we prepare press packages and forward copies to each of our clients. Public relations? Perhaps your people do the same sort of thing. Maybe it's effective... But we cannot force them to spend more money protecting their treasures. Lots of paintings go missing, both the great and the lesser. As I say, often they'll just live with the loss—which isn't really a loss if it's a piece that's no longer admired or even known. At least that's how they think when putting it against the size of the collections in their vaults and the cost to their reputation.'

'At the museum? ...You say Bettelman was on duty during some thefts?'

Taub reached for yet another binder, found a page. 'A dozen times. Small pieces, mid-range value. Off the wall and out the front door. No discernable pattern. Or market, for that matter—not according to people like Inspector Perella. We reviewed it in each instance and found nothing to hold him at fault. The client will confirm this.' The client being the Museum. 'They know they have a problem. They've got their own security department, of course, but...well, Frau Zeidler...' Dieter Taub's smooth face cracked a rueful smile, 'that's why they need us.' He re-opened the Human Resources file on Martin Bettelman. 'So long as our personnel are cleared through the entry screening and all goes well, we are not inclined to look. Martin knew his job. All enquiries said he was honest. I do find this very odd.'

She passed him the police photo of the battered shoemaker. 'Found in the river with your employee. We're having it restored. We'll go public, if need be. Someone will come forward.'

Dieter Taub perused it. He had no idea who had made it or who might own it. Handing it back, he said, 'I'd be very grateful if you'd keep me informed.'

It seemed the meeting was concluded. She again thanked him for his time.

Dieter Taub leaned forward with an offer. Would she like to view the museum surveillance tapes? The Kunst was a public institution, not so problematic where it came to disclosure rules, and he would personally arrange it. 'With Della. You'll like Della.'

Aliette accepted. Not sure what she'd see, but it was something.

His agent would meet her at the Kunst reception at nine sharp next morning. Beyond that, Herr Taub was sorry but they had different priorities here and a man in his position sometimes had to split himself down the middle where it came to responsibilities.

'This is not France, Inspector.'

PART 2

FANTASY WEEKEND FOR ONE IN BASEL

- 16 -
A Bit of Pleasure

No, not France. Not France at all... It had been a long day amongst the Swiss. Inspector Nouvelle walked out of the sleek blue tower and into a pleasant late afternoon. Clear sky. A warmish southwest wind. She headed back toward the river. She needed some supplies.

Aliette didn't know if she was going to sleep with Agent Rudi Bucholtz—but it was a notion she was willing to explore. Because she needed to. But it would be for him to make her want to. But if he did... She found a boutique in Claraplatz where she bought a change of underwear. Black, and not too skimpy. *Au contraire.* Black and slightly reserved.

Next on her list was leckerli, the ginger-flavoured cookie that was a justly famous Basel specialty. She looked inside a chocolate shop and asked where she might find some. Anywhere, was the reply—from your corner grocery to highest-end gift shops, but the ones in the grocery store were all you needed. Aliette bought a huge bar of hugely expensive pure milk chocolate by way of showing her gratitude to the lady for the tip. She paid with her card.

'Merci, Madame Bettelman,' the woman said, handing back the card. 'Enjoy yourself.'

She was planning on it.

She stopped at a pharmacy and bought a toothbrush, paste, and a bar of goat's milk soap.

There was also a phone card among Martin Bettelman's rejected personal effects. She found a phone and called the office. Monique answered. The garage had called looking for the Opal. The inspector said tell them probably Monday, and asked to be passed along to the boss.

Claude, without so much as a hello, said, 'Everyone outlives their cat, Aliette, and everyone deals with it. Why not you? Unless you get a cat when you're eighty, you are going to outlive it. This is nature. This is —'

Aliette hung up the phone. He had no idea. Being in Basel helped her see this.

She removed the card, then reinserted it and tried another number — in Nantes, on the far side of the world. Her mother answered. '*Salut. C'est moi.* What are you doing?' She and Papa were going to eat at the club with some old friends. Aliette felt the usual twinge that came with each reminder that her life was so different from Maman's. There were no 'old friends' on this side of her life. She pried news from her mother. Bridge group, exercise class, new neighbours. What are you reading? Some wretched bestseller that was nothing but sex, it made you wonder how far the notion of taste had fallen. Aliette hadn't read it. 'How is Papa?' When Maman finished her usual droll litany of complaints about the man she had loved exclusively for almost sixty years, Aliette told her about Piaf.

'Ah, *ma pauvre...*' Maman knew Piaf. He had started off, white and helpless and so cute in a basket in the kitchen, directly below her mother's feet where they rested on the bottom rung of the ancient kitchen stool. Piaf had been nine, a well-seasoned veteran, by the time he had started life on the third floor by the park in a dull mid-sized city on the eastern edge of the universe. So Maman commiserated in the way only a mother can. The subtext was: life changes, life ends. Maman and Papa were both closing in on eighty.

And Aliette was crying, silently, huddled with the phone in the corner of a chic café.

When the lesson in life was concluded, she informed her mother, 'I'm in Basel.'

'*C'est bon, ma chère...* A change of scene will do you good.'

Yes and no, Maman. She mentioned some interesting biscuits she and Papa would love. 'I'll bring a box at Christmas.' She did not say a word about Claude and her mother didn't ask.

Then she crossed the street and went into a corner store and found a 1.3-kg tin of leckerli. *Memories of Switzerland.* A photo of a Swiss mountain scene on the lid. Forty Swiss francs. Outrageous. But the nice Swiss lady assured her, 'These are very special cookies, madame. Lots of pure honey. Just wonderful.' It was exactly what she needed to hear. In appreciation, she added three bottles of Boxer beer to her purchase. Did that mean she did not trust Agent Rudi to show up? No, it meant she couldn't wait to enjoy her treats. She put the beers in the crepe bag with her underwear and chocolate and continued on, wandering up and down charming and immaculate Klein Basel streets, considering boutique windows, laughing quietly at the absurd prices. She stopped again at a kiosk and bought an *apfelküchlein*. An apple donut.

Hands full, the inspector began circling northward, in the direction of the secret apartment. She hoped. Once she'd found Mulheimer and knew she was almost home, as it were, she pulled up in a small park and sat on a bench... She beckoned a passing teenager. Yes, he had a bottle opener—on his Swiss army knife, where else? Merci. *Danke*. She sipped and chomped.

Boxer beer and an apple donut. With a ginger cookie for dessert.

Claude could fuck himself. This evening she was entertaining Rudi.

Where that might lead, well, they'd have to wait and see.

She cried again as she sat there on a bench with her treats and a beer.

No one would notice. No one would know her. She cried because she didn't know...

Aliette Nouvelle knew the value of relationship. Her own mother had conveyed this elemental message since before she could remember. It had been internalized and tested. Then tested to the nth degree with a man called Claude Néon. But it wasn't right... It wasn't right.

If sex is central to the bond—and it has to be—then sex is a way of destroying it. A way of breaking free of an intolerable mistake the body can't let go.

Two hours later, FedPol Agent Bucholtz gazed, rapt, as the French cop told the story of her life and her beliefs. In French, of course, and Rudi followed, willing, enchanted as she spoke of love in the higher echelons of the French police, the profound thrill of going into action hand in hand. Rudi believed every word. Her story, which was also her confession, included the death of Piaf, the shoemaker's dedication to craftsmanship, a mysterious ivory-skinned man naked on a rock at midnight, and her double life as Lise. She wondered if Rudi was cop enough to take an undercover turn at Zup. He insisted he was. 'Turn around,' she commanded. He did. The moment was preternatural, in a place that had nothing to do with her life yet felt essential to her soul. From ten steps away, in the dim light of the fifth-floor window Rudi's back and buttocks were lean and deathly white. 'You could almost be him,' she murmured.

'The guy on the rock?'

'Almost.'

They had consumed a quantity of beer, laughing, playing the games of mutual attraction. The expensive lingerie had served its purpose and was now discarded. She wore only the department-store quilt with which Martin Bettelman had covered his second-hand bed. She had allowed this young Swiss to see her, even touch for a moment here and there, and she had enjoyed kissing those sensuous soup-lapping lips.

But Rudi wasn't an angelic ghost by a river. A docile Saint Bernard could never be.

And, more cogent to the matter sorting through her foggy soul, he wasn't Claude Néon, who was hairier, much larger, and so much more intense — all that sublimated power. Rudi was nowhere near to being a man like Claude. He was an overly intellectual Swiss art cop with milk-white, mole-spattered skin.

It wasn't that Aliette Nouvelle was a bigger-is-better kind of girl. It was because she could not shut down the machine in her mind comparing men.

In seeking what, Inspector?

She only knew the feeling was warm, but far from warm enough. Swathed in her blanket, she moved across the space of the chilly room and pressed herself against him. 'Time to get some sleep, Agent… Big day tomorrow, you and me.'

He turned, so willing.

Inspector Nouvelle smiled the kind of smile all women have to master for moments exactly like this. 'I mean you in your bed, me in mine.'

'No…'

'Yes. We will continue on tomorrow, Rudi. We will see where this investigation leads.'

'But…' prying at her blanket, just like a loyal Saint Bernard, nudging.

'Please… Nothing like this is ever solved so directly. It can't be, Rudi. Mm?' Pulling gently away from his hands. '…Come on, get dressed. We'll build on what we know tomorrow.'

Of course he acquiesced. After a few more longing kisses, Rudi went, slightly groggy, down the long stairs, having been ordered to meet her at Freiestrasse at 08:00 hours. She waved from the landing and closed the door. She briefly wondered, Did he have a wife he was willing to lie to? A wife and beautiful Swiss child? It was not her problem. Her problem was her sense of responsibility. She cared about the thing she needed to break apart. Her own erstwhile masterpiece, now destined for love's scrap heap. Her problem was her anger and the need to keep moving, though she had no idea where. Except to learn more about this crime.

17

RUDI'S DAY IN THE TWILIGHT ZONE

'Your eyes, Rudi. I'm going to need your eyes.'

'Yes.' But can a cop see his mistakes before they happen? Only vaguely.

Last evening, whispering the details of her metamorphosis, she had articulated a compelling link between attention to method and the vocational sense of duty, arguing that these two were bottom-line prerequisites, how the one fed the other, creating true professional integrity and a compassionate love of mankind. No woman had ever told Rudi anything like that before. And so FedPol Agent Bucholtz awoke believing he was in love. In love with this French inspector who had smiled and patted his head and called him my beautiful puppy. The woman beside him, who sleepily scolded Rudi for smelling of beer even as she reached to keep him in bed, she was a good woman, a long-time lover—but this Aliette was something special. Rudi pleaded a long and difficult stake-out with a colleague—they'd deserved a beer or two. He left advising that it was a tricky case and he might well be late again.

And that magic feeling only grew on a bright, crisp Saturday morning. They walked through the streets, headed toward the Kunstmuseum, feeling autumn arriving in Basel. They stopped for coffee and apple donuts, two investigators on the case, sharing information, discussing strategy. Coming through the museum courtyard, Rudi Bucholtz felt monumental, there forever like the *Burghers of Calais*. Rudi's eyes were definitely at the service of Inspector Aliette Nouvelle.

VigiTec security agent Della Kypreosus—Greek or Macedonian, it sounded like—was there to greet them at nine o'clock sharp. Minimal German, a touch of English, no French at all, it seemed, but a large, proud smile as she led them down to the second basement.

The monitoring suite was dimly spectral under the flat glow of three dozen screens and various tiny lights on the face of the controls. Inspector Nouvelle gave basic directions: a pale man. Pale and very slight. Alone or with Martin Bettelman. If there was footage of Agent Josephina Perella, this would be of interest too. Della assured her, 'Me, I know.' Rudy took his place beside Della. He was not worried when Aliette leaned close, whispered, 'Counting on you, Agent Bucholtz. I'll be back,' gently patted him on the head and left the room. He thought she was going to the bathroom. It was over an hour later when it occurred she'd left him with a job.

Fine. He settled in. But...

But Rudi was trained to study paintings. Watching other people do it on a video screen was another thing entirely. This search through endless views of people passing through rooms, standing, gazing, then wandering away was excruciatingly tedious. The occasional appearance of Martin Bettelman, arms folded, drifting into a scene, then out again, was becoming a high point.

VigiTec agent Della Kypreosus sat still and businesslike, eyes poring over every frame.

At first Rudi felt an instinctive sense of competition with the immigrant worker. It did not last. The more Della focused, the more his discomfort increased. Agitated, he got up, stretched and paced, sat for a few more minutes, then went to pee. Then found his way up to the main floor.

Where was Inspector Nouvelle? Had she gone for a tour? Rudi watched as museum goers entered, got their bearings, headed off toward the rooms. He fought the urge to leave, to walk out into the sunny Saturday... he went right up to the door and looked out at the *Burghers of Calais*. They appeared so free out there in the courtyard. But he returned to his chair beside Della.

The inspector said she needed his eyes. Rudi had watched *her* eyes as she gazed at him the night before, half-smiling, half-wondering, so serious: they were a crystalline silver-blue. Rudi needed another night with this woman. To consummate it. To move it forward. It felt like destiny to Rudi...

It occurred to him to ask Della, 'Is she here—in the building?'

Della sighed, hit some buttons. A quick scan in real time did not locate the French cop. She returned to their search. 'We find this man for your boss.'

'She's not my boss.'

Della laughed quietly in an unknowable-foreigner sort of way. She left to pee, leaving Rudi to stare at the back of a man's head, a man in the Early Modern room who was in turn considering a painting of a young boy kneeling, prayerful by a single tree, rendered naïve and stark beside a naively rendered river. It was a Swiss painting, Rudi knew it well. Who? His brain was growing foggy and the artist's name eluded him. And was this screen image real time? Or sometime days or weeks ago? 'You eat,' said Della, returning with a cookie tin and a thermos. The coffee was from somewhere east of Switzerland, the pastry was too sweet. But his boredom stoked his hunger and he quickly demolished five. 'I make myself,' Della said. An hour later the tin was empty. Rudi felt himself nodding off, lost in dull, sugar-induced catatonia.

'Sad Martin,' said a voice.

Rudi shook himself awake. Della pointed to Martin Bettelman standing unobtrusively in a corner observing visitors. It couldn't be real time—Martin Bettelman was dead. What about the pale-skinned man? Rudi allowed himself to fade again, till, 'Sad Martin.' Della added a musical intonation, a cue, a wake-up call. Rudi snapped to, watched dutifully, quietly ashamed of abusing the inspector's trust. Until his requested eyes dropped shut again.

'Wottel,' Della announced. Agent Bucholtz was jolted back to awareness by a segment of video footage showing people moving quicker, some running. He watched Martin Bettelman running, then watched Bettelman explaining something to Agent Perella and Dieter Taub. In this dim room, in this twilight state of awareness, it was very real. But Agent Perella was also dead. He gave his head a brisk shake. Wake up! In her special way, Della explained that this had been the day a small Watteau had suddenly not been on the wall.

Did Watteau have anything to do with anything? Rudi made a note. 'Let's see the lead-up to that.' Della pushed some buttons. They watched the general in-and-out flow at the front entrance in the days before the theft. Martin Bettelman was nowhere in that footage. Historically it was all in reverse and Rudi was lulled again. On Rudi's command, Della brought them back to the actual day. 'Not *this* day, *frau!* ...the day of the theft!' Rudi wanted to scream at someone.

Della quickly relocated Dieter Taub and Agent Perella, Bettelman and several other flummoxed Kunst employees of various rank, silently conferring. Then Taub and Perella were alone together in front of the empty space on the wall. Rudi mused bleakly, 'They look like the butcher and his wife.' The notion was the result of too much television, an unfiltered tendency to generic typecasting after half a day in a subterranean video jail. Flat images and utter boredom left you dangerously open to the vagaries of dreams. But it was apt: Taub and Perella, both large-sized, middle-aged: Herr and Frau Butcher, looking well scrubbed for a day off from the shop to get some culture, then perhaps a sausage and some beer.

'I don't think this man like women,' Della mused in response to Rudi's musing.

'Why would you think that, Della?'

'I feel.'

Rudi shrugged. Maybe Dieter Taub was gay. So what? Maybe Agent Perella had been too.

They plowed on, at jerky speeds, sometimes in real-time reverse, on and on through a silent sea of desultory movement, formless, an ongoing logic-free portrayal of humanity that belied all noble adjectives, too much like watching cows at pasture, or those experiments observing dogs that have been allowed to wander free and always wander nowhere special: Arf!...until Della, inured to day-long onslaughts of brain-numbing black and white wide angles pushed a button that stopped the flow. 'This man is very white.'

Rudi woke up, leaned toward the screen. 'Have we seen him before?'

'I have seen. He is very white.'

'With Martin Bettelman?'

'No. With paintings. In rooms. Never with no one, I think.'

'Fuck!' They had to start all over again. They had to isolate this man.

Everyone is white in grainy black and white. Wide angle, it is impossible to define the look in a person's eyes. But Della was trained for this and they began to find him. An adolescent, or slightly older? It was difficult to say. Invariably dressed in nondescript Saturday clothes, jeans, trainers, an oversized hoodie obscuring a face already obscured by loose locks of darkish hair. He would sit on the armless banquette in the middle of the room and gaze. He would stand and come close, intimately close, hands seemingly poised as if to grab… Or was it to embrace? But they never saw him touch a painting. Not once. This young man with the veiled, pale white face.

Della managed to freeze a side-angle close-up of his face as he was coming through the front door. The lips were his defining trait. Full, some would say feminine, in their set pout and shapely aspect. Della studied the image, then looked sidelong at Rudi. 'He like you.' It bothered FedPol Agent Bucholtz to hear it. Last night he'd happily indulged a French cop's fleeting fantasy that he could be that man. Or boy? Checking date, time code, Della found a extra-wide perspective of the entrance area. This view showed Martin Bettelman watching this same visitor from his place by the door to the Romantics. They knew this with a simple switching of views. Della's time code confirmed the same moment. Then, moving forward: That same day, inside the otherwise empty Romantics room the pale visitor stood and gazed, rapt. 'Switch, please.'

Della expertly obeyed. Rudi watched Martin Bettelman at his designated post, watching the pale visitor. Bettelman appeared sleepy (like himself), dreamy. He seemed to be swaying like a plant in the wind. Of course there was no wind — just a dozy contemplation creating movement, ever so slightly, languorous, the outer layer of an inner pulse. Agent Rudi Bucholtz did not understand what he was seeing till Della muttered, 'Awful, Martin!' She touched a toggle switch, the shot zoomed in and down to Bettelman's crotch. His partially opened fly, his hand inside. It *was* awful. Disgusting. In a public place! And Martin Bettelman was supposed to be working.

18

TRAPPED IN THIS LIFE

Crossing the Wettstein Bridge, heading back to the Kunstmuseum, there was no pleasure in the charm of the four o'clock sun against the Basel rooftops, the strolling citizens, the busy river flowing past below. Aliette had spent the day traipsing from one private gallery to the next seeking traces of a fraudulent nexus tying art restorer Justin Aebischer to security guard Martin Bettelman to FedPol Agent Josephina Perella. Futile! It seemed Herr Dieter Taub had told it right: She had been politely stonewalled at every stop. At her last call, Herr Rutger Mettler had politely advised her that if the police persisted in this unseemly intrusion he would proceed to have his entire inventory moved to a secure bank vault at Bern. His security firm could have the job done by Sunday noon. (That would be Herr Taub.) The mention of an international mandate elicited the politest silence. Recalling the sorry sight of Franck Woerli's confused and defeated eyes, Aliette could only think, Poor fool. Putting Dieter Taub's negative prediction beside Hans Grinnell's damning evidence, it was almost sure Perella had deliberately sent her naïve colleague into a void of bland Swiss discretion and impenetrable business code. Then gotten herself killed. Little wonder the place was as much a haven and transfer point for shadowy art as it was for dirty cash. Little wonder some police officers just gave up. Little wonder Inspector Nouvelle was in a foul mood when she stepped back into the dim security suite in the bowels of the museum.

So was FedPol Agent Bucholtz. 'Where the hell have you been?'

'Working! On my feet since this morning, wasting my precious time with a bunch of smiling *connard* Swiss... Do you know how many Flemish shoemakers of the late Romantic period there are out there?' This was rhetorical. 'Thousands upon thousands!'

His smile was snide. 'I did know that, yes.' His tone said, You deserve it, bitch.

VigiTec Agent Della Kypreosus was busily logging reference numbers. She looked up from her board and into the middle of an escalating French-Swiss confrontation. 'We find him.'

Which defused the situation, at least momentarily. Aliette took a seat, pointedly ignoring the surly Rudi while Della presented a series of black and white scenes featuring the same slight, stoop-shouldered youth whose bony, pale features were perpetually obscured by an oversized training hood as he stood motionless...for long periods it turned out, in front of works of art. The dates on the timecode went back more than a year. In the last few months, the lanky figure of Martin Bettelman in uniform became a regular sidebar to the non-action in the centre of the screen. Aliette cringed when they arrived at the horrid climax, so to speak. But it certainly could be the boy on the rock at her crime scene, and Martin Bettelman had been dangerously smitten. The link, though circumstantial, was now definitely there.

But the third side of the triangle? 'Is Josephina Perella anywhere in this?'

It was Della, efficient and bright, who reported instantly. 'No.'

Standing, she extended a hand to Della, 'Excellent work, madame. Merci.'

That bothered Rudi. He picked up the fight exactly where they'd left it, whining, 'It's not fair to leave me sitting there without so much as a—'

'I left you with a job to do, Agent Bucholtz.'

Rudi blinked, blushed deeply enough to be seen even in the half-light of that room, and, clearly angry at being embarrassed in front of a mere security guard who wasn't even Swiss, blustered, 'He loves Art Nouveau naïf. And ultra-metaphysical Romantic. OK?'

'*Bon.* I trust you've made a detailed list.' Shrugging away another muttered stream of Teutonic cursing, she picked up her bag and headed for the door.

Relations were distinctly cool as they made their way back to the FedPol offices on Freie.

In the lift, he faced her. 'Why exactly are we here?' Same surly whine.

Same cool French response. 'As I mentioned yesterday, and as you might have noted, Rudi, our forensics indicate the possibility of a female shooter.' That was a lie, both today and yesterday; it was strictly a feeling on her part. But, 'Video presence or not, I need to pursue this further.' Aliette led him through the empty office to Agent Perella's desk and, exhausted, sat heavily down in her chair. 'I need her key chain. If I remember, it's in the top drawer.'

He blanched, caught between petulance and rules. 'I'm not authorized. I need to call Inspector Woerli. I —'

'Are you working with me or not, Rudi?' Swivelling slowly in Josephina's chair, knees opening and closing, methodically messaging her thighs, qualmless, only trying to keep the Swiss police moving forward. Adding, somewhat shamelessly, 'All I really want is a nice warm bath. But we have to do this first. We have to.'

The we and the warm bath plus white French thighs seemed to assure him. Rudi opened the drawer, produced the keys. Aliette smoothed her skirt and got to her feet with a groan.

They retrieved her delinquent car from the basement parking. Rudi drove. Turning into Nestléplatz, a tiny crescent off Haltinger, which in turn met a corner of Mulheimer, Inspector Nouvelle, who was not as bad at directions as some men (Claude) sometimes insinuated, assessed the route, the larger layout, and declared, 'All quite walkable.'

Bettelman's dormer. Perella's flat. And Zup.

A man sat alone and forlorn on the steps to Josephina's building. Franck Woerli had the look of a man who's been locked out of his own home and is waiting for someone to show up. Helpless. Useless. 'Hello, Franki,' Aliette said, exiting the car, ducking under the police tape.

'I wanted to see for myself.' Not locked out. He obviously had his own means of entry.

'And?'

'Nothing. Not a hint of a life beyond work,' he murmured. 'And her mother.' It had an angry kind of finality. Woerli's bitter proof of a futile life. Like his. 'Maybe you'll have better luck.'

'Won't you join us?'

Franck Woerli only gestured, woeful, worn out: You go. I give up.

Yesterday's tears had dried, but he was dazed. 'What is it, Franki?'

'We get trapped in this useless life, Inspector. Completely trapped.'

19

PARSING A MOTHER'S MESSAGE

Woerli went home. Nouvelle and Bucholtz went up.

Franck Woerli was not wrong in his gloomy assessment of Josephina Perella's life. The place was stodgy and drab. Apart from some brightly illustrated books on art that were probably for work, everything from the lamps to the fraying, faded carpet was old. Worn out. An art cop with no imagination. No verve.

Rudi seemed personally offended, noting that it reminded him of films about nervous people living grimly in East Germany.

Aliette instinctively defended Josephina. 'Maybe she liked it.'

'What's to like?' he scoffed. 'She was a senior officer. With what they get, you'd think she could have done better than this.' FedPol Agent Bucholtz pronounced the place 'depressing.'

That didn't mean there would be no clue here to her killing. Inspector Nouvelle was circling slowly, touching things, lightly, barely, like a gypsy with her fingers hovering over a crystal ball. Failure. Love. Death by violence. A home contains the seeds of everything. It's always there.

Rudi sat on the dreary sofa. 'You know, we haven't really talked all day,' he ventured.

'We're working, Rudi.'

'I'm sorry if I got mad.'

'Shh!' Standing dead still in the middle of the frumpy salon. Feeling Josephina's space.

Rudi watched her, wondering how to atone. After locating Martin Bettelman lost in obscene ecstasy while the pale boy/man lost himself in Romantic art, Rudi had confidently called his girlfriend to tell her, yes, the investigation demanded his presence for a second night, likely all of it this time. He'd lied to her twice. And she'd believed him. So easy... Not so, the French inspector. Last evening Rudi thought he understood her perfectly. Now he was not at all certain.

She moved. In quick succession she looked in the bedroom, bathroom and kitchen, in and out — it was like watching a cuckoo clock character on a track. She finished her quick tour by the window, where she stood looking out at a residential street, soft in the muted evening light, a quiet quarter settling in for Saturday night. 'She had a boyfriend,' Aliette declared.

Rudi nodded dumbly. He shrugged — so what?

'Do you know what that means, Agent?'

'No.' ...yes, the French inspector was getting seriously strange.

From across the room Inspector Nouvelle stared at Rudi fiercely for a heart-stopping moment. Then moved three steps to the small *secrétaire,* badly scratched and in need of refinishing. It was set against the window wall to give Josephina Perella sunlight as she worked on her bills on a lonely Sunday afternoon.

Or maybe not so lonely. If she had a boyfriend.

The inspector picked up the only post-modern object in sight. A cellphone. 'Recognize it?

'No.' It was not government issue. They'd found that one with her body.

Aliette pushed buttons. No names in the directory. One message waiting. She put the device on speaker, and played the message. A woman's voice. Elderly. Fragile: Something in Italian, but nothing she could identify. 'Ticino dialect,' advised Rudi. He knew a little. She played it again. He recognized the words '*cara mia,*' the Italian version of 'Toussaint...' Then, '*Ciao.*'

'It's her mother.' Just as poor old Woerli had said.

Rudi shrugged. Agent Perella's mother didn't kill her, surely.

Aliette played the message again. Rudi was meant to be listening, but it was at that moment he noticed movement — a shadow shifting along the crack of hall light in the space between door and floor. Yes, a shadow moved across it. There was someone on the other side of the door. 'Look,' he whispered, gesturing. She shook her head, lost in her deductions. She played the message again and listened, pacing the room. Rudi gestured at the door. 'I think we have an issue.' He saw the shadow shifting, coming closer, then withdrawing, like a sinister wave.

She stopped. 'Of course we do, Rudi. We only need to fasten on. That's the trick, what I was telling you last night, mm? Attention to method. And the method of the world. It's our job to bring these two into alignment. Please...' Pay attention. She played the message yet again.

'I'm talking about here, right now.' The shadow on the other side of the door moved again. 'Inspector...' Rudi tried to keep it calm, conversational. He did not want to force the matter and alert the lurking presence. Perhaps there was more than one.

She made another trance-like turn of the room and stopped in front of him. Rudi pointed at the shadow diluting the light in the crack at the foot of the door. The inspector did not react. She pushed the button and played the thing again. Despite the presence beyond the door, Rudi caught the name of a place — 'Savosa?' And a person. 'Signora Biaggi. Angelina. Amigo...'

The inspector confirmed. 'Some woman, right? Angelina. Her friend?'

As the question hung there between them, Rudi heard the softest shift of a leather sole. 'Toussaint,' he whispered, 'something about Toussaint.' All Saints Day, three weeks hence.

Aliette listened again. Rudi heard another sound outside. Aliette listened again...

In the silent instants between cueing the machine and the fragile voice leaving information for Josephina, Rudi began to deduce a game — a high-stakes game of timing that would come down to a split second of precision force. Again the old woman's voice flowed by in its tired sing-song cadence. He focused on the apartment door. When it finished, Rudi indicated negative: he could not make out any more of a mama's message to her daughter — only the sad thing underlying it. So sad when you come across messages to the dead, messages doomed to stay in no-space, unheard forever. This sense was reinforced with a sixth...then a seventh hearing.

While the shadow in the crack continued to feint and slide.

'An invitation?' Aliette pondered.

Rudi was too distracted to consider it. A prying concierge? The shadow on the other side of the door was now showing deliberate motion, back and forth, as if it did not care who saw it.

FedPol Agent Rudi Bucholtz was perspiring freely when the message ended its tenth reprise. An art cop, like all cops, had been taught some basic martial moves — mostly defensive, but it was not as though he practised breaking bricks with the edge of his hand.

The French inspector gravitated back to the window, puzzling over the message, apparently unconcerned as to the crisis waiting at the door. She was looking out at the sky when she said, 'I did not say anything to my mother about Claude. And *she* did not say a word about him either. Do you understand what I'm saying, Rudi?'

Not exactly. Was this tactical, a ploy to keep the lurking presence lulled while they got themselves into a more proactive position? Rudi's work as an art cop had never brought him to a moment like this. As brightly as possible, and certainly so it would be heard on the other side of the door, he chirped, 'I don't believe I've had the pleasure of meeting Claude.'

Turning to face him, the inspector's thumb hovered over the replay button on Josephina's cell. Rudi sensed pressure on the door handle. He rose from the musty corduroy divan, caught between fear for life and limb and fear of being a fool. She did not respond to his signalling.

She said, more to herself than him, 'And *her* mother did not say a word about *her* boyfriend.'

Far too loudly, Rudi blurted, 'Inspector, there's — '

'Hush! …So it means she was not telling her mother about him. I mean probably never.'

As she paused to assess her conclusion, Rudi heard a distinct 'click.'

Not a door handle. The possibilities quickly grew darker, deadly.

'It means it was not going well between them,' Aliette surmised. 'Something wasn't right.'

Rudi grasped an empty vase from the side table. A tacky Polish folk-art piece. *Why did Josephina live with an ugly thing like that?* Rudi shuddered, aware of a useless thought. The situation was splitting his thinking in a dangerous way.

Inspector Nouvelle finally moved toward the door, musing, 'If it *was* good, I mean a good relationship, her mother would have known all about him and invited him for Toussaint too. No? What

I mean, Rudi, is why didn't I say word about Claude? Because it's turned to shit, that's why. No, let's not put too fine a point on it. Let's be honest here, mm?'

Rudi deduced a signal. Let's do it. Heart in overdrive, he reached for the door handle.

Aliette said, 'Mothers urge daughters to bring their boyfriends home. I know this, Rudi.'

Door yanked open, Rudi Bucholtz stepped into open space, arm raised, ready to strike.

Hans Grinnell punched him square in the face. Rudi made no sound. For some reason he did not drop Josephina Perella's cheap vase. Perhaps he should have. Perhaps Grinnell perceived a continued threat. He kicked Rudi in the gut with the hard toe of the leather shoe which Rudi had correctly identified. Now Rudi dropped the vase. It hit the floor and smashed. Rudi did the same.

A French cop did not understand the German epithets spewing from Inspector Grinnell's mouth as he hovered over Rudi Bucholtz, but she had no doubt at all as to the device he'd been in the process of affixing to the door handle casing. From one cop's patch to the next, a listening post is universal. In his free hand (it had only taken one to knock poor Rudi senseless) Hans Grinnell still held the tiny heat rod that would fuse the miniscule wafer to the brass casing.

Ceasing with his invective, resisting an obvious desire to give Rudi another kick, Grinnell went into a pocket, found a packet, removed a piece and recommenced his operation.

Staying calm, the French inspector commented, 'But surely you did all this. Your team? You said you had a team here.' She watched bemused as he carefully lifted a tiny disc from the floor where it lay near a puddle of blood and saliva from Rudi's mess of a mouth.

The Basel Lands investigator wiped it on his sleeve, put it in his pocket. 'Wrong frequency.'

She commiserated. 'Two crime scenes *will* stretch your resources.'

'You want it right, you have to do it yourself.'

'True enough, Inspector. True enough.'

They both contemplated Rudi Bucholtz, curled on the floor, a bloody tooth near his nose.

Rudi appeared to be watching them from one eye—waiting like an injured dog. That Saint Bernard had been hit by a truck. Hans Grinnell removed a facial tissue from his pocket. Crouching, he appeared slightly remorseful as he manoeuvred the art cop's front tooth onto it, and folded the tissue once. He left it by Rudi's nose. Rudi's eye took it in, but he made no move to claim his tooth. He waited. Grinnell was finally compelled to help Rudi to his feet. 'Come on, get up, you're going to live.' He put the wrapped-up tooth in Rudi's pocket.

Agent Bucholtz stood before them, wobbly, swollen face askew, the missing tooth creating a glaring gap in his credibility. In a slurred, lisping voice he accused Grinnell. 'You arrogant bastard.' Or German words to that effect. 'Bastards like you are the reason she did what she did. You're the reason she was killed.'

The Basel Lands cop shrugged his denial. 'I never met her before Wednesday.'

'You're all the same, with your shitty little patches. Too fucking proud to ask for help from someone who actually knows...' Rudi was fighting tears. '...all the fucking same.'

'You're not really trained for this, are you, Rudi?' Grinnell smiled. 'Agent Perella sure as hell wasn't—no matter which side she was playing.' He came across like a kindly, if slightly psychotic, scout leader. 'Believe me. Far, far out of her depth and she paid for it.'

The battered Rudi made a universal gesture: Hand to elbow; fist up hard: Fuck you.

Aliette said, 'Rudi, you could learn a lot from Hans.'

Eyes burning with shame and anger, there was horrid saliva flying through the gap in his teeth as he told her, 'And you are a bizarre French cunt!'

Grinnell moved to intervene. Aliette put up a hand. She knew Rudi would never hit her. And she could not be bothered to slap his face. She said, 'I was counting on your help, Rudi. But there *is* a learning curve that has to be respected here. Mm?'

'Bullshit! You need my *eyes*? Why? You need someone to watch you making speeches in your underwear?' He spat blood on the floor. 'I am such a fool. Such a total fucking fool!'

That made two, and perhaps three, fools on the FedPol roster. What could one say?

'Go home, Rudi. Hans and I will take it from here.'

Agent Bucholtz was truly wretched as he slouched away, down the apartment stairs.

20

DEEPER INTO IT WITH HANS

Basel Lands Inspector Hans Grinnell eyed her. 'What was that about?'

'Not much. A fantasy?' Shrugging Rudi away. She watched him, down on his knees installing a new listener. He had a steady hand. She said, 'Looks like it's just us now, Inspector.'

Gathering his tools, he muttered, 'There is no *us*. There are two different cases.'

'Why don't you trust me?'

'Short answer? Because I don't need to.'

'I would say you're a man without much curiosity. Eh, Hans?'

That hit a nerve. He stood and dusted the knees of his pants. 'And I would say you are one of those women who cannot handle being wrong.'

'*Au contraire*. I am *usually* wrong, at least in part. But there was a man in her life and that will be part of our solution here. And I bet you think so too. Why else would you be here making sure this place is wired right? On a Saturday evening, no less.'

Hans Grinnell sniffed the same half-nasty, half-exasperated little snigger he'd expressed in demolishing Franck Woerli. 'If there was anyone, it was a woman.'

She put her hands on her hips. 'I'm betting boyfriend.' Police Judiciaire Inspector Aliette Nouvelle was not some abstract Swiss FedPol agent. She could and would stand her ground.

Perhaps Hans Grinnell accepted this as fact. He moved past her, into the apartment and over to the salon window. He surveyed the street. 'We did some canvassing. A neighbour—just there,' indicating the building opposite, 'says she saw a woman in the street some time in the early evening the day Perella died. Pink topcoat.

Had to have a key because she went in and up. Neighbour saw lights go on. Then off. Wasn't there ten minutes. She left on foot.'

'Description?'

'Hardly. The pink coat... Middle-aged. Blondish. Biggish...'

'Like Josephina Perella.'

A moment of silence as two cops stared out the window.

Aliette reconfirmed her bet. 'Everything here says a man.'

Grinnell repeated, 'We are *not* working together, Inspector.'

'Come.' She marched to the kitchen. Grinnell followed, skeptical but amused. She took two bottles of beer from the refrigerator, proffered them. He took them. She gestured. 'Two steaks for a Thursday night? One definitely large. First, a girl does not have her girlfriend over for steak, Inspector. At least not where I come from. And if she does, who gets the bigger piece of meat?' Shutting the fridge, pointing at a drawer: 'Opener.' She headed for the bedroom. She waited till he joined her. 'Her side...' Big dramatic whiff of the left side pillow; 'and his...' sticking her nose into the right side pillow. 'A man smell. I know this. Your wife does too.'

Grinnell gave her an opened beer. They touched bottles.

He smiled. 'Why are you people such a pain in the ass?'

'Good question. We ask each other all the time. The fact remains, someone came in here to wipe her phone and clean the place of everything indicating another presence in her life. The things that person forgot or didn't think to remove all indicate a man. A man who's more than likely in this city.'

'And don't forget her mama's message, Inspector. Irrefutable proof if ever there was.'

His Swiss sarcasm did not quite work in French.

She met his twinkling eyes. 'Does that mean your fist was meant for me and not poor Rudi?'

He actually looked abashed. She absolved him. 'At least you were paying attention...' Then she went for the kill. 'Inspector, if you don't need me, you need Commander Boehler. And surely you don't need him. Mm?'

'All right!' Hans Grinnell sat himself on the threadbare corduroy divan. 'I'll tell you why I don't need help from the French police. Or Boehler. And then you will bugger off. Yes?'

Dodging the commitment, Aliette plunked herself down beside him. 'I'm all ears.'

'Three things. One: I have the painting, and it's not moving till I get a resolution.'

'And I have the gun and it is staying in France till *I* get a resolution.'

Grinnell gave a quick shake of his close-cropped head. 'It's the *painting*, Inspector. Perella's reason for going out to Aebischer's was to get that painting back here. She thought she'd badger me into being overwhelmed by Reubens and say, Please, take it!' He shrugged. 'Why do they always think we're so stupid? Always. It never ceases to amaze me… Two. I have Perella tied to this thing. She's on tape removing that box of business cards from Aebischer's desk — caught red-handed. And three,' taking a sheath of folded paper from his breast pocket, 'I have these.'

Two sheets. Copies. A letter. The other was an official document. In German, of course. A French cop humbly requested, 'Please translate.'

He obliged. The official document was a complaint processed on a Basel Lands Police form, made out in the name of Hildegard Federer, resident of Benken. It concerned false representation regarding the work of Justin Aebischer, an art restoration practitioner, performed under contract to the Federer family, specifically on a painting entitled *Caresses* by Frans Snyders, dated circa 1625. 'Last winter this woman comes to me looking for help. Old family. Very rich. Collects these paintings of dogs licking themselves. Apparently some are very valuable.' He sipped beer, continued. 'They'd had their collection authenticated by modern means and she'd started the process of refurbishing. Aebischer was recommended by Marcus Streit, who's an old family friend and has often acted as a kind of advisor and curator whenever the world became interested in the Federer collection. I got the sense she knows and trusts him. That's two years ago. Aebischer took delivery of the Snyders, reported on his progress when asked, and returned it according to the schedule. Good and fine. Then she gave him the Reubens. Same job — clean it, bring it back to its original state. At your service, *frau*. Aebischer gets to work. Meanwhile, Streit comes to look at Aebischer's work on the Snyders. And he noticed something worrisome.'

'Such as?'

'A colour discrepancy of some kind.' Grinnell shrugged. 'It's well beyond me.'

'Are we talking about a fake?'

'Not at that point. Streit just thought it wasn't very good work—that the refurbished colour wasn't right. It's all related to value. When Frau Federer contacted Aebischer demanding an explanation for Streit's consternation, he just laughed and told her Marcus was getting old. He told her to take it to the lab at the Kunstmuseum and let them look at it. The *frau* told me Aebischer wasn't worried in the least. But her friend Marcus kept coming back and staring at her cleaned-up Snyders. And fretting. So she came to see us for advice on how to guard her painting and at the same time compel Aebischer to provide more comprehensive disclosure with regard to his work on said painting during the ten months it was in his keeping.'

'Why did she not take it for a second opinion?'

'Actually, Streit brought some of his contacts through to see if they saw what he saw. But it's so specialized, not to say subjective, and no one could agree. As for taking it to the museum, well, if she did that, Aebischer's reputation would be cast into doubt regardless of the result. I'm not talking about the public. I mean his standing in the community that gives him most of his work. He could sue. But worse, the value of the work would come into question. Aebischer told *me* the same when I went to see him on her behalf, though not in so many words. In a backward way, he had control. Upshot: Herr Rooten, that's her lawyer, told Frau Federer to go lightly.'

'So you met Aebischer. What was he like? What did he tell you?'

'That it was ridiculous, that Marcus Streit should retire, it was long past time, and that if the *frau* made trouble for him, he would reply in kind. Completely knowledgeable, completely arrogant. He more or less told me to get stuffed. Justin Aebischer was a haughty little prick.'

'So you advised her to go ahead with the complaint.'

'I did.' Then, after a thoughtful pause and what-the-hell sort of shrug, Grinnell added, 'I also convinced her to reclaim the painting. The Reubens.'

The complaint was dated in September. It was witnessed by Marcus Streit. 'This is a week before he was killed.'

'Indeed.'

'And the letter?'

A personal letter from Marcus Streit to Inspector Josephina Perella, Federal Police, Cultural Crimes Division, Basel. Grinnell translated,

Agent Perella,

I am the last person to know the proper form or procedure in this matter. Because we have worked together on several occasions, I feel I may approach first on a personal level, and you will tell me how and/or where to proceed. Attached is a copy of a complaint made out by a friend to the Basel Lands Police—I have removed the name for reasons I'm sure you understand. It is self-explanatory. The Basel Lands authorities have advised they are taking steps to help my friend gain a more clear sense of her predicament. I myself have doubts their steps will lead anywhere, and certainly not quickly. As we both know, the longer the process, the greater the odds against a satisfactory resolution. I believe the matter I would like your advice on is related, and perhaps directly. I am growing increasingly certain there are colleagues in my profession using their status and perceived integrity to perpetrate the most grievous fraud. There is of course a huge amount of financial gain underlying this. More important, and which I believe you will appreciate, is the integrity of some our community's—and the world's—most treasured artworks. Forgive the hyperbole, but I am deeply concerned. As you also know as well as I, discretion is a necessity when looking into such matters. I have no notion how to proceed or whom to contact in order to bring effective attention. Perhaps yourself. If you could spare an afternoon, I believe you might find my worries most disturbing. Call to let me know you have considered this letter and give me your thoughts on the possibility of a meeting and/or names of any other contacts who might be able to move the matter forward. Yours in good faith...

Grinnell looked up. 'No date, but it's obvious it was written within the last two weeks.'

'Then Aebischer is killed.'

'We start our investigation. Our turf, our case. Then she shows up. The Bettelman angle was interesting, but it didn't affect my position. Or my strategy.' Grinnell tapped the two documents laid out on the coffee table. 'Finding these on her body later that day only confirmed it.'

'But you said she was pressuring you about the painting. And she declared it original.'

Hans Grinnell grinned and swigged his beer. 'You should have heard her giving me hell. She really wanted to get that painting to Basel. The problem of a problematic masterpiece entrusted to our murder victim would move into a completely different milieu. Invisible. Far beyond my scope. I'd be automatically marginalized. Some little murder out in Basel Lands. Probably a gay thing. No one would give much of a shit, not the least our noble prosecutors.'

'But the painting wasn't there. You said —'

'Not the original. It's verified. It's safe.'

'*Alors?* A fake.'

'Justin Aebischer's specialty was restoring Baroque period paintings. Very valuable Baroque period paintings. He also, as an even more particular specialty, made exquisitely perfect copies of these paintings. He returned the copy to his client. Someone else sold the original to god knows who for a very large sum. Marcus Streit noticed a mistake on the Snyders copy. The orginal is long gone, unfortunately. But we saved the Reubens. And we will get these people.'

Aliette sipped beer, considering Grinnell with an emerging admiration. 'But...' she suddenly experienced the vague existential hole that frames a bad mistake; 'if Perella shows up and declares this fake original, then maybe she's not part of it. Maybe Franki's right and you —'

'She was lying. Or guessing. I say lying. When we were called to Aebischer's, the very same painting we'd removed a week before was sitting there on his work table. At least to my eyes. So I fetched Marcus Streit. I guess it's a matter of professional tricks. Now he knew Aebischer's. In two minutes he showed me how the Reubens on Aebischer's bench was a fake. Perella had the same expertise as Streit, more or less. I say she was in league with Aebischer.' A wise smile. 'And whoever else.' A cabal, covering all the bases.

Hans Grinnell was probably right. But again, Aliette Nouvelle took the part of this sad woman — this time for selfish reasons, as yet unclear. 'But if you had the real Reubens, why would she even bother going?'

'Because she didn't know. *They* didn't know.'

'Didn't know?'

He stared into his beer. 'You told her there was a painting found with Bettelman?'

'Yes.' And Aliette felt her error coming into the light.

'Did you tell her which one?'

'No.'

'No.' Tipping the bottle to his lips, he drained it. 'And Aebischer didn't tell his people the real Reubens had gone home. Obviously that would end the deal. He probably thought, no problem, mine's just as good. Trust me, Inspector — you would not believe how arrogant this man was. And they, whoever they are, would likely not know one from the other. One good reason among several for corrupting a cop like Perella... Then Perella receives the letter from Streit with a copy of Federer's complaint about the Snyders. Boom! Aebischer's under suspicion. She does what she's been recruited to do and tells her friends. They can't live with that. They decide to kill Aebischer, stop the flow of information, take the Reubens, and his bogus copy, and lie low. They must have expected to find two jobs in his studio the day they killed him. But there's only one painting there and they don't dare take it. They don't want to sell a fake. In that world, that's a sure death sentence. They need to find out. I was waiting for someone and I was surprised it was her. But then, why not? A bent art cop's the perfect partner. An insider. News of Bettelman and a painting in France provide a door for Perella. They send their insider to find out where they stand. They don't care who killed Martin Bettelman but they have to know which painting has gone to France. For business purposes — you see?'

Aliette got up, sought some space alone, looking out the window. 'You're saying Bettelman was a bit of good luck for you.' She spoke to his reflection. She saw him shrug again. 'If Bettelman hadn't been killed, Josephina Perella would not have come to Aebischer's that day.'

'Perhaps. But it's all moot.'

'But why would they kill her?'

'Maybe they saw what I saw: a panicky amateur who's even more of a risk than Aebischer. Better kill her too — after she's done Aebischer. Kill Streit. Set up a frame, back away.'

'If I had mentioned it's a shoemaker and not a dog she might still be alive.'

Hans Grinnell rolled off the divan and joined her by the window. 'On the strength of our meeting, I believe she was headed for the same sorry end at some point. Sad, but inevitable. Not a game for amateurs. Please don't tax yourself on that score, Inspector.'

You can stare into the darkness, or at reflections. There was a shadow on the other side of the street. Instinctively, Aliette drew the curtain. Reflections vanished. She faced Hans Grinnell.

He told her, 'And I have to say I think someone else killed Martin Bettelman, someone not involved at all.'

'The people behind this could be over on my side,' she ventured.

'Client maybe,' Grinnell conceded. 'Not the ones managing it, Inspector. Too delicate.'

If she was honest, she had to take his point. 'Two different cases.'

He smiled, but it wasn't smug.

She smiled back. 'You could call me Aliette.'

'Aliette... Any more beer in there?'

'I may be searching for someone who's already dead.'

A cold cop shrug. 'Would it be the first time?'

"No." She went to Josephina's kitchen.

Beers replenished, back on the dusty sofa, another chin-chin... 'And so?'

The Swiss heaved a sigh. 'And so I have to bring the prosecutor a feasible link to Aebischer — his work more than his killing. I need the people who've done business with Aebischer to come forward. Frau Federer, obviously. But she has already lost one of her disgusting doggies and can't abide the thought of the Reubens becoming questionable and Rooten her lawyer backs her. He knows how to work the rules and he's using every one of them to keep the thing under wraps. With her blessing. But I need an unequivocal link to that level before I can realistically ask a prosecutor to direct a magistrate to order certain people to open their vaults, accounts, not to say their mouths. It's tricky.' So saying, Hans Grinnell went to the ancient television facing Josephina's shabby sofa.

It took a while for the image to come. It was clear enough for an old machine. Two teams were lined up as the Swiss anthem played. Basel against Lucerne. A French cop perceived an opportunity to continue the game. Her game. Her mystery. 'Are you hungry? Someone ought to eat those steaks. And I noticed a bottle of decent wine. Some salad...'

Hans Grinnell did not take long to signal yes. He rushed to the bathroom before the kick-off.

As she was preparing their meal she heard him on the phone, making his excuses to his wife.

LIKE GOLDILOCKS ON SUNDAY MORNING

The inspector's Saturday evening was different from her Friday evening. Hans was not Rudi. Neither was he Claude (all that mattered at the moment). It was still very pleasurable. Suffice to say that before they parted Aliette had showed Hans how it was in the nature of the beast to be different things to different people in service of the job.

When she awoke to a greyish Sunday morning in Agent Josephina Perella's bed, she felt like Goldilocks. She knew this was an image left over from Hans Grinnell's snidely amusing attack on his famous compatriot Jung while in the process of venting over the never-ending and very costly therapy his wife had become addicted to and applied at every turn of her life—which meant his life too. So the inspector enjoyed it as she showered in Perella's shower, then made coffee and boiled the last of Perella's milk. Why waste good milk? Why waste steak or wine? She made a thorough search through Josephina's drawers and laundry hamper, found several synthetic-based bluish items she would offer to IJ for analysis against the one found thread. She knew Hans was right, Josephina Perella probably hadn't been to France a week ago Friday, but she took them anyway. To justify a fantasy weekend in Basel? The inspector felt no guilt at all as she tidied up and left, locking the door behind her. Was someone already listening? Hans had promised not to restart the surveillance till after ten that morning.

As she stepped into the wet street, the last traces of fantasy disappeared. It was the requisitioned car, waiting dutifully. The car would have to be returned—one could not simply drive away. To where? Deeper into the heart of Switzerland? In returning the car, she would in turn be delivering herself back to reality. Guilt would be waiting for her there. Likely several other painful emotions too. She knew this. But who can prepare for painful emotion?

The car that would bring her back to reality was parked opposite the building where Hans Grinnell had received information about a woman in a pink coat briefly visiting Perella's flat the evening she was killed. A lady, in a housecoat tightly bundled against the cool and humid morning air, came out as Aliette approached the car. She asked something in Swiss German. Aliette caught the word 'police.' She begged her pardon. The woman switched to French.

'Are you with the police?'

It was how Aliette's mother would always say it. My daughter's *with* the police. A corporate-like perspective. Really? My husband's with the bank. But in that tiny twist of language there was a deep personal echo and the inspector sensed no harm in affirming that she was.

'I saw her again last night,' the woman whispered, though they were alone in the empty street. 'The woman in that pink coat. She was just there,' pointing to a spot below Josephina Perella's salon. 'She was watching the apartment. I was too afraid to go out. To come and tell you. You and the other detective. I'm sorry. I suppose I might have run.'

'Yes?'

'Then this man came along. He was watching too. The woman didn't like it. She left.'

'And the man?'

'Left after you pulled the drape.'

'You're sure it was the same woman?'

She was sure. 'That coat. Pink...too pink. From forty years ago.'

'And the man?'

'Wretched. All bloody, like he'd been in a fight. Or maybe drinking, fell on his face.'

'Thank you, Frau...?'

She did not give her name. She looked into the French inspector's Sunday morning face for an almost impolite duration. Then said, 'You stayed up there a long time.'

'All night,' Aliette replied.

'I know.' Then whispering even lower. 'You have a difficult job in such a horrid world.'

Aliette Nouvelle felt the woman's curiosity. It flowed out of her. It had a desperate energy, made the more so by the pinching armour of Swiss tact. She felt a reflexive urge to tell the woman the truth — that it was a *very* difficult job seducing Basel Lands Inspector Hans Grinnell. But how to describe it to a curious lady? Like time-travel. Forward, backward? More like a sudden step sideways through a rip in the years to the life that might have been, an interlude in normality. Saturday night in Basel. Blasting through an emotional sound barrier, from Claude Néon to Hans Grinnell. Doppelgangers? Not physically. But the one liked Lucerne, the other Paris-Saint-Germain. There were even the children Claude so badly wanted — Hans was a very proud father. There was something almost heroic in compelling a man like that to take his own step sidewise and meet her in Josephina Perella's bed, something infinitely more profound than a whimsical Friday night with Rudi. The fantasy of wretched Rudi, the reality of Hans. And for many, a doppelganger portends ill fate. But could this lady who spent Saturday evenings at her lonely window understand? Right now, Aliette expected Hans Grinnell would be at mass with his family, praying for equilibrium — leaving her to face this good citizen who was desperately wanting to know. Aliette thought that if she could tell the lady, she would, but of course she could not. The public cannot know these things. She said, 'Yes, but citizens such as yourself (i.e., looking out windows, into other windows) are a great help.'

The woman stepped back, shocked, and Aliette knew the shield of propriety had been breached. Guilt or not, she had to get back home. The car. The car must be returned.

She handed the woman a card. 'If you see that woman again, please call me.'

'But this is in France.'

'We'll accept the charges.'

'What about the man?'

'The man is under control.'

Not really. Never really. Safely in the car and away, she punched a number into her cellphone. A woman answered. Rudi was in bed. Not well. But the French police were persistent, and eventually he came. When asked for a description of the woman in the pink coat,

FedPol Agent Bucholtz breathed, 'Stay the fuck away from me,' and cut the line.

She probably deserved it. Maybe needed it too.

...But she needed Rudi. Or would.

Heading across the bridge and through the checkpoint back into France, the inspector tried to visualize the fifty or so works of art she had flipped through with such (unnecessarily) hurried disbelief four nights ago in the squalid pied-à-terre on Mulheimerstrasse. Perhaps she had looked at some Early Modern naïf representations, some ultra-metaphysical Romantic images as well. But she couldn't really remember, and even if she could, she didn't really know. In any event, she doubted a stolid Flemish shoemaker taking a break for tea fit either category.

Perhaps that was why he'd been so rudely treated. And Martin Bettelman killed.

PART 3

SEARCH FOR R

22

RATHER BLAKEAN

Inspector Nouvelle left the requisitioned car in front of the garage door in the courtyard at rue des Bons Enfants, deserted on a Sunday afternoon, and walked home. Leaving the old quarter, she crossed at the *rond-point* and let herself into her almost empty apartment. She showered for the second time that day. Feeling sullied? Her *raison d'être* was disappearance, personal erasure with a minimum of pain, a maximum of love escaped. But you need far more than a careless weekend in another world to self-inflict an existential *coup de grâce*. The problem was having to discuss everything twice — once at breakfast, and again at the office. Then she sat alone, idly towelling her hair. Along with much else, her dryer was in the north end.

There was a knock and she froze. Would Claude come looking for her?

'Mademoiselle Nouvelle?' Madame Camus used the formalities of a previous generation. The inspector relaxed and greeted the aging, sometimes snarky, but always honest widow who filled the double role of landlord and concierge. 'I heard movement. Just wanted to make sure.'

Which is exactly what concierges are meant to do. 'No, it's only me.'

It would be nice to cast Madame Camus as the kindly older confidante, but life is not so pat. Aliette informed Madame that she might be hearing more movement in the coming days. She said nothing of Piaf, nor Claude, and Madame did not ask. The rent was paid, the place was clean, the woman would never dream of enquiring after her tenant's private affairs and likely wouldn't want to know — one always sensed Madame Camus had made her own mistakes. She wished Mademoiselle a pleasant Sunday and went back downstairs… Hair dry, Aliette went out to Madame Chong's to pick up some beer, bread, a hunk of Cantal, *saucisson*. Madame Chong said it had been a while. No cat food today? Not today, thanks. She cried as she walked back.

At her Monday morning briefing, Claude said, 'I thought you wanted children.'

It was far from an opportune time and place for such a statement, but he could not say it in the privacy of their shared home. Because she had not returned to their shared home.

'So did I,' she replied. Then added, 'I do…but I don't.' Then added, 'Sitting there all day?'

These opaque silences between disconnected thoughts. This stop/start rhythm, no direction.

'It changes your point of view,' Claude said.

She agreed it probably did. He was sad but, no tyrant, did not pursue it. She managed to let him understand that she would remain at the south end of the park for the next little while, then headed back to her office, where she wrote her report, submitted her expenses.

Gas, mostly. She had slept for free since Thursday.

She vaguely wondered about Martin Bettelman's credit card. She would wait and see.

She sent an email to Inspector Grinnell at the Basel Lands police detachment at Oberwil summarizing her conversation with Josephina Perella's neighbour, the return of the woman in the pink coat, her retreat when Rudi had passed by. She sensed an email would be more efficient than a phone call so soon after the fact. She added 'Call me!' to her sign-off. She sent separate emails to FedPol Agents Woerli and Bucholtz outlining the 'real progress' they had made in isolating Martin Bettelman on the Kunstmuseum surveillance tapes in the proximity of a pale-skinned museum patron who was definitely a person of interest, and promised to continue to pursue the matter on 'this side' (France). In her communication to Rudi she did not specifically mention Saturday night or Hans Grinnell — only that she would appreciate anything salient regarding the pink-coated woman. She added 'Call me!' to her sign-off… She emailed Herr Taub at VigiTec and thanked him, mentioning that he was very fortunate to have Della Kypreosus on his team. She promised to keep him informed about their progress in restoring the shoemaker and the search for his true home. Formulating, then sending these various communications left her exhausted. For all her angst and effort, the only communication coming back was a memo, handed to her by Monique. *From the desk of J-P Blismes*: He would be delighted to make some time for her. The psychologist specialized in young offenders but consulted to all departments housed at rue des Bons Enfants. Monique let it be known the request had gone out via Claude.

Aliette was touched. Claude Néon was not what you'd call a touchy-feely sort of man. But she doubted J-P Blismes could remedy their situation. *Notre crise de couple.* A problem with our relationship. So normal. So totally unique.

She knew passion would not be passion if it didn't die. Still, one believes in the foundations laid within passion's throes. Or one tries. And if there is permanence, it's a permanence of recurring signs. She'd been convinced that two cops' paths had converged to a perfect match. What did Claude communicate now? They no longer worked together — not actually, they way they had. There has to be an *actual* for there to be a sign, a shared symbol from one day to the next. A belief? A belief in *us*? How vague and ambiguous it all seemed after a weekend of sex and other games in Basel. She could hear herself confessing to J-P Blismes. She could see him nodding, the way he did. And smiling with his huge teeth. J-P never stopped smiling.

No, won't work... Aliette put the memo in her pocket and got on with her job.

She mulled a plan. She ran it by Chief Magistrate Gérard Richand.

He agreed it could be the cleanest (i.e., least-encumbered) means of moving forward.

Bon. The inspector summoned Inspector Milhau. Bernadette was a handsome, large-boned woman from the south. And tough. She had no problem offering an encouraging shove to police 'clients' who needed one. She would cheerfully wave her sidearm under any hard man's nose. After a rocky start (a tactical screw-up in the matter of the Hashish Twins) Inspectors Nouvelle and Milhau had become allies, if not friends. Natural for the only two women on a small PJ brigade. She was Aliette's instinctive choice as a partner for her intended operation. The young cop was attentive and unquestioning as she instructed, 'We need to put someone inside Zup—this club in Klein Basel. Someone who fits.' Problem was, there was no one on the PJ roster who 'fit.' At least not that they knew about. Nor, as far as they knew, anyone on the Municipal force downstairs. A very straight police force guarding a very conservative Alsatian city.

Bernadette suggested they might find a match within the PJ ranks at Strasbourg.

The inspector and the judge had considered the notion of seconding a gay inspector from the regional capital. Then backed away. Too much politics. Too much risk in that. 'We're thinking it would be better if this someone actually knew Martin Bettelman, even if only marginally.'

'And so?'

'Our judge is waiting to conduct interviews.'

'Got it.' Inspector Milhau went into the streets in search of suitable interviewees.

Aliette turned her attention elsewhere. Two busy days planning a bust in a warehouse in Saint-Louis, then, because she needed to be busy, she led the team. The operation was not fun—one killed, one badly wounded, but it was successful. She watched from a distance as Inspector Richard Roig led the guys through their brutal steps. The operation took place three blocks from the Bettelman residence but Aliette did not stop by to see how Lise was getting along. It could have been guilt concerning the credit card. Or just no interest in that woman? She drove straight back and got working on the next thing. A quarrel in the Vietnamese community over a family resto that was turning violent. Being busy helped her resist a simmering urge to sit in front of J-P Blismes and tell him about running away to Switzerland and having sex with the Swiss Police.

Evenings, she sulked in her apartment, trying to see it clearly. How? Why?

Then Monique walked in with a printout of an electronically transmitted image of a partially obscured white face at the entrance of the Basel Kunstmuseum. And a full-figure image of a slouching figure in sloppy jeans and oversized hoodie. Thank you, Dieter and Della!

She had the police artist down on the second floor do a rendering combining these elements to make a pale boyish man, naked on a rock, a three-quarter view from behind.

'Rather Blakean,' opined Chief Magistrate Gérard Richand.

Though none of the three images were at all specific, when placed together on a poster-sized sheet that included an official plea for help from the public, it felt like another small step. A step that helped her justify her weekend in Basel—at least for another day.

Inspector Milhau was also busy. Gérard Richand interviewed two dozen members of the local gay community. They ran the social gamut, from an eminent chemical engineering prof at the École Supérieure, three respected members of the legal community, a popular gynecologist, an array of service industry types—a plumber, a postman, waiters, an executive chef, a bus driver—to a handful of lowlifes known to the police. Each was rounded up on the strength of an anonymous tip and delivered to the Palais de Justice on an *interpellation* order. Not all were willing, for obvious reasons. But the Police Judiciaire have powers of interrogation and the public is obliged to comply in aid or furtherance of an enquiry. Once they understood their lifestyles and livelihoods were not at issue per se, most cooperated without a fuss.

They all expressed varying opinions and emotions as to the violent end of Martin Bettelman—the news was now public. (Had there been a moment of silence at Zup?) But none admitted to knowing him. It seemed Bettelman had sowed his wild oats in Basel.

On the other hand, when presented with the composite image, several interviewees admitted hearing tell of this pale-skinned, youngish man. A few had seen him—dancing, chatting at a table, and yes, swimming at the 'beach.' None had had the pleasure of being introduced. He was indeed beautiful, interesting stories had circulated.

He was known only as *R*—from a garish, gothic-styled tattoo on his shoulder blade. The inspector had not discerned this from thirty metres that one spell-binding moment in the middle of the night. She had the police artist add an *R* to their man on the rock.

But without a Bettelman friend or former lover, Gérard Richand did not yet feel they had the proper asset. Maybe he had no friends. Maybe lovers were only conquests. That had been the implied message from the guys at Zup. Aliette told Bernadette Milhau, 'There has to someone around here. Martin Bettelman was a swordsman. Bring me another like-minded swordsman.'

Perhaps their swords had crossed.

— —

She requisitioned a car and took their poster down to the communities closest to the scene.

First stop, Kembs. 'We believe he might be local. If you happened to see him at the baker's?'

Gregory Huet shrugged and put the image aside. Despite the industrial-grade air-filter mask he insisted she put on, his work area exuded the cool, searing reek of solvents combined with the familiar thick and not unpleasant odour of leaded paint. 'I've barely started,' cautioned Huet, ever so gently lifting the gauze-like wrapping in which the shoemaker was now swathed. 'Three more weeks, a month before he's halfway presentable.' Yes, he knew it was the case, not the painting, that had priority. He assured her that he was proceeding as quickly as professional integrity would allow. 'But there is one thing I can tell you, if it still matters. This work is not a fake.'

'It still matters.'

Huet had cleaned away the layer of silty film. The workshop scene was brighter, more details of a life fixing shoes and boots were now apparent. The dull grey green of the smock was now revealed to be a well-worn blue denim, the bib of the apron a rich chocolate leather.

But new clarity did nothing to reveal the mystery of the shoemaker's rapt gaze. The stolid eyes would be forever looking down through the lenses of his rimless specs at the flow of tea from the spout of a copper teapot into the cradle of a silvery glazed bowl, and people like herself would be left forever wondering what was on his mind.

He seemed smaller now, without his ornate gilt frame.

'He's the same size as the *Mona Lisa*,' Huet noted.

'Smaller but brighter.'

'Likely too much so.' He moved his hand along the shadowy space above the shoemaker's lamp, the central source of light. 'I cleaned all the varnish away, all on account of the gash...' He lifted the shoemaker and turned him. The rip was mended with a swatch of cloth affixed to the back of the canvas. Huet carefully set him back. 'It'll take several layers of paint or the gash will always be a scar. We'll have to put some kind of varnish on to get back that muted quality. I can make a varnish that will be much like the one this painter used.'

'Does that give us a better sense of where he's from? Our judge insists he's French.'

'I still say Dutch.'

'Not Flemish?' From behind her protective mask Aliette smiled at Gregory Huet's educated guessing. Like everyone else, he had no idea. She imagined the shoemaker was pleased by that.

It did not seem Huet would offer tea and kugelhopf this time. She was backing away, leaving him to it, when he mentioned, 'I heard Justin had some trouble. With his work.'

'Really?'

The eyes above the rim of the mask met hers. 'A friend who works at the museum. There's a cop over there—not in Basel, down where Justin lived. I heard he's been bringing a parade of people like me—what they call experts in the field—through some private gallery.'

Why play games? She trusted him. She conceded with a shrug. 'Surprised?'

'Not really. Not anymore.'

'How many Justin Aebischers are there?'

'I don't know. A lot. More than is good.'

Aliette risked telling him, 'It's not sure. They still have to prove it.'

'Of course. And that could take forever. Justin was very good.'

— —

She drove on to Village-Neuf. Her knock on the door in circle Georges-Simenon was met with resistance. 'Please, not now, he's actually doing his work.' A small miracle. But it was very important, about the case, it would only take a minute, she promised... With a huffy sigh, Madame Hunspach relented and allowed her son to be yanked away from his homework.

He studied the poster. On the one hand, a beautiful man naked on a rock. On the other, a shambling male figure in droopy garb, face mostly hidden from the world. Hubert Hunspach was uncertain. 'Could be...I mean...' The difference was disturbing: the one an inspiration, the other a... a nothing. Hubert did not want to think the two were one and the same. But he agreed they could be.

'You keep this. And you keep your eyes open. He might come walking into the local McDo. You're my eyes. OK?'

He was not high. There was no music in his ears framing the romance of true crime. In his still too-stuffy room, Hubert's smile was snide. 'You mean your *cousin*?'

'Exactly.'

He was dryly accusing. 'But you won't lift a finger if someone kills me. I've seen cousins a thousand times. They all end with their faces bashed, lying in piles of trash.'

'This is not TV, Hubert. No one's going to kill you. No one's going to know but me.' But it gave her pause. 'Is there a reason someone might want to kill you?'

'Hope not.'

He accompanied her out to the car. She strolled for an extra minute with her young informant, trying to help him understand the reality of looking for a single person amongst sixty-odd million French. Add in seven million Swiss... 'See what I'm up against? Television only takes an hour. Where could he be?'

The boy seemed suitably deflated. 'Not in the clubs?'

'Apparently not. But you've seen him more than once. Right?... Well, I'm betting he's a local boy. Like you.'

Like me? You could see the river from the foot of the circle. Hubert thought about it, trying to imagine another local boy's life. 'I bet he's in jail.'

'I would have told you, Hubert.'

'Not *your* jail. I mean his mother would have him all tied up at home.'

'What do you mean?'

Big fateful adolescent shrug. 'I mean, if he really is like me.'

Hubert Hunspach stunned her with his elemental sense.

23

PREPARING TO RE-ENTER SWITZERLAND

P J *interpeller* power may extend to what they term 'coercion.' If they ask and you're not in the mood to talk, they're allowed to physically drag you in off the street. Thus Inspector Milhau hauled Bernard (Beppi) Crerar, known in the bars as Beppi la Braguette, cuffed and cursing, into the inspector's office. He unleashed wild, sporadic kicks and would not stop spouting loud and horrid profanities. But the brawny southerner was built for hauling. Aliette gave Bernadette all the room she needed as she wrestled Beppi into the interview chair. 'Have a seat, *mon cher.*'

'Fucking retarded Amazon!'

'You be polite now.'

'*Pute!*' He spat.

'Sh!...sh, sh, SH!' A few swift whacks to the back of his greasy head, then her large hand gripped his skull like an orange and she shoved him into the chair. 'Sit...*voilà.*' Beppi sat, spewing more profanity till Bernadette finally slapped his mouth, '*Tais-toi!... Connard!*' (Shut your mouth, asshole.) And he stopped.

'Beppi.' Aliette knew him. A brief stint as a cousin. She had used Beppi Crerar's loud mouth as a way of drawing in a German pornographer whose wares had started to offend the deeply Calvinist Alsatian sensibility. A scrawny guy in all but one key aspect, Beppi spent his days in the gyms and his nights in the bars, making sure anyone and everyone knew about his super-sized sexual equipment and its availability. He accepted drinks and invitations home for sex with his prey, then stole from them. Then fenced his takings wherever there was a market. Beppi was marginal psychologically—this was obvious in his incessant self-promotion. One feared early-stage syphilis, or else the accumulative effects of lousy cocaine. He had served a couple of years for illegal import/export of stolen or illicit goods. He lived on the edge of trouble.

The inspector confronted Beppi and told him directly, 'It's about Martin Bettelman.'

'So?'

'So you knew him. Mm?' Beppi's eyes moved in a way he could not control.

'Sure, I knew Marty, poor guy. Marty had some good moves the time I checked him out.'

'You checked Marty out?'

'More like he checked me. *La braguette?*' Everyone wanted to get their teeth into Beppi.

'When was that?'

'Oh…well…Marty…I don't know. Busy guy like me tends to lose track of time. This summer, for sure. Swimming party.'

'Down the road? Village-Neuf by any chance?'

'Somewhere…I got a drive. Kind of out of it that night.' Adding, 'Braguette still worked fine, no problem there.' Beppi patted his crotch.

'Where?'

'Under the stars. It was good.'

'And the next time?'

'Next time what?'

'Well, if it was so wonderful…'

Beppi was suddenly rueful. 'My place.'

'How long were you together?'

'Couple of weeks.'

'And then?'

'And then we weren't.' Shrugging, moving from rue to suspicion. 'What's the point of all this? I did not see Marty ever again after the last time I saw him. OK?'

'OK. But did you go back down there looking for him?'

Beppi couldn't lie and knew it. 'Yeah, I went back.' She waited. He thought it through and told her, 'Look, no one fucks as good as me. OK? I'd been hearing about this chicklette, been flogging his little ass around the scene. I heard Marty had it on for him. I heard he's a total ball-breaking bitch. I was thinking I would love to run into him and settle his hash.'

'R?'

'Mm.'

'Are you talking about hurting him?'

'I'm saying I would show him who's boss.'

'Boss of what?'

'*B'en*, boss of *les braguettes!*' A man has to do what a man has to do.

'Did you find him?'

'No.'

'And no Marty, either.'

Beppi Crerar shook his head, stared out the window and crossed his arms.

The inspector considered the power of the *braguette*. 'Ever party in Basel, Beppi?'

'No.'

'Not with Marty?'

'Never.'

The inspector thought about it, but not for long. 'Beppi, I'd like you to repeat what you've just told me to our judge.' Inspector Milhau stifled a gut laugh at the prospect. Aliette ignored it.

'Why?'

'Why? So we can get the bastard who killed poor Marty.'

'Yeah. Sure...poor fucking Marty.'

'*Bon.*' Bernadette Milhau hauled Beppi Crerar away.

In her memo to the Chief Magistrate, Aliette advised a search of Beppi's place, as they might need collateral to close the deal. She noted Beppi was a good choice, at least as far as matching their selected profile went.

— —

Judge Richand interviewed Beppi Crerar, then called her in. 'Highly risky,' Gérard cautioned. 'Hoping for any sort of subtlety with this man is wishful thinking.'

The inspector sidestepped that obvious limitation. 'It's hardly the most subtle place, Gérard. He really will fit right in, believe me.' And though she agreed Beppi was far from ideal, he was the only one they'd found with an issue directly connected to Martin Bettelman, and, a bonus, the mysterious *R*. Beppi would not have to be overly clever, or subtle for that matter—his talking points were part of his recent life. Without divulging Hans Grinnell's side of it—because you never knew how Gérard Richand might use such information in a way that would obliterate Swiss trust—she pushed. 'Everything I've seen points to a love affair at the nexus of a high-end art scam. Someone is taking desperate steps to cover all traces. We have to do something to move this thing along, Gérard, or we'll lose it.' The issue of Martin's love would be Beppi la Braguette's calling card and cover. Beppi's apartment, full of illegal items, was their bargaining position to ensure he volunteered. For better or worse, Beppi was their man.

Gerard remained leery, but he too wanted progress. 'When?'

'Friday.' A shrug. 'The guys'll be letting loose after work.'

Inspector Bernadette Milhau and Beppi Crerar were waiting in the hall. Richand buzzed his secretary. A moment later, Crerar was being apprised of the situation. First item: Beppi's apartment full of illegal goods. He had no choice. But if he came through, the charges could be reviewed. That was fine, and totally normal. For Beppi, bribery was part of life. He was more worried about practicalities. 'But how do I get there? You lot took my permit.'

Beppi would take the bus. They knew the inspector at the checkpoint, she would not risk driving him. He would wear a listening device. 'Your job is to gather information. Being natural is the best way, so be as open as you can be. There's no need to be nervous, Inspector Milhau and I will be right around the corner.' Bernadette smiled at Beppi. He sniffed his contempt. Aliette repeated, 'This is a job, Beppi. Doesn't matter who likes who. You're working. OK?'

Beppi bargained. 'And you're going to pay me back for the bus and my drinks and clean up these outstanding bullshit charges.'

Gérard folded his arms. 'I will recommend we think about it. Depends how you perform.'

'Perform? You kidding?' He stroked himself impulsively. 'But what if I meet someone and...' A lewd smile. Gérard looked away.

'We won't interrupt your fun,' Aliette assured him. 'We *want* you to have fun. Just don't let anybody kiss your ear.'

'Or bite it off,' Gérard added. His notion of gay culture was skewed.

Beppi was warming to it. 'Think I'll wear my J-P Belmondo jeans. Like in *Le Marginal*.'

The judge could not help muttering, 'Such garbage.'

Aliette said, 'That could be perfect. The white T-shirt, leather jacket?'

Beppi pulled an oily comb from his pocket and with a few deft strokes — ta-da! Beppi la Braguette as maverick cop Commissaire Philippe Jordan. It had a certain twist that fit the venue.

'We're counting on you to control the action,' Aliette said.

'And you will not say a word to anyone,' Gérard advised. 'I mean no one. Clear?' He sighed heavily, it seemed sadly, watching Beppi's skittish fingers working the insides of his thighs. 'In fact, I'm thinking of *garde à vue* till tomorrow evening. That might be the best idea here.'

Beppi flared, 'That's not fair!'

Aliette Nouvelle tended to agree and convinced Gérard Richand that trust was the better way of nurturing Beppi's commitment to the operation. By way of closing the meeting, Gérard instructed, 'No blabbing. You go alone on the bus, you keep your receipts. And if you're not at the rendezvous point Friday evening, monsieur...' Beppi promised he'd be there. Bernadette escorted Beppi out. Gérard expressed second thoughts. Were they being a bit hasty here?

The inspector held her ground. 'What's the worst that can happen?' A call from Magistrate Weiner, counterpart to Richand in Basel City, on behalf of Commander Boehler?

Gérard rose to that, relishing the thought. 'You're right. Let's move this thing along.' Then he settled back, musing, 'Monsieur Huet's doing quite the job with our shoemaker. Been down twice to see. Amazing, the work they do.'

Aliette agreed. And thought, Good. Gérard's sneaky interest in the painting of the shoemaker was tangible support for her.

- 24 -
KLAUS NOMI NIGHT AT ZUP

Bernadette drove and they arrived with plenty of time to kill before their rendezvous with Beppi. They left the car close to Zup and walked back into the centre of Klein Basel, off on a leisurely tour of the stores along Claraplatz, busy on a chill but dry Friday evening in October. Bernadette bought a pricey *soutien-gorge* with a yellow flower motif and the same gift box of leckerli biscuits for her maman in the Midi that Aliette had bought for hers in Brittany. They walked down another street, had a beer and a bite. Then coffee at the next place. It got colder as they headed back to the drearier part of town, the sky lowering. It looked like there could be snow.

The two cops sat together on a bench by a bus stop on the Rheinweg promenade overlooking the river, surrounded by shopping bags. The air was colder by the water. Beppi Crerar showed up, looking suitably absurd and possibly obscene in jeans that showcased all. They strolled past the club and got in the car. Inspector Nouvelle commanded Beppi to sit still while Inspector Milhau fitted the listening post on his ear stud. The Tech guys at Division in Strasbourg had gone the extra mile and mounted a tiny plastic pistol on top of it, black and lacquered, an actual bit of boutique jewelry that would be perfect for a maverick commissaire out loose on a Friday night.

Beppi liked it.

Inspector Milhau waited in the car with the receiver as Aliette escorted Beppi down the street. When they were almost opposite Zup, she whispered, '*Grosse Corvette, petite quéquette.*'

Beppi blurted, 'What the fuck is that supposed to mean?'

'Shh!' Aliette squeezed his arm. 'That's code, Beppi.'

Bernadette flashed the headlights once. The thing worked well.

'Remember: you and Marty. What happened? That's your basic question. You're just looking for news of Marty. Because you care about him. And you had business with him. And this R. Be cool, but see if he's part of the scene. You'd really love to meet him. OK?'

'I'm there.'

'If anything starts to feel not right, just start humming and we'll be there.'

Beppi waved away the offer. 'I know how to handle Swiss fags.'

The inspector was stern. '"La Vie en Rose"...*au cas où*.' Just in case. 'Got it?'

'Yeah, yeah, yeah.'

'We'll be here till midnight. If I don't see you, you're on your own for getting home.'

'If you don't see me, I'm having a real good time.'

Beppi sauntered up the street just like Jean-Paul Belmondo and rang the bell.

Aliette heard Adelhard squawk 'Zup!' Then Beppi was in.

Back in the car, she was pleased to hear Beppi Crerar, loud and clear and gregarious as he ordered a beer from Max. German, Beppi! They knew he was capable of the local dialect.

Beppi la Braguette switched to German as he began to chat up Max.

Aliette wondered how *la braguette* would translate. And what was that bizarre music?'

Shall I stay / Would it be a sin/ If I can't help/ Falling in love with yoooou...

— —

Inside Zup, Greta Garbo sipped champagne and grumbled. 'Who put on that noise?'

Fred Astaire cast an urbane smile toward the door. 'Adelhard.'

'It's horrendous!'

'It's his place,' Fred responded. 'He gets to spin the discs, my dear.'

Adelhard and Max adored Klaus Nomi.

Take my hand/ Take my whole life too...Because I can't help / Falling in love / With you!

A deeply tender ballad camped up beyond forgiveness into a shrieking, dying Wagnerian swan. If you don't like Klaus, it is hard to take. It put a damper on a Friday evening meant for fun. Fred and Greta were dressed superbly for a night of dancing. They had to be — otherwise, who were they and what did they mean? Fred has to have his tux on. Greta must be elegant, those lashes lushly suggestive, pencilled brows forever arch. Although, if truth be told there was nothing in Greta's look and bearing remotely resembling Greta, and Fred was a less than average dancer. And Fred sometimes wished his Greta could be Ginger. Greta could have been Ginger — the possibility was there in his partner's shiny glow, the rounded lines. But one must follow one's heart and Fred knew that Greta was an ideal his love had lived for too many years without properly exploring, and so now there was no turning back. Fred accepted Greta for what she was. Fred knew he fit fine with Fred, except where it came to the smooth moves — something Greta mentioned mercilessly if she was feeling bitchy. Yes, they had their scraps, but they were settling into it and getting along in a difficult world. As often as domestically feasible, Fred and Greta retreated from their respective high-level, highly respectable lives, to meet in a place not far from here that was cheap but warm, and mainly discreet. Greta's decorative tastes were not Fred's, but forgiveness is essential in matters of love. They helped each other dress...and then undress after some carefree fun at Zup.
'...What? What is the problem now, my love?'

Klaus Nomi had finally stopped, but Greta remained out of sorts. It was the newcomer. Over at the bar, chatting up Max — who was neglecting his duties. Greta wanted to know, 'Why are there suddenly so many French in this place?'

'Word gets around,' Fred said. He was fascinated by the man at the bar.

'Do we need them? This should be a much more private sort of club.'

'Oh, they're fun.' Hadn't they both enjoyed some fun with Martin? 'This one's huge!'

Greta sniffed, 'Is that a reason to like somebody? It's obscene.'

'It's just for fun.'

'It's an insult! Who do those people think we are?'

'Personally, I like to meet new people.'

'I need another glass. Max!'

'Let's switch to Scotch.'

'I could kill him.' Greta was getting a head of steam on. She pushed back her chair.

Fred urged, 'Calm down. You don't even know him…Where are you going?'

'To get a drink. These fucking French will wreck everything.'

'You sit still,' Fred commanded. 'The last thing we need is a brawl and police.'

Greta huffed, but sat. Then whined, 'I'm not happy. Will you take me home?'

'Oh, Greta,' Fred sighed, rising, adjusting his bow tie and smoothing his tails. 'Sit tight, my love. I'll get you a nice drink.'

'Adelhard!' Greta screamed, but to no effect as Klaus Nomi's unearthly voice swelled again, fortissimo.

— ◆ —

In the car they were receiving, recording, but the screeching music made the listening doubly difficult. One cop's German was sketchy, the other's non-existent. But now here was another one wanting to meet Beppi. It was getting interesting. Aliette struggled to get the gist.

Beppi: Me and Marty, we had some business.

Max: Me too.

Other: Big business, it looks like.

Max: You're such an old whore.

Other: Oh, Maxi, you know I'm just enchanted to meet your friend. Monsieur…?

Beppi: Beppi. Beppi Crerar.

Other: Beppi. I do admire your ear stud…Two Scotch-rocks, please, Max.

Max: Sure.

Other (Very close; in French.): Lovely. Wherever did you find it?

Beppi: Strasbourg. Little shop in the student ghetto.

Other: Strasbourg is one of my regular stops. I'll keep my eye open.

Beppi: Your ears aren't even pierced, man.

Other: Not for me, Beppi. I think my Greta would enjoy it.

Beppi: Oh. Yeah. OK... Better give me another one these, Maxi man.

Other: On my tab, Max... So Beppi, might one ask what business you and Martin were in?

Beppi: Art. Import, export, like.

Other: That sounds exciting. I dabble in art a bit myself. Poor Martin.

Beppi: Yeah, well, give me your card. I'm trying to pick up the pieces... *Danke*, Max... It's not easy without Marty. He worked the Swiss side.

Other: I understand.

Beppi: Had a Swiss client all lined up. Big deal. Sad. After all my work. Guy's disappeared.

Other: No, it's not easy. Does he have a name? I could ask around.

Beppi: That's a problem. R.

Other: R?

Beppi: That's it. Marty was very cool as far as his side of the business.

Other: Business demands it, Beppi. The client is king. At least that's how we see it. If Martin worked the Swiss side, as you say, he would have to know this.

Beppi: Sure. But I have a horrible feeling Marty and this client were into other things, you know what I'm talking about? I mean it's what I'm hearing. I heard they partied here.

Other: All the best people do, monsieur. Eh, Max? *Danke*, dear. Keep the change and bring this one to Greta. And could you maybe whisper a little something in Addie's ear? This music is very hard on Greta's nerves.

Max: Not a chance. It's Klaus Nomi night. You knew that walking in.

Other: Please? At least down to a dull roar... There's a good boy.

Max: He'll just scream at me.

Beppi: *Mon Dieu!* Nice ass! I been standing here for an hour and didn't even notice.

Other: One of the nicest, monsieur. Your Martin was a big fan...
Yes, I've known Martin to let himself become involved with his heart
when it should have been just his head. Too many times, Beppi.
We're almost starting to believe this is a French weakness.

Beppi: Hey, *monsieur meister*, we know how to handle it. It's our
client I'm worried about.

Other: Tell you what, Beppi. I gather you're not a regular. Is
there a message? If he comes in. A discreet message, of course. For R?

Beppi: Well, I guess. You're a nice old fag.

Other: Old and wise, monsieur. So?

Aliette Nouvelle struggled to hear. It was the noise of this Klaus
Nomi — screaming.

Lightning is striking again! And again and again and again...

'God, that's horrible...' Bernadette Milhau was cringing with
each beat. 'How's he doing?'

'Making contact.' Obviously. Beyond that, the inspector
shrugged. 'I have no idea.'

When the song ended, she heard a voice — a different voice — ask
Beppi if he wanted to earn one hundred Swiss francs. Beppi's reply
was in French and very obscene. But he didn't say no.

25

SNAFU

Allies, almost friends, it didn't matter — after nearly three hours in the car Aliette and Bernadette were growing bored with each other, and listening to Beppi talking non-stop about the glory of himself while having sex somewhere in the back or upstairs was just not interesting. Time for a break. The inspector made sure Bernadette Milhau had a clear fix on their location, then, exiting the car, sent her off in search of coffee and buns. Aliette kept the receiver. And two shopping bags, for cover. The night was now quite nippy but it felt good to walk and get some air. She was adjusting the sound level as she shuffled up the tiny street, heading for the river. A couple emerged from Zup — stumbling away from the door as if blown out of it by a blast of that excruciating music. She noted in passing that it was that cross-dresser — what did she call herself? — and the man in the tux who'd chatted her up that first strange night at the club.

Greta. That was it. Greta and her debonair friend. Who was he supposed to be?

They were arguing.

'It gives me a headache!'

'Please!…You're ruining a lovely evening.'

Aliette hurried past, heading for the bus stop.

The disputing couple hardly glanced at the woman in the beret with an armload full of packages on her lonely way home after an evening of shopping, perhaps a drink with a friend.

Barely a glance. But enough of a glance —

'Is that not Martin's poor wife?'

'I tell you, there are far too many French hanging around!'

…before they went off the other way.

Aliette Nouvelle sat on the bus stop bench and watched the inky river. She soon wished she'd worn wool slacks, warmer socks. She got up and paced along the promenade. The machine was working perfectly, but Beppi's friend was not interested in Martin or the mysterious R. It was coming on half an hour when she walked back, past the club's front door and around the block.

Where was Bernadette Milhau? Well, it was a bit of a labyrinth around here…

It seemed their man inside had returned to the bar. Aliette circled a block, staying within range of Beppi's inane monologue. The annoyingly frantic music came and went as Beppi chatted on, with the occasional response from Max. She got the impression Beppi was getting quite drunk. She was getting cold. And worried about Bernadette. She'd promised till midnight. But if Beppi got past the point of walking, how would Max and Addie deal with that? If they tossed him in the street, the French cops would risk their cover… She walked to keep warm, distracted, impatient for the car. Turning into Morsbergerstrasse, there was the sudden sound of metal ripping the paving three steps from where she walked.

Silenced or not, it was a sound she knew too well. She leapt for the safety of a doorway.

None too soon. Another bullet grazed the wall where she'd been walking.

She dared to peek. A man, a black balaclava shielding his face. Aiming. Another zippy ricochet off the wall above her. Was he trying to scare her? Or missing because he was a lousy shot? Yes to either still left her only one choice. She tossed Bernadette's packages containing an expensive new bra and Basel leckerli into the far side of the street. It cracked against the far curb, prompting another shot from the silenced gun. Hugging the near wall, she ran for the corner, fortunately only ten steps from the doorway. Another shot. Too close. She felt it brush her calf, and dove for the shelter of the corner. Steps approaching. She scrambled to her feet and ran, moving in and out of doorways, heading for the open space of the Rheinweg and the bridge.

No! Stūpid, Aliette…stupid, stupid. stupid. She turned sharp left, risked a dash across the open street and sprinted down another tightly curved medieval *gasse*. She pounded on a door.

…and on the next and the next and the next, calling *'Au secours!…au secours!* Help! Police! Call the police!' The German for these words was just not there. She had no time to see if she had succeeded in rousing anyone before turning another corner into another small street. A lane that appeared to go behind the main block. She stopped. Considered it. A cul-de-sac?

Another bullet! More steps. He was keeping pace.

Aliette ran on. A steady barrage of silent shots poked holes in the night behind her. Several corners on, totally lost, she came out of the quarter, raced across the river road and sprinted down the promenade. More than lost, she now was on the far side of Dreiorsen Bridge, in the beginnings of the port area. All traffic off the bridge was heading the other way, south to the centre of Klein Basel, where Friday night was still in progress. She was alone on open ground.

Another bullet ripped the ground a metre behind her. He came across from the shadows.

She could try for shelter among the stacks of bins in the yards. She had to. She ran.

More bullets… Suddenly lots more, another gun, the second not at all silent.

The river was twenty paces to her left. She was tempted to swim. But it had to be icy cold.

Then a car drew up beside her and slowed. The driver's window came down. He took aim.

Aliette took desperate steps left and dove.

…It was dark. But not so frigid. Not immediately. She managed to free herself of her mac while still inside the fluid darkness. Managed to stuff her blonde hair into her beret before slowly pulling her way toward lighter darkness and much needed air. Just her face. A breath. Split-second orientation. And a voice, alerting someone. Another large gulp of oily air, she let herself sink again. A bullet sounded against the surface. Another. And another, closer. They were tracking her without much problem — because she stayed within sight of the wall. She had to, she could not allow herself to head for midstream.

The chill in her limbs was quickly growing equal to the adrenaline that kept her moving.

Is the mind working at a moment like this? Or are we on instinctive auto-pilot? Most likely the latter. Adrenaline creates a mode of thinking that is sub-conscious. All we can really hope for is a series of useful actions as opposed to the counterproductive kind (like those drowning souls who struggle when help is literally at hand, often inducing double desperation, double tragedy). It's hard to know which part of the mind understands the useful from the destructive. The inspector's hands were clawing along a slimy metal surface, whether the hull of a boat or the steel plating reinforcing the concrete quai, she didn't know, but her body knew it had to get free of the water and her hands and arms worked in a deliriously methodical series of clutch and reject motions doing whatever they could to respond to her need. The thought of pulling herself free to face the barrel of a pistol did not enter into the equation. Survival first. Then death. If—

A rung. She clutched it. And the one above it. She went up into the night air.

The sound that came from her inner reaches was something she could not have imagined producing. She did not truly hear herself moan, not as a human does — she only felt the air fill her lungs, only wanted more of it as her hands pulled her up another rung, her foot and leg now contributing to the project of moving up into the air… air! getting more of it, more of it…

Till a hand clasped her wrist, pulling her so forcefully her body agreed to let go of those cold but blessed rungs and rise. Then collapse on wet concrete, face down.

And yet more of this utterly foreign sound flooding out from inside her heaving guts. Her body, having done its work, was wanting to shake itself into a thousand pieces.

'It's all right…*Ça va, ça va*…' French words. Hands on her shoulders, turning her over, sitting her up, now enfolding her in a strong embrace, rubbing her heaving back, a vaguely warm rhythm against the shuddering coldness that threatened to spilt her. 'It's fine, just breathe calmly, calm…calm…calm, it's fine.' Her mind began to register. It showed her Bernadette.

'*Ça va?*'

'*Ça va, ça va…*' Fine. Fine, over and over, as Bernadette Milhau worked to warm her up and calm her down, till the large southerner eased her stroking motion and gently released her from the hug that had kept her senses from exploding. 'Can you stand?'

'Of course I can.' When Bernadette hauled her up, she collapsed. One leg was not doing its job. The pain she felt when she insisted on trying again brought another unrecognizable cry.

Bernadette held her vertical. 'Just use your left.'

Aliette obeyed. She was still soaking, but now realized the upper part of her right leg was *warm*, not cold. She had been hit.

Arm in arm, just as they had started out that evening, the two women made halting progress across the storage yard and up the lane to the street. Inspector Milhau wielded her gun in her free hand, at the ready. The port was deserted — but a car could emerge at any moment. There was only a thrumming sound. Machines somewhere. The sparse lights of a factory fifty paces across the tarmac appeared like a picture of finality, a dull castle at the end of everything.

'I'm sorry. I got lost…I was out on the river road trying to get my bearings. I saw someone race across and head for the yards. And someone else shooting. I felt I should help.'

'Good instincts,' breathed Aliette.

The car was waiting. The coffee was cold.

'We should get you to a hospital.'

'No!'

'You're losing blood.'

'No…It's not that bad. I wouldn't be here talking if it was.'

'But it's an hour back home.'

'We're not going home.' Inspector Nouvelle forced herself to focus. Ordered Bernadette to drive them back to where she'd found the coffee. Concentrated against the onslaught of shock while her partner bought more coffee, lots of sweet things, a large pizza. Then directed her to the address on Mulheimer, where Bernadette retrieved the police first-aid kit from the boot of their requisitioned car and they went up, five flights, the hardest part of the journey, intending to dress the wound, get dry, filled with food, then drive home.

The wound to the inspector's thigh was ugly but it was just a frightful graze and it eventually stopped bleeding. Bernadette had sure but gentle hands as she applied a dressing. Lucky.

And a bonus: There were still five bottles of Boxer beer in Martin Bettelman's fridge.

Somehow two French cops were still there in the morning, together, well wrapped in coats on Martin Bettelman's secret bed. Aliette awoke with an aching leg, became aware of shivery aches in every part of her as she tried to piece the thing back together, but found herself frustrated by a shock-scattered memory. Bernadette was lying there staring at the ceiling.

'Did they return fire?'

'The first one. We had a little battle along the quai while the other kept trying for you from his car. Whoever he is, he knows how to work an area. Maybe in the military? But I got him.'

Aliette said, 'You sure?'

'Pretty sure. He fell. His friend put the car in front of him, he got in and they left. I got myself to where you seemed to be and luckily—'

Aliette touched her arm. 'Merci.'

Two French cops put themselves together and went down, Nouvelle more or less carried by Milhau. Although she'd eaten the best part of a huge pizza, Aliette was starving for something sweet and lots more of that excellent Swiss coffee. But first they returned to the area near Zup. They knocked, then pounded on the door. A passing local said there was rarely anyone there till mid-afternoon. By some Swiss miracle, the bags containing Bernadette's new bra and cookies were waiting, sodden but untouched in the gutter in the street around the corner from the club.

Bernadette picked up a shell. Then three more.

They discussed their position over breakfast. No way they would take what happened to the Basel City force. 'They don't like the French police,' Aliette said.

Bernadette did not argue. She asked, 'But do you think someone is *on* to the French police?'

'Yes.' Obviously. The question rankled worse than the ache in her leg. Was it Beppi Crerar or herself who'd showed their hand? 'God knows where he ended up.'

'He knows the deal's not done till he reports back in,' Bernadette noted.

'Probably not the smartest move on my part,' Aliette said, more to herself than her friend.

Crossing the bridge on their way out of Basel, Aliette looked down at the grey-coloured flow of the Rhine. 'That was my first time.'

'First time for what?'

'In ten years I never once even put my toe in that filthy river.'

'Apparently they're cleaning it up.'

'I don't like rivers. I prefer the sea.'

'I lost my virginity on the banks of the Orb,' Bernadette reflected...a river flowing through the wine lands where she'd been raised.

'Salt water,' mused the inspector. 'Cleans you.'

Rolling home, Aliette Nouvelle could not stop thinking about bad judgment.

Stupid sending someone like Beppi Crerar into a place like Zup to do a job.

She kept telling herself, I should leave this place, I should go back to the sea.

26

EFFECTS OF BAD JUDGMENT

They patched her up at Hôtel Dieu and gave her a cane. She returned to the flat by the park and lay in bed all Sunday. On Monday morning she limped to her desk.

Claude watched. Did not request a briefing, didn't say a word.

Identité Judiciaire used the Aebischer/Bettelman ballistics profile to establish that the shells they'd recovered from the streets of Klein Basel were from the same general batch — numbers filed by the same hand, even with the same tool. But where did that point? Neither of the two men who'd sent a French cop diving into the chilly Rhine could be R — not according to her own sighting of a delicate boyish figure naked on a rock, much less the slight, sloppily dressed man contemplating art for hours on the Kunstmuseum security log.

She made a call to VigiTec. 'For the record, the ordnance you purchase for your people: it's numbered and logged?'

'Of course.'

'Some of your people are good with guns, beyond shooting? Maintenance, and the like?'

'We have many ex-military. They fit right in.'

'Can you send a list?'

'I suppose I could. Progress, madame Inspector?'

'Perhaps. Our shoemaker's almost ready.'

'Keep me informed.'

'I will, Herr Taub.'

She sat there. Waiting. But Beppi Crerar failed to report.

Beppi's recorded chat with an unknown man at Max's bar pointed to the elusive R at Zup with Martin Bettelman. That was progress. But the recorder and anything of forensic value it might contain was lost in the Rhine, in the pocket of the inspector's beloved blue mac.

Come on, Beppi!... They needed to know more about the unknown man who promised to pass a message along to R.

'Immoral bastard.' Instructing Judge Gérard Richand deeply resented Beppi's blatant breach of trust. He would write an order for Beppi Crerar to be collected and placed in *garde à vue*.

When, later that day, they received word from Basel City police that a Bernard Crerar had been fished out of the Rhine on Sunday morning, it touched the inspector's fragile spirit. Befuddled with guilt and creeping desperation, Aliette picked up the phone. The ID was confirmed — one very defining physical characteristic left her in no doubt. Did she know him?

'He's on our books, yes…' They asked her to hold.

The next Swiss voice was not so polite. 'Inspector Nouvelle, is it? Inspector Morenz, Basel City. What was he up to?'

Automatically, she lied. 'I wouldn't know, Inspector. The name came up from downstairs. He's one of our contacts. I called to find out for sure…What? Out of his mind from a night on the town and straight into the river? That's poor Beppi, all right.'

A pause. No doubt Inspector Morenz was trained to hear an automatic lie. He decided to challenge. 'That, and minus an ear. Someone sliced his ear clean off, then threw him in. Any thoughts on that, Inspector?'

A pause — to squelch a rush of horrified bile. Then, 'None, Inspector. No idea.'

'I'm sure. Well, Inspector, we'll be looking into it. If you can find anything that might place your poor Beppi here last weekend, we'd be very glad to know.'

She promised. Thanked him. Sat frozen. She was not solving this. She was making it worse.

Poor Beppi. Someone had not been fooled at all by her little ploy. Someone was quite intent on warning her away. And now Inspector Morenz would be looking into it. Bad judgment. Totally bad. She felt like quitting then and there. Going home. Or *some*where. Leave! — get away from this place. This love-foresaken life. It was clearly time. It was all she wanted to do.

But no. The case. The shoemaker. She had not been raised to walk away half-done.

Judge Richand was not overly bothered by the news. The Beppis of the world failed to touch his heart. 'People like him are their own worst enemy.' He shrugged at her whiny self-recrimination, dismissing her insistence that it had been a bad idea, a stupid decision. 'Not at all.' Gérard was grim, righteous. 'A logical step in the right direction. Sad, but useful.' It had been his decision too, after all. Picking up his pen, 'Finis. No more talk of Monsieur la Braguette.'

'His name is Bernard Crerar.'

'Whatever.' He would not play her miserable game. '*Bon.* The way I see it, now you have to confront the two gentlemen who run this place.'

'Gérard! How can I possibly go back in there?' Fretting, hating Gérard, morale in the toilet.

'As yourself, of course. A police officer. Full view. An interview regarding a crime.'

'And Boehler's man?' The nasty-sounding Morenz. 'I bet my name's at every checkpoint.'

'They're only Swiss, Inspector. You have your mandate. Use it.'

Thus goaded, she went — she knew she had to. But alone, on the noon bus next day.

—   —

The door to Zup was open. The place was empty, gloomy in the early afternoon. They were behind the bar, unloading the dishwasher. They stopped their work, watching her limp toward them. Max said, 'Bonjour, Lise. What happened to your leg?'

'Work. And it's not Lise, Max. It's Aliette.' She showed her ID card, her mandate, and came straight to the point. 'Forgive the deception. Or don't forgive. In any case, I suppose you know by now Martin Bettelman was murdered.' They knew. 'Now Beppi Crerar has been too.'

'Murdered? When?'

'Probably Friday, after he left here.' She decided not to mention that Beppi had been there on her direction. The less deceived and invaded they felt, the better. She was following up on a second murder linked to the murder of Martin Bettelman. Her information led her to understand that Beppi Crerar had been partying at Zup on Friday night.

Max was shocked into silence. Adlehard glared. 'French aren't very honest, are they?'

Aliette met him head on. 'Honesty is relative, monsieur.'

'Slimy cop.'

Sure, sure, slimy cop. 'Are you going to help me?'

Max slowly rotated a dish towel around the inside of a wine glass. 'I can see how someone would get mad enough to kill Martin. But why kill that Beppi? I liked him. I mean I think I liked him. What was not to like?'

Adelhard huffed, 'Yes, and you liked Martin.'

She cut in before they could start bickering. 'Who did Beppi leave with Friday night?'

The two Swiss looked at each other. 'Fred,' Max said.

'Fred… The one in the bow tie? I remember him. Him and Greta Garbo.'

'Just Fred,' Adelhard sneered, '…hoping for something. Disgusting. Unnatural.'

For all his leering Heidi act, Adelhard would fit right in with the righteous Gérard Richand. Interesting where male insecurities aligned. 'I gather they're regulars. Yes?'

'Very,' Max admitted. 'Spend a fortune. And add a certain class, I'd have to say.'

Adelhard did not agree. 'Anyone who does not like Klaus Nomi is a peasant. Money and evening gowns cannot hide the fact.'

Aliette waited for an explanation.

Max slid the glass into the rack, began to polish another. 'Greta couldn't handle Addie's music, so they left. Fred came back later, near closing, when things were quieting down. Your Beppi was far gone by then, and alone. Fred took care of him. They left together.'

'Did he say anything?'

'Said he was going to take him home to Greta.'

'But who are they?'

Max shrugged. 'Fred and Greta.'

'I mean during the day.'

'No idea.' Accurately reading her doubting gaze, he added. 'Because they don't want us to know, Inspector.' He slid the next glass into the rack. 'And we don't really need to, do we?'

Aliette supposed not. She asked for a glass of beer. It was provided. She pressed the issue. Did either Fred or Greta ever mention what business they were in? Where they lived? Any names they happened to drop from time to time? Max and Adelhard told her: Rich. Corporate, for sure—probably from Gellert or the like, an *haute bourgeois* Basel quarter. The way Fred talked—you could hear it. But Greta too: used to giving orders. Pick a business that fits with that.

She sipped her beer and scribbled. 'The art business?'

Adelhard shrugged, 'Why not?'

Max said, 'I heard Fred say he sometimes dabbles. I mean, he said it to Beppi. Beppi said he and Martin had some kind of deal going. He wanted to find Martin's client.'

'So do I.' Aliette studied her notes. 'Martin never came back here after he broke with Max?'

'One night,' Adelhard responded. 'In August. With his new *petit ami*.' A new boyfriend.

'Swiss or French?'

'French. *Son beau petit* Robert. Didn't stay long. Everyone was pissed at Martin.'

'Young? Bone white?'

'Beautiful,' Max whispered, sounding slightly spooked by the thought of French beauty.

Adelhard, past his pique, held his Max's hand on the counter. 'We never saw Marty again.'

Robert. It sounded like the truth. 'So where does Justin Aebischer fit in?'

'Justin?' Max paused to place it. 'Justin was way back last winter... before New Year.'

'After Greta,' specified Adelhard.

'Greta was with Martin?'

'Greta's been with everyone,' sniffed Max, eyes sliding sideways toward his lover.

Adelhard shrugged. 'Hearts are tricky things. We provide a room in the back.'

Aliette finished her beer. 'Have you seen them this week? Greta… and Fred?'

'Fred Astaire?' Max prompted.

'Ah.' Remembering how her mother loved to watch those movies. Adelhard thought about it. 'No, we haven't… Have we?'

'No,' Max confirmed.

Presenting her card, she implored the two proprietors of Zup to call her if Fred or Greta made an appearance. 'Doesn't matter what time, I'll get it.'

Max took her card, smiled. A real French cop. 'You never said what happened to your leg.'

'Oh, line of duty.' She hobbled out, then to the bench, where she waited for the bus.

━ ━

So: Robert. A name. And French. But at what price?

Bernard Crerar came back to France, minus an ear. Beppi's mother lived south of the city, in a village in the Sundagau. But Inspector Aliette Nouvelle did not have the guts to go to Beppi's burial, let alone talk to his maman. Pleading too much to do, she sent Bernadette Milhau.

Gérard Richand said, 'Buck up, Inspector. This is not like you at all. What matters is, What now? You know the ground. You choose the best way forward.' He sat, pen poised, awaiting her call.

'We look for a French boy…man, whatever, called Robert. He is our suspect.'

He made a note. 'Very good.'

27

TIME AT THE CENTRE OF THE UNIVERSE

The job does not care if you're happy or sad. Senior Inspector Nouvelle had three teams in ongoing operation mode against the gangs. They needed constant legal advice and investigative strategy. After a preliminary investigation, Inspector Christophe Tavernier was advising that she recommend a murder charge against the Vietnamese patriarch's illegitimate son. The beating of a manager at Peugeot, no doubt related to the recent downsizing and restructuring measures, had left the victim in a coma. She assigned Inspector Richard Roig to the preliminary, and went with him to oversee initial interviews at the plant. Every move involved paper work, much conferring with various powers at the Palais de Justice, with City uniforms downstairs, with forensics in the basement. Sure, the job will keep you busy, no problem there. But a conned, then brutalized and summarily discarded Beppi Crerar had tipped the balance in the war for meaning. Aliette limped through the halls at rue des Bons Enfants trying to analyze shame as it relates to love, self-love, moral imperative. *The story of myself.* She knew she was the centre of the universe.

It was all unspoken. How could she explain to Claude when she could barely understand it herself? He wasn't stupid, he did not push, and she knew he wouldn't unless she forced the issue. Which she had not. They both knew they were on the verge of something and it would be hers to shape. She was polite, neutral, professional. Indeed the limp, a wound suffered in the line of duty—this lent definition to the thing that hung between them. She did not explain. Or apologize.

Saturday night she sat in the bath and studied the scar on her thigh, touching the stitched-up gash, the now forever less-than-perfect skin, a new element in the mix that was herself. She soaped her breasts and analyzed her remorse—which is not the same as shame. But shame and remorse are definitely cousins, and shame seemed to be the abiding point of reference. How to deal with that? She lay there, soaking. Asking, Why can't I bring this to a civilized end?

Or a dead end? Your choice, Inspector. One way or the other, these were long-term questions and her heart could not see clearly. Wrong decisions will bring you there.

Sunday morning she took the vacuum for a limpy tour through the apartment: cleaning as the catch-all fall-back position, something to do in lieu of sleeping late and having sex, a long and lazy breakfast. Quiet vacuum but noisy bashing, relentless, into door frames, chair legs…

Smash! Crash! Whirrr…What a crazy bitch I am.

The people downstairs started yelling. Madame Camus banged on the door.

OK, all right, she got the message.

And so Monday, after efficiently getting everyone on the PJ team pointed in the right direction, the inspector hobbled down to the second floor and knocked at the door of J-P Blismes.

⟫   ⟪

'I have nothing to say to him. If he won't acknowledge my soul.'

'We live in an indirect world, Inspector. Everything good is metaphorical. Nature operates through oblique tangents. This takes time, you see?' J-P smiled, his huge teeth an unavoidable trope. He assured his sullen client she was not the first cop to feel trapped in a labyrinth of misplaced pride and relational walls. He refused to let her believe she might be unique.

'No, of course not.' But she *was*! The centre of the universe? 'Oh…*merde*!' She wept.

J-P Blismes sat by, silent behind his perpetual grin till she pulled herself together.

She wiped her nose. Together they meditated on the reality of love. She confessed to her weekend of irresponsible behaviour in Basel.

Rudi Bucholtz had fallen in love with her and had been deceived.

Smiling, Blismes assured her: Rudi had been deceived, but not by her. The FedPol art cop had fallen prey to who he'd thought she was. 'Projection. Some skewed Swiss thing within himself,' J-P advised. She argued: No, she had coerced poor Rudi, blatantly tempting him to form this unreal image of a French hero. A few carefully dropped lines, a few careless tears, a chilly pied-à-terre, new Swiss underwear, Swiss beer, it had all been far too simple—and utterly phony. J-P challenged her self pity. 'But is this your fault? How could he have been so callow?' Or...the psychologist massaged it: perhaps the better question was, Was she really so naturally skilled at creating such deep-seated illusion?

'That's not a fair question!'

Yes, perfectly fair. It played to her disaster in the house in the north end, the root of her problem. J-P Blismes elaborated: 'It's not: What did I ever see in Claude? It's the opposite: What did Claude see in me? You see?' She was not unique, yet it all came back to herself.

Aliette Nouvelle sat silent, defiant. Wasted half an hour of the Ministry's time.

J-P did not seem worried. She was here to dig deep and confront. '*Bon*...See you next time.'

Just so. Aliette came back. Told him of her Goldilocks fantasy. Carefree. Untouchable. The messes left. 'Jung said the foundation of all mental illness is an unwillingness to experience legitimate suffering.'

J-P Blismes displayed a rare frown. 'Who was it put Jung inside your head?'

'Him. Hans. My other Swiss cop.'

'The soccer coach? These people live in very cramped little worlds.'

'My life is connected to the case.' That was the point. No?

Je m'en fous pas mal de Jung.' I don't give a damn about Jung.

'Fine.'

J-P Blismes said, 'The point is, you have to live in the place your life has put you. You've ended up beyond the pale. This is your life's new starting point.'

'Fine.'

'Whether you want to go back inside, or farther out, that's your choice. Your instinct.'

'Fine.'

'Just remember: life does not last forever.'

'Fine.'

'*Alors:* fine, fine, fine, fine, fine!' J-P Blismes grinned. 'I believe we're making progress.'

Next time she confessed that she felt she was a failure.

J-P Blismes said, 'Failure is like air. It surrounds us from the first day to the last. As such, it is probably vital for survival. You can try to hold your breath…' Blismes drew a large breath and smiled at her, eyes gradually bulging till he expired, gasping, 'But how long?'

Connecting J-P's psycho-dots, she told him about her timeless interlude beneath the surface of the inky Rhine. He gasped and breathed. 'Yes, and you surfaced! You came up prepared to face it, the failure of your operation. Even if it meant a bullet in the face, you came up because you had to breathe and face it. So why not this? Failed operation. Failed relationship. You see?'

'That's hardly a fair analogy.'

'Stop asking for fair… Life is not fair, Inspector. And failure is to be expected. All couples fail. Love is not *ideal*. It is *a deal* you constantly renegotiate and fix. Or walk away from.'

'I feel broken. I feel *us* is broken. I see no way of fixing our deal. I think he sees that too.'

'What makes you think that?'

'I feel it. He knows *us*—who we are. How we happened. Where we came from. He knows.'

'Where is that you came from?'

'Two cops.' A pause. 'Two working cops.'

'A lot of people meet at work. It's normal. Very normal. Can't you be normal?'

'No.' She sounded fourteen, and knew it.

J-P heard it, smiled. 'Don't you want it to work?'

Aliette Nouvelle did not answer. She didn't know. J-P Blismes waited, smiling.

'I want *him* to acknowledge what we are.'

J-P Blismes reminded her, 'You just said he knows *us*.'

'But that's the problem! He knows—and he's let it go by. *Us.* The essence of us. He has left it behind, completely, willfully, like *us* was just a game. Not real. And I resent that.'

'Fair enough. It's your job to recreate the environment.'

'Why me?

'*B'en*, because you're the centre of the universe?'

'Where's his responsibility? I want him to *show* me that he knows us. I insist on that.'

J-P was smiling, but sadly. 'Won't happen. Not him. Not the Néon I know.' J-P Blismes knew Claude. He'd helped him through his own crisis. It had to do with trying to work with her.

But that was in another life. She said, 'What about the Néon *I* know?'

'Voila, my point exactly... Your show, Inspector. You call the tune.'

She wept as he guided her into the hall. He said he would see her next time.

Thus time passes, flowing through the job's emotions, some cases advancing, others not.

- 28 -

SPOTTED!

The Toussaint holiday week came and went. One grey November afternoon, around the time Inspector Aliette Nouvelle was gazing out her office window at the first snow on the peaks of the Vosges and thinking if she didn't leave by Christmas she would die, Hubert Hunspach was inspecting sunglasses arranged on a hallway display rack opposite the Carrefour grocery checkout lanes in the mall at Village-Neuf. Hubert was skipping school again. His best friend René had sucked out. Best friend? Any kind of friend? René was not meeting Hubert's standards much these days. Hubert had still not told René his big secret — now it looked like it might never happen. He wasn't worried. Hubert's play list offered hard but beautiful advice on the inevitability of change and the soul's need to go it alone — and, if nothing else, Hubert believed in the music. Love was out there somewhere, but the journey could be long.

Hubert had smoked a bit of decent pot he'd scored at the bus station, then headed for the mall in search of more tunes. He was an expert at securing his music gratis, hadn't paid for a disc since he was ten. And maybe shoes. Hubert's orange trainers were getting that old feel. Free shoes were easy *if* they had his size (both) out on display. And perhaps a new pair of shades?

The blade on his Swiss knife would cut the wire that kept them attached to the rack with one smart tug — he'd performed the operation more times than he could count; but the guy who ran the notions shop beside the lingerie store owned the glasses display, and he was there at his cash, keeping a steady eye on Hubert. So it was a test of patience. Fine. Wasting an hour assessing each pair in the tiny display rack mirror was not a problem. Hubert manoeuvred in front of it, smiling, frowning, adjusting his hair. He was thinking a pair of blue-tint aviation shades might be just the ticket for a soulful mood when a woman's voice caught his ear:

'Robert, those men will hurt you!'

It was a voice in a cranky upper register that effortlessly broke the sound barrier erected by the music in Hubert's headphones—and to which he reacted instinctively. Maman. Not his. But they all sounded the same and Hubert heard her loud and clear.

This mother wanted the world to know. Those men *would hurt her Robert.*

A guy and his mum were in checkout line number three. He was clearly very pissed at his mother. She didn't care that the woman at the cash and five bored shoppers behind them were tuned right in. She nattered at him in high volume while she transferred groceries from the cart to cash conveyor belt... He was taking dangerous risks! And those men would hurt him!

Hubert Hunspach knew the feeling. Really nice to have your life spilled out for the pleasure of everyone waiting in line, spilled out by someone who's supposed to be on *your* side. Hubert raised the blue-tint shades for a better view. He saw a deathly white face under an oversized grey training hoodie, partially obscured, but not so Hubert couldn't see the anger there.

And Hubert was not surprised when the poor guy lost it. He bellowed, '*Bordel!* Maman! *Bordel!*' and he grabbed a jug of milk from the cashier's hand and whipped it.

French milk is well packaged in strong plastic, the jug did not break. But it smashed through a floor display of wine like a bowling ball through pins. Bottles exploded. The cashier screamed. Robert's maman stood there, stupid. Two male store employees raced to the scene.

The boy called Robert hesitated for an instant. Then ran.

He sprinted past the sunglasses display, hood falling back from his pure white face and off his longish, darkish hair. Hubert Hunspach was stunned, sure that he recognized the angel of the river, the same white face he'd marvelled at from a secret distance late one windy night. Hubert had to follow.

But the sunglasses he was trying on were secured to the display with a wire that constrained him. He heard the clattering. Because he was more than slightly stoned, it took him a step or two to understand he'd yanked the entire glasses display over. The blue aviators lay on the floor. One arm of the frame lay near them, broken off.

Oh fuck!... A security guard trod on both pieces as she rushed to secure Hubert.

Mall security escorted Hubert Hunspach and Robert's mother into separate rooms in an office between the public washrooms and the key cutter's kiosk. It took an hour, but Hubert managed to calm the sunglasses guy's rage and avoid a call to the gendarmes by forking over thirty-five euros for the aviator shades. And by agreeing he was totally lucky there was no real damage to the rest of the stock on the display. *And* by agreeing he was totally stupid. Agreeing was always the best strategy. 'Yes, I do have the brain of a tired goldfish. I saw a friend. I reacted, man. I was not thinking. I mean, how could I steal them? They're attached, right?' And being totally, totally sorry. And totally grateful. 'Merci, monsieur, it will never happen again.'

Whew! Lucky.

Robert's mother was being let go at the same moment. She was still pretty wobbly, wiping tears when she emerged, a security officer dutifully patting her arm. Hubert wondered what kind of deal she'd cut. He supposed she had paid for the wine destroyed in Robert's outburst. Or maybe they'd been sympathetic. Mothers got away with things in a way that wasn't fair... He followed Robert's maman to the parking lot. Not so high anymore — no matter the quality of your weed, an interrogation in a windowless Security office will dampen the effect. He took note of a bashed-up navy blue Opal hatch-back, scribbled the plate number in one of his school exercise books. And then, not to push his luck, Hubert Hunspach returned to school in time for his last two classes, where he spent the entire time lost in space trying to devise an organized way of searching the town for that car. It would surely lead him to Robert. The angel.

And debating with himself. Should he call that cop? His cousin, Aliette.

...Well, that's what a cousin does, monsieur. It's an agreement. The police are waiting.

Hubert thought perhaps he would investigate a little first. Zero in. Then call.

PART 4

EN NOVEMBRE

29

INVITATION

Inspector Aliette Nouvelle received an email communication from Basel Lands Police, Criminal Investigations Brigade: *FYI: We now have a solid majority expert opinion as to the authenticity of J. Aebischer's first commission for the Federer family: Caresses, F. Snyders, Antwerp, c.1625. We will be holding a press conference at the Oberwil garrison Wednesday next at 11:00, at which time we will be making an announcement re. positive identification of the piece returned by J. Aebischer to the Federer collection as a reproduction of the original work. Hildegarde Federer, registered owner of the work in question, has fully consented to a public announcement of this finding. I believe this act of stepping forward in public could lend new support to our investigation. I note Marcus Streit was right in his original suspicion. I am taking this as circumstantial proof that Streit was not part of the scheme and is therefore not absconded but dead. We owe him a debt of gratitude and will ensure the public is made aware of Streit's contribution. You and interested colleagues will be most welcome.*

Inspector Hans Grinnell did not ask how she was. He did not even bother to add his name. That stung, though not much. The man was a soccer coach, with a wife and two sons. This was work. Well into dreary November in Alsace now, the Martin Bettelman case had gone quite dormant. Regular calls to Zup had yielded no sign of Greta and/or Fred. Her shoemaker remained unknown as he made his slow return to life in the studio of Gregory Huet. Grinnell's case, murders included, was not her case. She had been coming to accept that, if only because he had not communicated and she been feeling too guilty, soul weary, whatever, to force the issue. But she was needing something to kickstart the spirit and she would go.

But Wednesday next was tomorrow!

...So she was an afterthought. That stung too.

So what? She would go. She even managed a positive thought — Good, Hans, good work — before calling to cancel her scheduled hour with J-P Blismes.

30

MISGIVINGS ON SERVICE & DISCRETION

The same widely disseminated communication from Basel Lands CIB found its way to a quiet flat somewhere in Klein Basel, provoking differing takes on service and discretion, and misgivings that led to a difficult night.

'I've been getting calls. Much worry about our guarantees of confidentiality.'

'Our guarantees all stand. There are many countervailing points of view. Five experts? We have an entire community. This will be stated clearly and forcefully.'

'Forcefully, *herr?*'

'Subtlety is force. Discretion is art — fortunately, the right people appreciate it. The rest of them? …You know me. The machine's much bigger than one wretched *frau*, five so-called experts, four not even Swiss. Will our friends allow a worried woman and a bumpkin policeman to throw a spanner in such elegant works? I think not. It just needs the right words.'

'Or one bullet.'

'Please stop worrying.'

'Maybe two…You make me worry. At the end of the day, what are we without integrity?'

'The gutter press will be with him. The media that matters will stay with us.'

'The client is sacred. And the client is *scared.*'

'*You* are scared. And I have to say it makes you less than beautiful.'

'I'm Swiss. I know the value of service and discretion. And our word. Ours more than most.'

'I can handle this. I will. I have to. I will do what's necessary.'

'We all have to do what's necessary.'
'Your tone bothers me.'
'It's because I care, *mein herr.*'

HANS DOWN

Inspector Hans Grinnell stopped in early at the Basel Lands Oberwil detachment to collect fresh copies of the necessary warrants, then drove up to the city. At 08:25 he turned into the secluded street and parked in front of the baronial gate shielding the residence of Attorney Frederik Rooten from the world. Not that there was much to be threatened by in the immediate vicinity. The district known as Gellert in the southeast area of Basel proper was the most highly sought, certainly the most expensive, a mini-world of spectacular design, from coolest Bauhaus to grand early twentieth-century and all things ostentatiously up-market that fell between. Extensive green spaces. Peaceful. Grinnell had been in the area a few times on police business. Many of the city's top advocates and solicitors lived in the quarter. And he had enjoyed showing some of the more beautiful homes to his wife and sons one Sunday after a visit to the Basel Zoo. This home could have been included on the tour. He smiled at the memory but could not remember — the Grinnell family had wandered from one street to the next, and with autumn's colour, new space where bushy green had shielded views, it all looked slightly different. Grinnell gazed through the gates at a renovated chateau surrounded by elegantly landscaped grounds, carefully planned patches of fall garden only now beginning to die. He waited five minutes.

Until a week ago, Frederik Rooten had advised his client to eat the loss attached to a possibly fraudulent painting and stay silent for the sake of future commercial possibilities. Worse, beyond Rooten's best business advice, the notion of 'going public' was foreign to Hildegarde Federer. Call it a lifestyle issue, an instinct bred in the bone, what you will, Hans Grinnell had been fighting a losing battle. Now, a 'Snyders' declared to be a fake by a five reputable experts was a new starting point in his case. Proof of the fraud helped him convince the *frau* that Marcus Streit was surely as dead as Justin Aebischer and the crooked FedPol art cop. Once she accepted that, he had persisted mercilessly. Did she not feel any responsibility, moral, emotional or otherwise in helping track down the killer of the man who'd spotted the flaw in Aebischer's brilliant copy? Her friend Marcus had done a service in the name Swiss patrimony, not just her family's gallery.

As was often the case, moral suasion turned on the results of discreet enquiries. Grinnell now knew the vanished Marcus Streit was much more than a 'family friend,' as described by the obstinate *frau*. They'd been lovers — the odds were good that Streit was the father of her youngest child, Maria. Of course, he did not come right out and say it. But he came close, and the lady heard him. And finally the better part of her dry old conscience got her to agree that justice for Marcus should be a priority. Going public would help the police confirm Streit's good standing. She *had* to speak out. But though Frau Federer would be present at the media event this morning, it would be her lawyer, Herr Rooten, who would speak for the family. As was only fitting.

Frederik Rooten tried to stonewall, threatening to sue the police for coercing his client into acting against her best interests. His client had wavered. Hans Grinnell had fought back with politely worded threats of turning the media against a well-regarded attorney who might be manipulating a client who was determined to do the right thing for the cause of both Swiss justice and Swiss cultural integrity. Rooten had relented, politely, smooth as you could want, but Hans Grinnell sensed fear, perhaps reasonably so after the cold-blooded elimination of Justin Aebischer and the hapless Agent Perella. He played on that, hard but subtle, quiet words a lawyer might appreciate, sealing the deal by offering to personally escort Herr Rooten to the media event in Oberwil, quietly or with an entourage: his choice.

It was horrible how nasty you sometimes had to get.

At exactly 08:30 the inspector got out of his car and touched the brass-encased bell fitted into the stone pillar supporting the gate. A few moments later there was a quiet buzz, the click of a latch, and the ten-foot gate moved automatically — not fully wide, but wide enough for Hans Grinnell to enter.

A maid in uniform pulled the door open at his first knock. He nodded good morning and briefly flashed his warrant card. Leaving him in a sparsely elegant sky-lit foyer, she clacked officiously across the patterned tiling and disappeared behind a door, whence drifted the smell of coffee…and chocolate. Hans Grinnell put his hands in the at-ease position and waited, a step removed from a three-storey shaft of morning sunlight, beside a vase filled with velvety orange Asian lilies. He watched the sculpture. Or whatever it was. The thing reaching up through the winding staircase to the skylight was made of buffed steel. It moved, whether by mechanical perpetual motion or electricity was not immediately apparent, but it made no sound. To a simple cop's eyes it seemed like two tall figures. They evoked the cartoonish metal things constructed from discarded mechanisms and strewn about the pool at Tinguely Park—he and the wife and kids had enjoyed that. But there was something vaguely sexual in the way these two figures interacted. If that was the right word. They made him think of the French inspector and himself. He had avoided thinking of her for the better part of a month. Was this the effect of art? Hans Grinnell shrugged and focused on the lilies. He knew a bit about flowers, still not very much about art. Or moments like that French woman had somehow induced…Aliette. A mystery.

He was wondering if Inspector Nouvelle would be there today, and what that might bring, when Frederik Rooten emerged from the kitchen.

The lawyer nodded a curt good morning. There was nothing cordial in recognition of a lovely day, nothing collegial in anticipation of a step forward in the resolution of a series of heinous acts, though both men were, in the broader sense, professionals in the service of the law. Grinnell did not take it personally. Rooten was none too happy with his client's decision to share with the greater public, even less so with the role that fell to him. Nothing to be said between cop and attorney? That was fine. Hans Grinnell smelled aftershave and coffee as Rooten went past him and into the study. When Rooten emerged, briefcase in hand, Grinnell fell into step behind him.

There was a woman in a peignoir waiting at the kitchen door, mug in hand. She sipped her morning beverage and peered across the foyer. The cold distance in her gaze fit perfectly in the vast and elegant space. Grinnell could feel it. Could Rooten? She did not wave or utter a word. Frederik Rooten did not look back in leaving. He paused at the door, patted his various pockets—glasses, keys, wallet, hankie. Since it was Rooten's house, it was for him to open the door and hold it for Hans Grinnell, who stepped out of that sumptuous vacuum and back into the bright and chilly tranquil Gellert morning. Silence held as they walked across the cobblestone courtyard and through the gap in the gate. Click. The gate closed behind them.

…Perhaps this was part of the maid's duties?

Grinnell offered a muted professional smile and gestured to his car. It was just an old Audi but he had cleaned it of litter. And he was not a smoker. The man would survive the humble ride to Oberwil. As a courtesy, he moved to hold the rear door for his passenger. The click of the door latch coincided with a quick flat crack that cut through the ambient rustle of chestnut leaves. Somehow it produced an instant trickle of blood on the side of the lawyer's well-groomed head.

Frederik Rooten looked very surprised. In fact, he was dead before he fell.

Hans Grinnell had his sidearm, of course, and he would have used it, although in which direction still wasn't clear; but there was another flat crack and he fell too, aware of a burning point in his belly. Indeed, it started small, barely pin-sized. Then it grew, too fast, bringing much blood seeping through his shirt as he slumped against the car. At which point all he was good for was a frantic pressing of the emergency key on his remote, in a shapeless, hopeless kind of panic as he slowly blacked out. And maybe died. At a certain point, one doesn't know.

— —

The event at Oberwil had drawn a crowd. Police, art people—both the sort in suits and the ones in jeans, including several from Zurich and Geneva, and even a tight-faced clutch of Basel bankers. With the grim news from the city, they would all have to turn around and go home.

Not immediately. There was coffee, local pastry. People lingered, murmuring, surmising.

Still hampered by a cane and limping, Inspector Nouvelle had come with Chief Instructing Judge Gérard Richand. Despite the fact everyone in this particular crowd spoke perfect French, the inspector got nowhere as she worked the hall. Well, this *was* Switzerland. She caught a glimpse of Frau Federer, a stick-like, not-quite-old woman with good taste in clothes, clearly muddled by a tragic turn of events. She was being guided by a younger woman who was probably her daughter. Same bearing. Same subtle sense of colour for a morning in November. But they were well protected by larger men, and gone before Aliette could get near.

Inspector Morenz of Basel City turned out to be a tough little man with rimless glasses.

Inspector Hilda Gross was presented as Grinnell's replacement. Aliette gave her a card.

After an appropriate amount of mingling, Gérard said he had to get back. Aliette thought she should stay for a bit. She would get a ride to Basel, catch a bus from there. A somber Franck Woerli was silent on the ride back to the city in a requisitioned FedPol car. Rudi Bucholtz was driving. He was hyper-silent. She sensed Rudi was more afraid of her than angry.

They dropped her at the hospital. Four hours later she left, hardly the wiser. They had taken a bullet from the gut of Hans Grinnell and were still working to save him. She gazed at his anguished wife (she had imagined Frau Grinnell almost perfectly) till the woman sensed her eyes and looked. Then she ordered flowers for his room and went limping off to catch her bus.

By the time Aliette boarded the bus she knew. She could hardly read the headline in German, much less the columns and sidebars of reportage focusing on the travesty that morning in the quiet, exclusive Gellert street—but she didn't need to. The front page photo of attorney Frederik Rooten revealed half of the extravagant couple who'd since disappeared from the happy scene at Zup. Frederik Rooten was the elegant Fred. Jokester. Half-assed dancer. Greta's attentive man.

Aliette wondered if better communication might have helped Hans Grinnell avoid today.

Or was that useless wishful thinking? Riding back into France with French shoppers and workers, Aliette said a silent prayer for Hans. And his typical wife. His soccer-crazy boys.

- 32 -

MANAGING IT

Monique buzzed. 'Max. From Basel?' The inspector shook away her guilty torpor.

Adelhard was on another phone. They were scared. No, the police had not been in. They knew they ought to step forward with the information. If they didn't, one of their regulars would, which could be worse for them. Either way pointed to disaster. Please help!

No police knocking at the door to Zup most likely meant Frederik Rooten's wife had not told Basel City Inspector Morenz of her husband's extra-curricular activities, and it had not occurred to Morenz to infer a link from the society lawyer to the seedy club in Klein Basel. Either Frau Rooten couldn't tell what she didn't know, or wouldn't tell what would surely heap shame and endless media attention on top of her pain. That was good. Max and Addie did not deserve the likes of Morenz bashing through their special world. Aliette could sense a bully.

She didn't tell them that. She told them, 'Don't say a word beyond your door. Just sit tight.'

They protested. They pleaded.

She commanded, 'You have to manage it, *mes amis*. Tell your people. Ask them what they want—Zup, or twenty seconds on the news?' Adding, 'My gut tells me your problem has left with Fred and Greta. Why invite it back?' She did not mention there was little she could do except hope that she was right. All in all, pretty irresponsible advice. But it made sense to them. They calmed down. They would manage it. She would be there for them.

Because it was not her case, but it was. Because Frederik Rooten was Fred and both Martin Bettelman and Justin Aebischer had been regulars at Zup. Because Beppi Crerar had died, and she had come too close herself. Would Hans Grinnell admit it now? ...He would live, but barely.

Attempts to be rid of investigating police had obvious motivation. But why assassinate the fraud victim's attorney? Probably for the same reason you'd want to silence Josephina Perella and Justin Aebischer. They were no longer assets, but had become a threat, a liability. Was jokey Fred one more piece in a suddenly vulnerable network, if not gang? A high-end attorney would be an even more perfect partner than a crooked police officer brought in to monitor things from the 'inside,' as it were. A high-end attorney would also be a welcome guest, a trusted advisor. He could actually touch the money, not to mention the art itself.

The Basel media did not go anywhere near there. Of course not. They were saying a tragic, heinous accident—in the sense of a cop-killer's errant first shot. Because a maid in the place across the street was sure she'd seen the neighbour go down first, and a community wants to believe that their best and brightest are also their true and good.

From the gravity of Grinnell's wound, Aliette was assuming a rifle had replaced Martin Bettelman's SIG 220. As promised, Dieter Taub had sent a file. Thirty names on the current VigiTec payroll with military background. It included seven Roberts, or variations thereof, three Italian, four French. One helpful gesture, one hopeless task.

Basel City played its boring game, keeping her on hold until she was at the point of screaming; then, 'Désolé, Inspector,' Inspector Morenz purred in his best French. 'I'm afraid that will be classified for the next little while.' The twerp would not even divulge the type of bullet.

Stupid man. If he knew what she knew... But no, she'd never share with a man like that.

She tried Basel Lands Inspector Hilda Gross but Hans Grinnell's colleagues had not been apprised either. The hospital had been warned not to speak to anyone without clearance.

Talking to Fred Rooten's widow, and not just about murder, would likely be interesting. Greta was the other *other* half of Fred and the poor woman might know this. Or something. Anything might

help in tracking down Greta. But Rooten's wife was being guarded
by two Basel City uniforms, posted at the baronial iron gate seen on
the evening news across the region.

Was Greta next on a list of liabilities? Was Greta already dead?
Who and where was Greta?

She called the boys. Max picked up. Addie opened his cell.

'There's one thing you can help me with.' Yes? 'Fred and
Greta—who wore the pants?'

Adelhard immediately got bitchy, but Max stayed cool. He
understood. 'Greta. That's what Greta is. No matter what, Greta
always wears the pants.'

That sounded true. Another question: Did Greta ever show up
in an ugly pink coat?

Adelhard sniffed, mocking the very notion. Such a thing was
never seen in Zup.

Of course it wasn't. '*Merci*. I mean, *Danke*. You have to hang
tough. And silent!'

Then Aliette sat back in her chair and stared out the window,
considering directions, still precariously close to the edge of torpor.
And wishes…

If only Hans had shared a little more.

She had tried to share. J-P Blismes helped confirm this (in her
mind).

33

READY FOR THE WORLD

A week later, on the twentieth of November, she received a call. *'Bon!'* She'd been waiting. She hobbled down to the garage. Though still using the cane, the inspector insisted she could manage, solemnly promising mechanics Joël and Paul she'd stay off the main roads. She signed for the car and headed for the village of Kembs. The chestnut trees along the river were losing their leaves at a rapid rate now. The willows and poplars might hold out against death for another few weeks. A drive by the water was good for her soul.

And the shoemaker was immaculate! Ready to meet the public.

'Almost ready,' Gregory Huet corrected. 'Don't touch, please.'

'What is this?'

'Vacuum table.'

'Feels warm.'

'That's the idea, Inspector. The vacuum applies a gentle pressure while the heat and solvent combine to soften the paint and it gradually flattens. Gets it back to where it was.'

'The original paint?'

'Yes, but interspersed with mine. Touch-ups. An entire new sector through here, where it was ripped...' His finger guiding her eye; 'consolidates old with new, though *my* paint is a beautiful replica of what this man was using, if I may be permitted a bit of self-promotion.'

Aliette had no objections. She saw nothing but excellent work. 'Is that it?'

'I'd prefer to give him another touch of lacquer...tone him down a tad more, add the shine of age. Give him back that lost and forgotten look. You'll see it. You'll be glad.'

'How long?'

'A week to settle. If circumstances were different, I'd say give him a month. But…' Huet shrugged. He was working for the police, not le Musée National.

She made a call, then asked Huet, 'But he'll manage in three weeks?'

'So long as no one starts pawing him.'

'Don't worry, monsieur, he'll have better security than Klaus Barbie.'

'Do you still love him?' Gregory Huet asked quietly.

'Yes.' This one thing still held fast and true.

Mended, clean of river mud, seductively golden in the contemplation of his tea. In every other aspect, Aliette's love was scattered, the reserves in her heart depleting fast. But her love for this lonely old shoemaker pouring tea forever was holding steady. No trite analogies. Just the image. The meaning of it. The *non*-meaning of it. The meaning that would never be known.

But J-P Blismes asked, 'Has anything good happened since you went down to Basel?' J-P's queries opened broad avenues of introspection. That was his job. Then it was up to her.

Anything good since she'd gone down to Basel? No (apart from momentary pleasures of the carnal kind—and J-P was not allowing those), nothing good had happened since she'd gone down to Basel. *Au contraire*. It was why she was sitting here. Fine. So then, why had she gone down to Basel? She was tempted to say, 'Claude.' She could have cited Martin Bettelman—French citizen, profligate in love, dishonest in marriage, art thief, murder victim. But, and at this juncture honesty was crucial, it was the shoemaker. Broken, unclaimed, a beauty deserving her attention. The painting had been her reason, not the sleazy man found beside him. The shoemaker was a project worth pursuing. Finding the mysterious Robert was a job, the purpose was to know the what and why of Martin Bettelman, found murdered by a painting no one knew or cared about. Her purpose. 'I went because I love this painting we found with our victim. Now it's time to go again, to tell them the shoemaker's ready; it's time to get him home.'

J-P smiled. 'Good. Go.'

34

RIVERSIDE BENCH

Lost! Unknown Masterpiece seeks home...

Do you know this man? A beautiful shoemaker, provenance unknown.

Believed to be post-Romantic, pre-Early Modern. Likely French, maybe Flemish, also shows strong hints of Dutch roots descending straight from Rembrandt, clear signs of English influence via Turner. The painting was recovered from the Rhine canal on 25 September last and may have vital links to another outstanding matter currently under police investigation. Repaired and refurbished, this work will be presented at 10:00hrs, Friday, 10 December, in the Media Centre, Hôtel de Police, rue des Bons Enfants.

Contact Monique Sparr at 34.77.70.44.
Refreshments will be served.

Nothing good had happened since she'd gone down to Basel, but here she was again, sitting on a bench on the Rhine promenade, chewing a sandwich from a kiosk and contemplating Helvetia — who was studiously ignoring a French cop, as she ignores everyone while she sits forever on a stone piling, watching the river, wondering where to head to next.

Like the Marianne in France, or Germania, Italia, Britannia... Columbia lighting the way to American freedom, Helvetia is the feminine avatar of the Swiss state. Like her international sisters, Helvetia is usually posed heroically, symbolizing strength. But not the Helvetia set in bronze on the riverbank in Basel. Not in the least. Helvetia's skirt is up at her knees, her tired feet are dangling, a weary traveller. Her suitcase, time-bound, ironic and mundane, is an integral part of the tableau. A shabby, well-travelled suitcase waiting with her sword and shield while Helvetia rests. Inspector Nouvelle was fascinated by Helvetia's suitcase. It spoke to her.

The Marianne was perpetually unreal—a heroine who would never dare to be ironic.

The inspector had spent the morning making her slow way through a web of downtown streets, stopping at galleries, promoting the shoemaker. Everyone was sympathetic to a limping cop. Most seemed genuinely intrigued to receive her personal invitation to come and view an 'unknown masterpiece.' Those were Gérard Richand's words. As was the suggestion of French provenance. Gregory Huet had laughed. But, from the coffee and cookies to secure transport from Kembs, Gérard was arranging the event, so he controlled the message.

Aliette had popped into Basel City police headquarters, left an invitation for Commander Heinrich Boehler and popped back out; she did not wait to exchange pleasantries. At the Kunstmuseum she gave out a dozen copies, receiving varied reactions and promises from staff. VigiTec agent Della Kypreosus, hard at work in front of her monitors, was thrilled and would love to come if she could trade shifts. Della promised to pass the page along to her boss. Merci, Della, it would save her a few steps. At the ultra-cool Mettler, a chic woman said she would pass the page along to Rutger but she could not promise he'd be there. A wide, slow circle brought Aliette to Clarastrasse and down to the Middle Bridge, heading straight for the FedPol offices on Freie. Before confronting Rudi Bucholtz, she needed to rest and regroup.

The previous day had brought light snow turning to rain. Wet leaves lay strewn along the promenade waiting for a Basel cleaning squad. The noon sky was cloudless, the wind negligible, and the city felt more open, clearly etched. The chicken salad in her sandwich was excellent, and there was a freshly baked leckerli cookie waiting in her bag.

She sipped water, watched the large man move haltingly toward her along the promenade.

'Inspector Nouvelle?' Dieter Taub extended a gloved hand. 'Bonjour.' She shook it. He held up a brown bag. 'Mind if I join you?' Adding, 'Seeing you've stolen my spot.'

'*Your* spot?'

Taub smiled at the sunshine. 'Days like this, I come all the way from Messeplatz. One small pleasure, eh? And not easy with this gimpy leg.'

'No. What happened?'

'Nothing to speak of. Fell from a ladder rearranging the garage. Winter's almost upon us, yes? Have to get our house in order.' She commiserated with a weary smile. Of course, Dieter Taub noticed the cane resting by her briefcase. 'And yourself?'

A polite shrug. 'Line of duty.' He didn't pry. Aliette gestured: have a seat.

He opened his package and settled in with a roast pork sandwich, a dill and coffee.

She knew Dieter Taub would not talk about his work in any meaningful way. Perhaps she could talk about hers. She allowed, 'I saw your associate this morning. Della. Nice woman.'

'Della Kypreosus. Yes, Della is sharp. Works hard. She'll do well with us. If she stays.'

'I hope so.' Laying her sandwich aside, carefully cleaning her fingers, she pulled a copy of the press notice-cum-invitation from her case and proffered it. 'I gave one to Della for you, but seeing you're here…We've decided it's time to go public with our shoemaker.'

Taub accepted the page. 'Ah, your shoemaker. Looking a lifetime better than the last time I saw him, I must say. Someone's done a good job for you.'

'Yes, very talented. We're very pleased.'

'Sent him up to Paris, I suppose.'

'No. Local man.' She would not reveal his name. A Swiss executive would not expect her to.

Taub smiled, sadly it seemed, contemplating a shoemaker at his table with his tools and a boot, pouring himself a bowl of tea. 'He looks alone, this man.'

'You can relate?' she ventured. A mistake. Herr Taub only nodded coolly, instantly and instinctively retreating to more formal ground. Leaning a miniscule feminine degree closer to his end of their shared bench, she nudged the notion ahead regardless. 'I feel the painter, whoever he was, is telling us something about the spiritual aspect of work. It's a mystery. Love it or hate it, your work becomes the centre of who are. I love this shoemaker. But he needs to go home.'

Which brought a quiet nod from Dieter Taub.

She eased back into her own space, smiled at the bronzed woman sitting opposite them and added lightly, 'And I think I love that suitcase too.'

'We all do,' Taub volunteered. In his ponderous way he explained that this Helvetia was a modern take on the allegorical character created with the founding of the Swiss state in the mid-nineteenth century. 'People think we take ourselves too seriously—that would be the fault of our banking industry. I believe our art shows otherwise. At least here in Basel.'

'It never seems to end,' Aliette rejoined. The man was a proud citizen.

'It is like a communal addiction, our art.' Laying the police announcement aside, he tasted his pickle, tentative, not sure he liked it. 'But better art than… what? Portraits of our glorious leader? Slogans about God? The revolution? Ours is an environment of beauty. Yes?'

'That's well put, Herr.' She wiped mayonnaise from her lips. 'I confess I don't really know much about art.'

'Nor do I.' A dark grunt that may have been a laugh. 'More of a cuckoo clock man, myself.'

Her smile was spontaneous. 'With a man and a lady who come out to dance?'

'Oh, yes. I adore them. If I were the collector type, it would be clocks, not paintings.'

She pushed—politely. 'But does he ring any bells, now that he's all patched up and shining?'

'Hmm.' Chewing, a large man, hungry after a morning providing security logistics, smiling sideways at her through soft blue eyes. Doleful. She discerned an abiding melancholy. He looked at the shoemaker sitting between them. 'Sorry. I see so many. Are you making progress?'

'*À peine, à peine.*' Little by little. 'Horrible what happened to the Basel Lands inspector and that lawyer. Think it was related?'

'Hard to say. The lawyer was certainly involved in the art trade, I mean by virtue of his connection to his client. Beyond that?' A slow shake of his polished head.

'Any suggestions as to other clients?'

Dieter Taub gazed at the river. 'You know, Inspector, I have to stop this conversation.'

'Why? …Dieter?' But she knew it was futile trying to con him with her gentle voice.

He offered a sympathetic smile. 'It's not personal.'

'I know, I know. Nothing's personal, it's just business.'

'I'm sorry you feel that way.' Again that sidelong look: slightly cold now, a wary dog. She saw it plainly.

But she wouldn't push. Aliette went back to her sandwich, sipped water, cleaned her fingers, bit into her cookie, listening politely as Dieter Taub spent the rest of their lunch on the bench explaining the DNA of Swiss neutrality, and the logical outflow of tact and secrecy that was bound to grow from this hard-won seed. Very speculative, but she'd never heard it put that way, and all in perfect French. When he stood to leave, she brushed crumbs from her lap and extended her hand. 'It was nice to see you again. I hope to see you next week.'

Cordial but distant, Dieter Taub dodged a personal commitment by promising to inform his clients of the police media event, Friday next in the French city down the river. Then he hobbled away, turned the corner into Clarastrasse and disappeared. He was another man entrenched in the none-of-your-damn-business approach to the world. But so far he'd kept his promises.

Collecting her things, the inspector limped over the Middle Bridge and on to Freiestrasse.

The FedPol offices on the sixth floor felt lifeless. Lots of mid-afternoon sun, but no energy. Dusty motes hanging in a vacuum, awaiting human motion. And emotion. The receptionist hardly smiled. It was just too much effort. And not a sound to be heard as the French cop limped along the corridor. If Rudi Bucholtz were there, she would dare to enter. Hi, Rudi. I really miss you… But he wasn't there. And she didn't miss him. Not really.

Franck Woerli was transfixed in front his computer screen. 'Bonjour, Franki.'

He turned, registering a minimal grimace before he gestured her in. 'How's the leg?'

'A little stronger each day.'

'Well, we have to do our job.' He scratched his nose. 'Bullets, accountants, bureaucratic jerk-offs, territorial fucks—we can get killed a lot of different ways. But what the hell, eh?'

'Smile, Franki. You're far better looking when you smile. What are you doing?'

'Not much, when you get right down to it. Do you know how much money our business class hides through guest worker payroll fiddles in the course of a year?'

'How much?

'No idea. They're far smarter than I'll ever be. I was hoping the French police might know.' Poor Franck. So dry and empty and dark as he turned back to the lists on his screen.

'I have this for you.' Maybe an outing to France would cheer him up. He took the sheet, read it without comment, turned glumly back to his screen. She asked, 'Where is Rudi?'

Woerli's bitter half-smile reflected off his screen. 'Spending his days with Reubens. Or the fake Reubens, depending on who you talk to. And Hilda Gross. Negotiating.'

'Negotiating what?'

'Trying to get her to pass Frau Federer and her problem along to us. To him, actually. To keep it moving along.'

'Makes sense.' In theory. Rudi's dreamy mind was another proposition altogether.

'You'd think so. The old woman and her painting are out there; everything else related to her case is here in town. The art part. Not the murders. Of course, Hilda sees it differently.'

'I can't believe you people.'

Franck Woerli turned away from his lists. 'What matters is that Rudi is feeling important. Hilda too, I bet. These lists don't make *me* feel very important at all.'

This man's relentless self-pity was the last thing she needed. She went to the window and looked out at the art-strewn city, the dirty timeless river running through it. Another couple had found the bench by Helvetia and her suitcase, armour and sword. 'You live in such a beautiful place, Franki. That has to be worth something in the daily grind, no?'

Agent Franck Woerli heaved a sigh and stood. He joined her at the window. 'Beautiful day out there. I'd love to go out and walk around, but I might never come back. Josephina used to go out for her lunch. Every day. Rain or shine. Parks, galleries, museum, wherever. Said it helped lighten this never-ending feeling. A day like today, she'd sit by the river.'

'I just enjoyed an hour with Helvetia.'

'That was one of her regular spots.'

'You go to the funeral?'

'Yes. Pretty quiet. Her mother, a few old Ticino neighbours. Hard to say much.'

'No man?'

'Or woman,' muttered Woerli.

It can be horrible how we are always slightly ahead of realization. Unless you're a genius. She was no genius. But still, it comes. Bound in a trance, Aliette gazed out at the spot on the far bank, just visible from Woerli's window. She conjured Dieter Taub and placed him front and centre in her mind's eye: a large man, the Swiss version of a Tati character, taking a large space upon the bench. It was harder visualizing Josephina Perella there beside him — a woman she had never met except in bits and pieces. But as she gazed, those bits and pieces came together and all fit there. Almost too well. She could see it: Dieter and Josephina meeting on the promenade.

In a city of images, was this a fantasy or something real?

She asked, 'What do we know about Dieter Taub?'

A shrug. 'Head of personnel or something at VigiTec.'

'But what else?'

Franki considered it. Shrugged. Sighed again. 'You tell me, Inspector.'

'We know, because he just told me, that Helvetia is one of his favourite spots as well.'

'And so?'

'You don't need a phone or email when you're sharing a park bench at lunchtime.'

Franck Woerli's dulled-over eyes lit ever so slightly as the notion filtered through to a mind dangerously anaesthetized by tax fraud. 'I will look into this.'

'It's just a thought.' But she was thinking, Good, Franki. Do it. Be a cop. In parting, she told him, 'You come next Friday. Rudi too. Order him—I know you can. My shoemaker will inspire him to great things. He'll have Inspector Hilda Gross in the palm of his hand.'

Woerli yawned. 'This is not my territory, Inspector. I've become a tax specialist.'

'Didn't Augustine say something about man surpassing himself, Franki?'

He looked at her blankly. 'And you know, I'm starting to appreciate it. I may not feel important, but I feel very safe inside my lists. Which is most important, yes?'

She did not dignify that with a reply. Said, 'We'll have lunch afterward. At the Rembrandt.'

– 35 –

AN ANGEL'S PROTECTOR

Monique buzzed. 'Officer Sachs. Village-Neuf Municipal Police.' …Officer Sachs? '*Oui?*'

Officer Sachs identified himself as the one who'd handed Hubert Hunspach into her care that first day at the river. They had received a call from a Christine Charigot last evening: a man was lurking on the edges of her property. They'd hurried over. Hubert Hunspach had tried to conceal himself in the branches of a plane tree at the back of the garden — futile in late November. 'We actually had to threaten to shoot him out of the tree like a pigeon before he'd come down. Kid insists he's doing a *planque*.' A stake-out. 'For you, Inspector.'

'I'm on my way.' In yet another sticky-seated, tobacco-smelling, requisitioned car.

The one-way mirror revealed Hubert Huspanch sitting at a table. No headphones today. A dishevelled teenager in need of sleep. 'Pretty young for a recruit, Inspector,' ventured Sachs. 'Can't say I blame his pa for losing it.' A sardonic laugh. 'Kid demanded police protection.'

'He's having problems at home.'

Officer Sachs escorted her to the interview room and showed her in.

She took a seat, confronted her informant. '*Alors*, Hubert?' Please explain.

'I saw him. The guy on the rock. '

'His name is Robert.'

'I know that too. Saw him in the mall a week ago. With his mother. I was going to call you, but I had to make sure. It took a while to track them. I had her car marked — finally saw it on the high street yesterday on the way home from school. Turned into circle René-Descartes, a development two down from ours. I took a little walk after supper, saw it parked, went round back. It's definitely him.'

'I did not and would never ask you to break the law, Hubert.'

Like a seasoned lowlife, the boy shook his head. Too late for moralizing.

'What did you see?

'*B'en*, him and his mother. Screaming at each other in the kitchen. Same as at the mall. Poor guy's really in tough with her.' Hubert knew all about the never-ending battle. 'He is *so* white!'

'Hear anything?'

'No. Not in the house. But in the mall — horrible! He wants to do what he wants to do, she's screaming about the horrible men, how they're going to hurt him. In front of everyone.'

'The horrible men?'

'It's what she said.'

'Was his father there? In the house?'

'Didn't see him.'

'Brother? Sister?'

'Seemed to be just the two of them. And then I didn't see him — I figured he went to his room to listen to some tunes. Only place to go. So I waited. I guess someone saw me. Suddenly the flics were shining lights, telling me I was under arrest.'

'Did Robert come out?'

'No.'

'And you told them you were working for me.'

'Because I was.'

Aliette left Hubert and conferred with Officer Sachs. 'Who is this woman?'

'Triage nurse at Three Borders.' The *Clinique des Trois Frontières* in Saint-Louis.

As Madame Charigot had not called back to formally press charges, Hubert was allowed to leave. In her care. The inspector guaranteed safe delivery to his mother. But not before a quick turn in circle René-Descartes, which was pretty much identical to circle Georges-Simenon, and a promise from Hubert not to push his luck. 'A bit of a cowboy, you — climbing trees is not exactly in the mandate.

But I have to say you did well, Hubert. You're a good cousin…' but she would take it from here.

She offered to accompany him inside.

The boy bridled. 'I can handle it. You keep me in the loop now!'

'Your parents love you, Hubert.'

Leaving her with a blasé wave, he slouched up the walk to his door.

Aliette found herself wondering what it would be like being the mother of Hubert Hunspach as she drove back to circle René-Descartes and parked in front of another nondescript bedroom community home. No sign of life. She knocked…several times. No answer. She went round back but her investigation was blocked by drapes and silence. And rules. No problem getting inside — she had tools in her valise, and she had facts and evidence surrounding the death of Martin Bettelman that might give her the benefit of the doubt in court.

But no. She had to resist, go by the book. There had been too many mistakes.

She returned to her desk and retrieved the appropriate form. Before the day was done Inspector Nouvelle had delivered an *interpellation* order via a uniformed officer to the address in Village-Neuf and a copy of same to reception at the clinic in Saint-Louis. Madame Charigot's presence was requested at her earliest convenience, police *politesse* for ASAP.

Next afternoon, while in the middle of a phone debate with Procureur Michel Souviron as to *assassinat* versus *crime passionnel* in the matter of the Vietnamese son-in-law, Monique peeked in. 'A Christine Charigot to see you?'

﹁   ﹁

Christine Charigot claimed she had never heard the name Martin Bettelman. 'Was he the one in the tree?'

'No, Madame. He was the one we found on the riverbank.'

'Which riverbank?'

'The beach, I believe they call it.'

'Robert is forbidden to go near there.'

'But he does.'

Her guest repeated, 'I will always protect my child.' This was Christine Charigot's fall-back position, regardless of where the interview led. Basic. Praiseworthy. But wearing thin.

'Madame, if your son is implicated in a crime, he must help in any way in setting the matter right. All citizens share this responsibility.'

'My Robert has not been part of any crime.'

'I'd like to talk to him.' And after all, this *child* was almost thirty years old. This was now established. The boyish, angelic face was a trick of nature.

Christine Charigot's clasped hands tightened. She shrugged. Her fatigued eyes focused on swirls of early snow falling lightly through the twilight outside the inspector's office window.

The woman's frayed presentation told the inspector everything. And nothing.

Everything, vis-à-vis truth and probably complicity.

Nothing, in the legal sense of solid evidence.

Had the inspector mentioned the word murder? No. She had to tread gently, finesse an admission, at very least a useful fact. There were always these special citizens who believe the so-called powers that be — tax man seeking unpaid accounts, doctor with bad news, the law with its immutable purpose — would go away if it were simply made very plain they were unwelcome. Clearly, Christine Charigot wanted no part of the police. She came across as if the police did not exist. The inspector was tempted to call J-P Blismes and invite him up to observe the interview. These people could be fascinating examples of psycho-social disconnect. At first. Then they quickly grew vexingly tedious and a challenge to a cop's patient good graces with their stubborn stonewalling. But if a cop pushed too hard, it could easily fall apart.

Which meant Aliette Nouvelle heard all about Robert Charigot's difficult childhood — borderline autistic, a condition exacerbated by the departure of his father when he was ten, a highly sensitive and vulnerable child who had grown up (so to speak) in his own world. Few friends, always transitory. Not comfortable in classrooms, never a school prof attuned enough to Robert's needs. Too delicate for team games. Girls were attracted, but none were right. '...I know I set a hard example, but I keep hoping one will measure up.' Robert's maman offered a weary, knowing smile, the kind often passed between women. It all came down to a boy and his mother against the world.

'But you did not press charges the other night?'

'I only wanted him off my property. Whoever he was, those are horrible men. I will do whatever it takes to protect my child,' she stated yet again, adding, 'You know, I've spent years listening to the doctors at work paint the most ghastly pictures. Always in the wake of disasters.' A repeat of that distant, hopeless stare. 'It's a war, and I have to protect my child.'

The war had left this fiftyish woman wan and raw. Her skin bore no trace of sun or, indeed, air. Taut and veined like a ninety-year-old's. Colourless. The midnight angel on the rock had clearly got his ethereal sheen from her. Aliette wondered if the angel's mouth was set as hard and fast. She doubted it—this woman was a veteran of grim pressure, tragic moments. She had come straight from her shift, obviously without bothering with makeup or even a quick brush through her grey-blonde hair. She could have done with a shower too.

'The officer who called at your home got no reply.'

'I prefer if he doesn't answer when he's alone.'

'Your son is not ten years old, Madame. I have it on good information that Robert spends a good deal of his time in some very challenging situations.'

'I have to protect my child, Inspector. This is my duty.'

'He visits Basel often, your Robert?'

'He has no idea how to protect himself. They will hurt him.'

'With respect, this is not the picture of Robert that I have gathered.'

'You are not his mother. Those men are not his friends.'

'And we are investigating a brutal crime... Tell you what, why don't we call Robert and ask him to join us?' She hated tormenting an already tormented mother. Having a much-desired beauty for a son could not be easy. It was plain the woman was close to a precarious place, psychologically speaking. But Christine Charigot was getting on her nerves.

'I must get back. On double-shift. Hardest time of my schedule.'

Complete denial. So strange in an otherwise functional human being.

'We will provide transportation. It won't take long.' Aliette picked up the phone. 'Can you help me here?' In the awkward silence the inspector saw another lonely woman grasping for reasons as to why the world was so mean. Christine Charigot finally muttered a number. The inspector punched it in and listened as it rang thirty times before cutting the line.

'He could be out. I cannot account for his every move.'

Bon. They had broached adult territory at last, a small step closer to reality. 'Does he work?'

'Not lately.'

'Not at the beach?'

'It is not a joke!' She stood and took her coat.

'Not at all, Madame. And I don't see the good of your persisting to dodge the issue. I can compel Robert—and yourself. You know that. And I assure you, it is quite inevitable.'

Madame only murmured, 'And I will defend him.'

'Just have him contact me. If all is as you say it is, your Robert has nothing to fear.'

The notion of fear brought a glaze of tearing to Christine Charigot's downcast gaze. She buttoned her coat as carefully as she probably did Robert's. 'I'm working till tomorrow evening.'

'Have you got a babysitter lined up?'

Sarcasm is a sign of failure, but Christine Charigot had already walked out. And Aliette Nouvelle was not the kind to give chase, throw her against a wall and shake her. Especially not with Claude and the rest of the brigade around to see. But that day she was tempted.

36

PIECES IN THE RIVER

Two days. No call from Robert Charigot. Friday, Inspector Nouvelle beckoned Inspector Bernadette Milhau, gave her a new *interpellation* order and the address in circle René-Descartes. 'Be nice,' she cautioned. 'Be careful with the mother if she's there—but bring him. Please.'

An hour later she took Bernadette's call: 'There's no answer.'

'Any sign of life inside?'

'None I can see. Every window has the blinds closed tight. Both floors. Back door, kitchen. Basement's dark as a cave. Gate, garage, both locked. Like they've left town.'

'*Merde.*' And no just cause to batter down the door. 'If he's in there, we can't make him open. Go to the clinic at Saint-Louis and serve her. And bring her. This is getting absurd.'

Twenty minutes later Bernadette called from Saint-Louis, 'She is not expected on duty till Sunday evening.'

'*Quel bordel!*...Go back to the house. I'm coming down.'

Aliette was feeling personally insulted. Which is, by definition, unprofessional. And dangerous. But it is an occupational hazard. The inspector hurried downstairs—a fast hobble, getting stronger every day—and grabbed a car. For better or worse, she knew she would enter that house in circle René-Descartes.

The previous evening's snow had fallen till the wee hours, covering everything. A magical Alsatian scene for early risers, but a hazardous, slushy mess for morning commuters. Her progress was marred by a regional plow tooling stolidly along the National. She turned off at the first exit, headed for the river road. No better—all motorists were on their guard and crawling through the humid grey mist. The radio was saying the expected rain would likely freeze.

Her phone buzzed. Bernadette asked, 'What kind of car was it?'

Aliette wracked her memory for Hubert's description. 'Old, nothing special…blue.'

'Navy-blue Opal hatch-back?'

'*Oui!*'

'Totally white and worried?'

'That's her.'

'Went past as I was pulling in. Car's filled up with something.'

'Follow her.'

Ten crawling minutes later, on the outskirts of Village-Neuf approaching circle René-Descartes, her phone buzzed again. 'She's going to the river.'

'Can you tell me where? Is there a sign?'

'A big factory…road going down opposite the gate. It's not plowed.'

'It goes down to the beach… our crime scene. Stay with her. I'm almost there.'

Two minutes later. 'She's unloading paintings from her car and tossing them in the river.'

'Paintings?'

'I'm standing fifty paces away. I think she even knows I'm here — but she doesn't care.'

'See what you can do. I'll be there in five. And leave your phone open. Please.'

'I will.'

She did. Trapped in crawling traffic, Aliette Nouvelle could hear Bernadette Milhau trying to engage Christine Charigot. 'Madame?… Madame?…Madame! Police!…' and a perplexed, frustrated, '*sacré!*… Madame, look at me!' More quiet cursing…steps, 'Madame, I am ordering you to—AGH!' It was the sound of one solid object striking another. And pain.

'Bernadette!' The inspector slammed the blaring siren onto the car roof, stepped on the accelerator, swerved around the creeping cars. A minute later, she finally left the road. Her wheels spun in the mushy tracks. She stopped, got out and ran. Her shoes and feet were soaked in an instant. She felt her healing thigh complain. The rain that had started falling stung her face with icy pricks. She passed Bernadette's car. No sign of Inspector Milhau.

The blue car was parked on the verge, the woman, in her housecoat it appeared, was methodically pulling flat rectangular objects from the back of it and flinging them into the waters below. Aliette made an emergency call to the Municipal Police. 'The beach?...Yes. Please hurry.' Then approached. 'Madame Charigot, I am commanding you to cease and surrender in the name of the law!' She may as well have been screaming at the rain. The woman took not the least notice. Soaked and wretched, she was obsessed with her bizarre task.

Aliette circled carefully wide. Bernadette Milhau was on the ground on the driver side of the woman's car, there was blood in the snow. 'Bernadette...can you respond?' Ten steps away, Christine Charigot was all business. She pulled another smallish, elaborately framed painting from the boot of her car and flung it. It spun briefly like a stunned bird before dropping into the swirling current. Then bobbed up and floated. At a glance, the inspector thought there were a least two dozen, floating away in a line.

But it was only a glance—because Inspector Milhau was on her knees now, struggling to her feet. Blood was pouring from a gash above her eye. Aliette hurried to help her colleague.

It was another one of those moments when an inspector might have made productive use of her hand gun. But it was in her underwear drawer, in the forsaken house in the north end.

Bernadette had hers. She muttered, 'In the glove box.'

Aliette did her best to support her much larger colleague as they moved around the fixated Christine Charigot—who continued unloading paintings and doggedly flinging them into the flow. It was pointless shouting at the woman. The gun was in the glove box. She fired it into the air. 'Madame Charigot!' To no effect.

There was also a rudimentary first-aid box. Easing Bernadette into the passenger seat, the inspector did what she could to stanch the blood. Then, apart from shooting her down in cold blood, two cops could only watch helplessly from fifty steps as the woman tossed the paintings.

Two pairs of local uniforms arrived almost simultaneously a long five minutes later. Several more in short order after that, sirens screaming. Christine Charigot was surrounded.

But she carried on, oblivious, as if unloading long forgotten basement crap at the village dump… until one brave officer lowered his stance, charged and tackled her to the ground.

Christine Charigot struggled silently, pounding at the man's thick shoulders.

Then stopped. Completely silent. The two of them lay in a wet heap in slushy snow.

A wailing firetruck finally bounced down the path. Two *pompiers* came running with medical aid. Aliette left Bernadette in their care and went to the water's edge to have a look. There were easily forty or fifty paintings — a flotilla of fine art drifting out past the mouth of the canal and into the open river.

PART 5

EFFECTS OF ANGELS

37

ROBERT'S THINGS

There was no sign of Robert Charigot 'in his room with his things,' as the wretched Christine had phrased it. But the irritating letdown of not finding Robert at home was instantly displaced by baffling wonder. The bolted door off the basement stairs had been crudely smashed with a hammer by a crazed and angry mother determined to enter at any cost. Inspector Nouvelle stepped into an expansive recreation room transformed into a private suite and exclusive gallery. The sunken windows had been painted over. The space was lit by banks of track lighting. There was a vacuum cleaner waiting by the desk. When he arrived, Magistrate Gérard Richand noted that the barometer/humidifier installed was top-line. Though the walls had been stripped bare—their contents now drifting toward Germany—everywhere else was art. In the cupboard, along the floors and on every shelf: paintings. Robert had also commandeered the laundry room adjacent, accessible only through his room. (Which partially explained the washer and dryer in the dining room upstairs.) The inspector found it crowded with carefully arranged lines of framed works, all small enough to fit under an arm inside a coat, and three pyramids of larger canvases which had been cut from their frames and rolled like scrolls. The distraught nurse would have needed at least another fully loaded trip to the river, probably two, if she hoped to rid her home of all the incriminating evidence. It was difficult to believe, let alone fathom.

But there it was. Somehow Robert Charigot had amassed it all—and locked it in his room.

How? For how long?

One hears tell of rich collectors who construct hidden, highly secured subterranean galleries, where they imprison their treasures, whether ill-gotten or legitimately, for solitary viewing. Whether through paranoia, grotesque greed or misplaced passion, the message of such stories is the tragic waste of beauty. Beauty doomed to an airless, antiseptic place cut off from the life that inspired it. There was a definite echo of that sad need in the basement of the house in circle René-Descartes.

Leaving Gérard Richand to browse and marvel, Aliette Nouvelle stepped outside. She had a feeling that Robert Charigot had fled from his mother's meltdown and would head for the source of his love. She made a call to the Kunstmuseum, hoping to find Della Kypreosus working the Friday afternoon shift.

A bit of luck: Della was on duty and eager to help. She would keep an eye out for the very white boyish man. Helpful Della also mentioned in her halting way that FedPol would have been supplied with documentation and video images related to all thefts in recent years.

'Merci, Della. And perhaps don't mention this request to Herr Taub? Please.'

'You trust me, Inspector. I do.' Meaning she would not.

Not without misgivings, Aliette punched in another number. Agent Bucholtz had left for the weekend. She had that number too. A woman answered, in German, she stumbled in the shift to French. There were sounds of a gathering in the background. A party? Rudi sounded surprised and not a little offended to receive a call at home on the weekend from the French police.

Surely he'd calmed down by now. Their moment together had been months ago — at least it felt that way to her. Forgiveness. Line of duty. An older woman... a more experienced cop, Aliette Nouvelle was ready with a wise word or two to help Rudi put it in perspective. Because he had to come. He *had* to. She needed him.

Rudi's first response was a knee-jerk 'No!'

'I assume you've seen the evening news.' When the pause at the end of the line continued, she added, 'A line of paintings floating in the Rhine like ducks — did Basel TV not show that?'

Of course it had. But Rudi resisted. Tomorrow he was expected back at Biel.

Aliette heard subtext. She would bet Agent Bucholtz had found another door to the romantic world of cold-blooded murder — this one through the heart of Basel Lands Inspector Hilda Gross. Well, good for him. And maybe for Hilda. But lovers come and go; this was something he had to see. 'Come, Rudi. You won't regret it. You'll be amazed, I promise.'

'Do I need another promise from the French Police?'

Had she offered him a first one? Men, Swiss and otherwise, they made these wildly wrong assumptions, then they compounded it by turning them into 'promises' somewhere inside their little minds. 'We have a house full of stolen art—I would say the vast majority of it comes from your side. And we have a very clearly marked suspect on the run—I would bet on your side.'

'My side, your side. Who is this person?'

'Name of Robert Charigot.'

'Where would I find this man?'

A sigh. 'I'm not suggesting you attempt such an operation, Rudi.' A gentle but pointed reference to his hapless performance at Agent Perella's flat. 'It's these paintings. I need you.'

'Ah, my eyes. Of course.' Touché. And not at all gentle. 'Is there no one on *your* side who could handle this, Inspector? I really do have a busy weekend ahead of me.'

'Swiss-owned art, Rudi. Swiss patrimony. If you can verify even one of them, you'll have the people in Geneva kissing your hand. But there are dozens!'

'I can't believe you.'

'My only other contact is Inspector Morenz at Basel City. I believe you know him? He'll take all the credit, Rudi. I'd much prefer to work with you… What time shall we say?'

'You really are the worst kind of person.'

'You could end up a hero. A national hero.'

'*Scheiße!*' Shit! This very discreetly in German. Aliette could hear steps across a hardwood floor, animated voices in the background. Guests for supper on Friday night.

Even quieter: 'I'll come tomorrow and have a look. Don't you dare ask me for anything before I have a look.'

'*Bon.*' She gave him directions to circle René-Descartes. 'See you tomorrow. Say, ten?'

- 38 -
NEW LIFE FOR RUDI

On his first pass through the collected works in the Charigot basement, FedPol Agent Rudi Bucholtz immediately identified twenty paintings listed as missing in his files. They included an Auberjonois, Hodler, Leinwand, Berber, Sperini, Herbst, Lenbach, Nattier, Remy — most of them names that meant little or nothing to a French cop, but left the Swiss flabbergasted. These paintings had been lifted from different galleries in Basel over the past few years, slowly, one here, one there, 'though I can show you video of that one walking out the front door of the Kunst' (the Lenbach) as well as galleries in Zurich, Geneva and Bern. 'We assumed they were gone. I mean, gone.' Adding, 'He has to be part of a gang.'

Aliette demurred. 'I believe Robert Charigot works alone, one painting at a time.' When Rudi raised a hand in protest, she qualified her statement. 'A gang certainly may have removed a large portion of them. 'This one on your video, leaving the *musée*, is it our waif in a hoodie?'

Rudi thought about it. Indicated negative.

'No... And Monsieur Charigot may well have taken advantage of one gang member's romantic interest in him. Martin Bettelman, to be specific. But he's not the type, this Robert.'

'What do you mean not the type? Look at it all!'

'Not the type to be in a gang.'

'What type is he?'

'A sensitive boy who prefers staying in his room with his things?'

'Right...' Rudi let that argument ride. What mattered right here and now was compiling an inventory. His inventory. His finds. His press conference. Rudi was not that hard to read. And Aliette was pleased that he was excited. (Hadn't she promised?) But she was compelled to break Rudi's self-induced spell for one hard moment: the trove of recovered works (including most from the river) were still on French territory. And while a flotilla of paintings in the Rhine canal made for a quirky item on the weekend news, the circumstances attached to the sad woman arrested for putting them there had been left vague — by design. (Fudging was one of Claude Néon's newfound and very necessary talents.) She needed Rudi to understand that with the help of all the available tools of legal game-playing, the treasure would remain here in France until well after Rudi's retirement if he or anyone in his office so much as uttered a word in public that did not fit with her timing and priorities. There was a French murder to be solved. First.

'Are we clear on that, Agent?'

'Mm.'

She hoped he heard her beyond a doubt. She would hate to disappoint him a second time.

Rudi made a call to a colleague. It was odd and somehow touching to hear Rudi ordering the person at the other end of the line to drop his Saturday plans and get himself to the office. Here was a boy turning into a man... Indeed, Rudi put down the phone, glowing with importance.

He immediately picked it up again, announcing to all present — Aliette and one very uninterested uniformed officer — that on second thought, two... no, three would better than one. Yes. He would need a team searching the files and working phones at the office if they wanted to make some decent headway. He made more calls, issued more commands. Aliette Nouvelle was impressed. She felt Rudi was finally ready to work with her in a meaningful way.

Then Rudi Bucholtz got down to business. It was a time-consuming process, calling in each item, describing it as thoroughly as his education permitted, waiting while his colleagues proceeded with a search: first through the FCP data base, then via their many InterPol links. But the calls trickled back. Many of the works on the Missing lists were here. And the thief's — or thieves' — range was increasing. Düsseldorf. Baden-Baden. Strasbourg. Churches, schools, city hall and court house lobbies along both sides of the Rhine in France and Germany, and upriver, deeper into Switzerland — Agent

Bucholtz called in his descriptions, and urged them on. A very big day for the art squad.

It soon occurred to the inspector that there was no real need of *her* presence here at all. She had no idea what Rudi was saying as he passed his information and instructions along to his people in Basel. All in brisk, idiomatic German. The local gendarme assigned to monitor would hear much more of Rudi's communications. But she stayed. Of course she did. Coming up from Robert Charigot's subterranean hideout for some fresh air and natural light—and to look at a normal Saturday being lived outside, the inspector announced to no one, 'This is *my* case.'

A mother pushing a pram in circle René-Descartes looked, gave a slight, puzzled smile. There were four uniformed officers assigned to keep watch on the house; the neighbours were obviously aware of the police in their quiet close, even if they did not know why they were there. More trouble at poor Christine's.

Aliette enlisted one of the uniforms to order some lunch. She received and served it.

She made her own notes as Rudi received details on each work.

She paced from room to room among the collected paintings.

At a certain point, a revelation: all of these stolen paintings were images of the human form. No landscapes, no city streets or parks or ports, no flowers in vases. *No dogs*, licking themselves or otherwise. And each and every one of these humans was alone. The figures rendered had been placed in nature, or in a room. Working. There were many of these mundane yet somehow essential scenes of people working, male or female, working with their hands or with their minds—a woman at her piano, a medieval cleric at his desk. There were the purely contemplative, some enclosed in interior shadow, others exposed to the will of nature. Some were set in heavily symbolic poses: she, naked in her boudoir; he in anguish at the base of a wintry mountain. The inspector recalled that stressful Saturday in October, in the monitoring suite at the Kunst. Agent Bucholtz's initial assessment that the pale-skinned thief loved the naïf strains of Art Nouveau and the more ultra-metaphysical Romantics was not wrong, just limited. There were many genres represented—she heard Rudi muttering terms like neo-Expressionist, Baroque and even Modern as he guided his searchers.

Robert Charigot had preferences, but, bottom line, he was not fussy as to period or style. Or setting. It was the person. Each of these human beings was solo, and eternally so.

Like the shoemaker they had found with Martin Bettelman.

The shoemaker was not beautiful in any Romantic or naïf sense of the word, but he would definitely fit in this hidden room of solitary souls. It cast the French cop back to the original conundrum: Was the shoemaker a gift from an adoring Martin to a beautiful Robert? Or was he a purchased theft being delivered that night? Was there a gang? Or at least a backer? Rudi wasn't guessing wildly — how could one boyish man possibly amass all this alone? *Those men will hurt you, Robert...* The inspector's 'cousin' had assiduously reported, sworn it was word for word, straight from the mother's mouth. Or, *par contre*, was the shoemaker in the process of being stolen *from* Robert when Martin Bettleman was killed?

Inspector Nouvelle murmured, 'Our Robert has lovely taste.'

Rudi Bucholtz hardly grunted a response. The Swiss cop was mesmerized, astounded at the range of the stolen collection. And perhaps overwhelmed by his dawning sense of responsibility. He plowed on, calling, noting, making lists...

The day passed into evening. She ordered another meal. *Tarte flambé.* Perhaps some salad. A cheese plate if they could do it. Some beer, a bottle of wine. No — two. A uniform on guard brought it in an hour later. She informed him they would certainly be working late, and gently closed the door. She used Christine Charigot's kitchen to heat and serve it out on her china plates. She brought it downstairs on a tray. They ate at Robert's desk, took their dessert on the edge of his (unmade) bed. Coffee and biscuits stolen from the house. There was plenty of wine and beer in reserve when Rudi picked up his remote and made another call. A French cop understood his kindly, slightly entreating German. 'I will be quite late.' Tomorrow was implied.

He offered her the phone. She shrugged. Claude Néon no longer expected to be informed.

She sat with her glass of wine. And Rudi. There was unfinished business between them.

Rudi Bucholtz put his wine aside. He lifted the glass from her hand, put it with his, but kept her hand — no longer the fool, this was clearly communicated. For her part, she was backsliding at a rapid rate, but the case was almost solved and her life as she knew it would be over.

So, why not?

She asked, 'Was your tooth expensive?'

He nodded.

She asked, 'Would you like to see my scar?'

He nodded.

In his memos to his colleagues Rudi had described Robert Charigot's collection as a 'secret'—an 'astronomically priceless!' secret. For a few spiritually obscure but not unpleasant hours on a Saturday night in a suburban basement, Aliette Nouvelle felt she was part of it.

Rudi was attentive. Gentle. He was deeply affected by her scar.

⟶ ⟵

Sunday morning they rose early and continued on. Smoothly. Rudi was intensely involved with his mission. No moping about 'us' this second time around. That did her empty heart some good. Touch for touch, cool for cool, merci, monsieur, now let's get on with the job.

They worked till mid-morning. Before going up to the IJ lab at rue des Bons Enfants to catalogue the paintings recovered from the river, they stopped at Kembs. Agent Bucholtz was not as impressed with the shoemaker as she'd wanted him to be. He was merely businesslike—though the Swiss cop did compliment the work of Gregory Huet. But he was as baffled as everyone else as to who had painted it and where and when, and the people in his office couldn't help. (Yes, another call, another command first thing Sunday morning. The new Rudi was not afraid of leadership.) Then he followed her up the River Road and into the city.

By the time they arrived, Inspector Nouvelle had more or less sorted through and accepted the difference between being in a basement jammed with beauty, and out in the world with only Rudi. By three, he'd done what he could with the remaining works drying in the lab. A Fra Angelico had been saved. That was something special too.

He shook her hand, 'We'll be in touch,' and left.

39

FINER SHADES OF MOTIVATION

After Agent Bucholtz departed, Inspector Nouvelle took herself down to Hôtel Dieu, thence to the Palais de Justice for a rare Sunday meeting. Christine Charigot was in a secured room at the hospital. She had been sedated and, on doctor's orders, allowed to sleep for a full twenty-four hours before a parade of experts, medical, psychiatric, legal, and psycho-legal, tried in vain to elicit a useful explanation. Magistrate Gérard Richand had a file of first opinions.

J-P Blismes, who knew something of the underpinning ties between criminals and mothers, had been asked to try his luck. Summoned, Blismes reported, 'Exhaustion is the least of it. Paranoia, anger, and a very deep and loyal love for her little boy, you have to give her that, no matter what else is riding here. I think you could pull her fingernails out, do some of that waterboarding, even apply some phone directories to the kidney area, and she wouldn't say a word. Although maybe she honestly doesn't know,' Blismes added with a thoughtful smile.

Judge Richand asked. 'But was she complicit?'

'Only in the sense of ignoring it.'

'An enabler. In my book, an enabler is complicit.'

'Apples and oranges, Monsieur Judge.' A smile. 'Sorry.'

'How could she ignore it?' Claude asked.

'Talk to her,' Blismes replied. 'She ignored it because she hated it.'

It was her Robert's amazing stash of art.

Gérard Richand noted that Christine Charigot had not once uttered the word painting, let alone art, over the course of their interview that morning. 'She has no sense of their value. None. She said it was to punish him. Teach him a lesson. A very typical mother.'

'But not. Let's hope,' Blismes amended. Typical mothers did not ignore their child's criminal career. 'Especially when said child is still at home. At least none I've met. There was no way she could ignore it — he'd commandeered her laundry room, yes?' This was confirmed. He added, 'Typical mothers want good boys.'

Aliette asked, 'Did she mention the men who were going to hurt him?' Her own second interview with Madame Charigot had been as unsuccessful as her first.

'She does not respond to the word homosexual,' Richand said. 'Doesn't even blink.'

'But she says she will protect her son,' noted Blismes.

'She won't admit to any knowledge of Martin Bettelman,' Aliette said. 'I'm prepared to believe she is honestly ignorant of names.'

Richand asked, 'Is she a sociopath?'

Blismes laughed. 'No, not in the least. But her son may be.'

'It's like a combination to the vault that's been ripped in half,' Claude Néon ventured. 'We won't get anywhere till we get to him.'

Richand nodded. 'They're a team.'

Blismes smiled. 'But not a criminal team.'

'A unit, then. A fundamental cog in a major crime.'

'A psychological unit. Your take on it will have to wait for court.'

Claude suggested, 'Let's just find him first.' Richand and Blismes were capable of playing the matter out *ad nauseam*. Claude turned to his inspector. '*Alors?*'

She could have, indeed should have, made another call to Basel. Should have made it Friday. Or yesterday. But Inspector Aliette Nouvelle had not called Basel City Police. She did not like Inspector Morenz. It was as simple as that and his own damn fault. People could try trusting. And communicating. People like Morenz and his boss Boehler, they worked at cultivating an atmosphere of suspicion. A French inspector's decision was the natural result. Sorry, we don't want your help, messieurs. She and Bernadette Milhau would find Robert Charigot and bring him back to France — to his mother.

True, he could still be in France. Or anywhere. But she knew where he had to be.

But tomorrow. They would go tomorrow, when Inspector Milhau's bandaged head was feeling better. Bernadette badly wanted and quite deserved to be part of the final operation in this affair. It was just a bang on the head; it had been stitched and the CT scan was negative. She looked a bit like Frankenstein's monster but had assured the inspector that with aspirin and a quiet day, she would be ready tomorrow. Aliette told them, 'I have a solid lead. Inspector Milhau and I will collect him tomorrow. Very quietly. Rushing in with sirens blaring won't work.'

Judge and Commissaire both knew she meant Basel. And Boehler.

They knew it was a wrong decision based on emotions, but neither challenged it.

Aliette felt comfortable. The murder of Martin Bettelman had been a crime of passion, a messy, amateurish one-off act of compulsion—nothing like the systematic killings on the Swiss side. As long as Robert Charigot stayed hidden from the glare of media, she was sure *her* murder would be solved. The Swiss mess she would leave to the Swiss.

So, moving on: 'Obviously, Friday is now a completely different proposition,' Richand said. They knew there would be people from as far away as Edinburgh at the media event on Friday morning. Art people as well as law officers. Now they had a treasure trove in the basement of a suburban house. For Gérard Richand, this was a huge opportunity. How could they capitalize on this confluence of international attention and an incredible cultural crimes breakthrough?

Aliette pretended to mull it. But her focus at that moment was personal. Gérard Richand's tendency (read Gérard's ego) showed much the same profile as Rudi Bucholtz's. Looked at historically, it gave one pause: Gérard had been her first lover in this nice but dull border city, and she knew Rudi would be her last. What did that say about *her* profile? One more strong bit of evidence confirming she should leave this place behind. What's more, Gérard Richand knew as well as she that the shoemaker was an orphan, and that when all was said and done he would likely still be. Then he would be discreetly claimed for a spot in a French magistrate's home.

To the judge's proposition, she replied, 'No, Gérard.' Senior Inspector Nouvelle was quietly adamant. 'Friday remains what it was designed to be: one murdered man, one unidentified painting recovered at the scene. That will be lost in a twinkling if we introduce this weekend's information. Which may or may not be related, don't forget.' Adding, 'My FedPol contact has agreed to this.'

Claude looked up. 'Rudi?'

Aliette nodded *Oui*, and cringed.

J-P Blismes was sitting there, smiling back at her. So was Claude.

Though from one man to the next, they were very different smiles.

'Of course it's related,' replied Richand. 'One little unknown painting hardly matters now.' In the face of Robert Charigot's grand collection, how could it?

It was a wrong notion, born of wrong motivation. Aliette challenged, 'What about one murdered man? A French citizen, Gérard.' Which was a right notion but not an entirely honest riposte. *Her* motivation had been the shoemaker, not Martin Bettleman... Oh yes, everyone at the table that day had a deep and ongoing relationship with the concept of motivation. Where it pointed. To *whom*. And she knew them all too well.

Yet another reason to move on, get out of town.

Still, the judge had to back down. 'Fine.' He smiled his own sort of smile and made a note. 'I presume all is in order at Kembs?'

'I was there this morning,' Aliette reported. 'All fine. Gregory's waiting for the truck.'

After the meeting, she and Claude went their separate ways, to Sunday nights alone.

40

IF DELLA HADN'T BEEN SO NERVOUS

Dieter Taub had seen the reports of the paintings in the Rhine. And he had overheard the French inspector's brief directive to Della Kyreosus. It was his business to overhear such calls. He had spent a solitary Sunday locked in a private room at the Kunstmuseum reviewing security footage of Martin Bettelman, such was his concern. In the interest of optimal security service, he of course had access to master discs that went back much farther than six months. No, as far as he could ascertain, Martin Bettelman had made no mistake till recently — it was there in the footage Della and the FedPol agent had uncovered back in October. A big mistake. A huge lapse in judgment. Taub hoped Martin was somewhere in hell, regretting it. But then, what do cretin French know about the deeper levels of service in the purest interests of the clientele? Monday morning he returned to the private room, his agenda freed up for the entire day.

Dieter Taub was in a state of controlled fury as he searched the discs again, determined to get a clear view of this pale boy who was the cause of all his grief. True grief, of a weight a shallow man the likes of Martin Bettelman could never know. Dieter regretted ever knowing Martin. Trusting him had been absurdly unwise… A knock on the door was almost too much to bear.

'What?'

Della Kypreosus could never really speak the language, but she had learned the business, the mentality that drove it. She'd felt Herr Taub's rage when he'd limped into the surveillance suite that morning. She'd heard the anger in the steady thump of his cane, too plainly, as he'd crossed the room and locked himself in the private screening room. It had left her confused and nervous. She had to follow orders—her livelihood depended on it. Herr Taub's order was the same order as the French inspector's secret favour. Was he watching her? Della was shaking as she faced her boss.

The ivory-skinned man had returned. She had found him installed in front of the painting of the kneeling boy in the Swiss Early Modern area. A kneeling boy, alone by a river. She had hit a button and immediately knew it was a work by someone called Hodler, titled *Adoration V*. The information meant nothing to Della—she was no art expert. But as she'd watched, entranced and bothered, Della realized the fragility she discerned in the pale man was echoed perfectly in the image on the wall. An instinct took hold. Della Kypreosus experienced a need to protect the fragile man as much as the painting she was paid to protect.

And the job she felt was sorely threatened.

She had to protect herself, her job.

But if she just sat there...

And if Herr Taub was observing her...

It had taken a good twenty minutes to get up the courage. She watched the day's first tour enter the room, swirl slowly around the pale figure on the bench, then leave. She watched the subject glance after them—saw his face clearly for an instant—boyish, but something else there—before he turned his gaze back to the image of the kneeling boy.

No... She had to. She had to report it. Della had keyed the image in the Swiss Early Modern area and dutifully crossed the room and knocked on the door. She liked the French inspector. She felt like a traitor. It was difficult to speak.

'What is it, Della? I'm very busy.'

Looking at him, at his hooded eyes, his fleshy mouth, it occurred to her that he always seemed like an animal with one foot on its prey, checking the air before killing and feeding. 'I find him.'

'When?' He thought she meant more footage from the recent past.

'Now. He is here now.'

Herr Taub moved past her. He hovered over her monitor. When she moved to take her place at the controls, he held out his cane like a railway crossing gate—Keep away! Muttering in a guttural German she still couldn't catch after ten years in this country, Taub enlarged the image, went in as close as the camera would take him.

Not close enough. The man was lost in the painting of the boy and his oversized hood kept the better part of his face in shadow. But the fixed jut of his delicate chin, the lips pulsing ever so minutely, these were signs of a person deep inside a moment of adoration.

Della watched her boss from inches away. She smelled the over-sweet tang of skin lotion on his freshly shaved and polished scalp, sensed his frustration, his need...and the perpetual sadness he always carried as he leaned closer and closer to the screen, as if that would enlarge the image. His piggy eyes narrowed in a way she had seen before and instinctively withdrew from.

Something mean there. Predatory.

She tried to sound coolly professional. 'I send a team?'

He seemed jolted from his thoughts. He smiled. The thing Della saw was grotesque as he rose and backed away, instructing, 'Carry on, Della. I will look into this.' He left.

Della Kypreosus sat stunned for a full four minutes before realizing the image in front of her was frozen. Fighting panic, she stabbed a button and resumed her watch in real time:

Herr Taub was standing in the Swiss Early Modern area observing an empty space on the wall. Della punched buttons. She found the thief on the stairs to the terrace, floppy hood hanging over his white face, calmly heading for the door. She did not see the painting, of course — it had been secreted away inside his baggy garment. But she knew he had it.

She did not sound the alarm. Herr Taub was handling it. She would wait for Herr Taub to instruct. On monitor one, Taub was still in front of the empty space on the Early Modern wall, scratching his nose, as if the answer were there, in the very absence he was studying. Della watched him bring his phone from his pocket and lift it, about to enter a code.

But Herr Taub decided against the alarm. He put his phone back in his pocket and left the room. The thief was on monitor two, blending into a tour group of camera-laden seniors filing slowly in past the woman on the door. He quickly became over-exposed and indistinct as he walked out into the daylight, then lost behind the

Burghers of Calais. Della switched to monitor three, picked up the thief as he entered the street and headed off in the direction of the bridge.

On monitor two she watched Herr Taub following, nodding good-day to the same woman at the door, then leaving the premises, limping at a carefully measured pace. In no hurry at all.

Della Kypreosus was left watching the museum courtyard, the steady trickle of visitors coming and going on a December morning. She was frozen, sifting dully—too slowly!—through a spectrum of feelings, none of them good. At the heart of it was this: She knew Dieter Taub did not like women. She had no proof, but after the years of being around him, she knew.

There was that, and the ugly thing in his eyes. And the fragile boy-like thief.

It brought her to an awful impasse.

Dieter Taub was going to hurt that boyish man. She had no proof, she just knew.

The impasse lasted. She battled through it, but not quickly. Della was feeling decidedly wretched as she took the business card from where it leaned against her monitor board and picked up her phone. Losing her job was not important. She was ashamed of her selfish fear.

— —

Senior Inspector Nouvelle had taken care of her Monday morning duties—two newly constituted teams briefed on two newly opened files: Inspector Patrice Lebeau was to take the lead in the matter of a murder in an HLM where the youth gangs were becoming dangerously territorial; Inspector Ricky Roig would head down to a forestlands park in the Sundagau and try to sort out the gravely serious beating of another gypsy. With a tap on the door, Inspector Milhau arrived. Bernadette's head was still wrapped in a bandage. Her eye was still swollen and ugly, but she had some painkillers in her pocket and the doctor had cleared her. She was eager.

'Good.' Aliette tossed the last file on the pile. 'Let's get going.'

But Monique buzzed. 'A Della...something. Sounds Greek. In Basel?'

'Merci... Yes, Della?'

It took VigiTec agent Della Kypreosus five irritating minutes in scattered English, almost non-existent French and several lapses into hysterical Greek to make her worries clear.

The two cops went down to the garage much more quickly than Aliette's still mending leg would have liked. Bernadette drove like hell for the checkpoint, pushing the battered old heap for all its dubious worth. Aliette called Franck Woerli from the car and woke him from his sorry spell.

She did not for a moment consider calling Inspector Morenz of Basel City.

41

WHAT ROBERT KNEW

Robert Charigot knew a few things, and none of them involved working very hard. Work was boring. Hard work was horrible — bussing tables at a suddenly busy Basel bar had probably been the most excruciating day of Robert's life. It was also the day he let Martin Bettelman fall in love with him. Robert knew how to do that without the least bit of work at all.

He knew how to keep his mother off his ass. Or had. Since the day his papa had taken off when he was ten, Robert had been playing to the notion, planted by her, that he was the only male in her life who cared. Who was there. Who would never leave her stranded. Say the same line for nearly twenty years and you're bound to get good at it, turn it into poetry in a bitter mother's ears. Unless you're a dolt. One of the things his mother insisted on, despite failure at school and in the part-time busboy sector, was that Robert was no dolt. He was sensitive. Extra-sensitive!

Well, yes. And he loved his pictures. His pictures made his life have meaning.

All Robert wanted was to be left alone with his pictures — to adore them.

Except when all he wanted was to be adored.

Robert knew women were too much like his mother. They never really connected with his pictures. His mother would never speak of them, which was why she was no longer allowed into his room. They'd moved the washer and dryer upstairs to the dining room. The basement was his. Maman had delighted in his first pictures. Now she was throwing them in the river. Hard to trust a person capable of that. But men...they recognized Robert's soul, which he got from his pictures, and they adored him — or said they did — and Robert let them. Until it got to be too much work. No, Robert was happiest alone with his pictures.

Finding a new one and bringing it home always brought another rush of joy, a jolt of pleasure.

And Robert knew the human eye always follows the action. He knew it instinctively, the way any lonely person knows it from watching the world. He knew it because people like Martin Bettelman had made it clear, unwittingly or otherwise. (Martin proposed a new scheme each time he saw him.) He knew it because he had seen it happen from his own very special place: put a most exquisite angel on a rock by the river and every boy in the bushes would be amazed. But if there was the slightest movement in the trees over by the cars, all eyes would immediately (instinctively) go there. Robert had observed this.

The eye follows the action. He knew it like a magician knows it.

And like a magician, he knew how to make the most of an elemental human impulse.

Robert Charigot knew someone would be watching him that morning, from the doorway, or through a camera, so he only waited and gazed, transfixed. Honestly transfixed. Robert truly adored the one called *Adoration V*. (The name of the painter meant nothing.) And in the back of his mind he knew that honest adoration made his gambit somewhat easier. When the tour came shuffling in to the Swiss Early Modern room, he closed his eyes and ears—and nose. God, how they smelled as they brushed past him, or sat down for a moment on the bench beside him, sometimes touching his knee. It was enough to make him scream. But Robert did as he always did. He hid inside himself till the lecture was done and they shuffled back out.

As the last of them were exiting, still one or two physically in the room, though their ears were turning the corner with the guide, Robert knew the watching eyes were moving with them, if only for ten seconds. It was exactly then that he rose calmly from the cushioned bench, stepped up to the naked boy kneeling by the river, lifted him off the wall and slid him under his jumper, then sat back down. And gazed transfixed at *Adoration III*, there on the opposite wall.

That was the hardest part. Five minutes. Sitting. Waiting to be caught.

But no one came running. It always worked, at least in museum-sized places like this.

Robert Charigot knew other ways and means for other places. So many ways, and each worked perfectly—just as there were so many perfect ways to depict a soul alone. As if it were God's plan. He felt at ease, indeed invisible, as he left the Early Modern room, moved through the formless crowd in the rotunda and out the door into the bright December sun.

42

If Franki Hadn't Been So Sad

Agent Woerli took the call from Inspector Nouvelle. He listened. He did not argue. He was too heart-weary to complain. He said he would look into it and rang off with the vaguest of goodbyes. Unpacking and preparing a firearm and rounds that had not been used in five years, Franck Woerli felt like a man heading out to his own funeral. He wished she hadn't called.

Agent Bucholtz was busy on the phone. Franck loomed in his office door till Rudi put the caller on hold and rather imperiously demanded, 'Yes?'

'What's your take on this Robert Charigot?'

Agent Woerli gave little credence to his colleague's notion of a boyish man at the hub of an international art fraud. The veteran cop heard Rudi Bucholtz's newfound self-importance oozing behind every word. No, it was not the man described by the French inspector. Rudi's take just didn't fit into a box filled with dead professionals. At best, this Robert Charigot was a dupe, his home a safe repository after the dormer apartment in Mulheimerstrasse had been cleaned out. His mother's home!... if the news had got it right. But Woerli did not argue with Rudi Bucholtz. Not worth the effort. He just nodded a thank you, then headed out. Alone. Not the most prudent way to proceed, but it was how he felt.

Based on the call from her contact at the museum, Inspector Nouvelle had been sure Robert Charigot would be heading for Mulheimerstrasse, and that Dieter Taub was likely following, albeit at a limp.

Stepping into Freiestrasse, Woerli went left, toward the Middle Bridge. Leaving from the Kunst, Charigot and Taub would have crossed at the Wettstein Bridge. Woerli's route would meet theirs halfway. Crossing the bridge, Franck Woerli noted a couple huddled against the river breeze, enjoying a private moment on the small lookout beside the homage to Helvetia. This simple sight caused the ageing FedPol cop to swallow hard. And choke on it. The ubiquitous beauty of the city, the vulnerability of his colleague Josephina. He felt the gun in his pocket as he moved through the Claraplatz, scanning the throng of mid-morning shoppers, face by face, searching for a now well-studied shiny head. He slowed…

There was Dieter Taub, his bullet-round top an easy mark. He was limping along supported by a cane, sipping coffee from a paper cup, a man in no great hurry. And it was apparent that he was not hiding at all. Franck Woerli adjusted his pace, feeling the stress.

There was no boyish man to be seen. Taub appeared so utterly relaxed.

Was he too late? More failure? Woerli followed, too easily, it seemed.

The French inspector had promised to be at the Mulheimer address within an hour.

Franck knew Dieter Taub would not need that long.

Inspector Nouvelle's notion of Dieter Taub and Josephina Perella on that bench by the river had struck a chord. Franck Woerli had done as she had asked and looked into it. He hadn't shared his information. Not yet. There were other things he still needed to know; he was a good Swiss cop, never one to jump to conclusions, indeed afraid of his rusty impulses after blithely running down to Josephina's office like an eager boy two miserable months before.

Franck now knew Dieter Taub had spent eight years with the Swiss special forces before being dishonourably dismissed, which usually meant on account of sexual impropriety. Whatever the reason, his very particular military affiliation meant Taub knew how to kill people. Dropping a well-connected attorney known to be involved in many art-related transactions from 'at least 300 metres' (one small but tantalizing morsel tossed to begging media and police counterparts by Basel City forensics), and almost ending Hans Grinnell with a second shot from the same place, was not beyond the realm of possibility.

Stabbing Josephina Perella in close quarters would have been easy.

Assassinating Justin Aebischer with a company gun. Disappearing FedPol consultant Marcus Streit. Neatly slicing off the ear of the French inspector's loudmouth plant in that squalid bar before tossing him into the river. And Martin Bettelman, a VigiTec employee who patronized that bar, probably a thief in his own right, a low-level and highly dubious man who provided a ready-made frame. All these possibilities calculated cleanly.

A near miss on the inspector herself. That fit too.

What made awful sense was Taub corrupting Josephina. Franck Woerli now accepted Hans Grinnell's proof. He'd detested Grinnell, but the man was only doing his job. The notion of love fit cruelly. A lunchtime love affair on a riverside bench as the entrée to someone with Perella's skills and access to police information. A love affair that was a heartless con.

Surely Dieter Taub had corrupted Josephina.

Franck Woerli *had* to act. For Josephina. For himself. For the commitment he and Josephina had made once upon a long-lost time. If this was the last thing he did on this earth, it might just be something a little more useful than tracking businessmen who cheated on their payroll tax.

A chill wind swirling willy-nilly in a labyrinth of Klein Basel lanes and closes injected energy into an old cop's step. But it dulled his tracking instincts. Fifteen minutes later Agent Woerli stopped, confused, watching Dieter Taub enter an apartment block in Gertegasse, a tiny lane not far from Mulheimerstrasse, but not at all where the French inspector had thought.

Franck Woerli stood in the quiet street, suddenly unclear as to where he ought to be.

Too unclear at a very wrong moment. Fear of failure left Franck afraid to think.

Twenty precious minutes later, a stout *frau* with shapeless hair came out the apartment block door wearing a frumpy pink wool coat and toting a flowery market bag. As she marched past him, Woerli gave her a cursory glance before returning his gaze to the window above. He thought he'd seen a bald head up there.

It was his own fault that no one told Franck Woerli about the woman in the pink coat. He'd been a useless mass of self-pitying emotion when the matter had come to light. He'd wallowed in it and the investigation had passed him by. Standing there, he sensed nothing for too long.

- 43 -
GRETA AND THE ANGEL

Dieter Taub worked on his face with brooding care. Lips first. He tried for beauty, though he knew he fell far short. But it was the thought that counted. It had to be. It was the heart that loved. Not the body... Smudging lipstick, trying again, Dieter felt the anger boiling. He cursed all preternatural beauty, the futile places it led to. It led to weakness. Which led to a fouling of respect. Respect for love. Respect for duty. A weakness for beauty had led Dieter to choose Martin Bettelman from among so many malleable and too-eager men earning an hourly wage. Dieter should never have allowed himself to go anywhere near Martin. One brief night almost three years prior, following his lithe employee to the little club on a dingy street.

Dieter had been observing Martin on high-tech surveillance cameras for some time by that point. It was an unforgiveable loss of self-control, mixing business with desire. Dieter's life was marked by these moments of indiscretion. Inside, they felt like explosions. Emotional explosions. Who would ever think it when Herr Taub sat down behind his gleaming desk?

But Martin had led to Fred. Eventually. After Justin. Adelhard. Some others. Dieter and Fred were a couple, a genuine pair. They understood each other, where they came from, what they needed. They understood passion's need to rip the bottom out of everything you stand for—at least one night a week. Add a project demanding trust and nerve: stealing priceless art made for some deliriously wonderful sex. Would Dieter have found Fred if he had not followed Martin into Zup? Another time, another place? Life was fraught with chance. Chance made Dieter nervous. Nervous of weakness, loss of self-control. There was a horrid symmetry to it all.

If the accursed Martin Bettelman had possessed the tiniest jot of self-control, the French police would not have come into it. There'd be no trail to Zup. No reason to lose faith in Fred's judgment and resolve.

There. Done. Lipstick should come last but Dieter needed it to be first. A clear statement was always a good starting point, and if nothing else, Dieter's lips were clear.

Now Dieter drew the makeup pencil hard and dark along his hairless brow, fretful, comparing one against the other. Symmetrical? Not easy on a face like mine, he thought…

Symmetry may not be comforting, but it does let us see clearly.

The enterprise had been working perfectly. Like clockwork. A finely calibrated Swiss clock.

Did they need it? Of course they didn't. They only wanted it. It helped them want each other. In that, it was one of life's necessities. And they were good at it. Justin and a few carefully recruited others were the portal to the major transactions. Dieter and Fred acted as their own runners. Fred, mainly—he had the contacts, he found the buyers through shadowy fences in places one would never dream, while Dieter built their retail inventory, responding to requests passed along by Fred, or calculating trends amongst his well-protected clientele. Martin Bettelman had seemed a right choice, smart enough to obey the rule of silence, savvy enough to fulfill his part without needing every syllable spelled out. A nod and a wink at Zup. Martin would gather quietly indicated works from the storerooms he patrolled, repositories packed with the old bumped aside by the new, works selected on the unlikelihood of their ever being missed, let alone shown again. But all of them worth something to someone. Martin was paid well for his risk—which Dieter controlled at considerable risk to himself.

Arrogant Justin was the only real threat. They'd dealt with it. They'd have let the thing be a lover's tragedy, with Martin strangling himself inside the frame. Not difficult to borrow his sidearm from his locker at the Kunst for a couple of hours on a Friday afternoon when Martin was off work. They would've dealt with Martin well before any investigation could get that far. Fred's skills at legal obfuscation could have kept them safe from the damning claims of Marcus Streit, the fiddly words of so-called art experts, that sneaky provincial police officer. The client would have been disappointed, but appreciative. Clients value attention to risk and absolute discretion in the protection of their anonymity. They had got him the Snyders. He knew they could deliver. They would get him a Reubens when they arranged new talent — there was always new talent — when the time was right.

Meaning safe. Secure. Anonymous.

And precise. Dieter craved precision, had done since adolescence, when the nervous-making push and pull inside taught him to stay tighter than a drum. Until the inevitable explosion.

Dieter twitched. The tiny brush flushing out his lashes jolted minutely in his outsized fingers and left a blotchy fleck that wouldn't do. He tried to flick it away and made it worse. He wiped his eye, and the tearing there, and started over.

The inventory at Mulheimerstrasse was a bread-and-butter sideline, a steady and solid hedge against disaster at the high end. Indeed, a source of gloomy comfort as the Federer catastrophe grew beyond saving. Thanks to Martin Bettelman, their bread and butter had been thrown into the Rhine. A shocking waste. Worse, the French fool had not even been stealing from them! This muted shoemaker was as unknown to Dieter and Fred and all their contacts as it was to the French inspector. Martin's rash freelance adventure had put everyone at risk.

And with his gun! Martin must have come for his gun just before the closing Friday evening. It was very much against the rules.

It was worse than that. If Martin Bettelman had remained discreet, Marcus Streit would not be somewhere in a pile of scrap metal, crushed to pulp inside a car that was now compressed to the size of a radio. Josephina could have remained in her support role, helping to deflect Fred's deft legal manoeuvres ever further off the mark… Poor dumb Josephina, the only woman since his mother with whom he could share shoes. A shameless charade, to be sure. But Dieter did not enjoy killing. He was not a monster. He was civilized. Respectable. Very private. Very Swiss. He was exactly what they'd always told him to be.

But he would always do what needed to be done.

The French inspector was an interesting woman. In other circumstances Dieter sensed he would have liked her. Lucky, too.

He had not been concentrating properly that wretched night on the docks, half-blinded as he'd been with anger and the need to punish Frederik Rooten. Fred's louche lack of constancy. Fred's ugly lust for that oversized buffoon. And Dieter had been more than angry when he'd sliced that grotesque Frenchman's ear to get that stud for Fred. He'd been in no small amount of agony from a bullet in his buttock. He'd been struggling with a severe pall of encroaching disappointment, hoping against his battered hope. For Fred.

Dieter's heart was delicate, always struggling from the tug of war within. And, inevitably, didn't Fred's disrespect bring on the doubts about Fred's judgment?

Yes, mein herr. These messy tears…this bloody mess!

Dieter's fears for their client's best interests crashed head-on into Fred's wrongheaded decision to face the media on behalf of the witchy *frau*. It left Dieter in a sheltered bow in a chestnut tree in a Gellert park on a sunny morning in November, service rifle trained. Perfect concentration that day. Yes, sick to his stomach and crying like a baby all that night, and all that lonely weekend; but never missing a day at work. Not Dieter Taub. The client had sent a politely coded note commending his sense of duty, his ability to act. Dieter took it to the toilet at the office and ripped it into pieces before flushing it away.

Threw up one last time and carried on, empty and alone.

No more dancing. No more Zup. Fred completed the soul's dark circle, so inevitable in Dieter's life.

If Dieter hadn't followed Martin Bettelman. If Martin hadn't loved that damned angelic boy.

Seeing that face on Della's monitor—deathly pale, exquisitely white, obscured in adolescent rags but unforgettable—Dieter Taub had finally twigged. That boy had been at Zup. Once, last summer. Martin had brought him in to show him off. His new toy. Robert. It was hard to see a fragile waif having the wherewithal to take Martin's gun and use it. But Dieter knew all too well how several fortunes' worth of beauty could bring a man to kill.

Adding just a hint of liner, Dieter finished his eyes. Nothing extravagant. He could not afford to be noticed today, and maybe never again. He opened the little compact, padded on the powder.

Too much, far too much, an effect made worse by the unseemly overlay of blush. But it was not night out there, it was just past noon. And it was an effect most people automatically looked away from.

The cheap wig ensured this. Dieter Taub fitted it with no joy at all.

Then he put on his clothes, took the market bag and went out the door.

Where the right side of Greta's shapely bottom clenched in pain with each quick step.

She held her stride. Now, Dieter, *he* moved slowly. He had to, the wound on his buttock still smarted deeply if he moved too fast. But Greta proceeded apace, clack, clack, clack, clack, clack, brisk and businesslike, past Josephina's tired colleague—who stood there gazing up at the wrong floor! No wonder anyone with anything of value to protect turned to the private sector. Did the poor man even turn to look? Greta did not risk a coquettish glance behind as she turned the corner. She brushed a finger under her blue eye. Was that another tear, welling in response to a humid December wind? Or was it from a heart that had been pushed too far? A burned-out FedPol agent might have been surprised to know Greta's sense of futility was equal to his own. If these things can be compared. He would certainly have feared Greta's anger.

Finally: the source of all her grief.

Greta knew she had missed Robert by a matter of hours, possibly minutes, the day she'd gone to Martin's apartment and found it empty. The spectacle of paintings floating in the Rhine on the evening news had shattered the numb shell that formed after Fred. They said Robert's distraught mother threw them in the river? The French were truly absurd. That little faggot had to kill Martin *and* steal their contingency assets. Beautiful Robert was the cause of everything. If his silly mother knew how Greta was going punish Robert for bringing all this waste and pain…

If, if, if.

Turning down Mulheimer, Greta flashed a smile for the Turkish grocer standing at his door, enjoyed the aroma of soup passing the Hungarian café. She wished she were younger. If Greta were younger, the world would be different. She knew this. The younger boys were so much more comfortable in their shoes. Perhaps she would even be able to enjoy that music. It was surely Adelhard's horrendous noise that pushed her patience past its limits that awful night at Zup. If, if if. But you can't go backward, Greta knew.

She let herself in and climbed the long, steep stairs.

Halfway up she paused and tamped sweat from her pancaked brow.

Halfway up, halfway in between. It took a lifetime to know oneself. Perhaps it took two.

Regardless of her fury, Greta was wanting to look her best for the beautiful boyish man.

— —

He was sitting on Martin's cheap divan, hands folded in his lap, for all the world like he was awaiting his turn at the dentist. He was contemplating his latest prize, propped in a patch of sunlight against the opposite wall. A naked boy kneeling by a stream. *Adoration V.* Swiss. Early Modern, verging on naïve. A variation on *Adoration III.* Same boy with the bowl-shaped mop of hair. Dieter Taub had often paused to wonder at it as he toured operations at the Kunst. At that moment the natural light (as opposed to museum lighting) enlivened the steely blue in the artist's flowing water.

'Robert?'

He barely glanced as the visitor entered then softly closed the door. He was not worried, or, better to say, not interested in the reaction he provoked.

Greta found herself irked by his blasé indifference. She announced herself again. 'Robert?'

He turned. His beauty was disarming. It left a mortal shaking. Worse, he seemed to know it. An edge of sunlight showed the limpid eyes, not so much shocked as disgusted. 'What are you trying to prove?' he asked in French. He meant Greta's meticulously *over*-made eyes and face and hair.

Rude. Thoughtless. An angel's fatal flaw? It left Greta feeling unnatural.

A girl's instinctual reaction was defensive—she took three strides and punched Robert in the face. 'Well, you're no angel, either!' And she kicked him hard in the back where he lay, curled defensively on the floor.

Greta knelt, too aware of the tight skirt riding high with the movement on her nylon-covered thighs. She laid her market bag down and cupped his jaw, forcing him to face her. It was true. Up close, the beautiful thing was just another man. A bloodied nose, probably broken by a highly trained fist, blackening creases around his clenched eyes as his nerves struggled to contain the pain: these things revealed a normal man. She touched his nose. He winced. Definitely broken. She asked, 'Why that one?' She meant *Adoration V.*

Robert did not respond. He tried to look away. Greta held his fragile face firm in one hand, grasped his puny shoulder with the other. 'Talk to me, *mon beau.*' The angel's eyes briefly flickered, then closed. Greta shook him. 'Why that one?'

Robert's tearing eyes stared into hers. 'Because it's me,' he murmured.

'Because it's you?'

'I see myself.'

'Isn't that romantic.' Greta drew her thumb along a stream of tears discolouring the deathly white cheek, leaving a pinkish trace. Releasing her grip, he lay motionless as she carefully removed the unframed painting from her market bag. 'And why not this?' she asked. 'This painting has caused a lot of trouble.'

The beaten eyes looked, then looked away. 'It's not me.'

Contemplating the shadowy image, Greta agreed, 'No…it's not you.'

'Ugly,' Robert whispered.

'Ugly?' The painting was shades of brown and gold and green. It was unknown and likely justly so. But it was not ugly. It was a shoemaker. 'You killed him because it was ugly?'

No reply. A dead-like stare.

'Eh? Talk to me, my beautiful Bob.'

'Ugly,' Robert repeated in a breath.

Greta tapped his broken nose. Robert cried out, jerked violently away.

Greta easily rolled him back so they were face to face. 'Answer the question, Bobby.'

'Don't call me that.'

A flick of a finger to the bridge of his nose. A scream. 'You've hurt me far more than I can ever hurt you. But I *can* hurt you a lot. Your client rejected it and so you killed him... Bobby?'

'I'm not Bobby.' So sullen.

'Sure you are.' Greta was perplexed by his defiance. 'To me, you're a beautiful Bob.'

'Fuck off,' he whispered. She touched his nose. He flinched, blurted. 'I have no client!'

'Come on, Bobby. Who wanted this shoemaker? Who was it for?'

'No one! ...for me!'

Greta sighed. 'Don't lie. It's too late to lie. How much were you going to make?'

The angel lay there, tears flowing, breathing hard against the pain. When it calmed, he muttered, 'Martin brought it.'

'To sell to you, for you to sell. To whom?'

'No. To give. To *me*.' *Obviously* was none too subtly implied.

Greta jolted. 'A gift?'

Robert's bleak stare signalled yes.

'Because Martin loved you. Martin loved your delicate ass... Well, that sounds right.' She put two thick fingers and large thumb firmly around a fine French nose, now bent and pulpy, pinky blue. 'Tell me about it. Tell me about killing Martin. You know, I was thinking of killing him myself.'

Robert wouldn't answer.

'Eh, my Bobby?'

'Don't call me that.'

'But I will. Bobby.' A slight toggle. Robert gasped. 'Tell me how this love story ends.'

'Call me by my name or go to hell!'

'Hell?' Greta twisted hard, Robert screamed, she put her free hand over his mouth and told him, 'You've no idea, Bob.' As Robert shook and writhed, Greta held him fast, repeating, 'My name is Bob. Beautiful Bob. I love beauty and I don't like pain.' Several times, like a rhyming song from a children's tale. *My name is Bob. Beautiful Bob. I love beauty and I don't like pain...*

Till finally Robert lay still, exhausted by pain, and breathed. 'I didn't kill him.'

'No? Who did?'

'It was dark. It happened so fast. I…I just ran.'

Greta patted the sweat-soaked, silky head. 'I don't believe you, Bobby.'

'Fuck you.'

'Did you love him? Did Bobby love Marty?'

'I love myself.'

'*Bon.* Down to the nut of it. And Martin's gift just wasn't right.'

'I didn't want that ugly thing. It has nothing to do with me.'

'Poor Martin. You're a mean little bastard, aren't you? Eh?…my beautiful Bob.'

'Don't call me that, you bizarre old hag!'

Too insolent. It earned him a hard slap that broke his perfect mouth.

Robert spat a tooth, more blood. 'I hate that thing.'

'And you told him.'

'Yes, I told him!'

'And you broke it.'

'It's ugly. Like you.'

Greta grabbed Robert by a knot of sweaty hair. 'And you killed him.'

'No! No! No!'

'And then you come up here and help yourself to the rest of Martin's art.'

Now Robert's eyes opened wide and fixed on Greta's. 'Why leave them here? Martin said they came from cellars where no one ever saw them. I thought, now that Martin was…' He shrugged again. Dead. 'So I took them home. For my collection.'

'But they're not yours, my Bobby.'

'Are they yours?'

'Mine?' Greta let go of Robert's bloody face and sat there on the floor of Martin's secret lair, staring at the stolen Hodler. As it will, artistic beauty calms: A naked boy kneeling by a river. A naïf. Humble. Pure. And nothing like this bizarrely twisted Robert—beyond the surface, no resemblance at all. Robert was in deep denial if he believed he saw himself in *Adoration V.*

…After a time, Greta mused, 'All I ever wanted was a cuckoo clock.'

'*Mon Dieu!*' Robert rolled his puffy eyes. He cared nothing for Greta's hopes and dreams.

Provoking Greta to slap him hard across an ear. 'Rude, rude cretin!' Robert curled into a ball of pain. Greta lectured crossly, 'Do you know how many people I had to kill? And all because you did not have the grace to accept a little gift from silly Martin.'

'Go to hell!…just go to hell.'

'Why couldn't you have just said thanks and kissed him?'

'It was ugly!'

'None of this would have had to happen.'

'Leave me alone!'

'Alone. I want to be alone. Is that a joke?' The clichéd plea echoed, burning through Greta's heavy-handed maquillage. Greta has to say that because that's what Greta always says. But only to Fred—who was dead, because of this whiny, selfish French baby. 'Are you laughing at me? Eh, my lovely Bob? You think I'm such a joke?'

'Don't call me that!'

Greta leaned close enough to kiss the exquisitely defiant face. 'Fuck you. Bob…Bob, Bob, Bob, Bob!' Robert swung a feeble fist. Greta caught him by the spindly wrist and stood, hauling him up, hugging him tight, embracing him like a dancer. The bashed-up eyes gazed back, morbid, indifferent. Greta whispered, 'I am going to fuck you, Bob. Then I'm going to break this thing again, right over your beautiful head. You ready for that, my Bobby?'

Greta meant the refurbished shoemaker.

Who ignored them both. Glowing, pouring tea…

Lifting Robert and spinning him in an embrace, Greta moaned, 'Oh, my Bobby. My selfish little bastard!' Turning him, turning him over and over like so much pastry on a board, ripping Robert's proletariat top from his porcelain back. 'My self-centred fucking angel, and why not?…so white, so perfect, so—'

Greta stopped, clasped the scornful, silent mouth and kissed it. Deep, wet, tasting blood, looking for reaction. Very aroused herself now. Robert dumbly shook his head, No…

Greta said, 'Believe me, Bob, you don't want to be alone. All the art in this ugly world's not worth it.' But it was definitely Dieter who threw Robert down on the divan, ripped his belt open, yanked his fly down, hauled Robert's pants off in one swift brutal motion. 'Look at you!' And, lifting Greta's skirt, always very proud in this erotic thrill. 'Look at *me*. Mm? Are you ready for it? Do we have a perfect fit, my Bob? Eh? Cat got your tongue?'

Greta was needing a response. Was getting nothing but a frightened moan. This passive thing was making Greta rage. She rolled him over and yanked him forward. The man/boy/angel screamed with pain as Deiter shoved himself inside, frenzied, shoving, grunting, 'Go, Bob, go!' Or words to that effect in German as the FedPol cop came through the door, gun drawn, aghast at the sight. And so clearly scared.

Greta, bucking, bellowed, 'Have you no shame? Get out! Get out!'

Instinctively, Franck Woerli retreated a step, affording Dieter Taub the chance to rip the automatic from the holster positioned under Greta's left breast. And fire.

Woerli fired too — though it could well have been just muscles. The shot went through Taub's mouth and he fell over. Still on top of, and well inside, a suddenly frozen angel.

— ∼

When he dared to extricate himself, Robert Charigot lay there touching himself, bringing his bloody fingers up to his perplexed eyes. The other man, slumped in the doorway, did not register in his calculations. He may even have still been alive, but Robert was not interested. Putting himself back together as best he could, taking his new painting, he stepped around Inspector Frank Woerli, and inched his painful way down the long stairs. He left the shoemaker. He hated it. He only wanted to get home, back to his room with *Adoration V*.

But Robert Charigot passed out on the street, waiting for the bus.

Too Late for Franki

Inspectors Nouvelle and Milhau arrived at the scene in Mulheimerstrasse much later than the promised hour—thanks to Commander Boehler and his paranoia. Aliette stood at the door to the tiny apartment, momentarily sick at the sight of two bodies, an ugly, tragic mess.

It was a different feeling when her eyes finally locked on the shoemaker, propped in a slice of sunshine against the humidity-stained wall. She registered a distinctly flat place in her heart, somewhere between stunned and stupid, yet somehow not surprised. She had no doubt it was the original, and beautifully restored by Gregory Huet. It was also obvious that Huet was another man she had completely misread. Where would this losing streak end?

Aliette shook herself and got to work. Replacing the painting in the flowery market bag, she instructed Bernadette to take it down to the car and wait there. Aliette would make the appropriate calls. One French cop on Commander Boehler's blacklist was plenty. Bernadette was to stay in the car until the Basel police arrived. If there was a problem, Berndaette should quietly leave. Upon her return to rue des Bons Enfants, she would leave the painting in the bag in a discreet spot in Aliette's office. 'Not a word to anyone, *ma belle.*'

Aliette would take the bus back, if need be.

'But—'

That was an order. Inspector Milhau obeyed.

Aliette canvassed the stairs. The dormer apartment was well removed from a busy street in the middle of a busy day and most residents were gone to work and elsewhere. No one even answered till she'd got to the second floor. No one there had heard or seen anything.

She called Basel City and asked for Inspector Morenz.

Then she waited, musing on futility. All signs indicated Franck Woerli had gone down in the line of duty. Foolishly perhaps, in fact probably, but one had to believe that in taking action Agent Woerli had moved beyond mawkish self-pity. Someone would be proud of Franki. A good police officer, a stupid waste of a man. Whether thirty extra minutes spent playing checkpoint Q&A could have made a difference would remain grievously moot and forever ironic given that the overly picky Customs officer was officially Woerli's FedPol colleague, while in practice his heart belonged to Boehler and surely (though never officially) a memo flagging a certain French inspector had been sent.

As for Dieter Taub, aka Greta: One of the frustrating aspects of police work was homicidal monsters who never got the chance to explain because they'd been shot down or shot themselves before being taken. Aliette Nouvelle had shared a bench with the man. She thought Dieter Taub might have said something useful. Not in the sense of justification; more like something to tuck away and use the next time. There was always going to be another homicidal monster.

And he too had seemed like a decent man…

The whiny blare of a *pan-pon* sounded in the street below. Morenz was arriving.

A subordinate entered first, gun drawn. Aliette smiled. His boss's sour little face appeared. He did not say hello. She responded in kind; forthwith she told him, 'Voila, two Swiss victims. Over to you, Inspector. I suspect a young man named Robert Charigot, French citizen, is somewhere in this city. I expect you to find him and return him to us. You'll probably get a good basic description from the security monitors at the Kunstmuseum. We have our own murder—we need to see him. After we've sorted out our business, we'll gladly send him back to you. *Ça va?* I'll say thank you in advance, and, well, maybe we'll have a long chat about it all in heaven. Even you and I might be friends up there.'

No response. She shrugged her disdain. *Tant pis*—tough luck for the rigid little man. Duty discharged, she made to leave.

One of Morenz's people blocked the door.

'You are under arrest.' In German.

'Are you serious?' Turning, Inspector Nouvelle told Inspector Morenz, 'As you can see, this was a gun fight, mutual shots exchanged.' Not her problem.

'You have no business here.'

'I have an international mandate.'

'We'll talk about it at the station. My boss would like to speak to you.'

He made a gesture to his man—who put a hand on her arm.

She stayed calm. 'Do you really want to drag your boss into an international mess? Because you will, I promise…'

Morenz met her eyes, daring her.

Aliette responded, 'Your boss is only your boss, Inspector. My boss…all my bosses, they will recommend to your Federal people that they conduct an in-depth interview with their team at the checkpoint. They will need to know as much as they can as to how their agent died and I happen to think shoddy service at the border may have been a factor. I have a witness to that.' She did not mention a roomful of priceless art, the matter of Swiss patrimony, the fact of French possession. But she would. She said, 'Swiss quality, Inspector. There is much on the line here.'

She smiled at the man with the grip on her arm. 'Please?' He looked to Morenz for instruction. Muttering profanities, Morenz waved a dismissive hand. The steel hand on her was removed. 'Merci. If I don't see Robert Charigot back in France within, mm, let's say a week?'

In fact, at that moment Robert Charigot was already under sedation in a hospital bed, no ID, still an unknown street person. Somewhere between the dormer apartment and a bus stop along Mulheimer, the Hodler had disappeared. But the French cop did not know that.

Neither did the Swiss. Apparently.

Aliette *did* know she had this nasty man thinking twice. And though she knew in her gut that Dieter Taub was not part of the murder at the 'beach,' she also knew she'd have to prove that beyond a shadow if she hoped to close her case. With help from FedPol she would eventually get a home address for Dieter Taub. But something told her that might not be the one she needed.

She took out a notepad. 'And I need directions to the home of the lawyer's widow. A call clearing the way would also be nice.' Naturally, Morenz balked. She eased him forward. 'I'm doing you a favour, Inspector. Try to believe it. Before I go back across the border, I need to make very sure you and I are well and truly done. Mm?'

He saw it. Didn't like it, but he liked *her* even less. Morenz scribbled an address. A uniform accompanied her down to the street, sent her and Bernadette in the right direction. On the way she called rue des Bons Enfants and asked to be connected to IJ. She pleaded for one or both of them to make their way to Basel. 'As fast you can make it. Call me when you're past the checkpoint.' Charles Léger promised she would hear from them within the hour.

Aliette and Bernadette found the address in the posh street. When Aliette pushed the button, the elegant gate opened without the usual disembodied demand for credentials and purpose.

Danke, Inspector Morenz. But what a pity such efficient cooperation has to be coerced.

They waited in the tall cool foyer, contemplating the steel couple copulating smoothly and endlessly beneath the skylight. The two cops both seemed to see it at the same moment... they rolled their eyes in rote reaction, oh-la-la! An interesting acquisition. Did Frau Rooten have the faintest clue? Her joyless face suggested she might. Then again, she was grieving the loss of a well-respected and very well-providing husband. Hard to intuit what a grim *haute-bourgeoise* Swiss did and did not know about her husband's secret life. Had they ever gone dancing? Aliette got straight to the point. The matter was painful but not complicated. If she had learned anything at all from this sordid business, it was that men have too many pockets for their own good and that wives will tend to go through said pockets and find some telling things. The lady's French was dull but perfect. Yes, Frau Rooten had found many unknown items in going through the pockets of Frederik's suits before sending them to charity. A receipt for flowers delivered to a number in Gertegasse made no sense to her—though she'd suspected for a long time that her husband had a lover. Had she shared this with Inspector Morenz? No. Why? 'Probably some tarty little clerical person from his office.' But where *was* Gertegasse? The *frau* was at a loss.

'Merci, Madame.' The two French cops left the poor woman to twig to that last detail of her husband's life in her own good time.

Desperately trailing a hunch, too aware that Inspector Morenz would be working his way toward the same conclusions, they raced for Klein Basel. Asking a stranger, they received precise directions. Gertegasse was just off Amerbachstrasse. The place was on the third floor of an ungentrified walk-up five minutes from Josephina Perella's drab domicile, ten minutes from Martin Bettelman's love nest in Mulheimerstrasse, and a pleasant walk the other way to Zup.

Entering, there was initial surprise. 'Is this all?' You would think a VP Resource Allocations and an establishment attorney would have put much more decorative care into their hideaway. It was too similar to Josephina Perella's uninspired flat—neglected wood that needed oil, furnished with old accoutrements from a thrift shop. No art on the walls. Beside the bed a photo of Fred and Greta resplendent in their party outfits, alone on the dance floor under the disco ball, grinning, locked in each other's arms.

Proof that love is all you need?

Her phone buzzed. She directed Jean-Marc Pouliot of Identité Juidiciaire as best she could.

It took two further calls for Jean-Marc to fathom the labyrinthine layout of Klein Basel, but thirty minutes later both he and Charles Léger were busy collecting items, taking reads. Aliette lingered in the bedroom, intrigued by Greta's dresses and shoes. There was a pair of hiking boots. On the inspector's order, they packed them for further analysis, a few other pairs of large-sized ladies' shoes as well. Bed sheets. Hiking togs. Underwear—many choices. All manner of things from the bathroom and the fridge. They did all this in peace… Who knew what (or whom) Morenz might be finding at Dieter Taub's listed address. It had yet to lead him here.

As they were leaving, the chintzy cuckoo clock on the vestibule wall was sounding the top of the hour. Two hand-painted dancers, he in a debonair tuxedo, she in a sheath-like golden gown with hair to match, came out of their separate doors, met for a turn, then went back in.

~ 45 ~
THE CHARIGOT WALL

Whether good to his word or afraid for his ass, Basel City Inspector Morenz located Robert Charigot and had him returned to France forthwith. France paid the bill for the ambulance and medic-attended ride. Robert was placed on a secure ward at Hôtel Dieu, far from his mother. Inspector Nouvelle requested they be kept incommunicado. Christine Charigot had wielded a gilt-framed artwork in a state of obsessed fury and used it to inflict serious damage to the head of Inspector Bernadette Milhau. That fact, and the woman's manically repeated vow to 'protect my child,' gave Aliette good reason to believe both Charigots had acted in concert to do away with Martin Bettelman. It was a question of who did what, and when. She needed to hear Robert's own story regarding the fatal incident that warm night in late September, then his maman's pure-hearted corroboration. The inspector began shuttling back and forth between wards, working on her bedside manner, as it were.

'Your mother was there, Robert. We know this…' Not strictly speaking.

'No. She was working. She's always working.'

'Your mother helped you kill Martin Bettelman.'

'My mother never helps me at all.'

'She took the painting of the shoemaker and smashed it over Martin's head.'

'My mother is mental.'

She could not move Robert past that. Though he divulged certain circumstantially helpful things about his encounters with Martin Bettelman both at the 'beach' and in Basel, Robert Charigot remained steadfast on the matter of murder. He could not say for sure, but it had to have been the Swiss. 'Old. Fat…' Robert provided a duly graphic replay of his painful date with Dieter Taub/Greta. The inspector patiently directed him back to September. Basic line: Robert had fought with Martin, 'I didn't want his ugly painting,' then he'd watched Martin destroy the shoemaker in a fit of rejected dismay. Robert insisted he'd walked away from this, '…the guy was losing it, totally, I didn't need that,' and he'd been well away when an unknown man rushed out of the darkness, grappled with Martin, then chased and shot him 'several times' before Martin fell in the shallows. Robert claimed he saw that from fifty metres. 'On my rock.'

'Your rock?'

He shrugged. The rock by the shore was his usual place.

Like a hooker's corner, Aliette was sorely tempted to add. But refrained. Insults had no effect on his seriously dulled heart. 'And then?'

'I dove in. Swam like crazy…' If the attacker further smashed the ruined painting over Martin's lifeless head, Robert did not see it. His mother had nothing to do with it.

'Did you ever take Martin home?'

'Are you nuts? My mother would—' But he stopped just there.

'What would she do, Robert?'

He looked away. 'Twice,' he admitted.

They already knew this. IJ had found good, if disgusting, evidence of Martin in Robert's less than pristine basement bathroom—where his mother was not allowed. But if she had come in, spying or otherwise, she would certainly have noticed the grubby signs of a visitor with sex and more sex on his mind. Any woman would.

Push as she might, this hint as to his mother's fears and volatile reactions was as close as she would come to hearing it from Robert. He knew he'd almost been tricked. From that point on, he denied and denied, always, and ever more definitely turning it back to the possibility of an outraged Dieter/Greta. At least it was clear that Martin Bettelmen knew all about Robert's obsession. The rejected gift of a stolen shoemaker fit cleanly with a confrontation at the beach.

Robert was wily but there were tricks he couldn't beat. Working from the opposite side of what she was sure she already knew, she presented images of Taub—both as shiny bullet-headed corporate VP, and as a less than perfectly conceived Greta.

'It was dark. I only ever saw him with his dress on — that day, at Martin's? And his wig.'

'But the face... Robert?' He was distracted, continually smoothing his hair, tracing the lines of his cheeks, examining his fingers, glancing skeptically at the mirror on the bathroom door.

'Ugly. All that makeup.'

'And those eyes — they don't change.' Silently reproaching herself. Dieter sitting at his gleaming desk stolidly mulling a murdered employee looked so much like Greta at a table in Zup, slightly worried as she contemplated her debonair and ever-jokey Fred. Aliette had seen it. But not. How could she have? 'I'm sorry, Robert — what did you say?'

'I said, It was definitely him. Yes.'

'Merci.' Like most in his position, Robert took the path of least resistance. They always did. And she could always see the easy lie. Whether a deliberate lie or a just calculated guess was harder to assess. She felt Robert Charigot could lie without a smidgen of conscience.

And he stuck to his story. What should have been a matter of course was anything but.

Down on Ward 3, Christine Charigot remained severely depressed, offering nothing save lethargic shrugs and tearful stares. Aliette took a chance, hoping the news of Robert's safe return might jar something loose. It was the opposite. (And another mistake, Inspector?) Christine pined. The fourth night she tried to go to her son, a zombie in a nightgown lost in halls of white, and had to be restrained. She made much pitiful, unearthly noise. Her depression deepened.

Whereas, plied with these bits of news — 'Your mother is suffering, Robert.' — her 'sensitive' son did not seem bothered in the least.

With leading queries, it became sadly clear. The star of the beach had nothing but contempt for his mother. Christine Charigot did not properly appreciate Robert's approach to life. 'She's a peasant. No taste! No sense of beauty.'

Yet he defended her. Strange, strange boy. And beauty was central.

Everyone who managed to get a meaningful word out of Robert Charigot was beginning to agree that he was not your usual criminal.

Money was truly the least of his motives. It was love. Self-love. The man who looked like an angelic boy (until you really looked) was motivated by a consuming sense of personal beauty and its reflection in the images he felt compelled to have. He was self-absorbed, a sensual monstrosity, grooming himself ceaselessly, never pleased. He needed those perfect works of art. But Martin Bettelman's link to the larger art fraud scheme (a Swiss problem, not ours) was incidental; he was a man caught in a passion for Robert.

After his third chat with Robert, responding to a befuddled mother's initial claims, an uncharacteristically grim J-P Blismes said, 'There is nothing remotely borderline autistic in that room. Emotionally, perhaps there is a resemblance. But really, that's the biggest load I've heard in a long time. I'll bet my licence. Immature. Rigid. Lazy, mostly—though the romantic obsession with self *can* be a blind. But nope, a straight case of arrested adolescent narcissism if I ever saw one.' And J-P, whose normal focus was on young offenders, had seen a few. 'Says he wants to go to Australia to get away from her. You know how many of my usual clients want to go to Australia to escape their unhappiness? I say leave him in there till he grows up!'

Aliette blushed. She too wanted to get far away. What did that make her?

'Don't worry—you will never be one of my usual clients.'

Merci, J-P.

The psychiatrist engaged to assess the accused agreed with child psychologist J-P Blismes that Robert Charigot was 'narcissistic in the extreme.' While the accused showed disturbing signs of both Antisocial Personality Disorder and what he termed Adjustment Disorder with anxiety, Robert was not unintelligent, he was not addicted to any drug—except the pure wonder of himself. However the eventual charges might be constructed, Robert could be considered 'responsible' despite the diagnostic fantasies his poor mother may have picked up at her job.

Aliette was no psychiatrist. She detected no anxiety in Robert—only in herself. Her need to end this thing, and end it cleanly, presenting the impending charges to the court in a way that accurately served justice was giving her a rash. But who does one tell?

Not Hilda Gross. The Basel Lands Inspector was not inclined to share information. That included DNA and other findings related to Justin Aebischer and Josephina Perella. Hilda was none too friendly on the phone, sounding suspiciously like a woman sensing competition from the French police. Or was it *female* competition? What had Rudi been telling her? A part of Inspector Nouvelle wanted to reassure Hilda, but any feelings of comradely empathy were in deep eclipse at the moment and she refrained from getting all sisterly about it. All she required were the DNA samples.

And they arrived. Promptly. Of course they did. Thanks to Rudi's team and network they now knew Robert Charigot's career as an art thief had started long in advance of Martin Bettelman's entry into his life and had included thefts from collections across Switzerland and beyond. The pale, slight man in the floopy hoodie had stolen significant paintings in France and Germany, even a small Fra Angelico from a chapel in Milan. Aliette knew Rudi wanted her paltry little murder case resolved even more than she did. Whatever else he may have been accomplishing with Hilda Gross, FedPol Agent Bucholtz would not let a provincial investigator forestall or otherwise undermine his big day in a Basel courtroom telling the world the extent of Robert's larceny and his own role in retrieving and identifying a substantial cache of major art.

A thorough collating of gathered signs left Jean-Marc Pouliot and Charles Léger 'ninety-eight percent sure' that the international line between two murder cases was at last clearly drawn. 'Unless he swam in and worked barefoot,' IJ felt confident in confirming that while Dieter Taub had murdered Justin Aebischer and Josephina Perella, there was nothing of Dieter amongst the things they had collected at the place on French soil where Martin Bettelman had been snuffed three long months before. Certain items retrieved from the Greta/Fred hideaway also revealed that Taub had switched hiking boots with Perella. And that they either shared several pairs of (her) shoes, or he'd helped himself the evening of his visit in the horrible retro-pink wool coat — which would have been only a few hours after he'd used his Special Services knife to put a hole in her compromised heart. Of course, intimate details of the relationship between Dieter and Josephina would remain forever unexplained.

But no one really needed to know, least of all investigators on the French side.

'No…' But to send the matter along to the court, she needed to assign proper guilt, to present the charges correctly, and for that she needed proof. Otherwise, Aliette could not close her case. 'Merci, messieurs.' She stared glumly at a table strewn with forensic items.

Christine Charigot had been there that night — she knew. But in what capacity?

A confession would help. But she needed proof.

Others tried — they tried their most devious interrogation tricks to at least raise contradictions. No luck. No one could induce Robert to admit to somehow getting control of Martin Bettelman's sidearm and killing him, much less that his mother was a party to the act. He said all manner of nasty things about his mother, but nothing that might include her in the killing of Martin. Christine did not contradict or add to what Robert said. If she said anything, it was about her duty to defend her child, especially where it came to 'those men' who would hurt him. Some days the inspector came away suspecting, but not positive, that Christine Charigot was willfully acting like lump of grey mud. The doctors defended her. J.P. Blismes just smiled.

Though separated, mother and son had built a weirdly impenetrable wall.

46

THE SHOEMAKER'S STAND-IN

On Friday morning, Inspector Aliette Nouvelle was watching from her office window, equal parts bemused and cynical. A steady stream of taxis and official-looking vehicles came and went from the courtyard. Quite the crowd was showing up to see their unknown masterpiece. Chief Magistrate Richand and PJ Commissaire Néon took turns coming out to greet and usher in. She did not expect to see a FedPol contingent. Agent Rudi Bucholtz had seen the shoemaker, or a version. Agent Franck Woerli was dead—buried yesterday in Basel. For Franki she had made the effort; so sad to see his greying wife, three early-twenties daughters, a tight family Franki had never even mentioned... She hadn't seen Gregory Huet arriving for the show and did not expect to. She wondered what she might have done had Gregory attended. She hoped he was at home in Kembs eating kugelhopf and shaking. Or had he run? Where would he run? She didn't care.

Silence was her best position. Looking down, she felt badly for Claude, a dry scorn mixed with pity for Gérard. The judge's vaunted love of beauty set his warts in high relief.

As she left for another go-round at Hôtel Dieu, the inspector saw VigiTec security agent Della Kypreosus hurrying up the front steps in rue des Bons Enfants. It was a jolt to suddenly behold the security guard in civvies. She had spent some of her wages on handsome boots and a chic December coat from the boutiques in Claraplatz. Good for Della. But Aliette Nouvelle did not call out—no, she kept moving, there was nothing she wanted to say. All meaningful movement was internal now, toward creating distance between herself and all of this.

In preparation for her leaving.

As expected, she returned in mid-afternoon to learn that while everyone enjoyed the fine baking and an excellent local wine, no one recognized the shoemaker. Some had looked very closely, but not knowing the work or its origins, they had no context, no point of reference, no means for comparison as to value, market-based or otherwise. Most educated guesses thought him likely Dutch — Monique whispered that Gérard Richand had engaged in some almost embarrassing debate on that. Historical aesthetic trends aside, no one from the art crime investigation community had the shoemaker on their missing list. No one amongst the contingent of curious dealers attending had any memos from clients seeking such an item. The shoemaker had his moment, then everyone went home.

Only one disheartened cop knew it was the shoemaker's stand-in that had stymied all the experts. The actual was still in a totebag leaning against her desk.

Bernadette had probably twigged. Or maybe not.

And Aliette thought, Well, if no one knows him, then he's worth nothing.

Yes, it seemed that the best revenge on Gregory Huet was to *say* nothing. He knew the fate of his real client. But he couldn't know where the bona fide product was. Gregory Huet would worry for a long time about the next knock on his door. The idea of silence pleased her.

At least as much as she was capable of being pleased in those raw days of mid-December.

Drifting snowflakes Friday evening, a drifting Aliette.

Monday, down at the courthouse reporting her non-progress after another weekend of futile visits to Hôtel-Dieu, she smiled as Gérard Richand reprised his lame charade of surprise and dismay (while so tenderly cradling Gregory Huet's immaculate fake). 'What a shame...what a sham! All these so-called experts.'

Inspector Nouvelle totally agreed, just as capable of shameless acting.

Gérard sighed. Notices would be posted on boards across France and, as a courtesy, in parts of neighbouring nations. A file would be shared with InterPol. The shoemaker would be carefully stored in a bank vault just down the street—Gérard himself had opened the account. If unclaimed after a year, the lonely artisan would be offered for a nominal price.

Aliette sighed too. She wondered if Gérard Richand could wait that long. Regardless, she knew that in the gentle course of time the shoemaker would appear in Gérard's home—a home just three blocks from the house in the north end where she had tried and failed to settle. Gérard would dream up some French provenance, turn him into a story that suited his study, if not his salon. We all have our little deceits, because life would be too flat without them, no? Deceits that become reality and turn into family history. So strange to think it, which is why we don't.

In any event, a dream provenance would fit well with an expert fake.

And a respectful cop would never dream of mentioning it to her judge.

47

BLUE *PANTOUFLES*

Suddenly it was two weeks till Christmas. She hadn't given a single thought to shopping, for anyone else, much less herself. After another useless walk through the spiritless rooms in the house in circle Rene-Descartes… looking for what?… she went to the mall at the Carrefour Store in Village-Neuf, thinking of a new blouse for the annual brigade party (her last!) and a pair of slippers. Living in a house in the north end, one could easily forget how Madame Camus kept the heat to the legal minimum, and there was no more Piaf at the end of the bed to warm her feet of a winter's night. Nor a man for the rest of her. There were so many things still in her cupboard at Claude's and she hadn't the heart to retrieve them. He was afraid to say a word.

Claude's fear, those averted eyes — it made her wonder how she looked.

…Not *looked*. How he saw her.

How *they* saw her. Monique, Bernadette, Raphaele, everyone. J-P Blismes was right: She was the centre of the universe. And right now she hated it — she only wanted out.

Depressed, uninspired, there was no blouse that caught her eye. She wandered into Footwear. A helpful shelf stocker turned a confused and distracted shopper a hundred and eighty degrees. Slippers were with the socks, not the shoes. Fifteen minutes later she was racing back to the city, pushing the crappy requisitioned car to its exhausted limit, sure she'd found the key.

'These!' Plunking a pair of chintzy blue *pantoufles* down on the desk of a startled Charles Léger. 'Please tell me these come from the same batch as that —' stepping to his workbench and pointing with newly hopeful determination at a plastic evidence bag waiting in box B.

Her plea was redundant. He saw it immediately. He plucked a tweezer's worth of synthetic fur from one of the presented items, then, in his methodical manner, carefully opened the bag in question and removed the strand of blue thread that had been harvested at the 'beach.'

'Polypropylene,' he noted. 'Horrid things.'

Half an hour later Charles Léger gave her an unequivocal 'Yes.'

'*Bon.*' Muttered low-key and workaday, masking another rush of hopeful energy. 'I'll have a sample of Christine Charigot's DNA here wihin the hour. Please see if that,' the found blue strand, 'contains some.'

This plea left him skeptical. He scanned his notes. 'There was no tissue apparent on this. No blood…'

'But sweat! These things don't breathe… it was a hot night. Her feet would have been soaking. Please.' She pressed. She knew his findings came from a first general pass. There had been no pressing reason to explore further with this one particular item. Now there was.

Of course he would try. But, warned Charles, 'sweat is not the best medium for DNA. Just salt and water. We need cells.'

'But all that movement—it comes from her!'

'We might get lucky. Perhaps some cells were shed and mixed with her sweat.'

'Thank you.'

Feeling better about (almost) everything, she ordered the sample sent from the hospital then took herself out, heading across town to the boutiques to make another search for a Christmas top. She would make this project last the remainder of the day. Charles said he would need some time and she did not want to be breathing down his neck. She browsed slowly, investigating every possibility. These shops offered nowhere near the variety and calibre of merchandise for sale in Basel, but if you looked, you could find good things. And she finally did.

Not especially Christmassy, forest green against beige, no red—but new, chic, fresh. She found it in the same place she'd found a wonderful dress worn the first time she'd gone out dancing with Claude. They had been working a case. Heading slowly back through the streets, vaguely considering gifts for her parents, her sister, the inspector reprised the memory again and again, focusing on the pleasing surprise that had been Claude Néon in motion. Because it had been a difficult case, that one, where she had given him the benefit of a very large doubt and eventually saved his career and what she believed might be their love. And look where it had got her… Falling victim to memory, she saw nothing that struck a chord by way of a suitable gift.

She would get it done when she landed in Nantes next weekend.

She went through the Commissariat door and directly to the basement.

Charles Léger was an honest and transparent man. He could never have been a cop in the streets. And she knew it was a No before he spoke. 'Sorry, Inspector, it's just not there.'

'Nothing?'

'Yes, there's some. If it has touched a human body there is always some. But in this case not enough to make a credible match… Mainly salt and water. Perhaps a trace of soap?'

He handed her the Carrefour bag containing the blue *pantoufles*. She murmured another thank you, thank you for trying, we have to try — at love and work and dreaming, what else is there but trying. Then climbed slowly back up the stairs. Brooding. Only wanting out.

− 48 −
How to Kill with Kindness

It did not really matter who killed Martin Bettelman. It was about closing the book and moving on. Despite the several clearly unprofessional mistakes deduced at the scene, a frustrated inspector was ready to let an anonymous professional carry the killing at the 'beach' and send the beautiful Robert back to the Swiss to face the music there. He would be punished for stealing art. She would be long retired before there was even the smallest chance of seeing his face again in the street. An old angel out on probation. It would depend upon where he served the last of several probable terms. Italy. Germany. France... Robert's suffering maman would likely still be suffering, might even be dead on account of it, but how much did an inspector who'd smashed her usually sympathetic head against the Charigot wall really care? Aliette wasted two days writing a report and recommended charges that fudged and in some instances revised or omitted facts she knew to be true, and accompanying circumstantials that framed the truth with utter clarity.

Then she pressed Delete and put on her coat.

No, it did not matter who killed Martin Bettelman. The cheap blue slippers were still in the shopping bag—taking them home and wearing them would have added to her sense of failure. She'd left them on the floor beside the shoemaker, still in his bag. Two items waiting in limbo.

She had only the vaguest vision for the one. Now she had a definite use for the other.

She did not need clarity, just movement, like a traveller on an all-night train.

She walked. She stopped at a favourite patisserie where she paid top price for their justly famous cake. Whatever else, it was Christmas. It might warm a heart to receive some cheer.

It might warm hers to offer it. She proceeded to Hôtel Dieu.

Christine Charigot looked every inch a wretched creature who could not even expect a Christmas kiss from the son she had protected and adored. But her empty eyes reacted when the visitor unwrapped a seasonally decorated kugelhopf. It may have been the sharpening effect of suspicion. Or the sudden sight of something deliciously wonderful. Christine's true position was still a mystery. At Aliette's suggestion, Christine's nurse brought a pot of tea.

Nibbling cake, the inspector went slowly, gently, a style and voice she was good at. Alone with Christine Charigot, in woman-to-woman mode, Aliette told her about the changes coming to her life, how it was painful but she was looking forward to moving on. *Everyone* had to move forward. Christine could too if she approached it with a hopeful heart and mind. A confiding cop even said some nice things about Robert she did not really believe.

Christine Charigot could not resist the offered treat — several pieces, refills of tea with milk, though she remained on edge, as if waiting for the police officer to emerge and attack.

Aliette talked on, confiding about the difficulty in going home for Christmas with the parents and her sister. 'My mother especially. She doesn't really agree with my life, you know?'

Some of it seemed to be getting through. She knew Christine also had a sister and a mother.

The kugelhopf was half gone, the teapot almost empty when Christine Charigot pushed back the covers, indicating it was time to pee. Since no males were present, she was quite casual as she eased herself off the bed. Her nightgown rode up to the top her thigh. Her thigh was white, muscled — she had spent a career on her feet. An inspector's eyes processed all these bits of personal information in a micro-second, even as she extended a hand to help the unsteady woman negotiate the space from bed to floor. It was impossible not to notice a scar about four inches above the knee on Christine Charigot's left thigh. About four inches long. It had healed but was plainly recent — Aliette had a recent wound of her own to compare. But where hers was a bullet wound, professionally mended, Christine's looked more the result of a fall against something hard and sharp, leaving a serious gash requiring extensive stitching. At a glance, about twenty. But an uneven line. Messy work. Homemade?

A veteran triage nurse would know how.

More clarity. Still no proof.

When Christine returned from the toilet and got herself back inside her bed, Aliette reached for the other bag. 'And I brought you these…' smiling flatly, presenting the blue slippers.

Lulled, bewildered, the woman took them in her veiny hands.

Aliette said, 'I know you were there. I know it was probably you… You came home from your shift and Robert was gone, and you knew where and you went straight to the beach in your slippers. And you found them, Christine, and you hated that, and you killed Martin Bettelman.'

No… Christine Charigot was blinking, fighting tears, clutching her blue slippers.

'Yes. I think so. But if you won't talk, I can't prove it.'

The tears started. The silence held.

'But it seems unfair, it really does. I mean, you were only trying to protect your child. That's worth something…to me, at any rate.' She reached for a last morsel of cake, put it between her lips and savoured it. Then washed it down with the last of her tea. 'So what I'm going to do is tell them Robert did it. Robert killed Martin. He's going away for a long, long time, in any event. Adding in a murder charge won't matter much at all. Mm? More to the point, you are a caring mother. He seems much more like a murderer than you. By which I mean to say, it fits.' She got up to leave. 'So that's what will happen. It's Robert who's the killer… Sorry, it's not the best, Christine, but it's the best I can do.' And she bowed, withdrawing.

'No.' Christine Charigot had closed her eyes. She seemed to be reciting when she stated, 'I killed him. I killed that gross man… Martin Bettelman.' And she added, 'It was me.'

Then the heart-rending noise began, piercing, inarticulate, but filled with truth.

It brought the nurses running. It gave Aliette, weepy herself now, a chance to slip away.

It was not sympathy for poor Christine. It was the release of pressure on herself.

It was given to J-P Blismes to present the picture, build a frame for Christine Charigot, and help her talk her way to a confession: How she had come upon Robert and a man, naked and doing things she did not want to remember—but she did, and how she took the man's gun and chased him, both of them falling and stumbling along the rocky bank, and killed him—finally; what did she know about shooting guns?—then broken the godforsaken painting over her knee, and yes, over his horrible head. And how she had dragged her Robert home.

Several nurses on the ward reported patients becoming dangerously agitated by the shrieking Christine Charigot unleashed in the process of unburdening herself. The head nurse called security. When they arrived, J-P held them off. He was used to anger. It was normal. Christine had to let it out. He advised that she should be tried as not criminally responsible for what she'd done. A half-dozen psychiatrists eventually agreed.

But all that was not till after Aliette Nouvelle was long gone. Direction: south.

EPILOGUE

One French citizen, one Swiss-owned painting. It was settled as much as it ever could be. Gérard Richand had held his peace and honoured the parameters of her case. Why not? Gérard had secured his little prize. Or thought he had — which is what mattered. So, good to her word with Agent Bucholtz, the inspector had Chief Magistrate Richand sign the forms releasing the sequestered art to the Swiss and wished him a happy holiday season. Robert Charigot's art collection began to be processed out in earnest, facilitated by Swiss FedPol agents and the Basel Kunstmuseum. Thanks to Claude's discretion and Gérard's forbearance, it was a non-event on the French side, nothing but a few unmarked, unnoticed trucks leaving town. At the other end, Rudi (or someone) made sure Switzerland knew. A victory for FedPol, good PR for law and order. Add in Inspector Morenz going about his duties and the calculated release of information, by Christmas Eve Basel media would be making gleeful hay of the incredible art fraud and series of murders based in the gay community. Inevitably, Zup did not escape. Aliette hoped the lull between Christmas and Saint-Sylvestre would kill it. Failing that, she hoped Max and Adelhard might seize the opportunity to spin their notoriety into pure Swiss gold.

But it had nothing to do with her. She requisitioned the grungy Opal and went up to Strasbourg for a meeting with the Divisionnaire. He never much cared about bad cop judgement so long as it got the desired result and did not implicate his office or the Ministry to which he filed reports. He shrugged in his dry way and said he would see to her request. Although he wished her well, he forgot Joyeux Noël, but that's the kind of man he was. She returned with a bag full of Christmas gifts — lots of good shopping in the capital.

She dutifully sipped champagne and munched Monique's cookies at the yearly party. It was not a farewell party, just a Christmas party, and her plans were not announced, so there were no parting tears. Who could bear it if the centre of the universe was disappearing? Commissaire Claude Néon managed to be both pleasant and completely distant. He was going to Paris, to spend the holiday with his mother and brother.

The only delightful spark in an otherwise cheerless week of tying loose ends was a card from Hubert Hunspach. One of those maudlin ones with a photo of the family. He'd circled his own smiling face, more or less obliterating his sister's. A note said he'd enjoyed working with her.

That touched the inspector's suspended heart, but she did not reply.

She took a flight to the coast, where she spent the loneliest Christmas ever. She came back before New Year and began to pack her things. Claude, in a civilized gesture, stayed in Paris with his family for an extra week, leaving her stress-free access to the house in the north end.

There was one bit of harrowing news over the holiday. Art restorer Gregory Huet was found in his garden with a bullet through his head. Clearly a professional job, according to Inspector Patrice Lebeau, who'd drawn the short straw and was looking after the otherwise deserted shop on the third floor at rue des Bons Enfants. Something to do with a Watteau.

So, the knock on the door had come. The client of his client Dieter? Or an entirely different tangent—all French? (Watteau is definitely French.) Either way, it was a dangerous business. She thought of Gregory's whimsy as she'd munched his lovely cake, evoking a shoemaker drifting away from a lover's quarrel, dreaming of freedom, peace and quiet, before being plowed to bits by an imagined potash barge. A beautiful imagination. But even his whimsy had been a lie.

Which raised the logical question: Did he really bake his own kugelhopf?

For that case she would have certainly assigned someone else, but it was no longer her job. Not that she mentioned as much to

Inspector Lebeau—she was only stopping in, en route to a Saint Sylvestre invitation in the south. Lucky her, said Patrice. Not exactly, she was thinking.

Though she only smiled, 'See you next year.'

Of course she would be back to offer her testimony in court. Because Robert Charigot would be extradited back to Switzerland in the early new year, where he would be tried for and admit to stealing priceless art. And when released from Swiss custody he would be bound to answer similar charges in Germany, Italy and France. And because Robert's mother would be convicted of murder in the Palais de Justice a twenty-minute walk away, though such was her destroyed condition that she would never suffer the coldness of an actual cell.

But all that was months, if not years, away. She knew that when she returned to testify, she would see Claude again. And Gérard, Raphaele, Jean-Marc and Charles, Monique and Inspector Bernadette Milhau…all the PJ team. Michel Souviron. The smiling J-P Blismes. But they would be different. So would she. In a moment, Inspector Nouvelle would be effectively gone.

She gazed around her office one last time. Ten years. Through her window were the snow-covered Vosges. That same snow covered Piaf, where he slept in an empty garden…

While she had a new life to start, as head of a small brigade.

It would be less than half the size of this small one, but she would be running the show. It would be in a town in wine country an hour from Spain. She'd never been there.

The shoemaker remained where Bernadette had left him, unframed, in a flowery totebag, which may have been useful to some people back in Basel, but it was far too late to worry about that. Aliette had not looked at him since that final, horrible day. Now she did.

Was the shoemaker beautiful? Who made him? Was the shoemaker the work of the man-in-the-moon, that unknowable artist of everything? Was the shoemaker's daily pause for a pot of tea a symbol of his daily dose of memory? Memory set against a life of intention, all ending in another boot? Large questions in a mundane moment. My life, my boot to fix and shine like new, thought Aliette

Nouvelle. Everything changed with hindsight. This case would be no exception.

She put the shoemaker back in the bag. She called a cab. And felt no qualms as she carried an unknown masterpiece out with the last of the sundries that were leaving here forever.

— *fin* —

OTHER BOOKS IN THIS SERIES

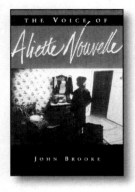

The Voice of Aliette Nouvelle

Jacques Normand, France's Public Enemy Number One, escaped from prison over ten years ago. But the Commissaire is convinced that the outlaw is alive. Find him, he commands Inspector Aliette Nouvelle.

"This book, by Montreal poet and filmmaker John Brooke, dropped into my lap and I was smitten: interesting premise, fascinating central character and good writing. Poetic images, film stills and literary writing, none out of place."—*The Globe & Mail*

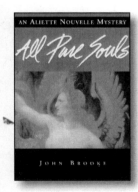

All Pure Souls

Inspector Aliette Nouvelle returns to solve the case of the murder of a Marilyn Monroe look-alike in a French brothel.

"*All Pure Souls* is definitely not a dimestore detective novel. The writing is good and the dialogue is sharp...the point of the book seems to be less about solving the crime than figuring out what motivates the characters."
—*Montreal Review of Books*

Stifling Folds of Love

When the ex-lovers of a former schoolteacher start dying at an alarming rate, Inspector Aliette Nouvelle is drawn into the investigation, not least because her boss is also in jeopardy.

"The relaxed pace supports the tone set by the dialogue as it exposes the complex layers leading to the murderer in this bucolic, small-town setting. The writing may feel impressionistic but the climax is as threatening as they come."—*The Hamilton Spectator*

About the Author

John Brooke became fascinated by criminality and police work listening to the courtroom stories and observations of his father, a long-serving judge. Although he lives in Montreal, John makes frequent trips to France for both pleasure and research. He earns a living as a freelance writer and translator, has also worked as a film and video editor as well as directed four films on modern dance. His poetry and short stories have been widely published, and in 1998 his story "The Finer Points of Apples" won him the Journey Prize. Brooke's first Inspector Aliette mystery, *The Voice of Aliette Nouvelle*, was published in 1999, followed by *All Pure Souls* in 2001. He took a break from Aliette with the publication of his novel *Last Days of Montreal* in 2004, but returned with her in 2011 with *Stifling Folds of Love*.